The Sh

His shadow self was as working to make him see di of everyone around him, an growing angry about the h whenever he addressed Vala. Was it possible that Galaeron had sent the phaerimm to Escanor not because he wanted to be certain of killing it, but because his shadow self wanted to see the prince harmed instead?

The Common Foe

"Maybe they don't know where we are," she suggested. "Or maybe they couldn't get here. Not everyone can just turn into a shadow and slip down a crack, you know."

"How long did they take to capture the Sharaedim? Five days—five days to take what Evereska has held for fifteen centuries." A hand came down on the edge of a mineral pad, shattering the whole thing and sending it fluttering to the lake's milky bottom. He appeared not to notice. "If I can find this place, *they* can find this place."

The Flying City

The witch looked at Hadrhune.

He glared amber flames at her, then turned to Galaeron and said, "The enclave is moving."

"Moving?" Galaeron echoed. "It's always moving."

"Deeper into the desert," Hadrhune clarified. "Away from Evereska. That's why—"

"Traitors!" Galaeron lunged for the seneschal but went down heavily, Vala on his back. "You promised!"

RETURN OF THE ARCHWIZARDS

Book I

The Summoning
TROY DENNING

Book II

The Siege
TROY DENNING

Realms of Shadow
EDITED BY LIZZ BALDWIN

Book III

The Sorcerer
TROY DENNING
November 2002

THE
SIEGE

Return of the Archwizards

BOOK
II

TROY
DENNING

THE SIEGE
Return of the Archwizards, Book II
©2001 Wizards of the Coast, Inc.

Distributed in the United States by Holtzbrinck Publishing. Distributed in Canada by Fenn Ltd.

Distributed to the hobby, toy, and comic trade in the United States and Canada by regional distributors.

Distributed worldwide by Wizards of the Coast, Inc., and regional distributors.

Cover art by Jon Sullivan
Map by Dennis Kauth
First Printing: December 2001
Library of Congress Catalog Card Number: 00-191039

9 8 7 6 5 4 3

U.S. ISBN: 0-7869-1905-1
U.K. ISBN: 0-7869-2678-3
620-T21905

U.S., CANADA,
ASIA, PACIFIC, & LATIN AMERICA
Wizards of the Coast, Inc.
P.O. Box 707
Renton, WA 98057-0707
+1-800-324-6496

EUROPEAN HEADQUARTERS
Wizards of the Coast, Belgium
P.B. 2031
2600 Berchem
Belgium
+32-70-23-32-77

Visit our web site at **www.wizards.com/forgottenrealms**

To Phil Athans
For Service Beyond the Call

Acknowledgments
I would like to thank Eric Boyd for his many contributions to the series, the entire WotC book department for their extra effort on this one, and Andria Hayday for her extraordinary patience and support.

CHAPTER ONE

26 Tarsakh,
The Year of Wild Magic (1372 DR)

Twenty Lords of Shade stood chest-deep in a lake that had never before known the color of light, pulling strands of shadow up from the milky bottom and splicing them into a curtain of umbral darkness that hung down from the cavern's thousand-needled ceiling. Save for the ripples of grime rinsing out of their travel-worn cloaks, the water was as clear as air, and thousands of limestone cave pearls could be seen gleaming in the inch-deep shallows along the shore. Farther out in the heart of the pool, a garden of white faerie stalks rose out of the limpid depths and blossomed across the surface in a carpet of alabaster mineral pads. Of the hundred natural wonders Vala Thorsdotter had witnessed since departing her home in Vaasa, this one was by far the loneliest and the eeriest, the one that felt most forbidden to human eyes.

"This will be the ruin of it, you know."

Galaeron Nihmedu was sitting on his haunches beside Vala, watching the shadow lords work. Tall and solidly built for a moon elf, he had the pale skin and regal features common to his race, but two decades of Tomb Guard postings along the Desert Border South had left his face rugged and weather-beaten enough to be considered handsome even by Vaasan standards.

"The ruin of what?" she asked.

"The lake," Galaeron explained. "The dirt washing out of their clothes will settle on the cave pearls and stop them from growing. The oil from their bodies will work its way into the mineral pads and break them up. A hundred years from now, this will be just another mud hole."

Vala shrugged. "It's in a good cause."

"Spoken like a human." Galaeron's tone was more remorseful than unkind. "And I find myself in agreement. How sad is that?"

"Not as sad as feeling sorry for yourself," Vala answered sharply. Elves worshiped beauty like a god, but there were more important concerns at stake than a lake no one ever saw, and she couldn't let its destruction sink Galaeron into one of his dejections. "If we could ask Duirsar what he wanted, I'm sure he'd tell us to go ahead."

"He would tell us to find another place to complete the Splicing—or not to finish at all. Elves do not destroy nature's treasures to save their own."

Vala rolled her eyes. "Galaeron, you *know* this is the only way. If the phaerimm aren't contained, they'll destroy more than this one lake. Far more."

"Being the only way seldom makes something the right way."

Galaeron looked back to the lake, watching the shadow lords weave their dark curtain, then laid a hand on Vala's arm.

"But what's done is done," he said. "You can stop worrying about me."

"Sure I can," Vala said. "Someday."

Her gaze followed Galaeron's out across the lake. The cavern was lit by three magic glowballs hovering among the stalactites. The shadow lords working most directly beneath the brilliant light looked most human, with swarthy complexions, dark hair, and gem-colored eyes. Others, laboring in the dim boundaries or shadowed areas, looked more like silhouettes, their lithe bodies bending and stretching in ghostlike whorls as they stooped down to pluck dark filaments out of the water. They would braid three strands together and give the resulting ribbon a single half twist, then splice it into the curtain fringe. After half a dozen splices, they would weave a few strands of shadowsilk into the fibers and speak an arcane word, and a dark fog would fill the empty spaces and solidify into a translucent veil of murk.

Galaeron and Vala watched in silence for another quarter hour, then Galaeron said, "They're sly, these Shadovar."

"That surprises you?"

"They always surprise me." Galaeron pointed at the shadowy curtain. "You see the way they're turning the fibers back on themselves?"

Vala gave a tentative nod. "I see, but I don't understand magic."

"Dimensional twisting," Galaeron explained, "to make the shadowshell one-sided."

Vala gave him a blank look.

"So nothing can leave," he said. "Anything that passes into the shadow goes all the way around the shell and comes out where it entered. It would be like stepping through a gate and always returning to the same garden."

"Not much gardening in Vaasa," Vala commented, trying to wrap her mind around the idea of twisting a dimension. "You can tell that just by watching?"

Galaeron looked at her askance. "The magic isn't difficult." His expression grew distant and dark, and he peered through a section of uncompleted curtain into the black depths beyond. "If I can understand it, so can they."

" 'They,' Galaeron?" Vala asked. She didn't like the emphasis Galaeron had placed on the word *they*—or the look that had come to his eyes. "The Shadovar?"

"No." Galaeron touched two buckles, and his Evereskan chain mail loosened its form-fitting embrace. "*Them*. You know." He continued to speak as he pulled off his armor. "They're out there, somewhere there in the dark."

"*Who*, Galaeron?" Vala asked, more concerned about what had come over Galaeron than what was lurking in the dark. "The phaerimm?"

Galaeron nodded. "Giant scaly slugs that've been down here in the dark for a long time, since before I felt the cave breathe, since before I followed that little crack down here to this place no one has ever left."

He let his chain mail breeches clink to the ground, then waded out into the water, kicking cave pearls loose with every step.

"They were out there then," he said, "and they're out there now, lurking in the dark, their tails just aching to stick someone with an egg."

"Galaeron, you know that can't be." Vala was fumbling at her own buckles, struggling to remove her heavy scale mail. "Wait!"

She was furious with herself for being caught off guard; she had seen him slipping toward dejection but allowed herself to be taken in by his reassurances.

"Galaeron, you're imagining things."

He half turned, a wild look in his eyes, and spoke over his shoulder. "You know how they like that, Vala, putting an egg in some wretch's gut and watching it grow until it's as big as his arm and squirming up his throat. They love that. It's the only thing they love at all."

Vala let her armor clank to the stone and splashed in after him, her shins still covered by her greaves. The Change had never been this deranged before.

"There aren't any phaerimm," she called, loudly enough to draw the attention of the Shadovar. "Prince Escanor checked."

"No, he didn't. Not well enough." Galaeron sank to his chin as the bottom dropped away beneath him, then floated back to the surface and began to swim toward the curtain. "They're out there. It makes sense. They *have* to be there."

Vala reached the drop-off and swam after him, half breaststroking and half treading water because the weight of her greaves prevented her from floating her legs to the surface.

"Maybe they don't know where we are," she suggested. "Or maybe they couldn't get here. Not everyone can just turn into a shadow and slip down a crack, you know."

Galaeron rolled into an easy backstroke. "How long did they take to capture the Sharaedim? Five days—five days to take what Evereska has held for fifteen centuries." A hand came down on the edge of a mineral pad, shattering the whole thing and sending it fluttering to the lake's milky bottom. He appeared not to notice. "If I can find this place, *they* can find this place."

"There is a difference between *can* and *have*, elf." It took a moment to recognize the raspy voice. While Prince Escanor was ten places away splicing strands into the shadow curtain, his magic made him sound as though he were in the water beside them. "If the phaerimm were here, they would have attacked by now."

"The phaerimm *are* here—they must be—and have they attacked?" Galaeron asked, facing the prince. "No, they haven't. So, you're wrong. Absolutely wrong."

Escanor's copper-glowing eyes flared. "How am I wrong, elf?" He began to wade toward them, a bugbear-sized silhouette limned in silver spell-light. "Explain."

Galaeron looked as though he were about to answer, then he cocked his head and, passing within a lance-length of an astonished shadow lord, vanished through a breach in the curtain. Vala followed as quickly as she was able, but the steel greaves on her shins made her slow. Escanor, swimming as well, beat her through the gap. She cringed at what was likely to follow. One did not ignore a prince of Shade Enclave.

Vala passed through the gap and found them standing close together in the shallows, Galaeron's lean form submerged to the waist and Escanor's to the knees. Like all the shadow lords, the prince was swarthy and powerful, with a mouthful of ceremonial fangs and a long, raw-boned face that lent a demonic aura to an already other-worldly mystique. They were standing close together, speaking intensely but quietly.

" . . . are spell collectors," Galaeron was saying. He sounded less irrational but just as intense. "They haven't attacked because they want to watch the Splicing."

"You suggest they're spying on us?" Escanor asked.

"If I can learn to use shadow magic, why can't the phaerimm?" Galaeron replied. "If they understand it, they control it."

"What you say stands to reason, as far as it goes." Escanor glanced over as Vala touched bottom beside them, then looked back to Galaeron. "But if the phaerimm were here, we would have detected their magic. They cannot hide that from us."

"Only phaerimm know what the phaerimm can do," Galaeron said. He was looking past the prince into the darkness, studying it as though he could find the enemy by sheer force of will. "And only a fool would believe otherwise."

Escanor's eyes brightened to a fiery red. "Watch that tongue, elf. A shadow crisis excuses only so much."

Vala slipped between the two, placing her back to Escanor and raising a hand to silence the elf before he could make a retort. "Galaeron, you know better. The Shadovar have killed more phaerimm than all of Evereska's High Mages together, and Prince Escanor has slain three personally. If there is a fool here, it is the one who speaks to him as though he were some Waterdhavian pikesman on his first march beyond the city gate."

The rebuke shocked Galaeron into silence, for Vala was the one person in the world whose loyalties he could never question, the one person in the world who could break through the Change to tell him such things. Together, they had traveled the dark pathways of the shadow fringe, fought beholders, liches, and illithids, seen their friends and comrades die in ways horrible beyond imagining. Vala had stood fast through everything and nursed him back to health when all was done, and that had connected her to his true nature in a way no shadow crisis could obstruct.

Galaeron continued to stare past Vala and Escanor into the darkness for a long time, then finally shifted his gaze back to the Vala and said, "I didn't mean to imply that the Shadovar are anything but the finest warriors."

He looked to Escanor, but his eyes remained distant and dark. "The prince is right. If the phaerimm were using magic to conceal themselves, I'm sure your divination spells would reveal where they're hiding."

Galaeron held Escanor's gaze a moment, then glanced toward the cave ceiling.

The prince seemed oblivious. "Good." His eyes did not even stray from Galaeron's face. "We're almost done with the Splicing. Evereska need hold only a few months longer, elf. The phaerimm are doomed."

"My city is grateful for the aid of Shade Enclave, Prince, but it would not do to underestimate our enemies." Galaeron furrowed his arched brows and again rolled his eyes toward the ceiling. "I recall one of our high mages saying the same thing shortly before a phaerimm larva tore its way from his throat."

This drew only a condescending smirk from the prince. "When will you learn, elf? We are not your high mages." He reached over Vala to clap a huge hand on Galaeron's shoulder. "The Shadovar have been preparing for this war for centuries."

Vala barely heard this last part, for Galaeron's efforts had drawn her attention to the mass of limestone fangs hanging down overhead, each with a single drop of water clinging to its stony tip. With broad roots narrowing down to sharp points, the stalactites were shaped more or less like phaerimm, save that they lacked spiny hides and four thin arms. There were hundreds in the lit area alone. At only three to six feet, most were too short to be phaerimm, a few were so long their flattened tips actually touched the lake surface, but a handful hung down in the ten-foot range. It didn't take Vala long to locate three with suspiciously dry tips and odd dark lines where their bases pressed against the ceiling.

" . . . that right, Vala?" Escanor asked.

"Is what right?" Hoping that all the blood had not drained from her face, Vala tore her gaze from the ceiling and tried to look calm. "Sorry."

Escanor cocked a disapproving brow but said, "I was just assuring Galaeron that we Shadovar were hardly likely to make the same mistake as the elves and Waterdhavians."

"I'm sure you won't," Galaeron said, still trying to draw the prince's gaze to the ceiling. "But new mistakes will prove—"

"Rare, I'm sure," Vala said, taking Galaeron's arm.

The prince should have recognized the elf's signal, and they didn't dare push things too far. Once the phaerimm realized they were discovered, they would attack instantly—and there were few mistakes more grave than letting a phaerimm have the first blow.

"If you will excuse us, Prince," Vala said, "it's time we let you return to your work."

Escanor dismissed them with an easy wave. "Of course."

Vala drew Galaeron away, her iron grasp permitting no argument. Once they were a few steps away, with their backs facing the suspicious stalactites, she released his arm and began to twist her hands through the gestures of Evereskan finger talk.

You're never going to get Escanor to look up. As Vala made the statement, she was careful to remain alert to any alien presences in her mind. The phaerimm were not so adept at telepathy that they could eavesdrop on a person's thoughts without revealing their own presence, but it never hurt to be careful—not around these enemies. *Are you sure they were phaerimm?*

No, Galaeron admitted, *but it's better to be sure they aren't. You saw what I was looking at?*

Disguised as stalactites, Vala said. Her tempo was slow and awkward, for it was a complicated language and she had only taken up its study as a way to pass the time while Galaeron lay immobile with a pair of broken ankles. *Dry tips and a dark line where they're pressing their bases to the ceiling.*

Galaeron raised his brow. *I missed the lines,* he said. *We can't run the risk of alerting them. We have to take them ourselves.*

Ourselves? Vala shook a fist downward to show emphasis. *How?*

You take the closest one, Galaeron instructed. *Throw your sword. I'll blast the other with a shadow bolt.*

Vala's fingers turned slow and clumsy. *I thought you were done casting spells.*

You have another way? Galaeron's gestures came so fast and sharp Vala could barely follow his meaning. *Maybe you can convince Escanor he's wrong—without alerting the phaerimm?*

The question required no answer. Vala knew as well as Galaeron that the prince could not be persuaded that he had made a mistake. They had no choice except to launch the attack on their own, and that meant Galaeron would have to use shadow magic to have any effect at all on the phaerimm, and using his shadow magic meant giving a little more of himself over to the darkness that was slowly devouring him from within.

Resigning herself to the heartache of watching the Galaeron she knew slip even deeper into shadows, Vala gave a curt nod, then asked, *What about the third one?*

You're joking, Galaeron replied.

I could be wrong, but I'm not joking. One above Escanor, one over the mineral pads—

That one I missed. Galaeron's fingers fell motionless for a moment, then he said, *I'll have to try a shadow door.*

Bad idea, Vala said, even more concerned. Shadow magic was far more dangerous for the wielder than normal Weave magic. If a magic-user overreached his limits, he invited in just the sort of darkness already consuming Galaeron. *You're barely holding on as it is.*

Then it's good you are watching over me. I am grateful—very grateful.

Vala looked away, then spoke aloud. "Galaeron, it isn't fair to hold me to that promise . . . not now."

"Nevertheless, I do hold you to it." Galaeron's voice was firm. "When the time comes, you must not hesitate."

"*If*, Galaeron." They reached the shore, and Vala sat down to remove her greaves. "If the time comes."

Galaeron turned away without answering and started down the shore, moving far enough away that they both could not be struck down by the same spell. Vala looked back across the lake to where the shadow lords were just closing the last few breaches in the shadow curtain. Though the shadow lords had left their armor on shore, all were armed with glassy black weapons similar to Vala's darksword—one reason, no doubt, that the enemy was being so careful to remain concealed.

The two phaerimm Galaeron had noticed hung about fifty feet apart in a rough line on the interior side of the curtain. On the flanks of their conical bodies, Vala could see a regular pattern of bumps where their body thorns lay concealed beneath the hardened lime-mud they had used to disguise their scaly hides. The third phaerimm, the one Galaeron had missed, hung over the mineral pads about forty paces away, barely noticeable in the gloomy boundary between dark and light. Though Vala had no way of guessing whether the creatures had seen enough to defeat the shadow curtain, the simple fact that they were making no attempt to stop the final Splicing made clear what they believed.

Finding no signs of any enemies beyond the three already located, Vala stood and waded back into the lake, angling toward Prince Escanor to avoid alerting the phaerimm. She had no idea how Galaeron had sensed the enemy's presence—or why that had brought on a Change—but she felt confident in his conclusions. Every good warrior knew the value of camouflage, and the thornbacks were nothing if not good warriors.

When Vala drew within throwing range of the nearest phaerimm, she stopped and looked back. Galaeron was just setting a loop of shadowsilk on a stone beside him. He peeled another strand off the mat of dull fabric he was holding, then soaked it in a drop of armor oil and glanced in Vala's direction. She nodded. He pressed the filament to the limestone wall, his lips already moving as he spoke his spell incantation.

A film of oily shadow spread across the ceiling, filling the cavern with a soft, rainlike patter as thousands of drops of water lost their tenuous hold and plummeted into the lake. Vala drew her darksword and in a single smooth motion sent it whirling up at the nearest phaerimm. The glassy black blade tore a three-foot gash across the thornback's body and became lodged with little more than the hilt showing.

The stain on the ceiling swept past overhead. The astonished phaerimm came loose one after the other, the hardened lime-mud camouflage falling in cakes from their squirming bodies and their strange language of winds stirring the air into whistling vortexes. The phaerimm hit the water almost as one and sank beneath the surface.

Escanor and his shadow lords stopped working and whirled toward the splash rings, shouting to each other in their own language and trying to make sense of what was happening.

"Phaerimm!" Vala stretched her hand toward the one she had attacked and thought of her darksword, and the blade rose out of the water and flew back into her grasp. "Three of them!"

She heard Galaeron intoning his second spell and looked over to see him flipping the ring of shadowsilk toward the place the third phaerimm had entered the water. A disk of black shadow appeared two inches above the surface. Vala was distracted as the startled phaerimm activated their floating magic and began rising out of the water. The two nearest the curtain came up in the midst of the astonished shadow lords, who quickly proved the truth of Escanor's boasts by assailing them with shadow webs and darkswords.

Even caught off guard, the phaerimm reacted like the terrors they were, unleashing a flurry of fire strikes and lightning bolts that left a dozen Shadovar bobbing dead in the darkening waters. A pair of scorched shadow lords popped up beside Vala, their arms and legs blasted off by the force of the strike that had killed them. Vala threw her sword again, only to see her target scythed down the middle by a falling wall of black glass as Escanor unleashed his own magic.

Vala glanced over to see the third phaerimm's tail vanishing into the circle of shadow Galaeron had placed over its splash ring. The elf himself was pointing across the lake roughly in her direction. Knowing the creature would be disoriented for a moment when it emerged from Galaeron's shadow door, Vala nodded and reached out to summon her sword back.

Galaeron's finger shifted in Prince Escanor's direction.

"No, Galaeron!" Vala cried. "Here!"

Too late. The third phaerimm had already reappeared, stunned and disoriented by its dizzying journey through the shadow plane. But Escanor happened to be turning to attack their other surviving foe, and so this thornback appeared behind him instead of in front. Vala's stomach turned to ice. With the prince at least twenty paces away and in a direct line beyond the dazed phaerimm, she did not dare throw her sword again.

She started toward him, yelling, "Escanor, behind you!"

The prince cocked his head in response but only stretched a hand toward the second phaerimm, who was assailing five of his lords with a roaring storm of meteors. A sphere of spinning darkness shot from his hand and streaked through the thing's torso, leaving a basket-sized hole in the heart of its body. The creature splashed into the lake and slowly sank out of sight.

The third phaerimm was already bringing its tail out of the water, ten steps away.

"Watch your back!" she cried.

A murky aura of darkness—more of Galaeron's magic, Vala guessed—enveloped the phaerimm, but the spell did not prevent the creature's tail from catching Escanor in the pit of the stomach as he spun to meet the attack. The barb sank to its root, doubling the prince over and drawing an eerie gurgle of anguish.

Vala hurled her darksword. The blade tumbled three times, then sank hilt-deep in the phaerimm's torso. The creature began to flicker between material and immaterial, and Vala was astonished to realize that Galaeron had not cast his spell to protect the prince but to trap the phaerimm beside him.

Had Galaeron finally been taken by his shadow self?

Escanor wailed in pain and slipped off the barb, then rolled to his back and floated, groaning. Vala called her darksword back to her grasp and began to angle in the prince's direction.

"Vala, no!" Galaeron splashed into the water. "The phaerimm! It knows too much!"

Vala glanced at the prince, who, unlike most of his wounded lords, was at least floating faceup. She decided to place her trust in Galaeron a little longer. She sprang at the phaerimm, her black sword blocking the tail as it arced toward her throat, lopping the dangerous barb off at the root. On the backswing, she removed two of the thing's four arms, then reversed her grip, jammed the blade into the creature's enormous mouth, and split it down the side.

The dark aura vanished from around the phaerimm—only to reappear an instant later as Galaeron recast his snare spell. The phaerimm flickered between materiality and immateriality again as it tried once more to teleport away, and again Vala sank her sword deep into its body. It pummeled her with one of its remaining arms, and the other clamped onto her throat, trying to crush her windpipe. She kneed it in the flank and felt sharp pain as one of its body thorns impaled her thigh. The phaerimm began to overpower her, pulling her face toward the fang-filled mouth atop its shoulders. She croaked in Galaeron's direction.

He was already pointing a sliver of obsidian at the creature and yelling a string of mystic syllables. A finger-thin ray of darkness left his hand, catching the phaerimm in one of its remaining arms and severing it at the elbow. Vala snapped the other with a palm strike, then kicked free and brought her darksword around in three eviscerating swings.

The thing's heart slipped out of the second gash, still beating. Vala sent it flying off with a flick of her blade, and the phaerimm dropped, motionless, into the water. She struck again and again, not stopping until she had opened it from tail to lip and left it floating in the water like a dressed eel.

Galaeron waded up. "Are you hurt?"

"I'm alive." She shook her head clear and gave herself a cursory glance, then looked over and found herself staring into a pair of black, empty eyes. "G-Galaeron? How many spells did you cast?"

Instead of answering, Galaeron pushed her toward Escanor's floating form. "See to the prince and the others," he said as he turned and started toward the shadow curtain. "I'll finish the Splicing."

CHAPTER TWO

28 Tarsakh, the Year of Wild Magic

The city appeared just before dusk, hovering low over a rosy desert butte, a distant diamond of umbral murk silhouetted against the purple twilight of the eastern sky. As usual, it was surrounded by wisps of black fog, giving it the appearance of a storm cloud, a mirage, or an angry djinn. The V-shaped specks of a hundred or so vultures wheeled in lazy circles beneath the city, chasing the constant rain of garbage that dropped from its refuse chutes.

"There," Galaeron said.

Though it had been two days since he'd completed the Splicing, the icy tingle of shadow magic still permeated his body—and he hungered for more, longed to cast spells until he was numb and cold from head to foot, until he was filled with the power of shadow and beyond mortal frailty.

Instead, he pointed at the floating city and said, "See it?"

"So far?" Malik complained.

A pudgy little man with a moon-shaped face and bug-eyes, Malik el Sami yn Nasser was the Seraph of Lies, a favored servant of the evil god Cyric and an oddly stalwart traveling companion who had saved Galaeron's life more than once.

"I apologize for my accursed luck," the little man said. "It has always been its nature that just when I think matters could seem no worse, a turn of bad fortune comes along to prove me wrong."

"In this desert, things look farther than they are," Vala said. Limping a little from her wounded thigh, she started down the dry wash at their backs. "We'd better get moving, or we'll lose sight of it when dark really falls."

Nodding, Galaeron turned to follow. As a precaution against attack, Shade Enclave appeared only briefly each evening and always in a different place. Given that Escanor's company had failed to finish the Splicing and raise the shadowshell at the appointed time, it made sense to put some distance between the floating city and the Sharaedim battlefields. Assuming they were lucky enough to reach the city before it vanished again, Galaeron only hoped they would not fall victim to any new defenses intended for the phaerimm.

In the bottom of the wash, they found the Shadovar survivors preparing the company's mounts for departure. Though most of the shadow lords had already recovered from the cavern battle, Escanor had taken an egg when he was impaled and remained incoherent with fever. The longer it stayed inside him, the harder it would be to remove, but his chances were far better than those of most humans would have been. Shadovar were fast healers. Most of their wounds had closed within an hour after the battle, so it seemed likely that the prince would survive even a difficult extraction.

Galaeron followed Vala over to the nominal leader of the group in Escanor's incapacity, a ruby-eyed lord so swarthy that he looked more like an obsidian statue than a live man.

"Lord Rapha," Vala said, "we've located the enclave."

"That is well." Rapha did not look up. He was looping a length of shadow strand around the hands of a dead comrade, using it to secure the man in his saddle. "We'll soon be ready."

Galaeron and his companions waited for Rapha to ask where or how far off the enclave was, or to give some indication that he was concerned about getting Escanor to the city quickly.

Rapha ignored them.

Finally, Galaeron said, "The enclave is a long way off. You might want to send Escanor ahead."

The Shadovar fixed his ruby eyes on Galaeron. "Concerned for the prince, are we?"

"Of course," Vala said.

"Most concerned," Malik agreed. He hesitated for a moment, then was unable to keep from adding, "But we are even more concerned for ourselves. We know who will be blamed if he dies."

This drew a sour smile from the shadow lord. Like everyone in the company, Rapha knew that Malik had been cursed by the goddess Mystra to speak only the truth or not all. It was an irony in which Shadovar seemed to take special delight.

Rapha clapped a hand on the little man's shoulder. "You have nothing to fear, my stubby friend. You were not even at the Splicing."

"But *you* were," Galaeron said, wondering what Rapha was playing at. "You know I meant no harm to the prince."

"I know what I saw," Rapha said. "You used a shadow snare to keep the thornback trapped beside the prince."

"Had I let the thing teleport away, the shadowshell would be no prison at all," Galaeron retorted. "Those phaerimm were there to learn its secret, and what they discovered was important, or they would have attacked us long before I found them."

Rapha considered this, then his voice grew quiet and menacing. "How is it you know so much about the phaerimm, elf? Why could you find them when twenty shadow lords could not?"

Galaeron glanced away. "I can't say why," he admitted. "It just seemed right that they would be there."

"It just seemed right," Rapha echoed dubiously.

"I think his shadow knew," Vala said. "He didn't say anything about them until his shadow self asserted itself."

Rapha shook his head impatiently. "The shadow self is only an absence of what a person is, a darker image of himself that he creates simply by being what he is. It cannot know more than its creator, any more than its creator can know it."

Galaeron shrugged. "Then I can't explain it," he said. "I just had a feeling they would be there—and I was right."

"And risking Prince Escanor's life?" Rapha asked. "You just had a feeling about that?"

"I had to do it to save the shell," Galaeron said. "I knew that, just like I knew the phaerimm would try to teleport away."

Rapha shook his head. "You can't be sure," he insisted. "Your shadow self has you in its grasp. Your thinking could have been subverted—"

"But I *can* be sure that he needs a healer—and soon," Galaeron interrupted. This Rapha was a sly one, accusing Galaeron of trying to harm the prince—and wasting valuable time. "Unless you have some reason for delaying? Perhaps you'd like to see Escanor hatch a thornback egg?"

Rapha's eyes flared from ruby to white-orange. "I have nothing but love for all the princes of Shade, elf."

"Then wouldn't it be wise to have someone return him to the enclave at once?"

"It would, had Prince Escanor been lucid enough to tell us today's word of passing," Rapha said. "As it is, anyone who tries to enter through the shadows will find himself plummeting through to the Barrens of Doom and Despair."

"So we must return the slow way," Vala said, placing herself between Galaeron and Rapha to cut off further argument. "Can Escanor ride?"

"It would be better if he didn't," Rapha said. "Perhaps your friend would be kind enough to take a passenger."

The shadow lord motioned across the wash, to where a grim-faced stone giant with sad gray eyes was kneeling over a ten-foot block of quartzite. He was clinking away with his sculptor's tools, fashioning a life-sized model of the struggle between Escanor and the phaerimm that had wounded him. Though the work was still rough, it was obvious by the snaking forms and undulating hollows that he had captured not only the details, but the spirit and swiftness of the battle—and from little more than a description of the events.

"I am confident Aris would be pleased to be of some small service to the prince," Malik said. "While we were watching the camp, he said many times—if once can be considered many—that he wished he were small enough to accompany the rest of the company into the

Underdark and do his part to seal the fate of the phae-rimm."

"Good. Will you be kind enough to ask him for me? I'll have the prince brought over directly." Rapha waved Malik toward Aris, then turned to Galaeron and Vala. "You can tell which mounts are yours? We'll be leaving shortly."

"We'll be fine," Vala said. "I banded a leg on each of ours."

The precaution was not a frivolous one. The Shado-var's flying mounts—veserabs—were odd, furless crea-tures that had no faces and uniform midnight-blue skin. With four spindly legs, fan-shaped ears, and a pair of gargoyle-like wings folded alongside their tubular bodies, they looked like an unfortunate cross between bats and earthworms. Once they impressed on a rider, their devotion was absolute—to the point that they would spit noxious fumes into the face of anyone else who tried to mount them.

Galaeron followed her down the draw until they found a trio of veserabs wearing copper bands on their legs. Vala pointed to one with a band on its right foreleg. Galaeron gave the wing joint a tentative squeeze and slipped a foot into the stirrup. The creature did not react until he lowered his full weight into the saddle, when—much to his relief—an undulation of pleasure ran down its long body.

A few moments later, Malik returned and climbed into his saddle, and Rapha signaled the departure. The veser-abs charged down the wash until they gathered enough speed, then spread their wings and rose into the air in flawless formation. Many of the shadow lords were tied across their saddles, but only Escanor's mount was rid-erless. The company had recovered all of its casualties and carried them through fifty twining Underdark miles back to the surface.

As they climbed out of the wash, a huge dome of darkness rose into view over their shoulders at Anauroch's western edge. Even from a dozen miles into the desert, the barrier was immense, curving away high into the sky and stretching north and south as far as the eye could see. Through its black translucency, Galaeron could just make out the stacked crests of the foothills of the Desert Border South and, looming behind, the familiar crags of High Sharaedim itself. He could not help thinking of what lay beyond those peaks, the vale and city of Evereska—and his sister, Keya, safe within the city's protective mythal. He knew better than to think that his warrior father had been lucky enough to survive his duties to return to her side, but Lord Aubric Nihmedu was as resourceful as he was brave, and there was no harm in praying it so.

Once the veserabs had ascended high enough to avoid being surprised by an attack from the ground, Aris rose into the air on an ancient Netherese flying disk. Though the bronze saucer was neither as swift nor as maneuverable as a veserab, it was capable of carrying not only the giant's weight but also that of the wounded prince, his campaign tent, and Aris's half-completed statue. Its one drawback was that Aris could not defend himself in an air battle. The disks had been designed as battle platforms for Netherese archwizards, not stone giant clerics.

As the company leveled off and fixed their course on the murky silhouette of Shade Enclave, the formation began to loosen, giving the veserabs room to relax and stretch their wings. The creatures did not fly so much as swim through the atmosphere, reaching forward to grab a piece of air, then pulling themselves past. The turbulence and slipstreams created by tight formations made it more difficult to stay aloft with this strange motion, so they usually divided into smaller groups and flew side by side when traveling long distances. Vala and Malik drew up on opposite sides of Galaeron, spacing themselves about thirty feet apart.

Even had they been close enough to speak comfortably, the pounding veserab wings would have made it impossible to hear. They continued toward the dusk with only their own thoughts for company, leaving it to their mounts to steer a course toward the enclave while they watched their assigned slice of sky. Though most of the phaerimm were trapped inside the shadowshell, their hosts of servants and slaves remained free and apt to attack at any time. Twice, Rapha dispatched fliers to chase down and slay asabi lizardmen lest they were scouting for a larger company, and once they themselves had to swing into the shadows beneath a long line of cliffs when Vala spied the flea-sized spheres of a distant beholder troop bobbing across the moon's face.

Galaeron spent most of the trip brooding over the bitter words that had passed between him and Rapha. When they reached Shade Enclave, the lord clearly intended to blame him for what had befallen Escanor, and part of Galaeron even wondered if that could be justified. His shadow self was as insidious as it was dark, always working to make him see dishonorable motives in the actions of everyone around him, and for some time he had been growing angry about the hungry look in Escanor's eyes whenever he addressed Vala. Was it possible that Galaeron had sent the phaerimm to Escanor not because he wanted to be certain of killing it, but because his shadow self wanted to see the prince harmed instead?

The thought sent a shiver down Galaeron's spine, for it meant that the darkness had begun to invade his actions as well as his perceptions. The idea was driven from his mind as quickly as it had arrived, though. The prince had already killed one phaerimm and was about to slay the second, so it just seemed wisest to send him the third as well. Besides, if he really thought about it, Escanor deserved what had happened. Had he listened to Galaeron in the first place, the company would have been ready for the attack, and—

"No."

Galaeron spoke the word aloud and, alarmed at how powerful his shadow was growing, shook his head clear. The rationalization had come so smoothly, felt so natural that he had almost accepted the reasoning as his own. He would have to speak with his friends about this as soon as they landed. Aris had suggested that the best way to combat the influence of his shadow self was to be completely open about what he was thinking and feeling and let the opinions of his friends guide him. So far—as long as he didn't listen to Malik—the stone giant's strategy had not only worked, it had kept Galaeron more or less in control of himself. It had also brought him closer to Vala than was probably wise, considering the fleeting and intense nature of human lives.

Galaeron's thoughts came to an end when the veserabs let out a single high-pitched screech and abruptly started to climb. Night had fallen and it was so dark that he could see clearly no more than sixty feet in front of his face, but the light of the stars above was being blocked by Shade Enclave's looming form. It was not long before a few bats from the growing colony on the enclave's underside began to flit about their heads. Rapha called the company back into a tight formation, and the shadowy crags of a capsized mountaintop appeared over their heads. They circled the funnel-shaped peak in an ever-growing spiral, exchanging silent salutes with the jewel-eyed sentries watching from hidden nooks and crannies. Finally, they came to the Cave Gate, hidden in the deep shadows beneath a massive overhang and all but invisible even to Galaeron's dark sight.

The veserabs climbed so close to the roof that the riders had to lean forward and press tight against the creatures' fleshy backs. Then, one after the other, the veserabs gave short screeches, folded their wings tight against their bodies, and dived through a square of nothingness so dark that Galaeron could not tell it from the black gates themselves. He felt his sleeve brush against one edge of the wicket gate, then the air grew muggy and warm and he knew they had entered the vast Wing Court.

His mount spiraled downward into a dimly lit mezzanine area and landed in formation, six places behind Rapha and between Vala and Malik. Galaeron was astonished to see the Princes Rivalen, Brennus, and Lamorak standing at the head of the landing yard with a full company of shadow warriors.

Following the lead of Rapha and the rest of the Shadovar, Galaeron slipped off his veserab and kneeled on the floor, pressing his forehead to the cold stone. He cast an apprehensive glance in Vala's direction and saw her looking at him just as nervously, but neither dared to speak the question on their minds.

When the rest of the riders had dismounted and assumed similar positions, Galaeron sensed the princes and their guards coming across the floor. There was no sound—no tramping feet or clinking armor, nor even the whisper of boots scuffing cold stone—only a growing sense of stillness and apprehension.

Finally, Prince Rivalen's deep voice sounded not ten paces ahead. "Who is in command here?"

"I am," answered Rapha's quavering voice.

He stood and gasped softly, then described what had occurred at the underground lake, making clear what he had observed with his own eyes and what had been reported to him by others. When Rapha came to the attack on Prince Escanor, he took care to relay only the facts, though his acid tone made clear—at least to Galaeron—where he was trying to lay the blame. The shadow lord finished by reporting the successful completion of the Splicing and venturing the opinion that the phaerimm trapped within the Sharaedim would perish within a few months.

"And what of Escanor?" The voice that asked this was sibilant and pervasive, like a whisper echoing into the chamber from some distant passage. "Where is he now?"

"On the flying disk with the native giant," Rapha reported.

Like Aris himself, the flying disk was too large for the wicket door that opened into the passage leading down to the Wing Court. The stone giant would have to wait outside the Cave Gate until it was opened, then land on the great Marshaling Plaza itself.

"Most High," Prince Brennus said, "I'll summon a healer and see to our brother."

If there was a response, Galaeron did not hear it. The air grew chill and motionless, and he sensed someone standing above him.

"You are the one who held the phaerimm beside Escanor?" asked the same wispy voice that had spoken before.

Galaeron started to lift his head, then—after a hissed, "Are you mad?" from Malik—thought better of it and pressed his brow back to the floor.

"I am, Most High."

"And you did this why?" The voice seemed more interested than angry.

"To prevent it from escaping with the secret of the shell." Galaeron did not enjoy speaking to the floor, and he could not keep his irritation from creeping into his voice. "That was why the phaerimm were there, to learn how to defeat the shell so they could take Shade Enclave unawares later."

"Truly? And how do you know this?"

"The same way I knew they were there in the first place," Galaeron replied. "To tell the truth, I don't understand myself. All I can say is that I knew."

The voice remained silent.

"It just made sense," Galaeron said, as confident that the voice desired further explanation as he was of his fate if he failed to provide it. "They had to know what we were doing, and they couldn't allow that. They had to be planning something."

"That explains why you held the phaerimm beside Escanor?" the voice said.

Galaeron started to agree, then realized that was not what the voice wanted. There was still a question to be answered.

"The prince had just killed one phaerimm," Galaeron explained. "I thought it would be easy for him to kill another one, especially when it was teleport dazed."

Again, the silence.

"The only other place to send it was at Vala," Galaeron said. "I thought if it *did* kill someone, better Escanor than her."

"Stupid elf!" Malik shrieked, forgetting himself and raising his head. "Think what you are saying, before you get—"

The objection ended with the dull thump of a halberd butt striking Malik's cloth-swaddled head. Galaeron glanced over and found the little man sprawled unconscious but still breathing.

The voice asked, "You are struggling with your shadow, are you not, elf?"

"Losing, I think," Galaeron said. This time, he needed only the hint of a silence before realizing that he was to continue. "Prince Escanor has been looking at Vala. I didn't like it."

"Ah."

Galaeron felt the weight of Vala's stare and tried to keep his eyes fixed on the floor, but the voice remained silent, and eventually he felt compelled to peer in her direction. He found her returning his gaze as best as she was able, a look of surprise and triumph in her emerald eyes.

"It is nothing to be concerned about." The voice sounded amused. "Shadows are by nature unconquerable and unknowable. You can defeat them only by defeating yourself."

More silence, but this time Galaeron did not feel compelled to speak. The air grew muggy and less still, and Galaeron felt as though he could dare breathe again.

When the voice spoke this time, it was farther away. "Hadhrune will see to it that you and your companions are lodged near the palace. If I am to avoid losing any more of my princes, it seems I must teach you how to live with your shadow."

Uncertain of whether that was a good thing, but hoping it was, Galaeron started to raise his head—and felt the butt of a halberd on the back of his neck. He touched his head to the floor again.

The voice asked, "That will meet with your approval, will it not, elf?"

"Of course," Galaeron said. His heart was pounding—whether with joy or fear remained to be seen, but definitely with excitement. "Thank you."

Silence, heavy and expectant.

"And, of course, I'll repay you any way I can."

"Good, Galaeron," said the voice. "Now we understand each other."

Though the month of Tarsakh had nearly passed and the Greengrass festival was fast approaching in Waterdeep, a fierce blizzard was roaring in from the east, battering the window panes with its angry winds and dropping more snow on a city already buried to the doorknockers. Nor was this the wet slosh that blew in from the sea early every Greening. This was needle-snow, tiny spears of ice crystals formed over the High Ice and swept across the continent in howling walls of frostbite.

There was no prospect of it melting any time soon. Melting required warm breezes and bright sun, and the closest thing to either that Waterdeep had seen in three months was the steady flow of pearl-colored storm clouds sweeping across the sky. Matters had grown so bad that the city guard had covered the frozen harbor in mountains of excess snow, the woodcutters were finding it impossible to keep smoke in the city's chimneys, and the area farmers had yet to till their frozen fields. In short, Waterdeep was facing a natural disaster of the worst proportions, which was what made the news Prince Aglarel brought so fortuitous—suspiciously so, at least to anyone who knew how such things worked.

The Shadovar stood before Piergeiron Paladinson and seven of the Masked Lords of Waterdeep, his eyes glowing silver and his ceremonial fangs flashing white as he addressed the imposing assembly in the marble-walled majesty of the palace's Court Hall. In addition to Piergeiron and the Masked Lords, the gathering included the Silverhand sisters Storm and Laeral, Lord Tereal Dyndaryl from the isle of Evermeet, Lord Gervas Imesfor of Evereska, and the inevitable host of gawkers that could be expected whenever such a group of dignitaries came together.

If Aglarel was aware of the power and influence of those whom he addressed, his easy manner and confident voice betrayed no sign of the knowledge. Huge and dark, with a blocky face and long ebony hair, he wore a flowing black cape and purple tabard that almost gave him the appearance of floating as he strode back and forth behind the podium, now and again emphasizing a point by stabbing the air with a black talon that looked more like a shard of obsidian than a human fingernail.

"The Sharaedim has become the prison of the phaerimm," the prince was saying. "Now that my people have completed the shadowshell, the wisest thing to do is to wait and let it do its work."

"Wisest for you humans, perhaps," said Lord Imesfor. Though a powerful, well-respected lord in Evereska, he was a withered and disheartened husk of an elf whose fingers had been so badly mangled by a group of phaerimm captors that he could barely dress himself, much less cast a spell. "What of the elves still trapped in Evereska? What of our lands?"

"The enemy has already ravaged your lands. The shell will do nothing to change that," Aglarel answered. "As for your elves besieged in Evereska, we can only hope we reach them before the phaerimm do."

"We will reach no one hiding behind this shadowshell of yours," Tereal Dyndaryl said. Relatively tall for even a Gold elf, he had a gaunt face that made his already sour countenance seem absolutely bitter. "We don't have time to starve the phaerimm out. We must carry the fight to them!"

"You know how to do that, Lord Dyndaryl?" Aglarel asked. Considering the accusatory tone Dyndaryl had employed, the prince's voice remained surprisingly cordial. "If the elves have a faster way to defeat the phaerimm, the Shadovar are eager to help."

Dyndaryl's flaxen cheeks darkened to amber. "We are working on a few ideas, but nothing I can share at the moment."

"When the time comes, then," Aglarel said, without a trace of disbelief. "For now, the shell remains our best choice. Please advise your commanders to give it a wide berth. Those coming into contact with it will lose whatever touches it, and anyone using Mystra's magic on it will accomplish nothing and may well regret the results."

"And why would that be?" demanded Storm Silverhand.

A striking, silver-tressed woman who stood more than six feet tall, Storm was garbed in form-fitting leather armor and armed for battle. Though she lived half a continent away and had arrived at the meeting uninvited, Piergeiron had nevertheless welcomed her attendance. When dealing with one of Mystra's Chosen, it was usually the wise thing to do.

"No one here cares for your Shadovar threats," added Storm.

"You misunderstand, Lady Silverhand," Aglarel said. He probably meant his smile to seem forbearing, but the line of fang tips hanging down behind his black lip made it look rather more sinister. "The Shadovar are not threatening anyone. I am merely informing Lords Piergeiron and Dyndaryl of the shell's dangers."

What are those dangers? whispered Deliah the White, one of the Masked Lords of Waterdeep. Like the other masked lords, her identity was concealed beneath a magic cloak, helm, and mask, and her words could be heard only by Piergeiron and her fellows on the council. *Knowing of these dangers does us little good unless we also know what they are.*

"What, exactly, is the nature of these dangers?" Piergeiron asked. As the Open Lord, it was his duty to serve as the council's common face and speak for the others in public. "It does us little good to know of them without knowing what they are."

Aglarel cast a meaningful glance over his shoulder at the gawkers in the public gallery. "It wouldn't be wise to reveal the shadowshell's nature at present," he said. "Suffice it to say that we all know what happened when a mere Tomb Guard's magic hit a shadow spell."

Along with Deliah the White and several others, Piergeiron found himself nodding. This whole mess had started when a patrol of Evereskan Tomb Guards interrupted a rendezvous between a powerful Shadovar wizard and what the elves took to be a company of human tomb robbers. A phaerimm had been drawn to the sound of the resulting turmoil, and during the terrible battle that followed, the patrol leader's Weave-based magic had clashed with the Shadovar's shadow-based magic. Nobody really understood what had happened next, except that the result had torn a hole in the mystic barrier that had kept the phaerimm imprisoned beneath Anauroch for over fifteen hundred years.

After allowing his audience a moment to contemplate his words, Aglarel continued, "Can you imagine the consequences if that spell had been loosed by one of Waterdeep's battle wizards?" He glanced at Gervas Imesfor. "Or perhaps a high mage from Evereska?"

"There is no need to imagine," Storm said darkly. "We all know what happened at Shadowdale—which is why I am finding your concern for our welfare so difficult to believe now."

"What happened at Shadowdale was a misunderstanding," Aglarel countered, "and it was *your* attack that opened the Hell breach. We lost one of our own to it as well."

"A small price to be rid of Elminster," Storm spat.

"That was never our intention," Aglarel said. "Rivalen and the others were there to talk—"

"Perhaps you forget that I was there, Prince," Storm warned. "I saw what your brothers did."

Before the lightning that flashed in her eyes became bolts flying from her fingers, Piergeiron raised a hand and said, "As concerned as we all are about Elminster's fate, that is not the matter before this council."

He could not allow Storm to turn this discussion into a quarrel over who had caused Elminster's disappearance. The argument was a sore one, and growing more so since the Simbul had turned up missing as well. There were some who suggested she had already recovered Elminster and spirited him off to some other dimension to recuperate. But Storm insisted on holding the Shadovar responsible for Elminster's continued absence, and she never missed an opportunity to rebuke them over the matter.

Piergeiron did not know what to believe—he had heard convincing evidence that supported both sides—and it really didn't matter to him. His only goal was to keep the matter from erupting into a full-blown magic duel anywhere within a hundred leagues of Waterdeep—much less within the walls of his own palace.

He locked gazes with Storm and said, "Whatever happened that day in Shadowdale, the last thing Evereska—or Faerûn itself—needs is war with the Shadovar, too."

"Whatever happened?" Storm fumed. "I have told you what happened! The Shadovar are as bad as the—"

"Come now, Sister," Laeral said. Almost as tall as Storm, she had the same silver hair but emerald eyes instead of blue. "Exaggeration serves no one, and I have seen for myself what the Shadovar can do against the phaerimm. We need all the help they can provide."

"Help from a nest of vipers will prove poison in the end," Storm retorted.

"We are asking for no more than was Netheril's in the days of our fathers," Aglarel said. "Leave us to Anauroch, and no one on Faerûn need fear Shade Enclave."

"Anauroch is not Waterdeep's to grant or deny," Piergeiron said, trying to guide the conversation back to the matter at hand. "Just as Evereska is not the Shadovar's to quarantine."

"I could not agree with you more, Lord Piergeiron," Aglarel replied. "Which is only one of the reasons we should establish a coordinating council. I'm sure we can all agree that it would be in Evereska's best interest if our nations shared in the responsibility of making these sorts of decisions."

"A magnanimous gesture, Prince Aglarel, considering that the Shadovar have dealt the phaerimm the few losses they have suffered in this war," Laeral said warmly. She knew whereof she spoke; her beloved Khelben "Blackstaff" Arunsun had vanished during a battle early in the war, and she was spending much of her time at the front trying to determine what had become of him. "I am certain Lord Imesfor would welcome such a council."

Before the elf could voice his approval or disapproval, Storm asked, "Who would lead this council? The Shadovar?"

Aglarel nodded without hesitation. "For now," he said, "it appears we are best equipped to assume that duty."

When dragons kneel before halflings! scoffed Brian the Swordmaster. As one of the Masked Lords of Waterdeep, his words came to Piergeiron as a barely audible whisper. *They're trying to take control of the war zone.*

Aglarel cast a brief glance in Brian's direction, then

looked back to Piergeiron and said, "If the Lords of Waterdeep find our leadership uncomfortable, we would not be adverse to naming Lord Imesfor master of the council. It is, after all, his home that is in peril."

Piergeiron was almost too astonished to reply. The discussions between the masked lords were shielded by the same magic that protected their identities, yet Aglarel had plainly heard what Brian had said.

"The lords will discuss the council you propose later—in private," Piergeiron said, "but we do appreciate your suggestion."

Many of the spectators in the hall would be mystified as to why he did not immediately agree to name Lord Imesfor the council leader, but they had not seen how the elf trembled at the slightest sound or heard the screams that echoed through the palace halls whenever he retired to his room to attempt the Reverie. Gervas Imesfor was in no condition to lead a horse, much less a political and military alliance of this magnitude. Piergeiron felt quite certain that Aglarel had known that when he proposed it.

I'm sure our deliberations would be more meaningful if we knew more about the nature of the shadowshell, Deliah said, still pressing for details. Like nearly every respectable wizard on Faerûn, she seemed more alarmed by the Shadovar's mysterious magic than by the evil of the phaerimm. *If the prince is concerned about spies, perhaps we could meet later—*

"I am at liberty to reveal the nature of the shell only to our declared allies," Aglarel said, drawing an audible gasp from three of the lords who had not previously realized he was listening in on their private conversations. "However, it is difficult to predict how the phaerimm will respond. It really would be better to establish the coordinating council at once."

"You have doubts that the shell will hold?" Lord Dyndaryl asked.

"Not at all. The shell will hold." Aglarel deliberately looked at Imesfor and said, "It is Evereska we are concerned about. We do not understand the mythal well enough to know how long it can withstand a sustained assault."

"It's still up?" The relief in Imesfor's voice was obvious. "You know that?"

The phaerimm had enclosed the entire Sharaedim within a magic deadwall that prevented any sort of travel to or communication with Evereska, and he was not the only one in the room who had been wondering if the city was still in elf hands.

Aglarel hesitated a moment, then gave a nod so slight it was barely perceptible.

"Thank Corellon!" Imesfor gasped.

"Then you are in contact with the city?" It was Laeral Silverhand who asked this. "Do you know if Khelben is there?"

Aglarel looked away. "Unfortunately, I am not at liberty to answer your questions, Lady Silverhand." He managed to sound genuinely apologetic. "That information would be available only to our allies."

"To your *allies*!" Laeral fumed. "Who do you think has been fighting at your side—"

"Were the choice mine, Lady Silverhand, I would tell you," he said. "Your contributions have not gone unnoticed by our Most High, but your allegiance is obviously to Waterdeep, and Waterdeep has not declared itself our ally."

Nor are we like to, said Brian. *Waterdeep won't yield to strong-arm tactics. Never!*

Aglarel looked directly at Brian. "This isn't strong-arming. How many of its secrets would Waterdeep reveal to a city that refuses to call itself an ally?"

"We are not asking for any of your secrets," Laeral said, straining to sound patient. "Only the simple courtesy of—"

"The Shadovar are showing you *every* courtesy, Lady Silverhand," Aglarel said. "That is what I'm doing here. It is Waterdeep that is being discourteous, that receives information given in good faith with suspicion, that rebukes our offer of friendship with high-handed accusations of coercion, that allows a visitor under its palace roof to call Shade Enclave a den of liars and vipers."

Aglarel allowed his gaze to linger on Storm Silverhand for a moment, then looked back to Piergeiron. "You have been advised of the shadowshell's danger. It is not our intent to interfere with any of your own missions. Should any of your forces wish to pass through, we will be happy to send an escort along to make that possible."

The arrogant devils! Brian ranted, either forgetting or ignoring the fact that the prince could obviously hear every word. *They're claiming control of the war zone whether we like it or not!*

Aglarel shot a glance in Brian's direction but chose to ignore the outburst. "While we regret that it will not be possible to coordinate our efforts, Shade Enclave does thank you for this audience."

The Shadovar bowed deeply, then turned toward the door to leave. Though Piergeiron could feel the gazes of the elves and the Silverhand sisters burning into his brow, it was what he knew his fellow lords were leaving unsaid that weighed most heavily on his mind. As usual, Brian the Swordmaster had cut straight to the heart of the matter. Whether Waterdeep and the elves liked it or not, the Shadovar had taken control of the war zone. What Piergeiron didn't understand was why they had bothered to send an envoy to announce an already obvious fact. Were they really hoping to establish an alliance, or was there something more, something broader and more nefarious?

There was only one way to find out. Piergeiron drew himself up to his full height, then called, "Prince Aglarel!"

To his credit, Aglarel looked properly shocked as he stopped and turned. "Yes, Lord Paladinson?"

"I did not dismiss you."

The prince looked as though he were biting a smile back. "Of course." He inclined his head. "I apologize."

Piergeiron resisted the temptation to let the Shadovar remain in the deferential position. The point had been made.

"Prince Aglarel, Waterdeep has not rejected your offer."

This seemed to catch the prince by surprise. "Then you have accepted it?"

"As I said earlier, the lords will discuss the matter later."

"That is the same as rejecting it," Aglarel said. "As *I* said earlier, the council needs to be established at once."

"Then you must be expecting something to happen soon," Piergeiron said. "Perhaps Waterdeep and Evereska should withdraw our armies."

Finally, Aglarel's silver eyes flashed in surprise. "Withdraw?"

"At once," Piergeiron confirmed. "We certainly wouldn't want to interfere with your city's plans."

Aglarel considered this for a moment, then lowered his gaze. "It is not our intention to drive you from the field," he said. "Let me consult with the enclave."

Piergeiron smiled. "Of course." He dismissed the prince with a gracious wave. "Take all the time you need. We will."

"Yes," Aglarel said, "I am quite sure you will."

The prince returned the Open Lord's smile, then bowed again and, with a courteous flourish of his dark cape, turned to leave.

CHAPTER THREE

9 Mirtul, the Year of Wild Magic

As with so much of Shade Enclave, Villa Dusari struck Galaeron as a monument to the allure of darkness and beauty half-glimpsed. The gates opened into a round courtyard paved in gray pearl—not stone exactly, but not quite glass either. In the center, a small fountain stood bubbling water into a black pool. The colonnade ringing the enclosure was deep and shadowed, with nine arched doorways opening like cave mouths into the house interior. In front of each pillar lay one of the precious urns wealthy Shadovar used for decoration, a hole knocked in one side to let the magic shadow spray gurgle out in a formless knob.

"A pity," rumbled Aris. The gate had no lintel, so the stone giant had no need to stoop as he stepped into the court. He kneeled and gingerly pinched one of the urns between his thumb and forefinger. "Who would do such a thing?"

"A sign of mourning," explained their guide, Hadrhune. A slender man dressed in a flowing black robe, he was swaddled in so much shadow magic that at times he seemed to vanish into his own umbral aura. He used the black staff in his hand to point at the half-completed statue beneath Aris's arm and said, "Your work is of suitable quality that no one would object if you replaced them with your own sculptures."

The giant nodded. "It would be my privilege."

"Indeed, it is always a guest's privilege to increase the wealth of his host with treasures of art," Malik said. He sat on the rim of the central basin and drew a disapproving frown from Hadrhune by using his hands to scoop water into his mouth. "May it please you to stay at my house sometime . . . when the One allows me the funds to purchase one."

"Until then, it is the hope of the Most High that you will find this one adequate," Hadrhune said. He took the dipper from its hook and pointedly offered it to Malik. "Consider it your home."

"Indeed?" Ignoring the dipper, Malik wiped his hands on his tunic and studied the courtyard with an appraising eye. "This is a little cramped for Kelda, but—"

"I am afraid your horse must remain in the stables," Hadrhune sniffed. He turned to Aris and waved his staff around the courtyard. "This is to be Aris's quarters. Will it do? We can have a roof erected, but space so near the palace is at a premium. Outside of the Grand Hall itself, no building in the area is large enough for you."

"I have no need for a roof, thank you." Aris studied the area with a growing look of discomfort, then tried to hide his disappointment and said, "There is room enough for me to sleep."

"Do not fear, my large friend," Hadrhune said. "Sleep is all you need do here. The Most High has declared that you may keep your workshop in the goodshouse where you have been staying. He was quite taken with your depiction of Escanor's fight."

This actually drew a smile from the grim giant. "Then he shall have it when I finish."

"Aris will fill the city with his work, if you let him," Galaeron said, stepping to Hadrhune's side. "When am I to begin my lessons with the Most High?"

Hadrhune ran a black thumbnail along a deeply worn groove near the head of his staff. "I thought you would first wish to make yourself comfortable in your new home."

"It took you a tenday to find this place," Galaeron said. "I have no time to waste."

"The Most High has been occupied with the war." Hadrhune's amber eyes were burning. "I'm sure you understand."

"What I understand is that he said he would teach me to control my shadow," Galaeron said, "and that *you* turn me away every time I present myself."

Hadrhune's staff rose as though he might strike Galaeron, who felt Vala's hand clamped around his forearm.

"Galaeron, get a hold of yourself!" She dug her fingers into the underside of his wrist and twisted, forcing him to open his hand and release the hilt he had not realized he was grasping. "If he doesn't want you seeing the Most High, drawing your sword would be just the excuse he needs to see you never do."

Hadrhune gave Vala a thin smile. "I do want him to learn from the Most High," he said. "We all do."

Moving more slowly, he waved his staff over their heads and aimed the tip at the gate, where a dark-haired woman dressed in the robe and veil of the Bedine desert people was attempting to sneak into the courtyard. Judging by her kohl-rimmed eyes—all Galaeron could see of her—she was a little older than Vala and not quite as swarthy as the Shadovar.

"You there," Hadrhune said. "Do you know what we do with thieves in this city?"

The hint of a cringe flashed across the woman's eyes, then she drew herself up straight. "From all I can tell, you harbor them." She spoke Common without a trace of Bedine accent. She locked gazes with Hadrhune and crossed the courtyard, a silver harp-and-moon pinned to her collar growing visible as she drew near. "I am searching for one rumored to keep company with these people."

She regarded Galaeron and Vala as though they did not deserve the honor of her gaze, then glanced past Aris's kneecap and into the shadowy depths of the colonnade. Galaeron was not all that surprised to realize Malik had vanished. The little man had an astonishing capacity for stealth, and he had mentioned his troubles with a certain Harper often enough for Galaeron to guess who this was. Vala caught his eye and barely raised her brow. He flattened his fingers in a signal to wait, and the Bedine Harper looked away, pretending not to see.

If Hadrhune noticed the woman's discretion, he hid it well. "How did you enter Shade Enclave?"

Her dark brows arched. "In the usual way," she said. "I have been serving Princes Clariburnus and Brennus as a desert guide, a position arranged in Waterdeep through Laeral Silverhand and Prince Aglarel. If there are closed districts, they did not inform me when they brought me into the city."

"The district is not closed," Hadrhune clarified, "but it is well guarded."

"And you would know everyone who enters?"

"Yes," Hadrhune answered.

A twinkle came to the woman's eyes, and she said, "I think not."

Galaeron liked her instantly.

"Ruha," he said, "it is a waste of your time to look for Malik with us. He is hardly the sort a wise company welcomes for long."

The witch turned her mocking gaze on Galaeron and said, "If you know who I am, then you must also know I am not so easily fooled. I found his horse in the stables." A small chain of gold dropped out of her sleeve into her cupped hand, though it was done so deftly that Galaeron doubted anyone else had noticed. "A pity—she was such a fine mount."

"Harper shrew!" Malik screamed. "What have you done to my Kelda?"

The little man came charging out of the shadows at her back, a stone loaded in his sling and his arm rising to attack. Ruha spun around deftly, holding the golden chain up before him and uttering a common imprisonment spell.

Galaeron was already halfway through the reversal. He timed his incantation to finish in the same instant as Ruha's, and a bolt of shadow magic rushed up through his body, cold and jolting, raw enough to sting his bones. A cord of brown magic spiraled up Ruha's body, binding her knees to each other and her arms to her sides, then the golden chain vanished from her hands and appeared in Galaeron's.

Malik loosed the stone in his sling. Galaeron gave the chain a quick tug and jerked Ruha out of the way. The rock sailed past, striking Hadrhune square in the chest.

The seneschal barely flinched, but Malik's eyes bugged out so far they looked like they might fall from their sockets.

"Your Darkness, a thousand pardons!" he cried. "But surely a man has a right to defend—"

"Enough!" Hadrhune lowered his staff at Malik.

Galaeron cursed under his breath and raised a hand to cast another spell—only to have Vala slap it down.

"Are you mad?"

Hadrhune spoke a word, and a tiny sphere of shadow shot from the tip and struck the ground at Malik's feet. He cried out and tried to leap away, but the dark circle expanded beneath him. When he came down, he fell in as though it was a hole. The shadow circle drew in on itself and vanished from sight.

Aris, who had been watching all this from far above, groaned and dropped to a knee, his big hand already reaching for Hadrhune. The seneschal raised his staff overhead and caught the middle of the giant's hand on its tip.

"There is nothing to be angry about, Aris. Your friend will return shortly."

"He better." Aris removed some of his hand's weight from the staff, but tried to sound threatening. "I owe him my life."

"There is no need to pay today, my large friend," Hadrhune said, lowering his staff. "I just wanted time to sort matters out."

He went to stand in the place Malik had vanished from, then motioned Galaeron to bring Ruha over. "Since you all seem to know of each other, perhaps you would be so kind as to enlighten me?"

Ruha glared daggers at Galaeron, then, with her hands still bound by the brown cord of magic, said, "I have no business with the elf or his harlot—"

"Harlot?" Vala stormed. "I've never taken a copper!"

She reached for her darksword and started forward, but stopped at a warning dip of Hadrhune's black staff.

"Let's finish this without bloodshed, shall we?" He turned back to Ruha and asked, "What do you want with Malik?"

"To take him to Twilight Hall to answer for his crimes."

"Which are?"

"More murders than I can count, but including that of Rinda and Gwydion, guardians of the evil *Cyrinishad*, and the theft of that same foul book," Ruha said. "If the Shadovar truly wish to be the good allies to the nations of Faerûn that they claim, you will release me and turn over this miscreant."

"I assure you, our desire is sincere," Hadrhune said, "but I was not aware that the Harpers controlled so many nations."

"We control none," Ruha admitted, "and influence many."

"A distinction we Shadovar understand as well," Hadrhune said, smiling politely. Unlike the grins of the princes and most shadow lords, his did not reveal a mouthful of ceremonial fangs. "We also know there are two sides to every argument. Galaeron, what say you? How would you advise the Most High in this matter?"

Galaeron considered Hadrhune, recalling his distaste for the little man, then said, "I know what you'd like to hear."

"Is that so?" Hadrhune cocked his brow. "Tell me."

"Do you think I'm that far into my shadow?"

Vala grabbed his arm. "Galaeron . . ."

"I know what's right," he said, shaking her off. "I won't betray a loyal companion for access to the palace."

"Galaeron, Hadrhune's not asking you to betray anyone," Vala said.

"I am only asking for the truth," Hadrhune said. "If you cannot see that, you *are* in the grasp of your shadow." Leaving Galaeron to fume, Hadrhune turned and craned his neck up at Aris. "What would you tell the Most High, my friend?"

Kneeling beside the fountain, the giant still loomed over the Shadovar by half-again his height. "It's true that Malik serves an evil god," Aris said, "but I am life-debted to him and honor bound to stand with him against any foe."

Hadrhune looked to Vala. "And you?"

"I wouldn't be here, were it not for him."

Galaeron still found it difficult to believe that Hadrhune was truly interested in his opinion, but he had no choice except to trust Vala's judgment over his own. He did not feel as though he was in the grasp of his shadow, but neither had he at the Splicing—and he had just cast a spell.

"Nor would I," Galaeron agreed. "He's saved us all."

"For his own reasons," Ruha interjected. "He's been playing you for fools—just as the Shadovar are now."

Hadrhune's eyes flashed. "You will not help your case by trying to poison the opinions of our guests against us, Harper."

"The truth is not poison." Though Ruha spoke to Hadrhune, she was looking at Galaeron. "You're from Evereska, are you not Galaeron?"

"What if he is?" Vala demanded.

Ruha's eyes narrowed. "How long has it been since you have been outside this city's murk?"

Galaeron frowned, wondering what the witch was trying to accomplish. "Not that it's any business of yours, but more than a tenday."

Even Ruha's heavy veil could not hide her smirk.

"What?" Galaeron demanded.

The witch looked at Hadrhune.

He glared amber flames at her, then turned to Galaeron and said, "The enclave is moving."

"Moving?" Galaeron echoed. "It's always moving."

"Deeper into the desert," Hadrhune clarified. "Away from Evereska. That's why—"

"Traitors!" Galaeron lunged for the seneschal but went down heavily, Vala on his back. "You promised!"

"And we will keep our promise," Hadrhune said. "The shadowshell has cut the phaerimm off from the Weave. Eventually, they will deplete the magic remaining to them—but it will take time, Galaeron, many months. You know better than anyone that we dare not attack until they have depleted their powers and begun to starve, until they grow too feeble to defend themselves."

"So, you are only abandoning Evereska for a little while?" Ruha asked, her voice surprisingly cynical. "Oh yes, that makes a great deal of sense."

Hadrhune kneeled in front of Galaeron, who was not struggling only because he knew how easily Vala could choke him unconscious with the arm already around his throat.

"We are not abandoning Evereska," Hadrhune said, "but the situation is stable now, and we must think of our own needs as well."

"When were you going to tell me?" Galaeron demanded.

Hadrhune hesitated and looked away.

"It's a fair question," Vala said.

Hadrhune let out a weary sigh. "As you wish," he said. "The Most High thought—"

That was when Malik appeared behind the seneschal, clambering out of a circle of shadow like a cat out of a well. He let out a bloodcurdling scream and dashed half a dozen steps across the courtyard before running into Aris's palm and stopping to see where he was.

Turban half undone, Malik whirled on Hadrhune and said, "If you knew what I had for a heart, you would not think that funny—not at all." Seeming to forget all about Ruha, Malik started toward the seneschal, wagging his finger. "It is a good thing for you that I did not die of fright in there, or the One would surely visit on you a hell a thousand times worse—or else laugh so hard at my miserable fate that he split his rotten sides."

This last admission, forced by Mystra's truth curse, seemed to take the fire out of him. Malik spent a moment taking in the scene in the courtyard, then slipped to Ruha's helpless form and raked his foot down her shin.

"Hag! What did you do to my Kelda?"

Ruha's eyes flared, but she showed no other sign of pain. "Why is it you care more for your horse than for your friends?"

"Because my horse is more loyal," Malik answered. He reached under his robes and pulled out his curved dagger. "Now answer, or your death will be even more painful."

"No!"

Vala and Galaeron were not the only ones to yell this, but it was Hadrhune's staff that came down across the little man's wrists and knocked the dagger from his hands.

"Not here," the Shadovar said. "Murder is as forbidden in Shade Enclave as it is in Waterdeep or Shadowdale." He cast a meaningful glance at Malik. "And our justice is swifter."

"Then you have no choice," Malik complained. "The witch will never leave here until I am dead!"

"Or my prisoner," Ruha clarified.

"That, we will never permit," Aris warned.

Hadrhune considered this for a moment, then shook his head wearily. "You place Shade Enclave in a difficult position, Harper. Either we harbor this miscreant against you or we allow you to violate our guest guard."

"There is no reason to concern yourself with that," Galaeron said, glaring up at Hadrhune. "We'll be leaving within the hour."

Hadrhune studied Galaeron for a moment, then nodded. "That is your privilege, of course, but as long as you or any of your friends remain in Shade Enclave, Malik is protected as our guest and may not be killed or taken captive."

"You would truly harbor a murderer?" Ruha demanded.

"He has not murdered anyone here," Hadrhune said. He touched his staff to her binding, and the magic cord dissolved. "Nor have you. The same law that guards him guards you—and if something unfortunate should befall either of you, we will know whom to execute."

Again, Hadrhune cast a warning glance at Malik.

"I'm free to stay?" Ruha asked.

"In this very house." Hadrhune seemed unable to avoid smirking. "Shade Enclave would never want it said that we made it difficult for a murderer to be brought to justice."

"Justice?" Malik scoffed. "You have no idea what you're condemning me to!"

"Not for long," Galaeron said. He scowled up at Vala. "If you'll get off of me, that is."

Vala studied him doubtfully. "You're not going to attack?"

"I'm going to *leave*," Galaeron said. "I'm going to go back to Evereska."

Hadrhune motioned Vala off, then offered a hand. "If that is what you wish, but the Most High will be very disappointed tomorrow."

Galaeron ignored the hand and stood on his own.

"He will," Hadrhune insisted. "He wanted to explain himself why the city was moving. That's why I didn't tell you."

"Sure it is." Despite his words, Galaeron took no steps toward the gate. "Tomorrow?"

Hadrhune nodded. "He would like to break fast with you. All will be explained."

Galaeron turned to Vala.

"One more day?" She looked around the villa and shrugged. "What could it hurt?"

The humans were at it again, clambering around on Malygris's mountain, kneeling and standing and kneeling again outside his cave, chanting, singing, groveling, begging his favor. That was a snort. He had told Namirrha he didn't want the cult members dallying about outside his lair, but did the mammal listen? What Malygris ought to do was clatter up there and bolt the whole lot, but then he would have to go out and devour something, and he just didn't feel like eating. Dracoliches needed food only to recharge their breath weapons, and Malygris hadn't discharged his (hadn't even left his lair) in over a year—or so Namirrha had told him the last time the necromancer deigned to visit.

Something alive—something human—appeared in the shadows over by his number three platinum heap. A bitter sense of outrage rising to fill his empty ribcage, Malygris swung his big horned skull toward the intrusion. Could the warmbloods leave him not even his seclusion? A pair of dark silhouettes rose out of the darkness, not emerging from the darkness so much as peeling themselves out of it, and turned in his direction.

How the mammals had bypassed his teleport traps, Malygris did not know, or how they had avoided activating his alarm magic. What he *did* know was that he could bear only so much and that this entering of his lair was the final insult. He opened his jaws and loosed a mouthful of lightning. In the crackling flash that filled the cavern, he glimpsed a pair of swarthy humans in dark robes cartwheeling across his hoard and smashing headlong into his wall. They collapsed among his diamonds and lay there scorched, smoking, and—amazingly— more or less alive.

Malygris continued to look in their direction. When Namirrha had made him a dracolich, he had grown acutely aware of everything alive within a wingspread of himself, and he knew the two humans were badly injured. Mammals were fragile, so they seemed likely to die within a few hours anyway, and he was not about to waste another breath attack on them. If he conserved, he still had two good lightning blasts left before he would have to leave his lair and eat.

But the pair did not expire. Instead, over the next hour, they grew steadily stronger, first crawling behind a pile of gold coins fused into a solid lump by the heat of his lightning, then hiding there and recovering by the minute, speaking to each other in some ancient human tongue even Malygris had never before heard. It was the ultimate warmblood insult—not being frightened enough to flee or at least to cower in silence. Malygris would have torn them limb from limb, save that over the last year, his hideless skeleton had sunken to his spine in his nest of sapphires, and he simply did not want to abandon such a comfortable bed.

A voice, deep and booming, at least by human standards, called out in Common, "Most Mighty Malygris, there is no need to attack. We come in peace."

Malygris considered this, then said, "If you come in peace, why do you cower behind my hoard piles like dragon hunters and treasure thieves?"

A soft clinking echoed of the walls as the pair rose from their hiding places. They stepped into view, revealing themselves to be a warrior and a priest, both dressed in the melted remains of some glassy, gleaming black armor.

Malygris blasted them again.

This time, his electric fury pinned them to the wall and held them there, stiff-limbed and smoking, the warrior's steel-colored eyes and the priest's bronze-colored glowing like mage-light. Their glossy armor ran off their bodies in runnels and gathered at their feet in black puddles. Their swarthy flesh melted and burned away from their chests, revealing the black organs and dusky bones beneath. Their heels and fists hammered themselves into pulp against the stone wall.

Still they were alive when Malygris ran out of breath—limp as scarecrows and reeking of charred flesh and in places naked to the bone, but alive. They dropped to the floor and lay there groaning for half an hour, then finally grew strong enough to pull themselves behind treasure piles as they had before.

Interesting.

It was the first thing that had interested Malygris since Namirrha had gotten his mate, Verianthraxa, killed in the senseless attack upon the keep-ists—an assault forced upon them by Namirrha's profane magic. Malygris searched out his legs beneath his nest of sapphires and bade them serve. He lifted himself out of the gems and clacked his fleshless bones across the cavern to where the two humans lay cowering.

No, not cowering.

The two were sitting, propped against the wall, staring up at him with their little molten eyes, not even trembling. The charred chest bones that had been exposed just moments before were already covered with dark flesh, and the scars were vanishing from even that. Malygris snatched up one in each claw, then watched in amazement as their shattered hands and feet returned to their normal shape.

"What manner of human are you that heal like trolls?" he demanded.

"We are princes of Shade Enclave," said the bronze-eyed one. "I am Clariburnus. My brother is Brennus."

"Do you think your names matter to me? Your arrogance is insufferable!" Malygris squeezed the one that had called itself Clariburnus and was pleased to hear the crackle of breaking bones. He felt the body go limp in his hand, but that was the only way he knew the mammal was in pain. He swung his bony muzzle toward the one with the eyes of steel. "I asked *what* you are, not who."

"We call ourselves Shadovar," this one said. "In our tongue it means 'of the shade.' "

"Ah, then you are shades." Malygris said. Shades were two-legged mammals that traded their souls for shadow essence. In the light of day, they seemed normal men, but as the light grew dim, they grew strong. "I understand now. I have met a few shades in my centuries."

Curiosity satisfied, he tightened his grasp to crush them—and felt his claws close on air. He sensed them emerging behind him and whirled around to find the steel-eyed one stepping from the shadows in front of his nest. The other, the one with the crushed body, lay in a hollow on top.

They were between him and his phylactery.

"Clariburnus and I are shades," the one with steel eyes said. "But not all Shadovar are shades, and not all shades are Shadovar. A Shadovar is a citizen of Shade Enclave."

"I see your game." Malygris started forward, his great tail launching whole mountains of coins into the dark air as it flailed back and forth. "Try, then. One way or the other, I will take pleasure in the end."

The steel-eyed one—Brennus—raised his hand and said, "Stop. We're not here to attack you, but you are done attacking us."

Malygris stopped, not because the human commanded it—he hadn't—but because he found himself snorting in laughter. "You threaten me?" Tiny forks of lightning began to dance around his nasal cavities. "Truly?"

"We are not threatening." This from the crushed one, who had already healed enough to sit upright. "We came to talk."

"Talk?" Malygris settled onto his haunches and waved a claw at the floor before him. "Very well, you may present your gifts."

The two humans—Shadovar—glanced at each other, then Brennus said, "We bring you no gifts."

"No gifts?" Malygris gasped. Even more interesting—insulting, but interesting. "How can you beg without gifts? How can you grovel with nothing to offer?"

"We're not here to beg," Clariburnus said. He stood—so soon after being crushed—and limped down to stand beside his companion. "But Shade Enclave does have something offer."

Malygris sensed Namirrha's arrival within the lair and whirled toward the entrance. The necromancer, a balding and wrinkled figure even by mammal standards, was already well inside, striding down the golden aisle between Malygris's carefully stacked chalices.

"You warmbloods!" he hissed. "Do you all think my lair yours for the entering?"

Namirrha made a show of appearing frightened, stopping to steeple his fingertips together and bow deeply. "A thousand pardons, Sacred One. I was informed that you have been hurling lightning about and thought you might be in need of assistance."

The necromancer cast a meaningful eye at the Shadovar.

"You think I need the assistance of a human?" Malygris sneered. "When that is so, you will scatter my bones across the Blight."

"As you command, Sacred One," Namirrha replied.

As Malygris had known he would, the necromancer stroked his amulet, and all of Malygris's anger drained away.

Malygris hated that, really *hated* it, but there was nothing to be done about it. He could no sooner attack Namirrha than he could regrow his long-rotted hide and scales. He was the necromancer's creature from nose-bone to tail-bone, and the fact that the sly old warmblood took pains to make it seem otherwise only added insult to injury.

Still, Malygris found himself saying, "Perhaps you can serve me, however. These shade things—" He flicked a claw in the Shadovar's direction. "—have come with an offer."

Namirrha's white brows rose. "Have they?" He advanced along Malygris's flank—a somewhat long journey that took the better part of a minute—and stopped across from the Shadovar. "And what is it that Shade Enclave wishes to offer Mighty Malygris, Suzerain of the Blight and all its wyrms?"

The two Shadovar glanced at each other, then Clariburnus shrugged and said, "We would be happy to remove the Zhentarim from Anauroch."

"Remove them?" Malygris growled. "What will my followers eat? I would sooner remove you—"

"What harm will it do to hear them out, Sacred One?" Again, Namirrha stroked his amulet, and again a numb calmness descended over Malygris. A smirk came to the necromancer's face, and he asked, "And in return for this small service, what do the Shadovar wish?"

"The service is more than a small one," Brennus said, addressing himself directly to Namirrha, "and so is what we expect in return: peace with the dragons, and their aid in the war against the phaerimm."

Malygris craned his neck to look down at Namirrha. "There is a war against the phaerimm?"

"Have I not suggested that you get out more, Sacred One?" Namirrha replied. "They have escaped their prison and captured the Sharaedim."

"Evereska's Sharaedim?" Malygris snorted in amusement. "The LastHaven of the elves? Well done, I say. Let them have it!"

Again Namirrha reached for his amulet. Malygris tried to flick a claw out to stop him, but found his foot too heavy, his toe too stiff.

"The matter is not as simple as that, Mighty One," Namirrha said. "The phaerimm pose a danger to us all. Even your shipments have been forced to detour far north or south."

"Ah, the shipments." Though Malygris had no idea what shipments the necromancer meant—and would not have cared if he did—he found himself nodding sagely. "We mustn't let them interfere with my shipments."

Namirrha smiled at the Shadovar. "If Malygris commits, the host he will bring to this war is without rival. Surely, his aid is worth more than simply driving the Zhentarim from Anauroch."

"How much more?" Clariburnus asked.

Namirrha grew serious. "Malygris would like to see them gone—wiped from the face of Faerûn."

"Then let Malygris do it himself, if his host is so mighty," Brennus said. "The Shadovar will not."

"Will not?" Namirrha demanded. "Or can not?"

The eyes of both Shadovar flared. "It is the same to you," Brennus growled. "We did not return to Faerûn to fight the Cult of the Dragon's battles for them. If you will not strike a bargain, you may be certain the Zhentarim will."

Namirrha stepped forward, perhaps trusting more than was wise to Malygris's imposing presence to back him up. "Then why aren't you speaking with the Zhentarim instead of me?"

Clariburnus craned his neck to look up. "Because the Zhentarim don't have Malygris."

"If it is my help you seek, then you should have brought gifts," Malygris rumbled, angered at being so obviously cut out of the negotiations. He knew as well as anyone who was in control of him, but he insisted on appearances. He still had that much pride. "You should be begging me."

"There is no need for that, Malygris." Namirrha stroked his accursed amulet. "This is something I should negotiate for you."

"Fine," Malygris said, and he meant it.

The Shadovar said nothing and stared at Namirrha.

Namirrha remained silent for several moments, then nodded and said, "Done." He offered his hand to Brennus. "We have a bargain."

The Shadovar stared at the appendage as though he wasn't quite sure what should be done with it, then glanced over the necromancer's shoulder at Malygris. "The Mighty One will honor the deal?"

Namirrha nodded, and stroked his amulet. "Of course."

"Good." Brennus smiled broadly, baring a mouthful of needle-tip fangs that even Malygris had to envy. "Done."

The Shadovar clasped Namirrha's hand then, in a move so swift even Malygris hardly saw it, pulled him forward onto the blade of a glassy black dagger. Namirrha screamed in surprise and tried to call on his servant for help, but the Shadovar's hand was over his mouth in a black blur, and Malygris felt no urge at all to defend the necromancer. Brennus finished the attack by first pushing his black blade down to Namirrha's crotch, then splitting him up the center and letting the two halves of the body fall separately.

When he was done, the accursed amulet was hanging from the back side of his dark blade. This he dropped at Malygris's feet.

"There is your gift, Malygris."

Malygris eyed the amulet warily, as he did the bloody mess in which the Shadovar stood. "If you think to ingratiate yourself with your warmblood treachery—"

"We think to avenge the insult he paid us by implying that Shade was not the equal of a piteous bunch of wretches like the Zhentarim," Clariburnus said, "and the insult he paid you as well, in treating the Blue Suzerain like a trained attack dog."

Had Malygris still had lips, he would have smiled. "For that I thank you—but why should I honor the bargain he made? My dragons need Zhents to eat."

"They will have plenty to eat in the war," Brennus said. "That I promise you."

"If you think on it, you will find yourself still bound by Namirrha's promise," Clariburnus said. "You sold yourself to the Cult of the Dragon, and even we princes of Shade cannot free you now."

CHAPTER FOUR

9 Mirtul, the Year of Wild Magic

Night in Shade Enclave came as a deepening of the general murk, when the air grew heavy and tepid and drew in on itself in inky mist. Galaeron sat on the balcony outside Villa Dusari's master bedchamber, not keeping watch, but watching. Despite the hour, the steady murmur and clatter of passing traffic growled up out of the ebony gloom, just loud enough to keep a company of restless householders from their pillows. Aris was down in the lower warrens of the city, plinking away in his workshop. Ruha was skulking about the house searching for Malik, who was obviously somewhere other than his chamber. Only Vala was in bed, on the other side of the door from where Galaeron sat. She was not sleeping, just staring into the blade of her black sword, a wistful smile on her full lips and a softness in her eyes alien to them during the day.

She was, Galaeron knew, looking in on her son in Vaasa. At night, her darksword often lulled her into a trance and showed her what was happening in the bedchambers of the Granite Tower—'dream walking' she called it, though it was more akin to spying. During their months together, he had learned to read her expression and tell when she was visiting Sheldon. That the sword seemed to be looking in on the boy more often these days was one of few things that made Galaeron think the weapon might not be entirely sinister.

Though he did not begrudge Vala these glimpses of her son, Galaeron did envy them. His own father and sister were lost to the fog of war—dead or beyond reach, he did not know which. The Swords of Evereska's desperate attempt to save the gate at the Rocnest had already become the stuff of legend. By all accounts, Aubric Nihmedu had been leading the charge, and Galaeron was not fool enough to believe a mere bladesinger likely to survive any combat in which Khelben Arunsun—one of Mystra's Chosen—had vanished without a trace.

His sister, Keya, remained trapped in Evereska—though Galaeron could not be certain of even that much, as the phaerimm had long ago stopped all communication with the LastHaven by raising a magic deadwall around the Sharaedim. He could hardly bear to think of his little sister—at eighty, barely an adult—sitting alone in Treetop, sad and frightened, probably hungry and perhaps even in despair, while outside the phaerimm circled the city waiting for a chance to enter. Yet, the alternative—that the mythal had already collapsed and Evereska fallen—was too horrible to contemplate.

And it was Galaeron's doing—the escape of the phaerimm, the besieging of Evereska, the whole war. He had caused it in one of those terrible moments a person replayed in his mind a thousand times, telling himself that if he had done this, or said that, or just left it all alone, everything would have been fine. Instead, Galaeron and his Tomb Guards had followed a band of crypt-breakers down into the long-forgotten workings of a dwarven mine and found Vala and her Vaasan warriors preparing to rendezvous with their shadow mage master, Melegaunt Tanthul. In the confusion that followed, Galaeron had given the order that breached the Sharn Wall, nearly two dozen men and elves had died, and the phaerimm had escaped to begin their assault on Evereska.

Vala and the Shadovar had told him a hundred times that he had only been performing his duty and wasn't to blame, but their words could not change what had happened—or how he felt about it. Eager to undo his mistake, Galaeron had joined forces with Vala and her shadow mage master and set out to summon the only help that seemed capable of defeating the evil he had unleashed. Along the way, he had learned to use shadow magic and had overreached his limits, opening himself to the corrupting influences of the Shadow Weave and beginning a desperate battle against his own shadow for the possession of his spirit. At every step of the way, it seemed, he had made the wrong decision, and now that he could not be certain whether the thoughts running through his mind belonged to him or his shadow self, he was almost afraid to decide anything at all.

But there was one thing he knew for certain, one decision he knew to be his own. He would do anything to save Evereska, make any sacrifice to amend his terrible mistake.

Galaeron settled back and tried to clear his mind, but found himself too agitated. His thoughts kept returning to the morning, wondering whether Hadrhune would arrange the promised audience or find yet another excuse to put it off—and whether the Most High's help would be the solution to his shadow problems, or just one more mistake. Certainly, it did not bode well that the Shadovar had concealed the fact that Shade Enclave was moving away from Evereska. But even Galaeron could see how his shadow would have used that information to feed his suspicions and make him distrust the one most able to help him win his spirit back.

While there was a time when he could have stilled his thoughts by retreating into the Reverie, Galaeron had lost touch with that facet of elf nature when he allowed his shadow to invade. Instead of slipping into a semilucid trance of memories and the shared emotions of other elves, he sank into the same insensible, nightmare-filled slumber as humans.

But this night even sleep would not come. He passed the black hours staring out into the darkness, listening to the city clatter past beneath his balcony, replaying the same thoughts and doubts over and over again until the gloom paled from night-ebony to dawn-gray and Aris came striding out of the murk carrying his statue of Escanor's battle against the phaerimm.

Already completed, the piece was Aris's finest yet, so flowing it seemed in danger of writhing from the giant's hands. The prince's figure was noble and majestic, one hand still stretched toward the phaerimm he had just killed as he twisted around to face his new attacker. The creature itself was connected to him by the tail piercing his abdomen, and also by two hands wrapped around his throat, an artistic license taken to impart the impression that the beast was hovering beside him unsupported.

"Aris, it's magnificent!" Vala said, joining Galaeron on the balcony as the stone giant stepped into the courtyard. "You did that in one night?"

"I could not have finished without Malik," Aris said. The statue was at balcony level, and the giant was speaking down from above. He half-turned toward the empty gate. "He did most of the polishing."

"And what has this favor cost you?" demanded Ruha, stepping out of the colonnade to meet them. "An arm, or a soul?"

"That is no business of yours, shrew," Malik said. "You cannot be expected to understand what one friend does for another, since you have none of your own." He craned his neck up toward the balcony. "You would do well to make yourselves decent. The prince is on his way here."

"The prince?" Galaeron asked. "Which one?"

"Escanor, of course," Malik said. "If you are wise, you will benefit by my experience and do nothing to encourage him to return. There is no thief worse than a royal."

Galaeron glanced at Vala, who merely shrugged and turned to don her armor—by Vaasan standards, a far superior mode of dress to any of the dusky gowns Hadrhune's servants had delivered. Galaeron opted for his scout's cloak, as even the coarsest Evereskan cloth was considered extravagant by non-elves.

By the time they had changed and joined the others in the courtyard, Escanor's entourage was pouring through the gate. Tall even by Shadovar standards, the prince was visible in the middle of the group, his coppery eyes glaring out over the heads of his escorts. Galaeron and the others dropped to a knee and waited while the guards took their stations around the perimeter of the courtyard.

Escanor went directly to Aris's statue and circled it slowly, running his fingers over its smooth stone. When he came to where the tail barb punctured his stomach, he winced visibly and turned away, craning his neck to address the kneeling giant.

"Very lifelike," he said. Though Escanor had spent three days in bed recovering from the removal of the phaerimm egg, he showed no sign of weakness. "I could swear it's moving."

"Thank you," Aris said. "That means much, coming from you."

"In truth, I am so fond of it I would like it for my villa," Escanor said. He motioned an unarmored servant forward. "Mees will pay whatever you think fair."

"Pay?" Aris seemed to puzzle over this for a moment, then said, "Unfortunately, I have already promised this piece to Hadrhune."

A collective gasp went up from the entourage, then Escanor snapped, "To Hadrhune?"

"For the Most High, Esteemed Prince," Malik said quickly. "Though I am sure Aris can make another in no time at all, especially considering that price is of little concern."

"Another?" Aris echoed. "Why should there be two?"

"There are many good reasons," Malik said, daring to rise and start toward Escanor's entourage without permission. "I'll tell them all to you later, but first let me speak with the prince's steward."

Escanor motioned his guards to stand down and glared at the little man as he crossed the courtyard. When Malik had nearly reached the steward, the prince said, "Malik, would you really want to affront the Most High by copying a palace treasure?"

Malik's face went pale. He began to stammer an apology, but Escanor waved him silent and started across the courtyard, motioning for the others to rise.

"Seeing the statue was only one of the reasons I asked

to show you the way to the palace." He stopped in front of Vala and took her hands in his own. "I wanted to thank you for saving my life. Rapha tells me you were really quite the trazt fiend."

Vala actually blushed, and Galaeron instantly resented the way her green eyes held the prince's gaze.

"It was nothing," she said, leaving her hands in Escanor's. "Your attacker was distracted."

Galaeron edged closer to Vala. "You turned away at the wrong time, Prince, or you could have killed it yourself while it was teleport-dazed."

"Yes, a pity I could not read your mind," Escanor said, fixing his coppery gaze on Galaeron and releasing Vala's hands. "You were right to hold the phaerimm in the cavern. It would have been dangerous to let them escape with the secret of the Splicing."

Leaving Galaeron to fume, Escanor turned to face Ruha. "You are the Harper pursuing Malik?"

"I am."

Escanor regarded the little man as though he found this difficult to believe. "Is he really such a terrible criminal?"

"It would not do to underestimate him, Prince," Ruha said. "Those who do often pay for the mistake with their lives."

This drew a fang-filled smirk from Escanor. "Then I am glad you are here to watch him, Harper, but mark well Hadrhune's warning—Malik has committed no crime in this city, and if he does, it will be our justice that settles the matter."

Ruha inclined her head. "My only desire is to see that he does no more harm than he already has."

"Good." Escanor turned to Vala and gestured toward the gate. "If you and your friends care to accompany Galaeron, it would please the Most High for you to see the palace this morning."

Vala nodded and started forward. Galaeron stepped to her side, making sure to place himself between her and Escanor as the others closed around them. Whether the prince noticed the maneuver was impossible to say, but Vala's frown was unmistakable.

As the entourage left the gate, she leaned in close and whispered, "Your shadow is showing, Galaeron. What do you think is going to happen?"

"Nothing I can help."

A twinkle came to Vala's green eyes, and she surprised him by smiling. "So you *are* jealous."

"Elves don't feel jealousy—and even if we did, there's nothing to be jealous about," he said. Though the feelings they shared for each other had grown too strong to hide over the last few months, Galaeron remained reluctant to act on them. Not only was Vala a human who would grow old before his eyes, she had promised to stay with him only until his shadow crisis ended—or she was forced to end it for him. After that, she would be returning to her son in Vaasa, and Galaeron did not think a few months of love worth the heartbreak of watching her leave—that was going to be hard enough already. "I don't want you to forget your promise."

"Why would I?" Vala asked.

Galaeron shrugged. "Because the prince is powerful and wealthy, and you humans have such a weakness for fleeting pleasures."

"Galaeron," she said, shaking her head wearily, "fleeting pleasures are not weaknesses! They're the stuff of life."

Vala looked away, and the entourage continued up the street. Paved in a duller version of the same black stone that lay in Villa Dusari's courtyard, the avenue was narrow and winding, meandering through a canyon-like labyrinth of dusky buildings so tall that even Aris had to crane his neck to look up at many of the residents who called greetings and fond wishes to Escanor as the procession passed. There were not many side streets, and those that they did intersect always ran uphill to the left and downhill to the right. It slowly grew apparent to Galaeron that they were spiraling up a gentle mound, though one so encrusted in looming structures that its terrain was all but impossible to discern. As they ascended, the villas grew ever larger and more magnificent, eventually becoming so enormous that it required the entourage close to a minute to pass by.

As they passed one of the largest, a many-spired mansion with flying buttresses and a line of long barrel vaults leading into the shadowed interior, Prince Escanor stopped long enough to wave in its direction.

"My abode," he said. "I hope you will attend me here soon, when we are not quite so occupied with our war duties."

Though Escanor took pains to address himself to all his guests, Galaeron—or his shadow—knew that the invitation was meant primarily for Vala. Biting back the urge to suggest that the invitation would come the first time only Vala was free to answer, he merely looked up the street and inquired how much farther it was to the Palace of the Most High.

Escanor waved him on. "Not far."

Indeed it was not. Just past the prince's home, the street opened into a broad hilltop piazza surrounded by similar mansions, all with their grandest entrances facing center. In a ring around the plaza stood a forest of gloom sculptures, all rooted in urns of polished obsidian with a single ribbon of shadow rising in the ever-shifting figure of a Shadovar warrior or wizard. Not far from Escanor's mansion stood the only likeness Galaeron recognized, that of the Shadovar who had helped cause the release of the phaerimm, Melegaunt Tanthul.

"The Ring of Heroes," Escanor said, waving his hand at the wall of figures. "Everyone represented here died accomplishing some great service to Shade Enclave."

"There must thousands!" Vala gasped.

"Tens of thousands," Escanor said. "Shade Enclave is an ancient city with ancient enemies, and much of our time in the shadow plane was spent defending ourselves from the assaults of the malaugrym."

"The malaugrym!" Ruha gasped. "Then the phaerimm must seem weak enemies to you, indeed."

"Different, but not weak. The first rule in the shadow plane is never to underestimate an enemy," Escanor said. He turned to Aris. "If you wish, I will have someone teach you to read the stories of the gloom sculptures in their changing shapes."

This drew a rare smile from the giant. "No gift would please me more."

The prince had only to glance in his steward's direction, and Mees said, "It shall be done this day."

Escanor nodded and turned to Galaeron. "You are wondering what Melegaunt's story says about you?"

Galaeron shook his head. "Only if it'll say he's honored for drawing Evereska and Waterdeep into the war against the phaerimm."

Vala started to hiss a reproach, but Escanor stopped her with a raised hand. "We must expect him to be suspicious." Despite the prince's patient words, the color of his eyes had deepened to angry red. "I think we should hurry to the Most High. Galaeron's shadow is making him foolish as well as distrustful, and that is a bad sign."

Escanor led them through a hundred paces of gloom sculptures and emerged on the far side of the Ring of Heroes. Directly ahead stood the dusky grandeur of the Palace Most High, its seamless walls fashioned of polished obsidian and its shadowed spires vanishing into the umbral haze above. Like so much in Shade Enclave, it seemed all sinuous curves and exaggerated proportions, with a shape that could not be named, nor even held in mind for more than a passing impression. Paying no noticeable attention as a company of Shadovar spellguards snapped to attention, Escanor steered his entourage into a keel-arched portal so high that Aris barely had to duck his head.

After passing through a short vaultway, the entryway opened into a vast hall of glassy curves and dusky translucence where every buttress soared into darkness and each corridor vanished into shadow. A hundred or more high-born Shadovar drifted in and out of the doorways, or stood rasping in tight knots of conversation, or sat patiently on the benches along the walls, their gem-colored eyes glowing bright against the murk at their backs. Ignoring the bustle of murmured greetings and inquisitive stares shot the entourage's way as it passed, Escanor marched his group down the center of the floor to a crowded seating area outside an enormous pair of guarded doors.

The detachment commander kneeled and informed Escanor that he had already sent word of the prince's arrival. A few moments later, one the doors opened and Hadrhune slipped out to inform them that the Most High was engaged and would see them as soon as he was able.

Escanor's eyes looked as though they might burn holes through the chamberlain. "You informed him that I am here with the elf?"

Hadrhune met the prince's angry gaze without flinching. "He is with—"

"Did I ask who he was with?" Escanor growled, stepping toward the door.

Hadrhune turned to cut him off. "I'll announce you now."

"We'll be right behind you," Escanor said, catching the door as the chamberlain tried to close it. "The elf should begin his studies at once."

"Of course."

Hadrhune waved Galaeron and his companions through, but Mees, Rapha, and the rest of the prince's entourage remained behind. They found themselves in a room even murkier than the great reception hall, where the gloom fell on their skin like ash and wisps of shadow-stuff floated past in long smoky ribbons. As Hadrhune and Escanor marched the group forward, the voices of unseen whisperers rose and fell in the surrounding darkness, and cold chilblains rose to prickle Galaeron's skin.

Finally, they approached a set of whispers that did not fade and, as they continued walking, eventually hardened into the fuller tones of normal speech. Galaeron recognized one speaker as a female and the other as the voice that had addressed him in the Wing Court. Before they drew near enough to understand what was being said, Hadrhune had them kneel and press their brows to the floor.

The two voices ceased murmuring, then the air grew chill and motionless.

"I know how busy the war is keeping you, Escanor," the Most High said. His voice was as sibilant and forceful as before. "My thanks for bringing these to me."

If the prince replied, Galaeron did not hear it.

Instead, Hadrhune said, "I have arranged an offering from the giant, Mighty One."

"An offering? Let us see."

The air grew less chill as the Most High moved away, then Escanor's feet appeared beside Galaeron's head.

"Have you power enough over your shadow to keep a civil tongue, elf?"

"If he doesn't, I can hold if for him," Vala said.

Escanor considered this, then said, "Good. Rise."

Galaeron and the others stood and found themselves facing at set of stairs at the base of a murk-swaddled dais. Escanor pointed toward the rear of the party.

"It is customary to face the Most High when in his presence."

Galaeron turned and saw a gloom-shrouded figure standing next to Aris's ankle, cowled head turned toward the statue. He began to circle it slowly, nodding in approval as he took it in. Galaeron glimpsed a pair of platinum eyes shining out from beneath the Most High's hood, but that was all of his face that could be seen.

After completing a full circuit, he stopped at Aris's ankle again. The murk in front of his body swirled and there was a clapping noise, then he tipped his head back to address the giant—and Galaeron still could not see his face.

"Truly, you are the equal of any gloom-shaper in the enclave," the Most High said. "I shall be proud to display this in the Gallery of Treasures with the city's finest works."

"You honor me beyond my skill," Aris rumbled. "If you could have seen the story galleries at Thousand Faces before they were destroyed, you would know how feeble my talents truly are."

"The phaerimm have taken much from us all," said the Most High. "I am sure their destruction cannot replace what you lost, but know that they will pay for it with more than their lives."

"So Melegaunt promised, and so am I here," Aris said. "Thank you."

Malik astonished Galaeron and—judging by the gasps of surprise—everyone else by appearing out of the gloom behind Aris's legs. "I also come bearing gifts," he said, reaching beneath his robes. "The One has charged me—"

"Stop!" Ruha was instantly rushing toward him, tossing sand at his hidden hand and uttering some kind of Bedine nature magic.

Before she made it far enough for Galaeron to infer what spell she meant to cast, the Most High gestured in her direction, and she was entwined in half a dozen murky tendrils. Her veil continued to flutter as she spoke her incantation, but the only thing that came out from beneath it were clouds of dark vapor.

"Did Hadrhune not warn you, Harper?" the Most High asked. "What Malik does here is no concern of yours."

Malik smirked in the witch's direction, then, still holding his hand beneath his robe, turned back to the Most High. "As I was saying, the One—"

"Your gift will have to wait until later." The Most High moved away from the little man. "Hadrhune will arrange a time. Now, I really must start with Galaeron. If you others will excuse us, Rapha and Mees are waiting to tour the palace with you."

So saying, he turned and vanished into the murk.

Escanor motioned Vala toward the others. "Feel free to enjoy the tour with the others. Galaeron will be fine with us."

Vala stepped closer to Galaeron's side. "That's not going to happen."

"It is." As polite as was Escanor's smile, it was also filled with fangs. "You have no need to worry while he is in the company of the Most High. The shadow has not been cast that Telamont Tanthul cannot tame."

"Tanthul?" Galaeron gasped. "The same as Melegaunt Tanthul?"

The prince nodded. "And Escanor Tanthul," he said. "All the Princes of Shade are Tanthuls."

Telamont's sibilant voice filled the murk around them. "Escanor!"

Escanor bowed briefly to Vala, then took Galaeron's arm and led him away.

"Galaeron?" Vala called.

"I'll be . . . fine," Galaeron said, choking on the last word. Whether he was excited or frightened even he could not tell, but his heart had risen so far into his throat that he could barely draw breath around it. "We'll meet back at the villa."

"When?"

"When he is finished," Escanor said. "I will bring him myself."

They passed the statue and vanished into the darkness, then emerged a dozen steps later on what felt like the mezzanine of a very high, very large atrium. Through the hole in the center, he saw what looked like half the continent of Faerûn lying spread out beneath him, from the Sword Coast in the West as far east as the great Shoal of Thirst in the desert Anauroch, from the ruins of Arabel in the south to the High Ice in the north. At the moment, most of the land west of Anauroch lay hidden beneath storm clouds, while all to the east was brown and parched with an uncharacteristic drought.

"I have brought you to our war room to show why Shade Enclave is moving away from Evereska," said Telamont Tanthul's wispy voice. "You wished to know."

"I do," Galaeron said.

"You suspect us of betraying my son's promise," Telamont continued.

Galaeron bit his tongue, fighting the urge to say that he *knew* they were.

"Speak freely," Telamont urged. "In the war room, no opinion is dismissed lightly."

"Very well." Galaeron's throat was so dry that the words stuck at the bottom. "As Netherese, you lost Anauroch to the phaerimm once."

He paused there, trying to sort out what he believed from what his shadow believed—but Telamont was in no mood to wait.

"And you believe Melegaunt intentionally loosed the phaerimm on Evereska so that Waterdeep and the rest of Faerûn would be drawn into our war," the Most High continued. "Say what you mean, elf. The only way to live with your shadow is to give it a voice."

"Did you?" Galaeron asked, anger rising.

Telamont remained silent for a time, and Galaeron began to hear other voices around the rim of the war room—whispering quietly or discussing heatedly, sometimes even laughing or shouting—but when he looked toward the voices, he never saw more than a few pairs of glowing eyes, usually gem-colored, but sometimes the metallic of a royal prince.

A few moments later, Telamont Tanthul finally responded. "Drawing the elves into the war would certainly have been a useful thing to do, but *you* were the one who breached the Sharn Wall. How could we have foreseen that?"

How, indeed? Galaeron wondered—then, "By breaking a crypt. Melegaunt may not have known I would come, but he knew someone would."

"That is certainly a possibility," Telamont admitted, "but could even we Shadovar be clever enough to be sure that you would cast the proper spell at the proper time?"

"And if we are, wouldn't you rather have us as allies than enemies?" Escanor asked.

"If you are allies," Galaeron said, struggling to focus on the question at hand. "So far, I have seen little enough proof of that."

"Have you?" Telamont asked. "Look again."

Galaeron returned his gaze to continent below and

was surprised to find himself looking at nothing but storm clouds. As he watched, the clouds grew larger and darker, with flashes of lightning stabbing through their roiling heads. Then he was through, diving into a vast, rain-soaked swamp where hundreds of lizardmen were swarming a much smaller company of Shadovar.

"The Marsh of Chelimber, on the far side of the Grey-cloaks," Telamont said, just a trace of pride in his voice. "You see, Shade Enclave does not need to be near to project its strength. Our warriors are shades who can walk the shadows and cross the breadth of Faerûn at will. Evereska will not suffer for our absence."

Armed as the Shadovar were with shadow magic and shadow weapons, the shade warriors were holding their own against the primitive lizardmen. Galaeron would even have gone so far as to say it looked like they would carry the day—but it was not like lizardmen to march so steadfastly to their deaths, and never in the even ranks of a disciplined army. There was something forcing them to attack, something that made them hate the Shadovar beyond all reason—or something they feared more.

"Can you call them out?" Galaeron asked, not bothering to conceal the panic in his voice.

"That will not be necessary," said the gravely voice of Prince Rivalen. "We are not afraid to lose a life or two in defense of our allies, and the scaly ones will lose an army."

Galaeron looked up and saw Rivalen's horn-helmed figure coming down the balcony, then found himself shaking his head. "There's more to this battle than we're seeing," he said. "You're the ones who lose—and to the warrior, unless you act quickly."

Escanor asked, "You know this?"

Galaeron nodded. "I do."

"How?" demanded Rivalen.

Galaeron could only shrug. "I don't know how I know, only that I do."

Escanor and Rivalen exchanged glances, and Escanor asked, "As you did at the Splicing?"

Galaeron considered this, then reluctantly shook his head. "It's a feeling, but not as strong. It just makes sense—lizardmen don't fight like that. Something must be driving them."

"Phaerimm?" asked Rivalen. "We always expected a few would be outside the shell when Escanor raised it."

"I am the one who raised it," Galaeron said, angry that the Shadovar kept slighting the role he had played in the Splicing. "And it's not the phaerimm. This is too direct for them." The words seemed to be spilling from his mouth of their own accord. "They prefer to remain hidden and work through intermediaries. It must be a beholder, or maybe a squad of illithids."

Both princes turned toward the Most High. Astonished at having won the argument so easily, Galaeron did likewise—and found Telamont Tanthul standing only a few paces away, his platinum eyes glaring down out of the depths of his cowl. Galaeron still could not make out the shape of his face, or even whether the Most High was bearded like Melegaunt or clean-shaven like most of the other princes.

Telamont looked over Galaeron's head to the princes and said, "Our question as been answered."

No sooner had he spoken than the Shadovar company began to bleed into the flashing shadows of the lightning storm, leaving the astonished lizardmen free to overrun the position—and the beholder that suddenly grew visible behind their lines so angry that it began to spray its disintegration ray around at random. Galaeron glared at the scene for a moment, then turned to find Telamont Tanthul still staring down at him with those platinum eyes.

"You were with Melegaunt when he died," Telamont said. "Something passed between you."

"I blanked out," Galaeron gasped, recalling the confused battle in which Melegaunt perished. "When I came to, he was gone."

"Not gone." Telamont drifted closer, until he was near enough to raise a murky sleeve and lay something dark and cold on Galaeron's shoulder. "Through you, he still serves."

"That's why you brought me here?" The air was so cold and still that Galaeron was finding it difficult to breathe. "Because Melegaunt passed his knowledge of the phaerimm to me?"

"That is not a bad thing," Escanor said. "Partners in need forge the strongest alliances."

CHAPTER FIVE

14 Mirtul, the Year of Wild Magic

In the dark sky, the sun was but an ashen disk peering over Eastpeak's craggy shoulder, too weak to burn through the dusky mantle Evereska's enemies had drawn over the Sharaedim, too pale to feed the few light-starved buds dauntless enough to emerge on the scorched and withered stalks of the Vine Vale. Murky as the morning was, it was bright enough for Keya Nihmedu's elf eyes to make out the faint swirl of ash and dust drifting down the other side of the Meadow Wall. A couple of lance-lengths from her hiding tree, it was moving slowly, quietly and carefully, bouncing along Evereska's protective mythal, trying again and again to cross the boundary into the un-touched fields beyond.

Every instinct screamed at Keya to throw off her camouflage and flee for the cliff gates. She stayed. The mythal would protect her, and she had promised to be there when Khelben and the Vaasans returned. *If* they returned. Keya looked at the pale disk in the sky and wondered if even the Chosen of Mystra could be that good. A full night among the phaerimm.

The swirl halted in front of Keya's tree, so faint she began to doubt she was seeing it. Perhaps the whorl had been just a breeze stirring up ash as it rolled down the Meadow Wall. Not every dust devil dancing down a scorched terrace was an invisible phaerimm—but a lot of them were. Had she been at her post inside one of the city towers, Keya could have waved a wand and known at once what she was looking at, but the thornbacks could see mystic energy the way dwarves saw body heat, and so the Long Watch did not use any magic—did not even carry it—this close to the boundary.

The swirl vanished, but Keya could still hear dead vine stalks stirring in the breeze and the distinct sibilation of air moving over the stones of the Meadow Wall, and she *knew*. The phaerimm were surrounded by an aura of moving air, which they used to communicate among themselves in a strange language of whistles and roars. There was not just one invisible thornback pausing on his circuit of the mythal—there were two, whispering quietly, lurking directly in front of Keya's tree—the same tree she had told Khelben Arunsun and the Vaasans to mark as their rendezvous point when they returned to the city.

Keya remained in her hollow in the linden's thick trunk, standing behind her screen of bark, hardly daring to breathe. She spent the next few minutes wondering why the phaerimm had picked this particular place on this particular morning to hold a conversation and what she was going to do if—when—Khelben and the Vaasans returned. She could not speak the word of passing with two thornbacks lurking outside—not even for one of the Chosen, not for her Vaasan friends, not even if her own brother Galaeron were to suddenly appear outside Meadow Wall. When an elf opened a gate in the mythal, she could not control who used it. Once the phaerimm were inside, it would take only a moment to cast the same life-draining magic that had already withered the vineyards of the Vine Vale and denuded the once-majestic spruce stands of the Upper Vale, and that was something Keya could not permit—not when the mythal was already growing weak.

It took Keya a moment to realize it when the phaerimm fell silent, for the difference between stillness and the sibilation of their whispering voices was no more than the flutter of a moth's wings. She thought for a moment the phaerimm had moved on, but when she looked along the Meadow Wall, she saw no swirling ash or any other sign of their departure. The thornbacks had fallen quiet for the same reason they were invisible, because they wanted to keep their presence secret, and their prey was close enough to hear them.

It had to be Khelben and the Vaasans, as invisible as the phaerimm, but walking into a trap. Keya knew Khelben would have his detection magic up and—assuming he was still with the group—see the enemy as soon as he came into range. The thornbacks would know that as well. The war around Evereska had become one of stealth and magic, with the combatants sneaking through the barren landscape, silent and invisible, searching for foes who were just as silent and just as invisible. More often than not, the victor was the one who detected his enemy first—and the phaerimm had obviously already detected Khelben and Vaasans.

Keya knew she could warn Khelben simply by speaking his name, for he had told her that the Chosen heard a few words whenever their names were spoken anywhere on Faerûn, but that was really not much different from a magic sending. She had to assume that the phaerimm would detect it just as easily. No, she needed to startle the thornbacks, to confuse them for just the half-second it would take Khelben and the others to discern the trap and react.

Assuming they were really out there.

Keya wished she had her wand of seeing—really wished she had it. Instead, she fixed her eye on the Meadow Wall and grabbed the shaft of her spear. It was a plain one with an oak shaft and a head of mithral steel, and it weighed almost a third what she did. She whispered a prayer to Corellon Larethian, then kicked her screen of bark aside and burst from her hiding place.

Two swirls of ash and dust went up behind the Meadow Wall as the startled phaerimm reacted. She angled toward the one on the right for no other reason than it was half a step closer than the other. The thing reacted by instinct, spraying bolts of golden magic in Keya's direction and growing instantly visible. The bolts blossomed harmlessly against the mythal, then Keya was at the Meadow Wall, shoving her spear through the magic barrier to strike at the creature's scaly midsection.

The phaerimm's magic defenses turned her spear as easily as the mythal had turned its golden bolts. A ball of Khelben's silver spellfire exploded into the thing from behind, pinning it against the mythal and holding it there as it was incinerated by the special magic of the Chosen.

Shielding her eyes from the silver brilliance, Keya stumbled away and turned to see the other phaerimm coming apart beneath the Vaasans' darkswords. One of the black blades was emitting a sort of musical purr—a brisk tune that sounded almost like someone humming. The song sent a shiver down Keya's spine. She had heard Dexon's sword talking while he slept and seen Kuhl's grow pallid because he had neglected to plunge it into a vat of mead that day, but this was the eeriest oddity of all. The melody was joyful and light, as though the weapon enjoyed its bloody work.

The three Vaasans finished the phaerimm quickly, then cut off its tail barb and fell to arguing as only Vaasans could about who deserved the trophy. Khelben appeared behind the trio and silenced them with a sharp word before turning to Keya with a grateful bow.

"Quick wit and brave deeds, Keya Nihmedu," he said. Tall and dark-bearded, Khelben had a grim manner that lent a sullen dignity to even his simplest acts. "You have our gratitude."

"It was nothing." Keya spoke the word of passing, then motioned the wizard and the others over the Meadow Wall. "I was never in danger."

"But we were," said Dexon, the darkest of the dark and burly Vaasans. "They would surely have taken us by surprise. I could kiss you."

This caused Keya to cock her brow. "Really?"

Weighing somewhat less than a rothé and possessed of a flashing white smile, Dexon was the handsomest of the Vaasans. She whispered the word of closing to seal the mythal behind them, then smiled up at the human. "Well, why don't you then?"

Dexon's jaw dropped, and he began to leer at her with that hungry look that seemed to come to the Vaasan eye at the slightest flash of skin. Though Keya knew her friends on the Long Watch were revolted by humans in general and by being ogled by them in particular, she did not withdraw her smile. The truth was that once a person got to know them, humans were really rather fun. She had even come to enjoy the glances that they cast her way—at least those Dexon cast her way—whenever they went to bathe in Dawnsglory Pond.

When the Vaasan seemed too shocked to do more than stare at Keya, Burlen stepped forward to take his place. "What's wrong with you, Dex? You can't keep our hostess waiting."

Burlen spread his burly arms wide and closed his eyes . . . and suddenly found himself holding a glowering Khelben.

"Keya is the one who deserves the reward, Burlen, not you."

Keya giggled at this, causing the archmage to turn his glower on her.

"And you, young lady, should be careful of baiting bears. I'm sure Lord Nihmedu would take a dim view of you kissing something with more wool on his face than a thkaerth."

Keya raised her chin. "I'm sure he would, Sir Blackstaff, but Galaeron is neither here nor my keeper." She sneaked a glance at Dexon, then added, "Now, pray tell how your scouting mission went?"

Something like humor may have flashed in Khelben's dark eyes, but it was gone before Keya could be certain. Speaking over his shoulder, he turned and started across the meadow toward the cliff gates.

"Lord Duirsar has reason to be concerned about the shadow sky," he said. "The Vale is dying outside the mythal even faster than it is inside."

Keya stumbled and, were it not for the speed with which Dexon's hand leaped out to catch her, would have fallen. The life of the Vale, both inside the Meadow Wall and beyond it, was what sustained the mythal.

"We must find a way to tear that shadow from the sky, and quickly," Khelben continued, "or we will soon be fighting phaerimm in the streets of Evereska."

❧ ❧ ❧ ❧ ❧

Galaeron stood in the cold stillness at the Most High's side, peering down into the world-window, watching a miles-long column of mixed volunteers trudge along the knee-deep mud trough that had once been the Trade Way. There were folk from all over the northwest—Evermeetian elves, Adbarrim dwarves, Waterdhavian men—but only the Uthgardt barbarians seemed untroubled by the blizzards and constant downpours that had been plaguing western Faerûn all spring. The rest of the volunteers were coughing and staggering, so weakened by fever and fatigue that the army could barely slog three miles a day, much less join battle at the end of the march.

Yet fight they must. Telamont's cowled head looked toward the High Moor, and the scene in the world-window shifted to a horde of bugbears being herded through a waterfall of rain by a troop of beholder officers. Supporting them were two companies of illithids and another of Zhentilar battle mages—though why the enemy would need human spell-flingers with five phaerimm overseeing their attack was beyond Galaeron.

Telamont's gaze shifted again, this time to a rocky ridge of ground that stood along the Trade Way opposite the High Moor. Laeral Silverhand and her sister Storm already stood atop the ridge, their long tresses streaming in the gale wind as they laid magic traps. Though it was far from certain that their army would cover the mile and a half remaining to it before the phaerimm's bugbears covered the eight remaining to them, the ridge meant everything. The army that controlled it would have the advantages of both height and solid ground, while the one that did not would be forced to wade into battle through a muddy morass.

Withdrawal was not an option for either force, not with

the kind of magic that five phaerimm or two Chosen of Mystra could call down on an army mired in the mud. There would be a battle that evening, perhaps the fiercest of the war, one that would annihilate both sides no matter who remained alive to claim the field—and why?

Telamont's attention turned to the phaerimm themselves, and the scene shifted yet again. Accustomed to the Most High's rapid changes of focus, Galaeron turned his own attention to the thornbacks and began to let his thoughts wander over the question of why so many had gathered in one place. He had been coming to the palace every day since their initial meeting, spending most of that time peering into the world-window and trying to get in touch with whatever Melegaunt had passed on to him during those last few moments of life. Sometimes it worked, and he was able to divine the enemy's intentions in time to save a few dozen—or even a few hundred— lives. More often, he had no more to offer than anyone else.

Regardless, Telamont Tanthul spent part of each day—sometimes most of it—with Galaeron, never teaching him directly, but always approaching the subject obliquely, as if concentrating too bright a light on his shadow self would only send it into hiding. No matter how long these sessions lasted, Galaeron always returned to Villa Dusari exhausted, numb, and irritable— so much so that Vala was beginning to question whether Telamont was helping him control his shadow or the other way around. Though she was not allowed into the war room—even Escanor had not been able to prevail on the Most High to allow her inside—she insisted on coming to the palace each day and waiting out in the throne room's whispering murk. Given how peevish that was making her, Galaeron was beginning to think she was the one struggling with a shadow crisis.

Telamont stepped away from the rim of the world-window and fixed his platinum eyes on Galaeron, and—as always—Galaeron felt the question on the Most High's mind.

"I can't see the sense in forcing this battle," he admitted. "When we raised the shadowshell, there were only ten phaerimm outside—"

"The figure is now twelve," Hadrhune corrected from the other side of Telamont. "Our agents located one in Baldur's Gate, and another in . . . that little kingdom south of the Goblin Marches—"

"Cormyr?" Galaeron asked.

Hadrhune nodded, his thumbnail digging into the deeply worn groove atop his ever-present staff. "In what was once the city of Arabel."

"Still, that is nearly half of their number outside the shell," Galaeron said. "Why risk so much to stop an army that may well die of the ague before it ever reaches the Sharaedim?"

"To slay a pair of Chosen?" Hadrhune asked.

Galaeron shook his head. "The phaerimm know better than that," he said. "The Chosen can be defeated but not slain—at least not by Mystra's magic."

Eyes sparkling at this last correction, Telamont said, "Whatever their purpose, this is a battle we cannot permit." He turned to where Escanor and Rivalen had appeared without any apparent summons, then raised a murk-filled sleeve toward the world-window. "You will take your brothers and your best legions and save those sick fools if you can. Leave the phaerimm until we understand their game."

"It shall be done."

Both princes placed their palms to their breasts, then turned and were gone.

Galaeron felt the weight of Telamont's unspoken question and knew that something was being demanded of him that had, until now, only been asked. He turned to the world-window and focused his attention on the High Moor, then on the horde of tiny figures swarming over it, then on the five figures drifting along behind it between the two companies of illithids. Each time, the window responded to his will, the image shifting and growing larger to show him what he wished to see.

When Galaeron was finally looking at only the thornbacks themselves, he shifted from one to the other, studying each one in turn, looking for scars or scale patterns or anything that might trigger one of Melegaunt's memories. Had the world-window been capable of carrying sound, he would have cast the spell that Melegaunt had taught him to understand their languages, but even the Shadovar could not eavesdrop without sending a spy. The Most High had already made clear to Galaeron that until he grew adept enough with shadow magic to find and pass on the knowledge that Melegaunt had entrusted to him, he would not be allowed to risk his life in any manner. For a Tomb Guard princep accustomed to chasing cutthroat crypt breakers down narrow passages strewn with magic death traps, the restriction was not an easy one to observe.

After several minutes of allowing his thoughts to wander over the phaerimm, Galaeron finally looked away from the world-window.

"I'm sorry," he said. "I can't summon anything."

Telamont accepted the failure with a patience uncharacteristic toward anyone except Galaeron.

"Do not let it concern you," he said. "I'm sure it is just your shadow interfering. The harder you try to control it, the stronger it becomes."

"I'm not trying to control it," Galaeron said. "I'm just letting my mind wander."

Telamont's eyes twinkled beneath his cowl, and there was a flash of what might have been a white-fanged grin. "You are always trying to control your shadow, elf. You are the kind who must control what he fears."

"What I fear is becoming a monster," Galaeron insisted. "Of course I want to control my shadow."

"As I said," Telamont replied. His sleeve rose, then a cold weight settled on Galaeron's shoulder. "It is no matter. The princes have their orders."

The world-window filled with a foggy expanse, which gradually grew less hazy as the Most High brought into focus what he wanted to see. Even after the scene stopped shifting, it took Galaeron a moment to notice a series of faint bluish lines that he recognized as crevasses in the High Ice.

The crevasses broadened into the dagger-shaped ribbons of deep, icy canyons, and Galaeron began to notice an odd patchwork of vapor columns rising off some sections of the massive glacier. One of these columns expanded to fill the world-window, and a square plot of snow gradually darkened from white to gray to ebony as it continued to grow larger. Finally, Galaeron found himself looking at something that appeared to be a huge, black carpet being unrolled by a company of ant-sized Shadovar.

"A shadow blanket," Telamont explained, answering Galaeron's question sooner than he could voice it. "A square mile of pure shadowsilk."

Galaeron frowned, as puzzled by what the Shadovar were doing as why Telamont was showing it to him. At the end of the blanket already laid out, a thickening vapor haze was beginning to rise into the air, while tiny rivulets of crystal water were flowing out from beneath the edge, braiding themselves into sparkling streams that merged into broad creeks and vanished down the blue crevasses in silver horsetails of falling water.

"You're melting it!" Galaeron gasped.

"Yes." If Telamont noticed the alarm in Galaeron's voice, his tone did not betray it. "The shadow blankets absorb all of the light that falls on them, then trap it below in the form of heat. We have already laid hundreds along the edge of the High Ice."

"Hundreds?"

Galaeron concentrated on a larger area of the High Ice. Sensing his change of focus, Telamont yielded control of the world-window, and the scene drew back to show the hundreds of vapor columns rising off the ice.

"You're changing Faerûn's weather!"

"We are rejuvenating what the phaerimm destroyed," Telamont corrected.

The scene changed again, this time to the southern edge of the High Ice, where dozens of huge rivers were gushing out of blue-tinged caves in the base of a mountainous wall of snow and ice. The water was pouring into enormous basins that had been dry for a thousand years, recreating the lakes that had once lain along the northern fringes of Netheril.

"Cold air is rolling down from the High Ice and picking up moisture as it sweeps across the lakes and grows warm," Telamont explained. "As the effect grows stronger, the winds will carry rain and fog farther south into Anauroch, forcing the hot desert air to rise and draw more winds down from the High Ice. The system feeds on itself. We are already seeing showers as far south as the Columns of the Sky."

Though Galaeron had no idea where the Columns of the Sky were—the name had a Netherese ring—he needed no explanation of what the shadow blankets meant for western Faerûn. He had already seen it in the blizzards plaguing Waterdeep and the deluges that had turned most of the farms south of the Ardeep Forest into hip-deep marshes.

"That is well and good for Shade," he said, "but what about the rest of Faerûn?"

Telamont's gloom-cloaked shoulders rose and fell. "Every good thing has a bad side. For Shade to reclaim its birthright, others must suffer."

"This is too much," Galaeron said.

He looked toward the west, and the scene shifted to Daggerford, where the River Delimbyr's frigid waters had risen into the streets, and residents kept boats tied outside their second-story windows.

"Surely, you could pursue a more gradual approach, one that would not force so many into homelessness and hunger."

Telamont seized control of the world-window from Galaeron, bringing the shadowy dome over the Sharaedim into view. "I thought your concern was for Evereska."

"The two are hardly related," Galaeron said.

"Aren't they?" Telamont asked. "Shade must be strong if it is to prevail. So whose people do you want to save, elf? Yours, or theirs?"

"That isn't the choice," Galaeron said. "Even at the rate you're melting the High Ice, Anauroch will take decades to restore. Evereska will be saved or lost in a year."

Telamont's murk-filled cowl tipped down toward Galaeron. "It is the choice I have given you, elf. Which will perish—Evereska, or the West?"

"I—I can't believe you would ask me such a thing!" Galaeron stammered.

He thought he had to be misinterpreting what he was hearing, missing some important nuance that would make clear what the Most High was really asking of him.

Something cold and angry rose inside him, and he understood. The Shadovar were trying to trap him, trying to corrupt him, perhaps, or test him, or move the burden of all those deaths from their heads to his.

Galaeron shook his head. "I see your game, and it won't work on me."

"You think this is a game?" Telamont lifted a sleeve toward the world-window. "Look and think again."

The scene had returned to the High Moor, where the princes of Shade and their legions were just rising from the dusky ground, thousands upon thousands of silhouettes peeling themselves out of the shadows and growing whole as they charged, flinging spells of umbral death and waving weapons of indestructible black glass.

Caught from the rear and the flank, the bugbears were roaring in confusion and fighting their beholder masters with far more ferocity than they were the Shadovar. One company of illithids was already under the black sword, while the other was rushing to fan out behind their battle lines and find the most powerful spellflingers to target with their mind blasts. The search was proving a difficult one, for most warriors of Shade Enclave fought with both spell and blade, often slipping from one to the other with a grace that even an elf bladesinger would envy.

No more eager to engage the princes than the princes were to engage them, the five phaerimm hung back, assailing their enemy's ranks with fireballs, lightning bolts, and sheets of burning light that felled whole ranks of Shadovar. Though this last spell was one that Galaeron had never seen before, it bore a semblance to certain elements of a prismatic wall, and he felt sure it was little more than a simple modification the thornbacks had developed especially for combat against shades.

That was when it hit him. "This battle is a diversion."

"An army that large may be many things, but a diversion is not one of them," said Hadrhune. "A force that size requires resources that our agents assure us the phaerimm dare not waste lightly."

"Your agents don't know the phaerimm well enough to make that judgment," Galaeron replied, somewhat surprised to discover he felt he did. He pointed at a flickering fan of azure light. "That spell is a new one, designed for battle against Shadovar."

"Even if you could know that," Hadrhune began, "I fail to see—"

"I can know it, and you do fail to see," Galaeron interrupted, confident of his judgment. "If the phaerimm were expecting to do combat with the Chosen, they would not clutter their minds with spells designed for Shadovar—and they would not announce their presence by floating into battle fully visible."

All of Anauroch and western Faerûn appeared in the world-window, clouds stripped away to reveal the swollen rivers beneath.

"What are they trying to hide?" Telamont asked.

Galaeron studied the divination for several minutes, focusing on the area around the shadowshell, Rocnest, and the Greycloaks for the longest period. Finally, he shook his head.

"I can't see it."

"Perhaps because there is nothing to see," Hadrhune said. "With these five in plain view, we know the locations of all twelve phaerimm who escaped the shadowshell."

"Your knowledge is current?" Telamont asked.

Hadrhune's amber eyes vanished behind their dark lids for a moment, then he nodded. "The shadow-watchers have seen them all within the quarter hour. Five are visible at this moment."

Galaeron nodded. "Of course. They would know we're watching."

"Our watchers would know if they were simulacrums or magic images," Telamont said. "Perhaps this is no diversion, after all."

"We cannot know what the phaerimm make of the shadowshell," Hadrhune said, smirking down at Galaeron. "It may be that they fear it is the Chosen's doing, and this army is part of their plan."

"Or it may be that the Myth Drannor phaerimm have a part to play in this," said Lord Terxa, whom Galaeron had not even realized was listening from the shadows. "What remains of the mythal there interferes with the shadow-watchers, and they are not even certain they have found them all."

Galaeron recalled how Melegaunt's shadow magic had failed inside Evereska's mythal but frowned and shook his head. "A good thought, but phaerimm are not social. They work together only when each one benefits personally, and there's no reason for the Myth Drannor phaerimm to think that helping the others would be worth their trouble."

Terxa's expression grew uncomfortable, and he peered into the darkness under Telamont's cowl. "Perhaps he should know, Most High?"

"Know what?" Galaeron was instantly resentful. "Now you are keeping secrets from me?"

Telamont's eyes twinkled as though he was amused—or satisfied. "Have you told us all *your* secrets, elf?"

He raised a sleeve, and a sleepy forest hamlet appeared in the world-window. Not too long past, a battle—or several—had been fought around it, for several new meadows had been burned into the woods around its boundaries. In front of a high tower not far from the heart of the village, a strange seam of distortion hovered in the air, emitting wisps of flame and dark fume.

"Many things are better kept secret," Telamont said. "Among them, deeds of shame done in moments of necessity."

Hadrhune moved to interpose himself in front of Galaeron and asked, "Most High, is this something—"

Galaeron stepped forward to block Hadrhune. "It is, unless you wish to let the phaerimm have their way with your legions."

"He needs to know," said Terxa.

Telamont spread his sleeves. Flames and smoke sprang up in the charred clearings, and Galaeron began to see familiar cone shaped bodies drifting through the trees. A moment later, Elminster's familiar figure appeared over the village and began to circle.

"After Melegaunt summoned his brothers to the Karsestone," Telamont began, "Elminster was proving most difficult to locate. In order to find him, the princes found it necessary to slay a few of the Myth Drannor phaerimm—"

"And leave the smell of Elminster's stinkweed in the air," Galaeron finished.

"As I understand, it was not necessary to leave anything," Telamont said, almost chuckling. "The thornbacks could not imagine anyone else capable, and went to take their vengeance on Elminster."

"And when he returned to see what was happening, the princes ambushed him and sent him to the Nine Hells?" Galaeron demanded. "How could you—"

"It was an accident," Hadrhune said firmly.

"In any case, its not relevant to the question at hand," Telamont said. "What is relevant is that the Myth Drannor phaerimm may have learned who was actually responsible—"

"And made a pact with their fellows to be rid of you," Galaeron finished.

He was growing angrier by the moment, and not just because of what they had done to Elminster. He saw how Telamont had manipulated him as well, deliberately drawing his shadow out by showing him the shadow blankets and telling him he must choose between saving Evereska or the whole west. Though Telamont remained silent, the force of his unspoken question pressed down like a boulder. So infuriated was Galaeron that he wanted not to answer, to deny what he saw so clearly, or lie about it, or do something to make the Shadovar pay—but he could not hold the knowledge inside. The pressure of the Most High's will was insufferable, as though he had somehow brought the entire weight of Shade Enclave to bear on that one pressure point.

At last, Galaeron had to ask, "You have a mythal?"

The air grew even more still and cold than usual next to Telamont. "Of a sort. There is a mythallar here, as were found on all the enclaves of Netheril."

"That's what they'll attack."

"Impossible," Hadrhune said. "They'd never make it through the shadow moats."

Galaeron shrugged. "Then you have nothing to worry about."

Hadrhune looked to Telamont.

The Most High turned to Galaeron and said, "You know our defenses. Can the phaerimm breach them?"

"They already have, or your sentries would be sounding the alarms by now." Then, in answer to what the Most High wanted to know next, Galaeron said, "It's likely a small company of infiltrators. If it was only one or two, they would have relied on stealth instead of trying to lure your strength away."

"An entire company?" Hadrhune shook his gaunt head. "Impossible."

"It would not hurt to be certain," Telamont said.

Hadrhune's amber eyes vanished beneath their lids, but Telamont was not waiting. He started for the throne room, motioning Galaeron to follow—and many others as well, judging by the cold swirl of darkness that accompanied them.

Hadrhune appeared at Telamont's side, his eyes opened again. "A veserab patrol did return unexpectedly, Most High. The officer cannot be found, and the mounts have burns where they were harnessed with Weave magic."

"Not impossible," Telamont said. "Recall the princes."

They were in the throne room, striding through the whispering shadows toward the reception hall, surrounded by a throng of increasingly substantial figures. Several of the silhouettes drifted apart long enough for Vala to emerge and step to Galaeron's side.

"What happened?"

"Phaerimm infiltrators," Galaeron explained. "They're after the mythallar."

Vala raised her brow, but said, "That's not what I was asking about."

"No?"

"You, Galaeron," Telamont said, speaking from a dozen paces ahead. "She wants to know what happened to you."

Galaeron frowned. "My shadow?" He glanced over at her. "You can tell just by looking?"

Vala nodded. "Galaeron, I don't even have to look anymore," she said, "and I don't much like that."

"Ready weapons!" Hadrhune called.

Vala reached for her darksword and asked, "They're coming here?"

They were somewhere else, dropping out of the shadows into a huge obsidian basin, sliding down the glassy slopes with purple sheets of light burning all around them, voices screaming, bolts cracking, air reeking of charred flesh. It took Galaeron a moment to recall where he was and why, a moment longer to realize the pain in his arm was Vala's free hand digging into his biceps, then he finally began to make sense of what he was seeing.

At the bottom of the basin sat a huge ball of obsidian, easily a hundred and fifty feet in diameter, with pale, ghostly shapes gliding about inside and a halo of deepening darkness radiating from its surface. A flight of phaerimm were descending out of the gloom above, flinging spells of fire and light as they came, trying to fight their way through the swarm of teleport-dazed Shadovar tumbling and sliding down the slopes of the glassy basin along with Galaeron and Vala.

An orb of darkness streaked up out of the basin and drilled a fist-sized hole through a creature close over their heads. It dropped onto the slope above and started to slide down toward them, roaring its pain in a swirling tempest of winds and lashing out with a wild flurry of lightning and burning light. Galaeron took a white fork of energy in the shoulder and went rigid, biting down on his tongue so hard that his teeth met through the flesh.

Vala hurled her sword, slicing off one of the phaerimm's arms and a good portion of its sinewy shoulder. The creature rolled away, then whistled something in the phaerimm wind language and vanished.

Galaeron felt Vala catch him by the collar, then their descent began to slow as they reached the bottom of the basin and the slope lost its steepness. She called her darksword back to her hand, and only after it had returned did she turn her attention to the smoking hole in his shoulder.

"How bad?"

Galaeron managed to unclench his jaw and, with a mouthful of blood, said, "Stiff, but all right."

He tried to rise, making it as far as his knees before discovering his muscles would not obey. Vala moved his leg into a stable kneeling position, then they both scanned the area. The battle appeared to have ended as quickly as it had started. Shadovar warriors and pieces of Shadovar warriors were sliding down the slope toward them, accumulating in groaning, knee-deep piles. Half a dozen phaerimm—or rather sections of half a dozen phaerimm—lay interspersed among the smoking bodies.

Telamont Tanthul stood a quarter of the way around the basin, Hadrhune at his side as always, calling for his princes and ordering the survivors to arrange search parties. There were no thornbacks in sight; once a battle started to turn against them, it was phaerimm instinct to teleport away. Galaeron knew the enclave defenses would prevent them from leaving the city via translocational magic—but he also knew the phaerimm would have anticipated that and picked a safe rallying point.

Galaeron grabbed Vala's arm and pulled himself up.

"Take it easy," she said. "You're not looking so good."

Though he was still angry with Telamont for drawing out his shadow and at that moment truly *wanted* to see the Shadovar mythallar destroyed—considering the number of deaths that would mean, he hoped that particular desire was his shadow's instead of his own—Galaeron also knew that Evereska's fate depended on Shade Enclave's continued survival.

"It's not done," Galaeron said. "They're still in the city."

Vala wrapped him in a supporting arm and started toward the Most High. "Telamont isn't going to like this. Didn't he order you to stay out of fights until you're able to pass on Melegaunt's knowledge?"

Galaeron nodded at the huge sphere of obsidian they were circling past. "He seems to have made an exception for the mythallar."

Vala glanced at the orb and raised her brow. "That's the mythallar? I was sort of expecting it to be the Karsestone."

"Me, too," Galaeron said.

After unleashing the phaerimm, they had journeyed into the Dire Wood, fighting liches and other undead guardians in order to help Melegaunt recover the famed Karsestone and use its "heavy" magic—from a time before the Weave and Shadow Weave split—to return Shade Enclave to Faerûn.

"I guess they only needed the stone to open a large enough gate between the dimensions," he said. "Apparently, the Shadow Weave can still support spells powerful enough to levitate a city."

"The Weave can't?" Vala asked.

"It hasn't," Galaeron answered, shrugging. "Not since the fall of Netheril."

If Vala saw the danger in that, her expression didn't show it. "That is good news for Evereska, if it means the Shadovar are more powerful than the phaerimm."

Galaeron nodded, but didn't say what it might also mean. If the Shadovar were more powerful than the phaerimm, then they were also more powerful than most of the great wizards of the realms. Only the Chosen themselves, or perhaps an entire circle of high mages, could rival their power.

They were almost to Telamont and Hadrhune when the first of the princes, with half a dozen Shadovar lords at his back, stepped out of the murk at the rim of the basin and began to descend the slick wall. Galaeron recognized Brennus by his large, crescent-shaped mouth and the orange tinge of his iron-colored eyes. Not slipping on the steep obsidian slope, he and the others began to angle more or less in Telamont's direction, their faces showing no reaction at all to the carnage around them. When they reached the body piles at the bottom they began to clamber across without drawing so much as a moan or disturbing even one arm.

"Vala, do you see that?" Galaeron asked.

"What?" she asked.

Like almost everyone else in the basin, Vala was focusing her attention on the murk near the rim, blithely awaiting the arrival of the rest of the princes.

"Lower. Look at Brennus's feet."

Vala looked, then frowned at the way no one seemed bothered that Brennus was stepping on them. "That's just wrong."

"So I thought," Galaeron said.

They were still thirty paces from Telamont, perhaps half that from Brennus and his companions. He stopped and pulled a small flake of obsidian from his robe pocket.

"Galaeron, no." Vala grabbed his arm. "You're—"

"Let go!" Galaeron ripped his arm free, then began to scrape the flake over his palm. "If that's really Brennus, he'll never know."

Galaeron began the incantation of a shadow divination—a more powerful one than he should have been using but necessary if he was to dispel a phaerimm's disguise magic. A surge of cold shadow magic rushed into his body, chilling him down to the marrow in his bones and filling him with a cold, bitter resentment at . . . well, everyone: Melegaunt and the other princes, Telamont, Hadrhune—even Vala.

The spell ended as the "prince" and his escorts were stepping over the last of the casualties onto the basin floor. The shadow drained from their bodies like water, revealing six phaerimm and a strange, three-eyed, three-tentacled orb with a huge, finchlike beak.

"Impos—"

That was as far as Vala's warning got before the basin erupted into flying shadow balls and sizzling fans of light. Two of the phaerimm and fifty Shadovar fell in the battle's first breath, and the three-eyed creature spun toward Galaeron, its tentacles whirling like the scimitars of a drow blademaster. Vala intercepted it, her darksword rising to meet the spinning tentacles—and fell back as the thing beat down her guard, slashing her up the cheek, above the eye, and then across the neck.

Galaeron pulled her back and drew his own sword, his elven steel severing one hooked tentacle as it struck at the hollow of her throat, then falling to his back as the thing's wicked beak clacked at his head. Another hook came whipping down toward Galaeron's unarmored heart—and was intercepted by Vala's darksword. She twined her black blade into the tentacle and pulled the creature toward her, bringing her iron dagger up to meet it. The blade sank a finger's depth, and the third tentacle came around, burying its hook in the back of her knee and trying to jerk her off her feet. Vala was too nimble. She gave it a dead leg, letting her foot rise while she pushed and twisted the dagger. The blade sank perhaps another knuckle.

Galaeron pulled a strand of shadowsilk from his pocket and wadded it into a ball, beginning the incantation for a shadow ball.

"Galaeron!" Vala yelled, hopping on one foot as the thing whipped her impaled leg to and fro. Somehow, during all this, she still managed to knock the shadowsilk from his hand. "No more—"

"Shut the hell up and fight!"

Galaeron kicked the thing's beak off of him and rammed his sword up through its body. Leaving it buried there, he pulled a small cylinder of glass from his pocket and rolled through the incantation for a normal lightning bolt and felt nothing.

Well, not nothing, exactly. There was a cold prickling as the shadow magic tried to rise into him where his body was touching the ground, but he pushed this down and opened himself to the Weave so he could cast a normal, bright, searing lightning bolt—and there was nothing. He had lost the Weave.

Vala exchanged her dagger for his sword's hilt, pushed, twisted, slashed, then cried out in alarm as the thing wrapped its dehooked tentacle around her ankle. Instead of allowing it to pull her foot out from under her, Vala dropped to her back, pulling Galaeron's sword from the creature's body and bringing a cascade of entrails with it.

The thing screeched in anguish and exploded into a bloody cloud as a huge shadow ball burst through its center. What remained plopped down between Galaeron and Vala, its slimy tentacles still twined around Vala and her darksword. She quickly used Galaeron's sword to cut herself free, then flipped it around and shoved the hilt at him.

"Don't ever—I don't care how darkly shadowed you are—don't *ever* tell me to shut up."

"And don't you ever—*ever*—interrupt a spellcasting," Galaeron snapped back. "Or the next time, I'll let it snap your head off."

"Better a . . ." She looked at the three-eyed thing and curled her lip in disgust, then continued, " . . . a monster I don't know than one I do."

She dropped his sword in the mess, then rolled to her feet and limped off through the carnage, leaving Galaeron to face Telamont and Hadrhune as the pair came up behind the monster's disemboweled body. The Most High nudged it with a dark boot.

"Our enemies from the shadow plane attack us even here," he said. "The 'monster' is called a malaugrym. You did well to unmask it. One might even say that we all owe you our lives."

"One might," Galaeron said, struggling to his feet, "but it seems a simple 'thank you' is too much to ask."

Telamont's eyes sparkled. "If that is what your shadow needs to hear."

"My shadow?" Galaeron growled. "It's just common courtesy."

Then, remembering how Vala had saved his life when his lightning bolt failed, he realized Telamont was right. Vala had been, too. His shadow had been completely in control—perhaps it still was.

Telamont motioned to Hadrhune, and both kneeled before Galaeron—causing every shadow lord who happened to be looking in the direction to do likewise.

"Galaeron Nihmedu, on behalf of Shade Enclave," Telamont began, just a hint of mockery in his voice, "please accept our most sincere—"

"Not necessary," Galaeron said, realizing how ignoble he was to be demanding thanks when so many had died. "Forgive me for asking."

Telamont did not rise. "You see, you *can* live with your shadow."

"Sure I can," Galaeron scoffed, looking past the Most High's shoulder. He owed someone an apology. "Where'd Vala go?"

Telamont rose and turned, then said, "There are some things even I do not know."

"Have no fear for her comfort," Hadrhune said, looking in the same direction as Galaeron. "Vala saved Prince Escanor's life. She will always be welcome in his villa."

CHAPTER SIX

15 Mirtul, the Year of Wild Magic

With Boareskyr Bridge hidden somewhere beneath the brown lake that had once been the plains north of the Trollclaws, Laeral's relief army was crossing the Winding Water on a fleet of rain-soaked log rafts. Laeral herself had flown three magic guidelines across two miles of muddy water, and along with her hippogriff-mounted scouts and several dozen of her best battle mages she was standing guard on the western shore, expecting a phaerimm attack at any moment.

This was the last river they would cross before reaching Evereska, and if the enemy meant to stop them, it would be there, and Laeral knew there was a good chance that they would.

In addition to slowing the progress of the relief army to a crawl, the horrid weather was taking a terrible toll on the health and spirit of the army. There was not a fighter among them who doubted that they owed their lives to the forces of Shade. Had the Shadovar not appeared when they did at the High Moor, the enemy horde would have beaten them to the high ground and obliterated the army to a warrior.

Many officers were beginning to question the wisdom of continuing the march at all. While the priests and healers were keeping deaths from illness to a bare minimum, most soldiers were feverish and—with the constant rainfall spoiling rations—weak from hunger. Even if they reached Evereska in time, it seemed likely that their poor condition would only be a burden on those already in place.

Laeral refused to hear these arguments. Sooner or later, the weather would break—it had to—and a few days of sunshine would do wonders to rejuvenate the army. More importantly, she felt certain the phaerimm would eventually find a way to defeat the shadowshell. When that happened, the thornbacks would learn from their mistake and scatter across Faerûn, and the only thing capable of stopping them would be the sheer numbers of Laeral's relief army.

Most of all, there was her beloved Khelben to think about. He had vanished at the Battle of Rocnest, defending a trio of Evermeet's high mages as they attempted to open a translocational gate that would have allowed Waterdeep to send relief forces in a matter of moments instead of months, and Laeral was determined to find out what had become of him. She would have known if he had died—as a Chosen herself, she would have felt his loss in the Weave—so he had either been sucked into another plane when the phaerimm captured the gate, or trapped inside Evereska with the elves. She was gambling on Evereska, if for no other reason than she had already done what little was possible to contact him in the planes beyond.

The first rafts appeared out of the rain, the deep voices of two hundred Uthgardt barbarians chanting a somber hauling song as they pulled themselves along the guide rope. Laeral began to think her army would actually make the crossing successfully. The rafts were spaced about thirty paces apart, just far enough to avoid being caught if a magic fireball, meteor storm, or some other area attack struck the raft in front, yet close enough that the warriors on any one raft could help the others if they did come under attack.

A distant thunder began to roll over the horizon from the direction of the Forest of Wyrms. Laeral assigned her battle mages to ground defense, then took her hippogriff riders into the air to establish a protective screen fifty paces ahead of the shoreline. The thunder grew into the unmistakable roar of pounding boots and growling voices, but the rain clouds were so thick that Laeral couldn't see their enemies even from a hundred feet above the ground.

The roar grew steadily louder and passed underneath her. Laeral dropped down until she saw first the hazy darkness of land, then thousands of oblong boot prints simply appearing in the mud. Someone had turned the entire army invisible, and that meant phaerimm—probably several of them.

She aimed her palm at the front rank and spoke a few syllables of dispelling magic, and a ten-yard circle of charging bugbears appeared no more than thirty paces from the shoreline.

Several of the battle mages raised their hands in spellcasting, and a mile-long wall of flame rose up to devour the first rank of bugbears. Most fell where they stood, but hundreds of the beasts stumbled forward, roaring in pain and raising huge double-headed axes as they staggered toward the thin line of mages. The first Uthgardts were already splashing ashore to meet the beasts, but the mud was deep, they were few, and time was short.

Laeral pulled a nugget of coal from her spell pocket and flew low in front of the burning bugbears, crumbling the coal into powder and uttering a complicated incantation. The ground turned black and viscous beneath the charging beasts, miring them to their knees, then to their waists and, as they continued to struggle, their chests. Wherever their flaming bodies came into contact with the black sludge, it began to burn as well, and the band was soon filled with roaring scarecrows of orange flame.

At the end of her attack run, Laeral rose into a storm of sling stones and hand axes. None of the attacks penetrated her shielding magic, but the sheer volume was enough to slow her ascent. She turned and found herself staring out over a sea of bugbears and gnolls, all visible the moment some had begun to attack. Pushing through the horde were small bands of beholders and tentacle-faced illithids, coming forward to punch holes in the magic defenses holding their masses at bay.

Of the phaerimm who controlled the army, Laeral saw no sign at all. It was even possible that the illithids and beholders themselves did not know where the creatures were or even that they were there. The phaerimm delighted in using their magic to make other beings do their will, and often the victims were not even aware they were being controlled.

A chorus of shouts drew Laeral's attention back to the flood-swollen river, where two flights of beholders were bobbing in from the flanks to attack the raft line. She flicked a finger over her thumb ring to activate its sending magic. She pictured the craggy face of the leader of her hippogriff scouts and thought, *Aelburn, they're trying to take the rafts from the flanks.*

As you predicted, Milady, came Aelburn's reply. *We'll turn that against 'em.*

Aelburn's mount voiced a series of sharp screeches that caused the scouts to divide into two groups and wheel around to dive on the two flights of beholders from behind. Laeral watched the gray sky to be certain that no phaerimm emerged from the clouds behind her scouts. A tempest of crackling and booming exploded over the river as the mages and clerics on the rafts began to fling spells at the attacking beholders. An instant later, the sound was joined by the screams and shrieks of drowning warriors as the creatures responded with disintegration rays and death beams. Hippogriffs started shrieking and crossbows clacking, and bodies from both sides began to splash into the water.

When Laeral turned back to the main battle, the first beholder was already at the wall of fire, spraying a green ray from its huge central eye and slowly dispelling the magic that had kept it burning. She pointed her fingers down at the creature and tore it apart with ten golden bolts of magic. The battle mages filled the gap with a new curtain of fire even as the first bugbears pushed forward to exploit it, but a dozen beholders more were already floating up to spray the flames with their magic-killing rays.

Laeral pulled a pair of wands from her belt and flew down the line, flinging bolts of magic with one hand and forks of lightning with the other. The nearest beholders died before they could open a breach, but those at the far end extinguished huge swaths of flame, and bugbears and gnolls poured through by the dozens. They were met by storms of fiery meteors and dancing chains of lightning, but the battle mages could not stop them all. The meager bands of Uthgardts were forced to meet them at Laeral's tar trench, and all too often it was the barbarians who fell. More warriors were rushing up from the second and third waves of rafts, but with the raft convoy still under attack from the beholders the flow would soon stop.

Laeral finished her run and took out the last of the beholders—then turned and found another two dozen assailing the fire wall behind her. She started down the line again and felt a mental jolt as an illithid tried to blast her with its mind numbing powers. Her thought shield held firm against the assault, but she knew it would only be a matter of time before the creature had one of its beholder companions turn its magic-dispelling ray on her and tried again, and *that* would work.

She would have to call her sister . . . again.

"Storm." Laeral did not bother to use magic. Like all the Chosen of Mystra, when Storm's name was spoken anywhere on Faerûn, she always heard it, and the next few words. "Need help. I'm in—"

Laeral was still speaking when Storm appeared, reeling from teleport afterdaze and plummeting toward the ground. Laeral barely caught hold of her wrist in time to keep her from falling into the morass of bugbears and gnolls clamoring to get past the fiery wall below.

"If you'd have let me finish," Laeral said, rising above the range of the bugbears' slings, "I would have said 'in the air.' "

"By the bleeding stars, where do they find so many brutes?" Storm asked, getting her bearings and staring down on the horde below. Having been warned about the crossing, she was fully armed and armored. "No help from Shade this time, I see."

"The Shadovar may have better things to do than look after me," Laeral said. "That doesn't mean they're betraying us."

"Doesn't it?" Storm activated her own flying magic, then drew a pair of wands and cocked her brow. "Heard from Khelben yet?"

"The Shadovar didn't have anything to do with his disappearance." Laeral pointed her sister toward the opposite end of the battle line, then added, "They weren't even here, yet."

"One of them was," Storm added. "Do you think we ought to call some more sisters?"

"Absolutely not," Laeral answered, diving toward her own end of the battle. "You're bad enough."

They spent the next quarter hour flying back and forth over the battle lines, blasting beholders and illithids with magic from on high, occasionally resorting to more powerful magic like sunburst spells and incendiary clouds when they fell behind and the enemy creatures broke through in numbers larger than the battle mages could stop. Once, Storm was caught in a beholder's antimagic ray when an illithid mind-blasted her, and Laeral had to use time-stopping magic to rescue her. After being restored to capacity by one of Tempus's war clerics, Storm returned the favor twice, once enclosing Laeral in a protective sphere of scintillating colors and the other time creating a magic hand that beat would-be attackers away until she arrived to carry her sister to safety.

Eventually, they simply ran out of beholders and illithids to kill. Laeral's plan for defeating the flank attacks against the raft convoys also worked, and the bugbears and gnolls were forced to stand idle while the relief army hauled itself to shore behind its protective wall of fire. The sisters knew by the simple fact that their monstrous foes remained to fight that there were still phaerimm somewhere in the horde, but they also knew that the creatures would be careful not to reveal themselves in the presence of Mystra's Chosen. The special weapon of the Chosen, silver fire, was one of the few forms of magic that was sure to harm thornbacks, and the creatures were nothing if not cautious.

Once the last of the rafts was across, Laeral and Storm descended to join the commanders of each of the different companies in a war council. It was raining harder than ever, their warriors were exhausted from the crossing, and their foes were both fresher and stronger. On the other hand, they had a slight advantage in numbers and a large advantage in magic, and Laeral felt confident they could carry the day.

Though the wall of flame was a good twenty paces behind her, Laeral could feel its heat chasing the dampness from her rain-soaked clothes.

"What do you think, gentlemen?" she asked. "Attack now or rest the night behind our wall of fire and take the battle to them in the morning?"

"We elves will be no fresher in the morning," said Lord Yoraedia, who commanded Evermeet's five hundred warriors and mages. He glanced at Laeral with an unmistakable expression of scorn, then turned to the black-haired leader of the Black Lion Uthgardts, Chief Claw, and said, "I cannot imagine that even your tribesmen would sleep well this night."

Claw shrugged. "Sleep or not, it is nothing to us," he said, "but night favors the yellow hides and the walking dogs. We will take more to the death fires with us by attacking before dark."

Uncertain whether she was more surprised or alarmed by the fatalism in their voices, Laeral scowled and started to rebuke the commanders—then caught herself and forced a smile.

"You gentlemen are letting the weather cloud your judgment," she said. "There are two of Mystra's Chosen here. Do you really think we can be defeated by a few thousand gnolls and bugbears?"

"You? No," Chief Claw replied, waving his hand vaguely in the direction of the army, "but the rest of us are not Chosen. The rest of us will die."

Laeral heard a nervous murmur building in the ranks but ignored it and kept her attention focused on the commanders.

"Even Chosen die," she said, "but this army is not going to die—not today."

"Forgive me if I find your judgment somewhat clouded," Lord Yoraedia said.

"Clouded?" Laeral was growing angry—and the rising murmur in the ranks was not helping matters. "In what way is my judgment clouded?"

"You fear for your man." Chief Claw glanced over his shoulder, then looked back to Laeral just as she found herself clenching her fists to keep from doing something she would regret. "Your devotion does him honor, but it blinds you to our danger."

Laeral felt as if she had been struck. Yoraedia, Claw, all of the commanders were looking at her as though they truly believed she had led them all to their deaths for Khelben's sake alone.

"I am not the blind one here," she said. "If you can't see—"

"Laeral, wait," said Storm.

She pointed upriver, to where a flight of dozens of huge, scaly wings was just appearing out of the rain. They were as large as sails and blue enough to show their color in the gray light, and even had the sisters never before seen a Rage of Dragons, they would have known what was coming by the sight of so many fang-filled mouths.

Storm said, "Maybe they have a point."

Through the world-window in Telamont Tanthul's palace in Shade Enclave, the dragons looked like an expanse of blue sea shining up through a hole in the clouds, their great wings undulating like waves, their blue scales flashing like light on water—all but the leader. The leader was naked bone, with blue embers gleaming in the empty eye sockets of its skull and claws large enough to grasp the heads of even its biggest followers.

It could only be Malygris, the foolish blue who had traded his soul to the Cult of the Dragon in order to slay his hated ruler, Sussethilasis, and claim for himself the title of the Blue Suzerain of Anauroch. Though Galaeron had never met the dracolich himself, the younger blues who came to the edge of the desert to feed on tomb thieves and their horses often made a show of defiance by speaking of their suzerain's folly. They were not too rebellious, though—several of the smallest wyrms in the Rage were the very ones who had taken such delight in deriding their ruler to Galaeron.

A tilted plain of brown appeared before the dragons, with an orange half-circle of fire lighting the top edge and thousands of tiny flecks blackening the surrounding ground. Galaeron recognized the specks as warriors, but he didn't identify the brown plain as a river in flood until a few moments later, when the diving dragons drew near enough for him to see the current pouring over a barn's roof.

Galaeron focused his attention on the fire wall, and the specks resolved themselves into two armies. The greater one, composed of larger figures as well as superior numbers, was being held at bay by the crackling wall of fire. The smaller army was trapped against the river, with a flotilla of log rafts beached on the muddy shore behind them and the much larger army in front of them. They were, by all appearances, aware of the dragons swooping down behind them, for their orderly ranks were dissolving into chaos, bleeding into the river or bunching against the wall of fire.

The image in the world-window began to grow blurry and coarse, with wisps of shadow closing in around the edges. Galaeron focused his attention in the center of the panicking army, where a small knot of figures stood looking up toward the dragons in relative calm. The world-window struggled to obey his will, but whatever was interfering with it was too powerful. He glimpsed a pair of women with familiar faces and long silver tresses, a frightened Gold elf, and a black-bearded, blue-eyed Uthgardt barbarian. Then the image became an unrecognizable blur and the shadows rolled in, and there was nothing but darkness.

A cold and familiar stillness settled over Galaeron. He turned and found the platinum eyes of Telamont Tanthul shining out at him from beneath his shadowy cowl.

"That's the relief army from Waterdeep!" Galaeron said. "What are you trying to hide?"

Telamont's sleeve rose, and Galaeron sensed a wispy finger wagging in front of his nose. "You mustn't allow your shadow self to draw your conclusions for you, elf."

Telamont waited, and as usual Galaeron felt the weight of the question without hearing it. "I apologize, Most High. When the world-window closed, I naturally assumed you had taken control."

"Because I wished to hide something from you."

Galaeron nodded.

Galaeron's skin prickled beneath Telamont's sigh. "Not everything is my doing, elf. The fear of the Chosen's army is to blame. The fools are sending thoughts to their loved ones, and the magic they use to carry them is interfering with that of the world-window. The image will clear in a few minutes."

And show us what, Galaeron wondered. He felt the weight of another question but could not quite sense what the Most High wished to know.

"Your attention is elsewhere today, Galaeron," Telamont said. "It is dangerous to let it wander. Your shadow will take advantage."

Galaeron nodded. "We have been watching them prepare for the crossing for some time now," he said. "I was wondering why you have still failed to send aid."

"You were wondering what I hope to gain by failing to send aid," Telamont corrected. "You must know your own thoughts, Galaeron, or you will never live at peace with your shadow."

Galaeron nodded. "Very well—what do you hope to gain by not sending help?"

Telamont's eyes brightened with approval. "Better, elf. The answer is nothing. I sent help."

Galaeron glanced at the world-window. The picture remained a black fog, but he knew better than to insult the Most High by questioning the veracity of his words.

"The relief army's losses will be small. They may even reach Evereska someday—though I can't see what good they can do there. It's you we must be concerned about, Galaeron. I do not like this preoccupation I sense. It's dangerous." Telamont lifted a sleeve to wave Galaeron toward his private sitting room, and together they went into the gloom. "What is it that troubles you?"

Galaeron was so astonished to hear the question

asked aloud that the answer began to spill out before he was conscious of formulating it.

"You know that Escanor has asked Vala to accompany him on the assault against the Myth Drannor phaerimm."

"She is a fine warrior, and her darksword has power," Telamont said. "It is a good choice."

"I want you to keep her here."

"Vala is not the kind to hide from death," Telamont said. "Even were such a thing possible, she would think less of herself for it."

"That's not what I'm worried about," Galaeron said. "She can take care of herself, even in a cave full of phaerimm, but I need her here."

"Ah, the promise."

They reached an archway and passed through into a small corner chamber with windows of thin-sliced obsidian on two walls. Beyond the windows, the customary murk that swaddled the enclave appeared to be almost nonexistent, allowing a spectacular—if rather darkened—view of Anauroch's sands rolling past below.

Telamont motioned Galaeron to a chair next to one of the windows and took the one opposite, then said, "The promise she made was to kill you if your shadow self takes over."

Galaeron nodded. "I need to know she's there to keep it."

"No, you don't."

Hadrhune appeared unbidden at the Most High's side, again running his thumbnail along the deep groove in his staff. Telamont ordered wine for himself and Galaeron, and the seneschal dug into the groove so deeply that the tip of his thumb paled to light gray.

Telamont continued, "Vala will never need to keep that promise, not while you are in my company."

Galaeron inclined his head. "You are capable of many things, Most High, but even you cannot solve my shadow crisis for me, as you have said—"

"Many times myself." Telamont raised a sleeve to silence him, and Galaeron saw the translucent form of a withered claw silhouetted in gray against the faint light of the obsidian windows. "But if you are going to lie, lie to me, not yourself."

Galaeron frowned. "What are you saying?"

"You know what I am saying," Telamont said. "At least your shadow does."

"That I don't want Vala to go because I'm jealous?"

Telamont remained silent.

Galaeron rose and strode across the room, nearly bumping into a small writing table before he noticed it floating in the murk. "Elves don't get jealous."

"Nor do they fall asleep," Telamont replied, "or dream like humans."

Galaeron swallowed his rising anger, then turned to face the Most High. "What if I am jealous? I still want you to keep her here."

Telamont looked out over the passing desert. "And who wants this?"

Galaeron considered a moment and realized he was thinking only of his own needs and not Vala's. She would feel diminished to think that he didn't trust her—and he still didn't want her to go.

"Does it matter?" Galaeron asked.

Telamont's cowled head bobbed in approval. "You are beginning to understand, but I will not interfere with Escanor's mission." He turned away from the window and fixed Galaeron with his platinum glare. "Forget this woman. Your shadow will use your love against you, and such emotional attachments can only interfere with your studies."

Galaeron's head was swirling. He had, of course, been aware of his growing attraction to Vala but had never called it love, even in his mind. Elves had to know each other for years—sometimes decades—before they felt anything close to what humans described as love, and he had only known Vala for a few months. To say that he loved her . . . well, most elves didn't sleep or dream, either. Galaeron felt the weight of a question and looked up to find Telamont's gaze still fixed on him.

"Studies?" he asked, hoping to cover what was really going through his mind.

Telamont's eyes twinkled. "Your magic studies," he said. "You are quite a gifted *innatoth*. Once you are at peace with your shadow, I will begin to teach you in earnest."

"Truly?" Even to Galaeron, the response sounded less than enthusiastic, but he kept seeing Vala in Escanor's arms, and that was an image he never wanted to feel comfortable with. "This comes as something of a surprise. Melegaunt warned me to stop using magic altogether."

"Melegaunt was ever the cautious one," Telamont returned. "A fine attribute for spies . . . but limiting."

Hadrhune emerged from the gloom with the wine. He served Telamont first, then crossed the room to offer Galaeron a glass of some vinegary black swill that would not have been used to pickle thracks in Evereska. Galaeron raised his hand to decline and bowed to Telamont.

"You have given me much to think about," he said. "If I may, I should return to Villa Dusari to meditate."

Telamont's eyes dimmed, but he raised a sleeve and dismissed Galaeron with a wave. "If you think that best. Perhaps Hadrhune will join me in your place."

"I would be honored, Most High." Hadrhune glared fire at Galaeron, then spun toward the window so fast that the goblet flew off the tray and spilled. "What a pity—I'll have to fetch another."

Galaeron left the sitting room with the hair prickling on his neck and his thoughts roaring like one of the sandstorms that occasionally forced the city to rise into the cold air miles above the desert. Like Melegaunt before him, the Most High clearly had plans to help Galaeron realize his full potential as a magic-user—and no hesitation about what it might cost Galaeron or those around him. Given the price he had paid merely for learning how to draw on the Shadow Weave, he was not at all eager to increase the depth of his knowledge—especially considering what Telamont had just said it would cost him. He was still enough of an elf to balk at the idea of giving up his emotions, but losing Vala was unthinkable—especially losing her to Escanor.

Galaeron arrived at Villa Dusari angry and determined. He found his companions gathered in the courtyard, sitting on cushions on the ground so they could share the evening meal with Aris, who was reclining along one side of the courtyard with his head propped on a palm as large as a saddle.

"Galaeron, what a surprise," Vala said.

There was no real enthusiasm in her voice. She had yet to forget the sharp words he had spoken to her after the battle at the mythallar, and every time Galaeron thought to apologize, the shadow in him seemed to turn the moment into something awkward or bitter.

"Fetch yourself a plate and mug," she said. "There's plenty to eat."

Instead of stepping into the shadowed colonnade to do as Vala suggested, Galaeron crossed straight to the group. Ruha glanced from him to Vala, then back again, and rose with ghostlike grace. Malik kept his seat, watching the witch with narrow eyes. Aris nodded a welcome to the elf.

"You sit," the witch said. "I'll go."

She vanished into the building. Vala reluctantly moved over to make a place for Galaeron, but he stopped at her side and remained standing, ignoring Malik and the giant altogether.

"Vala, you can't go with Escanor tonight."

She looked up at him with an expression of disbelief. "Who are you to tell me what I can't do?"

An angry heat rose to Galaeron's face. "I . . . I . . ."

Surprised to find it was a question he could not answer, he let his reply trail off. What right could he claim over her decision? He had never spoken the words of love to her, had in fact denied even to himself that he felt such a thing—until Escanor had begun to take an interest in her. Only one oath had ever passed between them.

"You made a promise to me," he said.

"Were I you, that is not something I'd be eager to remind me of."

Realizing he would get nowhere butting heads with a Vaasan, Galaeron took a moment to calm himself—and to quell his shadow, which was whispering dark warnings about the sincerity of the threat implied in her words.

When he finally felt under control, he said, "Vala, I need you to stay."

"You've a funny way of showing it—and I'm not just talking about what you said at the mythallar," she said. "You've been treating me like some two-copper wench and everyone else like house servants. I don't much care for it."

The outrage Galaeron felt from his shadow quickly gave way to a colder kind of anger, something more

subtle and cunning. He found himself nodding and looking at the ground.

"You're right," he heard himself say. "I owe you an
apology."

Vala cocked an eyebrow and said nothing.

"And I'm going to give it to you at the proper time,"
Galaeron said. His shadow would not let him say he was
sorry. He actually wanted to, but those were not the
words that rose to his lips. "And in the proper place."

Vala frowned. "Now is fine."

Galaeron shook his head. "No, when we're out of this
cursed city."

Vala's jaw dropped. "You want to leave?"

"As soon as possible."

Galaeron sat beside her. He felt a little sick inside
because the words were only what his shadow knew Vala
wanted to hear, but what was the harm, really? If Telamont would not do a small favor like keep Vala in the
enclave, then Galaeron *was* ready to leave.

"We'll start planning after dinner and be gone as soon
as we can collect everything we need," he said.

Malik rose so fast he spilled his plate. "Leave? What of
your training?"

"As far as I can tell," Vala said, "Telamont is less interested in teaching Galaeron to control his shadow self
than in turning him into a tool of Shade Enclave. He's
getting worse, not better—we all see that."

"*I* have not seen that!" Malik tried to stop there, but
his face contorted, and he continued, "Except, of course,
that what I mean by 'better' is much influenced by the
current needs of the One."

"There can be no doubt of what Vala says," Aris said.
"Galaeron is turning evil."

"And so what if he does?" Malik demanded. He turned
to address Galaeron directly. "Have you forgotten

Evereska? Telamont needs the knowledge inside your head to defeat the phaerimm."

"The need cannot be that great," Vala countered, "or he would not have moved the enclave so far from the battlefront."

"You can't know that . . . though there is much to be said for your argument." Malik grimaced at the curse that forced him to add this last part, then tried another tack. "Even if the need is not great, there is an implied bargain. If you desert the Shadovar, why should they defend Evereska?"

"I don't think anything Galaeron does will influence the Shadovar one way or the other," Aris said. He sat upright and spoke even more thoughtfully than usual. "The Shadovar serve the Shadovar in all things. They will defend Evereska because that is the best way to destroy their enemies."

"Can no one here let a man make his arguments without spoiling them with logic and common sense?" Malik demanded. Fuming, he began to shake a leg of roasted fowl at Galaeron. "And who is this 'we'? I am going nowhere."

"You *are*," Galaeron insisted, feeling vaguely betrayed. "Do you think Hadrhune will let you stay in this comfortable house after we're gone? You are here only because I am."

Malik drew himself up to his full height, which was only a little taller than a dwarf. "I have means of my own," he said. "And even if they fail me, I have lived in gutters before, when service to the One demanded it . . . or when I could afford no better."

"And you prefer that to our company?" Aris asked. "My friend, I do not understand."

Malik sighed. "I do not prefer that at all. You are the best friends I have ever known . . . at least without paying."

Face darkening, his beady eyes caught Ruha as she returned to the courtyard with a mug and plate for Galaeron. "It is what is safest. The minute we are gone from this city, the hellwitch will plant a *jambiya* in my back."

"Only if you are fleeing the Harp's justice," Ruha said from behind her veil. "But why be fearful? You are safe in Shade Enclave . . . unless you are planning to leave?"

"That is no affair of yours," Malik said, face contorting as his curse compelled him to continue speaking. "Except that my friends are the ones leaving, not I. The One demands my presence in this city so that its denizens may bathe in the light of the Black Sun."

"Ah." Aris nodded as though this made perfect sense. "My behorned friend, I know too much of your god to wish you success, but duty I understand. Your assistance will be missed at the shapings."

Galaeron continued to feel betrayed but knew better than to think he could argue the Seraph of Lies out of obeying his god's will.

"Do as you must, Malik. Can we trust you to keep our secret?"

"Of course," Malik answered. "I am sure I could profit handsomely by running to Hadrhune the moment you are gone and announcing your escape, but in truth Aris's talent has already made me a wealthy man, and I have learned enough of his art to continue the business until his departure is discovered. You may be sure that I will be as loyal to you as I am to my own god and for the sake of my own profit remain silent on the subject of your departure . . . at least until someone tricks me into revealing it against my will."

"We can ask no more," Aris said. "With luck, we will be far out in the desert by then."

"Desert?" Ruha asked. "You will try to cross Anauroch . . . on foot?"

"I do not think Galaeron has the magic to carry us across any other way," Aris replied, looking to Galaeron for confirmation.

Galaeron shook his head. "That is beyond me."

"And it would be unwise for him to push his limits," Vala added.

"Wiser than trying to walk across Anauroch," Ruha said. "You know nothing of the desert."

"No matter—they must leave, and the sooner the better." Vala took his hand. "You have been scaring me, Galaeron. I was beginning to think you meant to hold me to my promise."

Galaeron barely heard this last part. The word "they" was still reverberating through his head. "They?" he demanded.

"I can't go with you," Vala said. "I'm due to leave with Escanor at midnight. If I don't show, he'll know something is wrong—and we all know they'll never let you leave willingly, not with Melegaunt's knowledge still locked inside your head."

"Then we'll wait until you return," Galaeron said. It was all he could do not to accuse her of *wanting* to leave with Escanor. "That's simple enough."

Vala shook her head. "It's not. I may hate what Telamont is doing to you, but the Granite Tower's debt to Melegaunt is not yet discharged."

"Melegaunt is dead," Galaeron objected.

"So his duty becomes my duty," Vala said. "And there is the matter of my men trapped in Evereska. I can't return to Vaasa until I know what has become of them."

"A convenient excuse," Galaeron said.

Vala's face clouded with anger. "Convenient?"

"So you can spend time with the prince," Galaeron said. He didn't really believe this, but the words were spilling from his mouth anyway. "If I were gone—"

"Galaeron, don't do this." Vala's expression turned from angry to sad. "You have to go."

"And leave you to Escanor?"

"Galaeron," Aris began, "she would never—"

Vala raised a hand. "Yes, I would, Aris." She turned to Galaeron. "You're right, Galaeron—I haven't felt anything for you since the mythallar."

"That doesn't matter," Galaeron said. Who was this speaking, he wondered, because it *did* matter. "You made a promise."

Vala's eyes narrowed. "And now I'm breaking it." She turned away from him and started for the interior of the villa. "I'm going with Escanor. Do us both a favor, Galaeron, and don't be here when I get back."

CHAPTER SEVEN

15 Mirtul, the Year of Wild Magic

Piergeiron arrived in Castle Waterdeep's unadorned Chamber of Common Command to find the captain of the City Watch and his senior armmaster and wizards-commander already in conference with their counterparts from the City Guard. Brian the Swordmaster was also present, hidden behind his Lord's cloak and helm. Even the Master of the Watchful Order of Magists and Protectors was there. Strictly speaking, the order was a civilian guild and not subject to military edict, but these were extraordinary times, and Piergeiron had often called private citizens to service when the security of the city was threatened. The question was, when the threat lay five hundred miles distant at Boareskyr Bridge, would they answer?

Piergeiron stepped over to a free seat—there was no head at the circular table—but did not sit. "You heard?"

Rulathon, the wiry, gray-haired captain of the watch, nodded grimly, waved a hand vaguely in the direction of his armmaster, and said, "Helve received a sending himself."

Piergeiron turned to the scarred veteran. "Lassree?" he asked.

Helve nodded. "She wanted to fight at Laeral's side."

Piergeiron's heart rose into his throat. Lassree was Helve's daughter, a watch-wizard who often fought at her father's side during major disturbances.

"I'm sorry," he said, turning to the others. "What can we do?"

"Against a Rage of Dragons?" asked Thyriellentha Snome. The commander of the watch-wizard forces, she was a dusky woman of proud bearing and uncertain age who had been Mage Civilar since long before Piergeiron assumed office. "Not much, I am sorry to say."

Though Helve's eyes were watering, he nodded. "Lassree said they were trapped against a wall of bugbears and gnolls, with all the blues of Anauroch dropping out of the clouds behind them. It's ending as we speak, I'm sure."

"Be that as it may," the Open Lord said, "we must do what we can."

Piergeiron ran his gaze around the table, pausing at each of the commanders to search for any hint of disagreement. They were brave soldiers all, but their duty was to Waterdeep, and if it was necessary to spell out how saving a relief army bound for Evereska contributed to the security of the city, he needed to know that.

With Waterdeep still buried under a constant wave of blizzards and ships in the harbor capsizing under the weight of their ice-crusted masts, no one present needed any reminder of the danger posed to their city since the phaerimm had escaped their prison in Anauroch. He found no questions in the eyes of the gathered commanders.

"Good," Piergeiron said. "As we speak, Maliantor is calling Force Grey to my palace. She will begin a scrying to determine what she can about the course of the battle. What I would like from you is to send a force of volunteers—a hundred battle mages and two hundred swordsmen—to meet her at the palace within the quarter hour. I have a store of teleport scrolls—"

"That won't be necessary," rasped a voice in the corner.

Piergeiron turned to find Prince Aglarel's swarthy form stepping out of the shadows beside the fireplace, his black cape and purple tabard almost seeming to solidify out of the darkness.

"How dare you!" Piergeiron demanded. What he really wanted to know was just plain "how." The room was supposed to be shielded against magic intrusions of any kind, though this obviously did not seem to apply to Shadovar shadow magic. "This is a private council."

"Forgive me," Aglarel said, stopping to bow, "but I wanted to save you the trouble of teleporting a company to rescue your relief army."

"I want to know how you can know our intentions," said Brian the Swordmaster. While it was customary for Piergeiron to speak for the other lords in the Court Hall, they usually spoke for themselves in less formal gatherings. The helm's magic transformed his voice into a hollow, anonymous baritone that even Brian's oldest friends would not recognize. "We have barely formed them ourselves."

Aglarel fixed a silver-eyed glare on the lord. "A short time ago, many of your citizens received farewell sendings from their relatives accompanying the Chosen." The prince did not bother to explain how he knew this. "Knowing the kind of men you Waterdhavians are, it only stood to reason that you would want to do something to help. I called at the palace and was told that Lord Paladinson had left to attend to an urgent matter of state."

"Which begs the question of how you slipped past the invader wards that guard the castle," said Thyriellentha, "or knew to look for Lord Paladinson in this chamber."

"I will be happy to demonstrate later," Aglarel said, dismissing the questions with a flip of his hand. "For the moment, I suggest we concentrate on the matter at hand."

He stepped to the circular table and stretched forward to circle his hand over the surface. A shadow fell over the center, then opened like a hole in the clouds to reveal a battle raging far below. The scene expanded to fill the entire table, and Piergeiron soon recognized Laeral's relief army trapped against the shore of a muddy lake that could only be the Winding Water in high flood. Much to his surprise—and relief—they were standing in good formation behind a wall of guttering flame, shields raised and weapons drawn but engaged in no combat more serious than swatting the flies and mosquitoes swirling around their heads.

The scene on the other side of the burning wall was far different. Dozens of blue dragons were tearing into an army of bugbears and gnolls, swooping down to gather up great clawfuls of warriors, then wheel out over the flooding river and drop them into the muddy waters. Despite the gaps being ripped in their lines, the monsters were holding ranks, doing their best to fend off the attacks with axes and flails better suited to smashing human heads than piercing draconian scales.

"The dragons weren't sent by the phaerimm?" Piergeiron gasped, unable to tear his eyes from the tabletop.

"Even in Anauroch, there are some things the phaerimm do not control," Aglarel said.

The wings of one dragon went limp, and it plunged toward the ground, tumbling end over end and tangling itself into a knot of tail, neck, and wing. Piergeiron glimpsed a huge black hole in its chest and realized that it had been killed by some very powerful death magic.

In the next instant, the polished bones of a huge dracolich dived down out of the clouds, discharging a thunderstorm's worth of blue lightning at a tiny, cone-shaped figure near the back of the bugbear ranks. A salvo of crackling red meteors streamed up to blast it in the flank, dislodging two ribs the size of trees and sending the skeletal dragon rolling through the air in a crackling ball of flailing claws and forks of flashing blue energy. Thyriellentha gasped at the mighty magic being hurled about in the battle—the magic required to send a two-hundred-foot dracolich tumbling would have reduced any normal wizard to a smoking cinder—then the thorny shape of a second phaerimm appeared behind the gnolls.

The first dragon had barely crashed to the ground before four long-tressed women rose into the air above the relief army's ranks. They streaked toward the visible phaerimm, balls of the Chosen's silver fire streaking from their hands. The two thornbacks vanished in a blinding explosion of light.

"*Four* Sisters," Aglarel said, clearly awed. "That was unexpected. When last I looked, there were only Storm and Laeral."

"The Chosen stick together," Brian said from behind his helm. "You Shadovar would do well to remember that."

Aglarel smiled tolerantly. "You seem to think we would have reason to fear them."

The bugbears and gnolls finally lost their courage and turned to flee, drawing the dragons down after them. Piergeiron had to look away from what came next.

"I think we've seen enough, Prince," he said.

Aglarel waved his hand over the scene, and the table returned to its normal brown surface.

"You're welcome," Aglarel said, assuming the thanks Piergeiron had deliberately omitted. "I'm sure Waterdeep has many genuine problems with which to concern itself."

"No more than we can handle," Piergeiron said.

He did not like this Shadovar, and because of that he did not trust him. Still, even he had to admit that aside from its part in releasing the phaerimm in the first place, so far the city of Shade had done nothing but help Waterdeep, Evereska, and their allies.

"Are we to take it that the dragons were your city's doing?" Piergeiron asked.

Aglarel nodded, then, without being invited, took a seat at the council table. "Our riposte force is occupied with other problems, so we had to call upon our ally Malygris to watch over your relief army."

"Malygris?" Brian demanded. "You would ally with the Cult of the Dragon?"

Aglarel turned and craned his neck to look up at the helmed lord. "Our alliance is with Malygris. His relationship with the cult is none of our concern."

"But you have allied yourself with a dracolich?" Thyriellentha clarified.

Aglarel nodded. "We hope to reclaim our home in Anauroch. It seemed wiser to ally with the Blue Suzerain than to fight him." He waved his hand at the blank tabletop and added, "I am sure Laeral and her sisters will attest to the wisdom of that decision . . . just as I'm sure that Waterdeep and its allies would benefit from a similar arrangement. Shade Enclave has demonstrated the benefits of working with us twice already."

"You let the Chosen speak for themselves," Brian said. He turned his helm toward Piergeiron. "There may be more to this than is apparent . . . or less."

"What are you saying, Lord?" Piergeiron asked. "That the prince misled us?"

Brian shrugged. "I'm saying it's possible. He could have shown us an illusion as easily as a scrying." The helm turned briefly toward Thyriellentha, who could only shrug and spread her hands, then he demanded, "How do we know those dragons aren't tearing Laeral's army apart right now?"

"Because you must have half a wit somewhere inside that helmet," Aglarel said, growing exasperated. "Why would we save the army at the High Moor, only to summon a flight of dragons to destroy it later?"

"I don't pretend to know the ways of shadow," Brian said, "but I do know better than to trust those who bargain with dracoliches."

Aglarel rose, then—to Piergeiron's amazement—responded in a civil voice. "Your point would be better taken, Masked Lord, had Shade Enclave not proven more reliable than any of your other allies."

"Reliable?" Brian scoffed. "We have seen how reliable you were in your dealings with Elminster."

Aglarel's hand knotted into a fist, and Piergeiron realized that he was allowing his own dislike of the Shadovar to interfere with his judgment as a diplomat.

"My Lord," he began, "your caution is well placed, but in truth the Shadovar have done nothing but serve our mutual cause."

Brian would not be called off. "No?" he demanded.

"And what of Blackstaff's disappearance? How do we know they didn't send him to the hells with Elminster?"

"Because we were not even here when Khelben vanished," Aglarel said, not unreasonably. He turned to Piergeiron. "Milord, this really is too much. I demand an apology."

Piergeiron almost let his chin drop. He had no authority to make a Masked Lord apologize, and—even were he sure that Brian was wrong—he knew what the brusque weaponsmith would tell him if he dared suggest such a thing openly.

"Prince Aglarel, there are those in this room who have relatives in the relief army," he began. "You can understand their concern. When our own mages have confirmed what you showed us, I'm sure the Masked Lord will reconsider his opinion."

Brian started to object, but Aglarel spoke over him, his raspy voice seeming to reverberate from all corners of the room at once.

"You will allow this insult to stand?"

"It is not my place to speak for another Lord," Piergeiron said, reminding himself not to look away. "Any more than it would be yours to speak for another prince."

"Were a Prince of Shade to insult a guest in that manner, he would be a prince no longer," Aglarel said. He turned to Brian and bowed stiffly. "I thank you for your candor. You have shown me that I am wasting my breath in Waterdeep."

"Think nothing of it," Brian said. Even the helm's magic was unable to conceal the smugness in his voice. "Though I wish you luck in your alliance with the dragons and scorpions."

Aglarel's eyes flashed, then he turned to Piergeiron. "With your permission, I will remain in the city long enough to purchase some things that have caught my eye."

"Of course," Piergeiron said. "All are welcome in Waterdeep. I'm sure this will blow over—"

"Please, Lord Paladinson, I think it is time to be honest with each other," Aglarel said, raising his hand. He stepped away from the table and crossed to the door, then turned and executed a formal bow. "In that spirit, it is only fair to warn you that the attention of Shade Enclave is required elsewhere. Your relief army will be receiving no more protection from us."

With the soft footfalls of the Guards Most High rustling in his ears and his own hands thrust in his cloak pockets to hide how they were trembling, Galaeron followed Telamont down into the murky passages beneath the Palace Most High. As they descended staircase after staircase, Galaeron was sometimes almost able to recognize the strange tinklings and odd raspings that resonated from the dark sanctums of each level and was sometimes unsettled by eerie gurglings and ominous rumblings too macabre for an elf's ear to discern. Though he had no idea where they were going, or why the Most High had picked the last hour of darkness on the same night as Vala's departure to have him fetched to the palace, Galaeron refused to ask. If his plan to leave the enclave had been discovered, he refused to give Hadrhune—walking a bare two paces behind him—the pleasure of seeing him squirm. If the summons concerned something else, any questions he asked stood a risk of revealing his intentions to Telamont.

They were twenty levels deep when the leading guards finally left the stairwell, then led the group down a winding tunnel through a large archway into a vast chamber with a high vaulted ceiling. At one end of the cavern lay a hundred-yard slit through which the purple light of the predawn morning could be glimpsed outside. Several dozen Shadovar were pulling a large, comblike device back toward the slit. Closer by, several dozen more were folding a huge section of shadow blanket into a compact bundle similar to several others stacked neatly along the near wall.

When the laborers saw Telamont Tanthul and his party in the room, they immediately dropped to the floor and pressed their brows to the floor. Though this hardly seemed the sort of place where the Shadovar confined their prisoners, Galaeron's heart beat no easier. Malik and Aris had left Villa Dusari before Hadrhune arrived with the Most High's summons. Once Aris had collected his supplies, Malik would stage a diversion to make it easier for Galaeron and the giant to slip away from the enclave unnoticed.

"One of our shadow looms," Telamont explained. He waved a sleeve toward the comblike device being drawn toward the slit at the opposite end of the room, then motioned his guards onward. "Not what I brought you to see."

They followed the guards around the edge of the room, then stepped through another archway into an even larger chamber where hundreds of Shadovar were busy sewing sections of blanket together with strands of shadowsilk. Again, the laborers stopped work to press their brows to the floor as Telamont entered. This time, the Most High turned to Hadrhune, his platinum eyes flaring with displeasure.

"We cannot have this," he said.

"I shall see to it." Hadrhune left the group and went over to the edge of the work floor. "Return to your work, lazy ralbs! Do not dishonor the Most High by shirking your duty in his presence."

The workers scrambled to return to their sewing, though all were careful to keep their gazes fixed on the area directly in front of their noses. Telamont motioned Galaeron to his side, then led the way along the edge of the work floor through a broad archway at the far end. In the room beyond, Prince Escanor stood on a bronze flying disk, holding a folded shadow blanket, while Vala, suspended by a new pair of magic wings, flew a line over the top.

"This is what I brought you to see, Galaeron," Telamont said, crossing to the disk. "I thought you might wish to say farewell."

"Is that so?" Galaeron asked, trying to sense whether there was a double meaning behind Telamont's words. Did the Most High know what had passed between he and Vala at Villa Dusari the previous night? Or was he only trying to gauge the depth of Galaeron's feelings for her? In either case, his answer had to be the same. "Why would I want to do that?"

Telamont's eyes brightened beneath his cowl, then a breeze brushed Galaeron's face as Vala swooped down to land. Escanor came to stand beside her, saying nothing but absentmindedly running his dark fingers along the feathers of one of her magic wings.

"We've said our good-byes, Most High." Her green eyes flashed, hard and cold, over Galaeron's face, then she directed her full attention to Telamont. "I'm sorry you put yourself to such trouble."

"No trouble, my dear." Telamont tipped his cowl in her direction, then turned and studied Galaeron for a moment. Finally, he said, "You surprise even me, elf. I had not expected you to release your emotions so easily."

"I doubt it was as difficult as you think, Most High," Vala said, with enough bitterness in her voice to bring a pain to Galaeron's heart. "As it happens, they ran more shallow than any of us thought. I'm glad to be rid of him."

"Indeed?" The purple line of a smile appeared in the shadows beneath the Most High's eyes. He turned to Hadrhune, then said, "This one may someday rival even you, my servant."

"Yours to see, Most High—but we must remember that only one of us serves the enclave." Hadrhune allowed his glare to linger on Galaeron just a second too long, then turned to Telamont and said, "I am afraid I must beg my leave, Most High. There is a disturbance in the Trades Ward that requires my attention."

"Of course." Telamont had barely raised his hand to dismiss Hadrhune before the seneschal melted into the darkness and was gone. The Most High turned to Galaeron and said, "If you will allow me a few moments, the battle with the Myth Drannor phaerimm is going to be a difficult one. I would like a few words with Escanor before he departs."

"Take all the time you need, Most High." Though Galaeron's voice was calm, his heart was pounding. The disturbance in the Trades Ward was Malik's diversion. Aris would be expecting Galaeron at the Cave Gate within a quarter hour. "With your permission, I can find my own way home. The route was not complicated, and the company here is not to my liking."

He cast a meaningful glance at Vala, who smiled cruelly and brushed the edge of her new wing against Escanor.

Telamont took all of this in with his metallic eyes, then raised a sleeve in dismissal. "Perhaps that is wise," he said. "I shall need you at the world-window by midday tomorrow, rested and alert. When Escanor lays the shadow blanket over Myth Drannor, we will need all of Melegaunt's wisdom that you can summon."

"As you command, Most High."

Galaeron bowed, more to hide his smile than to show subservience, then turned and left. He did not say good-bye to Vala or even wish her well in combat. He could think of nothing but of how she had betrayed him for Escanor, how Escanor had stolen her from him, how Telamont had permitted it . . . and, most especially, how he was going to make them pay.

All of them.

The greatest danger, Malik realized, was not that the witch's stolen *haik* would slip through his grasp—though it might—or even that the merciless winds would beat him unconscious against the enclave's stony under-side—though they might. The greatest danger was the lazy vultures who spent their lives in search of easy meals from the city rubbish chutes. Already, one crea-ture was perched atop his right shoulder pecking at his fingers, and two more were circling above his head fight-ing over the left shoulder, and a dozen more were cir-cling beneath his dangling feet, ready to snatch up any bloody morsels the others let fall.

"You are sure this is a good idea?" Aris called down.

"Undoubtedly one of my best."

Malik craned his neck and ran his gaze up ten feet of camel-wool *haik* to the jagged breach they had punched through the exterior wall of the workshop. Aris had care-fully sculpted the hole to look like the crater of a power-ful blasting spell, ingeniously fashioning two cragged teeth into the edge to bind the upper end of the cloth.

"Who would believe I would dangle myself here on purpose?" Malik asked.

"I'm more concerned that you still be there for them to find," Aris said. "It is a long way to the ground."

Malik did not look down. He had already done that once and through a hole in the murky haze glimpsed Anauroch's sands drifting past a thousand feet below.

"I will be here," he called, taking one hand off the *haik* to swat at the vulture pecking at his fingers. "Just sprinkle the sand and be gone. By the time this is sorted out, you and Galaeron will be far away."

Aris did not withdraw. "You are certain Ruha will not suffer for this?"

"Did she not say she wished to help?"

Aris nodded. "Yes, but—"

"Then let her help. No harm will come to the witch— I am not that lucky—and you know I cannot lie." Malik struggled to hold his tongue but was compelled by Mystra's curse to add, "Except by my silence, and when have you ever known me to hold my tongue for more than two minutes?"

Aris considered this, then said, "Only when you are sleeping." He tested the *haik* to make certain it was securely wedged in place, then waved. "Fare you well, my friend . . . and thank you."

Before Malik could reply, the battling vultures obscured his view, and Aris was gone by the time he could beat them aside again. He spent the next few minutes fighting off birds and cursing all creatures with feathers as the wind slammed him into the enclave's rocky exterior time and again. Though his body ached from a hundred horrible bruises and his cramped muscles burned like someone had pushed hot pokers into them, Malik did not worry that his strength would fail him. As the Seraph of Lies, he had been gifted with the ability to suffer any amount of pain and still perform his duties to Cyric, and while helping Aris and Galaeron escape the city did not necessarily serve the One, the second part of his plan most assuredly did.

When he judged he had allowed the giant sufficient time to leave the trade warrens and be on his way to the Cave Gate, Malik began to scream for help.

"Save me! *Help!*"

After a few minutes of screaming, someone finally poked her head out of the hole. She had long sable hair, dark sultry eyes, and, above the veil that covered the lower part of her face, a dusky complexion. The face was the last one he had hoped to see.

"So there you are," Ruha said. She squatted above the teeth where her *haik* was caught, scared the vultures off, and reached down to grab the cloth. "And with my *haik*, no less."

"Meddling witch!" Malik said. "What are you doing here?"

"Looking for you, of course. And now that we are alone, I think the time has come for us to take our leave of this flying city."

Still holding onto the *haik*, she held her free palm in front of her face and blew on it lightly, then began the incantation of one of her Bedine nature spells.

"Stop!" Malik began to climb the *haik* hand over hand. "Shrew! Harpy!"

Ruha finished her spell, then wrapped her hand into the *haik* and looked down, a smile in her dark eyes. "Is that how you talk to the one who holds your life in her hand?"

"Who will feed my poor Kelda?" Malik cried. He was halfway up the *haik*, almost within striking range. "I am going nowhere with you!"

"You prefer to fall?" Ruha twisted around, reaching back to collect something behind her. "Because that is your only choice."

"Not my only choice." Malik wrapped a hand into the *haik*, then reached under his *aba* and grabbed the hilt of his *jambiya*. "I have another I like much better."

Pulling her *kuerabiche* shoulder bag around with her, Ruha spun around to face him, exposing her throat just as he had hoped, and started to reach for her own dagger—then she fell backward as a swarthy Shadovar hand caught the strap of her *kuerabiche* and jerked her away from the edge.

Malik shoved his *jambiya* back in its sheath and began to scream. "Help! I am down here!"

Hadrhune's amber eyes peered over the edge. "I know where you are, Malik."

The Shadovar whispered some barely audible shadow spell, then Malik floated up through the hole into the goodshouse that had been serving as Aris's workshop. The place was crowded with Shadovar warriors but still looked as though a troop of bugbears had crashed through it. Statues lay toppled on their sides, some— mostly half-finished pieces that had little value anyway— shattered or irretrievably broken. The walls were marked with streaks of soot and pocked with hollows the size of a giant's head, and a broad smear of Aris's blood ran along the wall, pointing out the huge hole through which Malik had just been retrieved.

After taking all this in, Hadrhune turned to Ruha. "Did I not warn you what would happen if you violated our guest guard?"

Eyes widening, Ruha looked around the workshop and shook her head. "This is not my doing."

"Do not lie to me, Harper. With my own ears, I heard you give Malik the choice between death and leaving in your custody. That is violation enough." Hadrhune looked to Malik. "Where is the giant?"

Biting his tongue lest he speak and give himself away, Malik simply turned and looked out the big hole where he had been dangling.

"I see." Hadrhune flicked a hand in Ruha's direction, and suddenly she was swaddled in black shadow web. "You will be executed as soon as the Most High pronounces your sentence. What do you wish done with your property?"

"Nothing. I killed no one, and he knows it." Ruha glared at Malik, and in her stare he felt the unspoken threat to reveal Galaeron's escape plans. "Ask him. He has no choice but to tell the truth."

Hadrhune considered this for a moment, then nodded. "A reasonable request." He turned to Malik. "Did she kill Aris?"

"I have no wish to see her executed," Malik said.

"You don't?" This from Ruha and Hadrhune both.

"Not at all. It will be enough to banish her from the city."

Hadrhune frowned. "I didn't know Cyric-worshipers were so merciful."

"Oh, we are not," Malik said, allowing a half-smile to crease his lips, "but I can think of no greater torture for Ruha than to know I am living like a king in Shade Enclave while she is sucking the dew out of sand down in Anauroch."

"That is not how justice works in Shade Enclave," Hadrhune said. "Tell me if she killed Aris or not."

Malik shook his head—truthfully.

"If I banish her, Aris's life will be your responsibility," Hadrhune warned. "Tell me now, or the weight of her crime will rest on your head."

"On *my* head?"

This was something Malik had not planned on. He glanced at Ruha and found her smirking at his predicament—that he had to either exonerate her or be executed for the crime he had accused her of. He shook his head in despair.

"Let me make certain I understand," he said. "If she killed the giant, then you will execute her, and I will remain in Shade Enclave living like a king?"

Hadrhune nodded. "Did she kill him?"

Malik raised his hand. "But if she did not, you will banish her and execute me?"

Hadrhune nodded. "Yes. When someone is murdered, someone must pay. That is the law."

"My miserable life is only one unfair circumstance after another," Malik complained. He took a deep breath, then said, "I have no wish to die, but the truth is this: No one killed Aris. He and I staged this whole thing so that he and Galaeron could escape into the desert."

"Malik!" Ruha gasped. "I should have known you would—"

"Silence!" Hadrhune raised his hand toward her. The shadow web rose to cover her mouth. The seneschal glared at Malik for a moment, then said, "As you wish, little man."

Still pointing at the Harper, Hadrhune swept his hand toward the jagged hole, and Ruha flew from the room and arced down toward the desert. When her black cocoon finally tumbled out of sight, he pointed at Malik and whispered something arcane. Malik found himself swaddled in sticky black shadow.

"Now you will stand before the Most High and answer for the giant's death," Hadrhune said. "To think, I nearly believed Galaeron when he said you could not lie."

CHAPTER EIGHT

16 Mirtul, the Year of Wild Magic

Escanor's army cascaded from the Cave Gate in a long river of flapping wings and shadowy pennants that curved down toward the east and vanished into the umbral mists beneath the city. Galaeron waited until the last rank of riders was well past the Livery Most High, then walked his veserab out to join the rear of the great formation. When no one objected—or even seemed to notice—he waved to Aris, who drifted into the Marshaling Court kneeling on a flying disk so overloaded with waterskins that it wobbled under the giant's slightest gesture.

Aris leaned down toward Galaeron, tilting the dish so precariously that it would have spilled its cargo had he not lowered a massive arm to hold the waterskins in place.

"You're sure the guards won't notice?" asked the giant.

"They'll notice," Galaeron replied, wincing at the gusty volume of the giant's whisper, "but we've traveled with Escanor before. A pair of gate guards isn't going to question our presence now."

"That I know, but this they would question," Aris said. He pointed at his knees, which were resting on a section of shadow blanket Galaeron had stolen as he left the looms. "You are certain we must take it?"

"I'm certain—very certain," Galaeron said. "That's how I repay them."

"Repay who?" Aris asked.

"All of them," Galaeron hissed. "Telamont, Escanor, Vala . . . everyone who's betrayed me."

"This is your shadow speaking, Galaeron," Aris said. "No one has betrayed you—especially Vala."

"Then where is she?" Galaeron hissed. "Why is she not here to keep her promise?"

"Because not being here is the only hope she sees of not having to keep it," Aris answered calmly. "You must leave this place before you are lost, and that would be impossible if she deserted Escanor to come with us. I am sure she will track us down later—especially if it proves necessary for her to keep her promise."

Galaeron shook his head. "You are too trusting, my large friend. Once we're gone, she will have no way of knowing when it becomes necessary."

"But she will," Aris said. "I will tell her."

They came to the watch balconies, and Aris clamped his mouth shut and stared ahead so rigidly that he looked suspicious even to Galaeron. The guards' gem-colored eyes fixed on the giant and followed his advance until they had passed under the great portcullis and launched themselves out into the sky, then they were curving down under the enclave with the rest of Escanor's army. Once they had passed out of view of the Cave Gate, they began to lag behind the others, and Galaeron used his shadow magic to make them both invisible. He was not really surprised to find the familiar chill of the Shadow Weave quenching a thirst that had lain buried just beneath the surface of his subconscious.

They dropped out of the shadow haze to find themselves over a mazelike warren of deep ravines and sheer pinnacles that marked the transition between the rolling sea of sand dunes over which the city had been drifting for most of the past tenday and the jagged spine of desert mountains toward which it was floating. Escanor's army was flying more or less in the same direction as the enclave but angling just a little bit south straight into the rising sun. Whistling an elven tune to help Aris keep track of him, Galaeron turned in the opposite direction—west toward Evereska.

"Galaeron?" Aris called.

"Here. Can't you hear my song?"

"If one can call that lip-trilling music, yes," Aris replied, "but shouldn't we have a look down there? It looks like someone might be in trouble."

Galaeron searched the sands ahead and saw nothing. "Where?"

"South of our bearing," Aris said. "Lying in the hollow on the crest of that dune, perhaps a mile back."

Galaeron looked and saw nothing but golden sunlight shining on the eastern faces of an endless chain of sand walls. "Where?"

"Follow me," Aris said.

The sonorous purr of stone giant humming arose beside Galaeron. He reined his veserab back and fell in behind his invisible companion, then followed the sound down toward the desert at a gentle angle. After a few moments, he saw the tiny dimple toward which they were descending, a circle the size of his fingertip with a minuscule fleck of darkness in the center. The fleck gradually grew large enough so that Galaeron could see it was indeed wriggling about like a chrysalis struggling to escape its cocoon.

"He lied!" Aris boomed.

"Who lied?" Galaeron called.

"Malik!" the giant exclaimed. "He told me Ruha would come to no harm."

Galaeron eyed the dark cocoon. It was about as long as his hand, and he could see that it had a vaguely human shape, with a head-shaped lump on one end and a feet-shaped tail at the other.

"How do you know that's Ruha?" asked the elf.

"How could it not be?" Aris demanded. "How many dark-haired women in veils do you expect to find lying about in this desert?"

"More than you might think," Galaeron replied. The giant's description could fit any Bedine woman Galaeron had ever seen, though it would have been an unthinkable coincidence to find one lying about trussed up beneath Shade Enclave's path. "But if you say it is Ruha, I will trust to your eyesight. It is obviously better than an elf's."

"Oh yes, it is definitely the witch," Aris said. "I recognize her now."

To Galaeron, she was still an indistinguishable lump of darkness. They descended to the crater in silence, and a minute later, Galaeron recognized Ruha's dark eyes peering out above her customary purple veil. Judging by the size of the crater in which she lay, she had hit the dune with a fair amount of speed, but she either had magical protections or was exceptionally resilient even for a Bedine. Swaddled in a cocoon of shadow web that would have dissolved in another hour anyway, she was writhing about, rolling back and forth in an effort to work her hands free so she could dispel the magic that held her bound.

"Don't hurt yourself," Galaeron called. "We're here."

"It is about time!" Ruha rolled onto her back and looked more or less toward Galaeron's voice. "I was beginning to think you meant to leave me out here to die."

"Meant to?" Aris said, speaking from the side opposite Galaeron. "We did not mean to do anything. It is a lucky thing we saw you at all. How did you end up here?"

"Do not feign innocence with me, Gray Face. You are not much better at lying than Malik."

"Lying?" Aris gasped. "He said that you would not be harmed."

"And so I am not," Ruha said, "but your plan has miscarried."

"What plan would that be?" Galaeron dismounted and tried to dispel the shadow web. To his astonishment, the spell failed—and even that felt good. "Who cast this on you? One of the princes?"

"As if you didn't know!" Ruha scoffed.

Galaeron had a sinking feeling. "I don't know," he said. "What do you think our plan was?"

"To make it look like I had violated the Shadovar's guest guard, of course," Ruha said.

"Why would we do that?" Galaeron asked.

"To have me exiled, so I would have to serve as your guide." Ruha was beginning to look less angry and more perplexed. "But Malik could no more keep your secret than he could neglect an untended purse."

Galaeron glanced eastward and finding Shade Enclave little more than a dark diamond barely visible against the shadowed slopes of the distant mountains, dispelled his invisibility spells. He found Aris looking more than a little chagrined.

"Aris, what happened?" Galaeron asked. "You were only to create a distraction."

"We *did* create a distraction," the giant said. "We made it look like Ruha had attacked Malik and knocked me out of the enclave."

"That much worked," Ruha said, "but Hadrhune isn't naive. He knew Malik was hiding something, and eventually Malik had to admit that you and Aris had left the city."

Galaeron and Aris immediately looked toward the city.

"You have a little time," Ruha said. "Hadrhune didn't believe him. But sooner or later, they're going to discover that you're gone—and when that happens, Malik will be in trouble."

"As will Vala," Aris said. "It won't take them long to realize we were all part of the plan."

"Unless we return to the city at once," Ruha said. "Hadrhune still believes that I killed Aris while trying to capture Malik. If we return to the enclave with Aris alive, matters will be confused, but there will be no crime. Things will be as before. You will be able to bide your time and escape when it is safe for Vala."

Galaeron shook his head. "Except for the shadow blanket." He pointed at Aris's bronze flying disk. "Once they realize that is gone, they're not going to believe anything we say."

"Shadow blanket?" Ruha asked.

Aris pulled a corner up from behind his waterskins. "Galaeron's vengeance," he said. "It will be the undoing of us all."

Ruha frowned. "What is that?"

Galaeron explained about how the Shadovar were

using the blankets to melt the High Ice and upset the weather all along the Savage Frontier and Sword Coast.

"Once they realize I've taken this, I doubt they're going to trust us much further."

"I believe that time has come," Aris said. He pointed toward the floating city, where a single dark line could be seen descending beneath the enclave. "They seem to be turning in our direction."

"In the name of Kozah!" Ruha cursed. Still encased in her shadow web, she began to roll toward the shadowy side of the dune. "Quick, send your veserab and flying disk into the west. We will hide beneath the sands, then sneak away after they pass by."

Galaeron nodded and sent his veserab into the sky, then turned and rushed across the crater to where Aris was unloading his waterskins.

"Leave the water. There is no time!" he said, jumping onto the disk. "Get the blanket!"

"The blanket?" Aris gasped.

"The blanket!" Galaeron said, hurling the heavy shroud into the crater. "Water, we can find later."

To the eye of Keya Nihmedu, the silver magicstar drifting past the window of the Livery Gate watchtower looked even brighter than the sun that once blazed down on Evereska from high above the craggy peaks of the Sharaedim. It hurt her eyes even to look under it to the yellowing meadow that surrounded the city cliffs, and its light flooded the cramped chamber with a white brilliance that brooked no shadows.

The magicstar was no sun. It hissed and sputtered like a guttering torch and drizzled a constant trail of cinders in its wake, filling the air with the acrid stench of brimstone and lamp oil. When Keya closed her eyes, she could not sense it at all, could not see its glow shining through her eyelids or feel its heat sinking into her skin. It was as though the magicstar cast only the illusion of light or that its radiance simply lacked the true substance of sunlight.

It lacked something. Though there were more than a hundred of the spheres floating in and around Evereska, the grass continued to yellow, the great bluetops and sycamores still dropped their leaves, and the liliap blossoms withered and grayed. Even Zharilee and the other sun elves were beginning to lose their color and turn sickly shades of saffron and ocher.

Something would have to be done to bring real sun to the Vale, and Keya was not the only one who thought so. Khelben Arunsun was standing at the next window with Kiinyon Colbathin and Lord Duirsar, staring out at dying lands within the mythal and quietly arguing for an assault on the enemy shadow mantle.

"We need only a company of spellblades, a dozen Long Watch sentries, and the Cloudtop Magi Circle," Khelben was saying behind her. He motioned at Dexon and the other Vaasans, who had become a more or less permanent escort—when they were not at Treetop, eating and drinking the Nihmedu larder into nothingness. "We just need to hold our position long enough to attach a magicstar—"

Lord Duirsar raised a finger to interrupt. "Did you not say the shadow mantle was *outside* the deadwall, my friend?"

"I did."

Keya turned just enough to see Khelben nodding as he spoke. While she was honored that Lord Duirsar and the others felt comfortable speaking of such matters in her presence, she was acutely conscious of the disparity in their ranks and tried to be as inconspicuous as possible in her eavesdropping.

"The shadow mantle's appearance suggested an interesting possibility," Khelben continued. "I'm beginning to think that the deadwall is actually three walls, a sphere of imprisoning magic sandwiched between two layers of dead magic."

Duirsar nodded eagerly. "That would explain why no spells can pass through it."

"Exactly," Khelben said. "So I may be able to burn through with my silver fire."

"Surely you've tried that before," Kiinyon Colbathin said, his too-gaunt face sneering in disapproval.

"I have," Khelben confirmed. "I've noticed a disturbance, but the imprisoning layer has always remained intact—the silver fire has no effect on normal magic—and the phaerimm have always come to chase me off before I had a chance to dispel it."

"Which is why you need assistance," Lord Duirsar surmised, "to hold the enemy at bay long enough for you to cast a second spell."

"A little longer than that," Khelben admitted. "The Cloudtop Circle would need enough time to cast a magic-star and attach it to the shadow mantle."

"I don't like it," Kiinyon said, shaking his sharp-featured head. "That will take easily a quarter hour. By then, my spellblades will be trying to hold off a hundred phaerimm. The circle would be doing good to finish its spell before they were all dead."

"The Vale is dying, Kiinyon," Lord Duirsar said. "We must do something, or the mythal will die with it. Keya, what do you think?"

Keya felt like her heart had leaped into her throat. "Milord?"

"About Khelben's mission!" Kiinyon snapped. "This is no time to play coy, Watcher. If we didn't want you to hear, we would have sent you to the rooftop."

Keya felt the heat rise to her cheeks. "Of course, Swordlord." She turned to address Khelben and found him looking at the ceiling with his head cocked and a vacant expression in his eyes. Eager to avoid another rebuke, she spoke anyway. "If Lord Blackstaff feels that our lives would be well-spent, I am sure I speak for Zharilee and the others in the Long Watch—"

Khelben raised a silencing palm, then spoke to the ceiling. "Laeral? Was that you?"

Lord Duirsar and Kiinyon exchanged astonished glances. They knew as well as Keya that while all Chosen heard the next few words when their name was spoken anywhere on Faerûn, the deadwall had limited the range of Khelben's ability to the Sharaedim. If he was in contact with Laeral, either she had entered the Sharaedim or something had weakened the phaerimm's barrier.

"Laeral, of course I'm alive," Khelben said. "I'm in Evereska."

The excitement was too much for the others in the room. Lord Duirsar and Kiinyon began to call Laeral's name and bark requests for weapons and magic, while the Vaasans inquired about Vala and whether the phaerimm had attacked their homes. Even Keya could not restrain herself from asking for news of her brother.

Khelben turned a dark eye on them all. "Do you mind?"

The room fell as silent as a tomb, then Keya and the others spent the next few minutes listening to a strange, one-sided conversation punctated by the use of Laeral's name every few words.

After establishing that she was still well outside of the Sharaedim, struggling through the Forest of Wyrms, the two Chosen spent a few minutes filling each other in on events inside and outside of the Sharaedim. Once they each had a basic idea of what the other had been doing for the four months or so, they began to test the extent to which the deadwall had been weakened, trying various forms of communication magic. When all of their spells proved unable to penetrate the barrier, Khelben decided to try another tack and used a spell to send his dagger to Laeral's hand. The weapon vanished when he uttered the incantation.

"Laeral, it's on its way." Khelben was silent for a moment, then frowned. "It didn't—er, Laeral, it didn't?"

A loud thunk reverberated through the ceiling, then an astonished Watcher cried out, "Hey, who's dropping daggers?"

Khelben closed his eyes for a moment, then said, "Laeral, no good. We'll talk later."

Khelben continued to stare at the ceiling, then turned to Lord Duirsar. "How much were you able to glean from my end of the conversation?"

"It would be better for you to retell all," Lord Duirsar said. "I take it Lady Laeral has found a way to weaken the deadwall?"

"Not Laeral," Khelben said. "The Netherese."

"The Netherese?" Lord Duirsar gasped.

"Shade Enclave, to be more precise," Khelben said. "They are the ones who created the shadow mantle—to cut the phaerimm off from the Weave and weaken them for a final assault."

"Then there is no need to sacrifice a company of spellblades to affix a magicstar to it," Kiinyon said. "If Shade Enclave is on our side, we need only ask them to lower it before the mythal is weakened."

Khelben's expression grew darker. "Matters are not so clear, I'm afraid." He glanced at Keya and the Vaasans, then took Lord Duirsar's arm and started for the stairs. "Perhaps we should discuss this in Cloudtop. There are difficult decisions to make, and you may have need of the Hill Elders' advice."

Keya bit her lip and managed to remain silent, even when Khelben started down the stairs with Kiinyon and Lord Duirsar.

Once they were out of sight, Dexon came to her side and wrapped a burly arm around her shoulders. "I'm sure Galaeron's all right," he said. "We'll ask later, after they've sorted out their strategy."

Keya nodded and squeezed Dexon's hand. "Thank you." She closed her eyes and raised her face toward the heavens. "I pray to Hanali that just this once, the Hill Elders will move with a speed more human than elf."

After just three days beneath the blazing Anauroch sun, Galaeron's tongue was swollen to the size of a rothé's. His head throbbed and his vision blurred unpredictably. His heart beat in slow, listless thumps that barely seemed to pump the viscous blood through his veins, and he was close enough to water to smell damp sandstone. Sometimes, through the screen of emerald foliage growing along the base of the cliff ahead, he even glimpsed a flash of rippling silver. Had Ruha not insisted that they pause to study the oasis before entering, he and Aris would have been at the pool already, doing their best to drink it dry.

Two minutes later, though, Aris and Ruha would have been dead and Galaeron on his way back to Shade Enclave in a pair of scaly claws.

It had taken Ruha only a few minutes of watching to realize the oasis was too quiet, there were no birds flitting through the treetops or hares scurrying through the underbrush. A few minutes later, Aris had spotted the dragon, a young blue tucked onto a hidden ledge just above the treetops, little more than its eyes and horns visible at one end and a tip of dangling tail at the other.

Galaeron motioned to his companions, and they slipped down behind the crest of the dune and retreated into the trough nearly four hundred feet below. There was no shade, so Aris dropped to his seat on the stolen shadow blanket, which lay folded on the face of the opposite dune. His eyes were glassy and sunken with dehydration, his lips cracking and his nostrils inflamed.

The giant glanced up at the midday sun, then said, "I need that water." His voice was a raw croak. "Even if I have to fight a dragon for it."

"The dragon will only be the beginning," Galaeron said. "It looks too small to have many spells, but I'll wager the Shadovar have arranged a way for it to communicate with Malygris."

"Maybe it has nothing to do with them," Aris said. "It seems like oases would be good places for young dragons to hunt."

"But not to guard," Ruha said. Though she had drank no more than a few swallows since their departure from Shade, her voice betrayed no sign of thirst. "Nothing will come while a dragon is here. When they are hunting, they must swoop in and take what they can. Otherwise, the silence of the birds betrays them."

Aris let his head drop. "I can't go another day," he said. "If I go in alone, maybe we can fool it."

"How many stone giants do you think there are wandering the desert?" Ruha asked. "If the dragon sees any of us, the Shadovar will realize we turned toward Cormyr instead of Evereska."

Aris glanced toward the crest of the dune, his eyes growing large and wild. "Then we have to kill it," he said. "We have to sneak up and kill it."

"You're sun sick, Aris," Galaeron said. "You can't sneak up on a dragon."

"There will be water in the Saiyaddar." Ruha stood and started south, walking on the trough's steep wall so the slope would collapse and slide down to cover her tracks. "We will be there soon. It is not far."

Aris groaned and buried his face in his arms.

"Come on," Galaeron said. "I'll take the shadow blanket."

Aris raised his head high enough to fix a single eye on Galaeron. "It is twice your size. How can you carry it?"

Galaeron pulled a strand of shadowsilk from his cloak and began to fashion it into a circle. "How do you think?"

"No!" Aris boomed the word sharply enough to loose a small avalanche on the slope behind Galaeron. "No shadow magic."

Ruha spun around. "Are you *trying* to call the dragon down on us?" She glared at the giant for a moment, then looked to Galaeron. "Leave the blanket. It is too heavy and hot for him to carry."

"It's proof," Galaeron said as he began to twist the ends of his shadowsilk together, "and I'm not leaving it."

"Then I'm carrying it." Aris stood and slung the huge blanket over his shoulder. "Because you're *not* casting another shadow spell."

With no place to hide from the sun and concerned about attracting vultures and giving away their position even if they did stop, the trio spent the rest of the day marching south. Every so often, Ruha would climb to the crest of a dune to study the terrain and search the sky for signs of pursuing dragons, then wave her companions up behind her and lead them eastward in a mad dash over one dune crest after another. The effort never seemed to tire the witch, but Galaeron and Aris would grow so weary after a dozen or so crossings that their legs gave out and left them crawling on their hands and knees.

Galaeron spent much of that time seething over Vala's desertion, relishing the prospect of the vengeance he would extract on Telamont for refusing to intervene with Escanor, and plotting how he would emphasize the prince's part in the melting of the High Ice.

The Shadovar had betrayed him, had stolen Vala away and made her turn a blind eye to the promise she had sworn to him, and for that they would pay. For that, he would expose their true nature to the world, reveal how they were melting the High Ice and upsetting the weather all along the Sword Coast. What that decision might mean for Evereska, Galaeron did not even consider. Shade Enclave had its own reasons for destroying the phaerimm, and his departure was unlikely to have any impact on their plans.

Finally, as the afternoon shadows began to extend their stretch toward evening, they crested a dune and found themselves looking over a vast prairie of pale green grasslands. In the distance, the brown blot of a gazelle herd was slowly drifting over the purple horizon, while the rest of the plain was speckled with the tiny flecks of foraging birds. Scattered here and there along the course of a dry riverbed were the puffy crowns of several dozen big cottonwood trees.

"Skoraeus strike me now!" Aris cursed. "The river is as dry as bones."

"Only on the surface." Ruha slipped over the crest of the dune and started down the other side. "There is water underneath."

"Underneath?" Aris cast a longing look north toward the cliffs where they had left the young dragon. "How far underneath?"

"Not far," Ruha said, waving the giant after her.

"You have said that before," Aris observed.

Despite his protests, the giant raced down the dune past the witch and started across the plain.

"Aris! Wait until dark!" Ruha called. "The birds!"

She was too late—and even had she not been, it was doubtful that the giant would have stopped. With the heavy shadow blanket still draped over his shoulders, he started for the riverbed in long, booming strides that sent a cloud of startled birds screeching and cackling into the sky.

Ruha looked to the north. "How close do you think—"

"Too close," Galaeron said. "I have heard blue dragons brag that they pick meals in the Sharaedim from a roost in the Greycloaks."

"You speak with dragons?" Ruha asked.

"On occasion," Galaeron said. "The Tomb Guard had an arrangement with several young blues."

Instead of asking about the arrangement, Ruha nodded and started across the plain after Aris. "Then we must hurry."

Galaeron caught her shoulder and pointed toward a fan of alluvial gravel spilling out of the foothills that separated the Saiyaddar from the parched slopes of the Scimitar Spires.

"We stand a better chance hiding," he said. "A young dragon will be arrogant in its approach, and we can take it by surprise."

"You would use your friend as bait?"

"He's the one who scared up the birds." Galaeron's tone was defensive. "I'm just trying to keep us all alive."

Ruha considered this, then started along the edge of the plain. "Your plan makes sense—though it would be better if he had been given the chance to volunteer."

"He volunteered when he let his thirst put us in

danger," Galaeron said, joining her.

"Perhaps so," Ruha said, "but had you taken his water-skins from the flying disk instead of your shadow blanket, his thirst would not be so great."

Galaeron's only reply was an angry scowl. They were only about halfway to the gravel fan when the birds suddenly began to flee southward. Ruha pulled Galaeron into a bramble thicket and crouched on her haunches, pulling a clump of thorny stalks over their heads so they would be concealed from the air. Aris did not seem to realize anything was wrong for another dozen steps, when he noticed the fleeing birds and stopped to turn around. He spent several moments searching the plain behind him, calling out to Galaeron before finally raising his gaze skyward and looking north toward the oasis where they had seen the dragon.

Though Galaeron was hiding close to five hundred paces away, he was close enough to see the giant's jaw fall and his shoulders sag. Aris spent another moment searching the plain behind him, then, still carrying the heavy shadow blanket, turned and ran for the foothills, angling toward a narrow gully not far from where Galaeron and Ruha were hiding.

"Good," Galaeron whispered.

He began to fashion a tiny stick figure out of shadow-silk. Ruha looked to the sky. It was only a moment before she nudged Galaeron and the cross-shaped shadow of a small dragon began to sweep across the Saiyaddar. Galaeron finished his effigy, then pointed it at Aris and uttered an incantation. A circle of shadows appeared around the giant. One after the other, they peeled themselves off the ground and assumed Aris's form, then fanned out in a dozen different directions.

An angry cackle sounded from the sky, then the dragon swooped into view, its blue scales flashing like sapphires in the dusky light. It leveled off a dozen feet from the ground and, starting at one end of the fleeing replicas, opened its mouth and loosed a huge bolt of lightning that stretched in front of three of the fleeing shadow giants.

Lacking any wits of their own, the images continued straight into the bolt and vanished from sight.

"This is a smart one," Ruha whispered, pulling a small flint and steel from her *aba*, "and it wants us alive."

"It wants *me* alive," Galaeron corrected. "Don't over-estimate your value—or Aris's—to the Shadovar."

The dragon breathed again, spraying another bolt of lightning in front of four more running giants. This time, they stopped and fled in the opposite direction. The dragon wheeled on a wing tip and extended its claws, slashing through two illusionary giants on its first pass. The dragon pulled up less than fifty paces from them, exposing its thin belly scales as it wheeled around to snatch up the fleeing giant. Ruha started to rise from their hiding place, pointing the flint and steel at the dragon's abdomen to cast what Galaeron knew would be a fire storm.

"Not yet!" Galaeron hissed.

He caught her arm and pulled her back down, then pointed his effigy at a figure he knew to be a false Aris. He whispered the same spell, and a circle of shadows appeared around each of the remaining giants on the plain. They began to rise by the dozen and flee in every direction. The dragon roared in frustration and blasted the nearest circle with its third and final lightning bolt.

By unlucky chance, his target proved to be the correct one. Aris bellowed in pain and went down on his face, then the dragon was on him, pinning him to the ground with a huge claw and hissing something angry that Galaeron could not quite hear from so far away.

"Coward!" Ruha hissed, throwing off the brambles. "You

should have let me attack when we had a shot at his belly!"

She started across the plain at a run, pointing her fingers at the huge dragon. Blood boiling at her insult, Galaeron started after her—then stopped as she poured a volley of golden bolts into the wyrm's flank. The resulting blast sent a fountain of blue scales spraying into the air, along with a fair amount of draconian blood and flesh.

The dragon roared and brought its huge head around—only to receive another volley of the witch's golden bolts in the snout. This time, the eruption sent a nostril, two horns, and one slit-pupiled eye tumbling away over its shoulder. As surprised by Ruha's power as was Galaeron, the creature spread its great wings and launched itself into the air.

It was clutching Aris and the shadow blanket in its massive claws.

Ruha switched to her flint and steel, crying out a Bedine fire spell and striking sparks into the air. A long line of tiny meteors streaked into the air, taking the dragon in the right wing and burning several dozen melon-sized holes through the leathery skin. The creature pitched right and plummeted a hundred feet toward the foothills, then leveled off and began to fly for freedom—still clutching Aris and the shadow blanket.

Galaeron was not going to let it escape with his shadow blanket. He fashioned a strand of shadowsilk into a noose, then uttered a long string of magic syllables and flicked the loop after the fleeing dragon. The filament stretched to nearly half a mile in length, allowing Galaeron just enough time to slip his end of the line under his foot before the noose expanded to the size of a wagon wheel and flipped itself up to slip over the dragon's head.

A version of a Tomb Guard enchantment used to capture fleeing crypt breakers, the spell worked even better with shadowsilk than with elven thread. As soon as the dragon hit the end of the line, the noose closed and the filament contracted to a small fraction of its previous length, both cutting off the wyrm's air supply and jerking it around to crash down within a few dozen paces of Galaeron.

The stunned wyrm impacted face first, then lay in a crumpled, convulsing heap as it clawed in vain at the magic line. Keeping his foot on his end of the line to keep the noose tight, Galaeron leveled his palm at its already mangled head and drilled a hole through its skull with a single shadow bolt. His body was filled with so much shadow magic that it was almost numb, but he didn't mind at all. The cold felt good.

Ruha came to his side and paused as though to say something, then thought better of it and went to the dragon's head.

"Dead," she confirmed.

"Good."

Galaeron stepped off the magic line, which vanished as soon his foot lost contact with it, and started forward as Ruha crawled over the wyrm's neck to its underside.

"And my blanket?" he asked. "Still in one piece?"

Ruha snapped her head around to glare at him. "Yes, the blanket is still in one piece." She dropped out of sight behind the dragon, then added, "Which is more than I can say for your friend."

"Aris?" Galaeron broke into a run. "He's hurt?"

"Yes, and badly." Ruha peered over the wyrm's back, then said, "That is what happens when you use someone for dragon bait."

Galaeron reached the dragon's back and clambered over to find Aris trapped beneath the wyrm's body. There were four talon punctures in his chest and one arm was twisted around behind him at an impossible angle. The giant's gray eyes were barely open, and when they fell on Galaeron's face, they looked away.

CHAPTER NINE

19 Mirtul, the Year of Wild Magic

By dusk of the day of its arrival, the Shadovar army was drawing the last corner of its shadow blanket over legendary Myth Drannor. The cracked spires and vine-wrapped columns of the city, already half-hidden behind a wall of spring mist, vanished beneath an undulating mantle of darkness, and a silence that had been eerie and foreboding for most of the day grew perfect and still. As the edges were affixed to the ground, a few birds and other woodland animals rushed to escape in ones and twos. These creatures were allowed to flee, but companies of warriors were waiting to slay any monster that might return later to harass the veserabs. From her airborne vantage point at the western end of the city, Vala saw them strike down a beholder, two gargoyles, and even a malaugrym in its true three-tentacled form.

The blanket would prevent their quarry from teleporting away or using the translocational gates rumored to be still functional inside the city, but that only meant the phaerimm would be even more dangerous and ferocious than usual. According to the Shadovar scouts and diviners, there were still close to thirty thornbacks inhabiting the ruins' subterranean levels, and if the attack was to succeed, most would have to be slain in their own lairs. For the first time in her life, Vala wished she could write. She would have liked to set down some thoughts for her son before the bladework began.

Vala dipped a magic wing toward the rolling meadow at the western end of the city and landed in the trampled grass outside Escanor's pavilion tent. The prince was waiting in the entrance, his coppery eyes watching every move as she undid her breastplate so she could remove the wing harness. His retinue of aides and subcommanders was there as well, though most seemed more interested in watching him watch her.

Though Vala had never been particularly shy—and even less so after her time among the elves—Escanor's gaze made her uncomfortable in a way that even the hungry leers of her own Vaasans never had. Instead of turning away, however, she smiled and cocked a playful eyebrow as she raised her tunic to undo the chest buckles.

"Never seen a girl take off her wings?"

Something that resembled a grin crossed the prince's face. "It was not your wings that caught my eye." Escanor left the pavilion tent, not coming to her so much as emerging out of the shadows at her side. "You are growing more comfortable with them?"

"Not comfortable enough to sleep in." Vala turned her

back to the prince, placing the wings more or less in his hands. She let the shadowsilk straps slide through the slots in the back of her tunic, then began to roll her weary shoulders. "We *are* going to sleep before the assault, aren't we?"

"That will be up to you." Escanor waited for Vala to put herself in order again. When she had, he said, "I have some news."

Vala's heart sank. Her thoughts flew at once to Galaeron and Aris, but when she turned, she asked, "Something has happened at the Granite Tower?"

It was impossible to say whether Escanor meant his fang-filled smile to be reassuring or mocking. "Not at all. I am speaking of Galaeron."

"Galaeron?" Vala said, feigning disappointment. She had been considering this moment since they departed the enclave and had come to the conclusion that there was only one way to play it. "He actually left?"

The prince's eyes flared red. "You knew of his plans?"

"Knew?" Vala shook her head. "I thought it was just shadow talk. He started it after you asked me to come along on this assault. You made him jealous, I think."

"And you didn't tell the Most High?"

"Why would I tell my personal business to the Most High?"

"It is not only your business," Escanor said. "The knowledge he carries belongs to Shade Enclave."

Vala smiled and patted him on the cheek. "I guess you should have thought of that before you invited me on this trip." She picked up her wings and started for her tent. "I've got to go wash. When's dinner?"

Escanor walked alongside her. "You're not worried about him?"

"Should I be?" Vala did not stop walking. In this, above all things, she had to appear indifferent. If

Escanor knew how she really felt, he would conceal his knowledge and play on her emotions to make her reveal what she knew. "The Most High had turned him against me. You saw."

"Then you can't tell me where he is?"

Vala almost smiled. If the Shadovar didn't know where Galaeron was, he was still free. "I'd watch for him at Evereska, were I you."

"That is the obvious choice, of course," Escanor said, "but he knows we have an army there. We were thinking he might have intended to go to Waterdeep, instead."

"Might have," Vala said. From the little she had overheard after leaving the dinner, that had in fact been Galaeron's plan. "It's going to be hell finding him. Anauroch's a big desert."

"Particularly on foot. We found their veserab and flying disk, with all of their water—but no sign of them." Escanor took Vala's arm and stopped her. "If you know where they're going, you must tell me—for their own sakes. Without their waterskins, they won't last a tenday, even if they can find the oases."

"Then they won't last a tenday," Vala said.

Though Escanor was right about their chances of surviving Anauroch—at least about Aris's—the Shadovar had already guessed the little she knew, so there was nothing to be gained by admitting her own small involvement.

She glared at the dark hand grasping her arm expectantly and said, "At least it will save me the trouble of hunting Galaeron down after he is completely lost to his shadow."

Escanor released her arm. "You truly don't know where they are?"

"Isn't that what I said?"

"And you are not in love with Galaeron?"

"I have more self-respect than that." As she told this lie, Vala made a point of staring directly into the prince's eyes. "All I am to him is a promise."

Escanor surprised her with an obviously sincere smile. "Just as I told the Most High." He waved her toward his tent. "Please, you will stay here tonight. It will be more comfortable."

"Comfortable?" Though Vala was cringing inside, she forced a playful half-smirk. "Don't you think we need our sleep tonight?"

"When we are done, you will sleep like a lioness after her kill," Escanor replied, showing his fangs. "In truth, I had thought your flirtations no more than a low attempt to mask your betrayal behind a veneer of desire, but I see now that Melegaunt's reports about the women of Vaasa were not exaggerated."

"Reports?" Vala demanded.

"That you are always in season," Escanor said. He took her hand affectionately between his. "Bodvar's daughter was a favorite of his."

"Bodvar's daughter?" Vala pondered this for a moment, then gasped, "Granna?"

"Have no fear. Even if Melegaunt is your grandfather, we are many generations apart. Our blood is hardly the same at all." He pulled her toward his pavilion. "Clear my tent!"

Vala stopped cold. "Wait!"

Escanor's eyes flared red. "You are not sincere?"

"I'm always sincere," Vala said, grimacing inwardly at the distasteful looks the Shadovar cast her way as they streamed from the pavilion tent, "but we've been on the wing for four days and pulling shadow all day for a fifth. I've got to wash."

"I have water in my tent," Escanor said. "You can wash here."

" 'Wash' is a figure of speech," Vala said. While hardly above sharing a man's bed for her own reasons, she was not in the practice of allowing herself to be ordered into one. The prince was pushing too hard, too fast. He was up to something, and she had to buy time to puzzle out what. "What I really have to do is—"

"You can do that in the garderobe behind my tent," Escanor interrupted. "It opens into the Gray Wastes."

"All right," Vala said, feigning surrender, "but we've got to eat first. I'm famished, and with the day we have tomorrow—"

"That will be no concern to you," Escanor said, leading her into the empty pavilion. "A prince's consort is not expected to fight."

"What?" Finally seeing her opening, Vala stopped. "Consort?"

"Of course," Escanor said. "We Shadovar are not barbarians. We do not cast a woman aside after we have used her."

"And I have to stop fighting?"

Escanor shook his head. "Not at all. A consort may fight at her own pleasure—but it is not expected." He waved her toward depths at the back of the tent. "If you please. I will have food brought later."

Vala refused to cross the threshold. "What about Sheldon?"

"Your son?" Escanor asked. "He will be brought to the enclave and raised in my house as a High Lord. Will that not please you?"

Vala needed to consider this only a moment before she shook her head. "No, he is Vaasan."

"Very well, he will remain in Vaasa," Escanor replied. "Whatever you wish, Vala."

Vala turned to look at him. "Whatever I wish?"

"For a consort of the First Prince, anything," Escanor

said. "You could even return to Vaasa yourself—with Bodvar's debt repaid in full."

It was nearly enough to make Vala step into the tent. She had been gone from the Granite Tower for more than a year and longed for nothing more than to return to raise her son and see her aging parents—and that was what made the prince's offer too good to be true. He wanted more from her than to share the fur. There were a thousand courtesans in the Palace Most High that he could have for a smile, and most were—though it stung her pride to admit it—far more desirable than she.

She stepped away from the tent and narrowed her eyes at Escanor. "What does all this generosity cost me? My life? My will?"

Escanor spread his hands. "Nothing, if your desire is true."

"Let's say it isn't."

"Then there is a much easier way to secure the same privileges," Escanor said, dodging the question. "Just tell me what you know about Galaeron's disappearance."

"I already have," Vala said. "Beyond that, I don't know anything that would help you."

"Allow me to be the judge of that," Escanor said. "You cannot know what might help us."

Vala was tempted. She was almost telling the truth anyway. If Galaeron wasn't going to Waterdeep—and apparently he wasn't, since the Shadovar couldn't find him—then she was at a loss. Escanor was right, though, in that she couldn't know what might help them find the fleeing elf—or implicate those who had stayed behind. However she looked at it, she would be betraying her companions at least in spirit, if not in fact.

"Let's try this," Vala said. "Tell me what you know, and I'll tell you if anything I know can help."

Escanor surprised her by laughing—not a cold, threatening chuckle, but a warm, almost respectful guffaw.

"You are a brave woman, Vala Thorsdotter," he said, clamping a big hand on the back of her neck. "I do not want to see what will become of you if the Most High learns you have refused to recant your betrayal."

Vala's legs grew icy, and she looked down to see herself melting into the shadows at her feet. "What are—"

That was as far as she made it before her consciousness vanished into cold darkness. Sometime later—it could have been a second or an hour, Vala had no way of telling—she felt the humid Myth Drannor air warming first her face, then her body, and finally her legs. She saw herself rising from a puddle of darkness, her body returning to its normal proportions. When she dared to raise her gaze again, she found herself standing atop the shadow blanket, surrounded by the murk-veiled towers and trees of Myth Drannor. Standing half-glimpsed at varying distances along the narrow street, were dozen of companies of Shadovar warriors.

Still holding Vala by the neck, Escanor pulled her around the corner of a huge, castlelike ruin into a tree-choked courtyard that had once served as the building's main entrance. There was a single attached tower to the left and an L-shaped wing on the right, all cloaked in the same mantle of darkness as the trees and the ground itself. A dozen Shadovar warriors stood near the entrance of the courtyard with their weapons and wands in hand and a nervous officer watching Escanor approach.

Sensing that she would not like whatever the prince had in mind, Vala allowed her hand to drift toward her sword hilt—and felt Escanor's iron grasp tighten on her neck.

"You saved my life once," he hissed. "Do not make me return the favor by snapping your neck."

"It's dark," Vala said. "Just wanted to see what's going on."

"Truly," Escanor sneered. He stopped in front of the nervous-looking officer. "This is the Irithlium?"

The warrior inclined his head. "It is, Prince."

"Good." Escanor thrust Vala forward. "Tell her what we've been able to learn about this place."

The officer nodded and turned to Vala. "Not much, Lady Thorsdotter. It was once a magic school, which naturally attracted the phaerimm. The upper layers seem to have been stripped bare, but there are at least six phaerimm lairing somewhere beneath the foundations."

"Six phaerimm?" Vala gasped, understanding why the patrol looked so nervous. "In one building?"

The officer nodded. "Our assignment is to map their lairs."

"No," Escanor said, "now your mission is to slay them."

The officer's topaz eyes paled to citrine. "Slay them, Prince?"

"There is nothing to fear, my servant." Escanor thrust Vala toward him. "I brought you a new scout. You may contact me to request another if she falls."

The officer raised his brow at this, then nodded and said, "As you order, my prince."

Escanor turned to Vala. "You said you wished to fight," he said. "If you change your mind, you know what you must do."

"I won't change my mind," Vala said, glaring at him.

"Of course not," Escanor said. He dismissed a young Shadovar from the patrol, then took the warrior's horned helmet and passed it to Vala. "This will prevent the phaerimm from controlling you—and if you should happen to change your mind, all you need do is touch the flat of your blade to a horn."

Vala accepted the helmet and used it to replace her own. "And if I don't?"

"Then I will report your death in battle to the Most High," Escanor said. "The Granite Tower will be informed of your bravery and devotion to duty."

"That's not what I meant," Vala said. "What do I get if we kill all the phaerimm? The same deal I would've by going into your tent?"

"If you kill six phaerimm?" Escanor's grin showed the tips of his fangs. "If you kill six phaerimm, then I will be *your* consort."

Laeral stepped out of the forest mud onto the damp sand at Anauroch's edge, nearly three hundred miles away. Though she had known in principle what to expect, so stunned was she by the size of the dark orb in front of her that, in her teleport afterdaze, she grew confused and thought she had somehow arrived outside the Plane of Shadow. Just translucent enough to make out the silhouettes of foothills rising ridge after ridge, the murky sphere was as wide as the horizon itself and so high that only a slim crescent of cloudy gray sky hung above it.

Laeral was jarred out of her awestruck muddle when Chief Claw stumbled into her from behind, nearly flipping his body over her shoulder and growling an Uthgardt curse. Recalling that there would soon be a whole stream of soldiers pouring out of the teleport circle, she quickly stepped aside and grabbed the barbarian's enormous wrist.

"It's the shadowshell," she said, trying in vain to pull him aside. "You're outside the Sharaedim, remember?"

"Charideem," Claw repeated absently, head rolling backward as he struggled to take in the enormous dome of darkness rising above him. "The Great Dark Mountain!"

Lord Yoraedia blinked into existence behind Chief Claw and slammed into the barbarian's back as he walked forward.

"Corellon's arrows!"

Yoraedia stepped back, reaching for his sword—and was promptly knocked forward again when Skarn Brassaxe crashed into him from behind.

"What? Who?" the dwarf cried. "Where in the Underdark—"

"The shadowshell, remember?" Laeral set her feet and jerked Chief Claw aside, then released him and grabbed both Brassaxe and Yoraedia. "Snap out of it, good sirs, or our army is going to start teleporting in on top of itself—and if you think the Trade Way was a mess, wait until you see what happens when an elf and a dwarf try to occupy the same space!"

"Don't want that!" Claw said, recovering his wits.

The chief turned and literally began to toss the other commanders out of the teleport circle as they arrived. Laeral spent another moment with Yoraedia and Brassaxe, helping them overcome their teleport afterdaze by reminding them where they were. When they finally seemed to recall what they were supposed to be doing, she assigned them each a sector to keep clear, then helped the next batch of arrivals through the transition. She had rehearsed the entire plan with her commanders before creating the teleportation circle in the Forest of Wyrms, but with only three hours to march the entire relief army through an area little more than five feet in diameter, there was no margin for error.

Finally growing confident that her commanders had the situation under control, Laeral turned to inspect the area. Though hardly pouring rain, the weather was still overcast and drizzly, and she could barely make out the main Shadovar camp, positioned for easy defense atop a low butte at Anauroch's edge. The murky silhouettes of several dozen sentries stood at the brink of the cliff, using their dark spears to point down at the arriving army while their astonished comrades rushed up behind them.

Laeral raised an arm and waved at the astonished sentries, then used a sending spell to address the closest one. *Give your prince the compliments of Laeral Silverhand and tell him the Army of the North has arrived.*

The warrior cocked his head in surprise, then raised his spear in acknowledgement and turned to go. *It shall be done.*

Laeral nodded and started across the damp sand toward the shadowshell. Though still more than a quarter of a mile away, the edifice's imposing size made it feel like something natural, more along the lines of the High Ice or the Spine of the World than something created by the magic of men. Stationed at its base every half mile or so were small patrols of Shadovar warriors mounted on their strange flying worms, paying more attention to Laeral and her relief army than to the rocky slopes inside the dark sphere. It was too murky to tell whether the drizzle was also falling inside the shell, but the few withered trees visible through the barrier suggested that *something* was turning the Sharaedim as lifeless as Anauroch.

As Laeral drew nearer the shadowshell, her faint shadow darkened and split into three identical silhouettes. A pair of gleaming metallic eyes appeared in the heads of the two outer shapes, then they slowly assumed the shapes of two Shadovar warriors. She stopped and addressed the broad-shouldered figure on the left.

"A pleasure to see you again, Prince Clariburnus."

The prince's lead-colored eyes lit with pleasure, then his silhouette peeled itself off the ground and, still expanding into its normal form, bowed.

"Clariburnus, please." He gestured at the other prince, a gaunt figure with talonlike fingers and eyes the color of rusty iron. "My brother, Lamorak."

Also returning to shape, Lamorak bowed and said, "Your arrival is a welcome surprise." He cast a meaningful glance toward the growing horde of warriors spilling from Laeral's teleportation circle. "We were given to believe it would be some time yet before you arrived with your army."

Laeral returned his bow with one of her own. "Yes . . . well, I was beginning to think you Shadovar would never stop coming to our rescue."

Lamorak frowned in confusion, but Clariburnus's grin was broad and appreciative. "Your long march was a ruse?"

Laeral glanced over her shoulder at the weary warriors spilling out of the teleportation circle. "Don't tell them," she said in a low voice, "but after the debacle at Rocnest, we decided it would be best to draw the remaining phaerimm out of the way before trying to bring another army in. According to my scouts, the last three free phaerimm are rushing down out of the Trielta Hills with their hobgoblins and illithids as we speak."

"By the time they realize that you are no longer in the Forest of Wyrms, your warriors will be resting in dry tents behind a screen of Shadovar pickets," Clariburnus offered. "My compliments. A sly plan well-executed."

"I thank you for the compliment," Laeral said, "but I fear I must decline your offer of protection."

Lamorak's eyes flashed crimson. "Surely, you do not believe the slander spewed against us in Waterdeep?"

"Only half," Laeral said, making light. "Tempus

knows, we need the rest, but Evereska's mythal is failing."

The two Shadovar glanced at each other, their eyes full of mistrust and suspicion.

"I heard from Khelben," Laeral explained. "He's in the city."

"Of course," Clariburnus said, nodding in comprehension. "The phaerimm deadwall has begun to fail—the shadowshell is working."

A terrible thought occurred to Laeral. "Are you sure? If the shadowshell is blocking their access to the Weave, it would be blocking Khelben's, too. I wouldn't have been able to hear him."

"We're sure," Lamorak said, addressing Laeral as though she were a several-hundred-year-old child. "There is still Weave magic inside the shell, and it takes far less energy to carry words than to maintain the deadwall."

Clariburnus's eyes grew distant. He fell quiet and turned toward the shadowshell. Not familiar enough with the Shadovar to recognize what was happening, Laeral remained silent herself and looked to Lamorak.

"My brother?" Lamorak asked. "What is it?"

Clariburnus turned back to Lamorak, then slid his eyes in Laeral's direction and shook his head ever so slightly.

Laeral frowned and said, "If something's troubling you, Prince, tell me. The last thing we need right now is to start mistrusting each other."

Clariburnus thought for a moment, then said, "Very well. Your story can't be true. The shadowshell would have turned Khelben's communication spell back on him."

Laeral nodded, recalling how all of the spells they had tried after establishing contact had failed. "As a matter of fact, it did," she said, "and not only the sending spells. We tried transferring items, opening dimensional doors, and about a dozen other things. Nothing worked."

"Then how could you hear him?" Lamorak asked.

"It wasn't a spell—it's a gift to the Chosen from Mystra." She waited until a look of acceptance came to the prince's faces, then said, "Now, I must ask you to allow my army into the Sharaedim. We are not going to let that mythal fall."

Clariburnus looked to his brother, who raised a hand and turned away to think.

"Prince Lamorak, your brother Aglarel assured Lord Piergeiron that we would be given access," Laeral said. "If you refuse to honor that promise . . ."

"Have no fear, we will honor the promise." Lamorak glanced back at the burgeoning relief army, then returned his gaze to Laeral and gave her an icy, fang-filled smile. "With your permission, we will do even more. We will help you destroy the phaerimm."

"Of course, I welcome the help of the Shadovar." Laeral returned his smile with one just as cold. "You might even say I've been counting on it."

As secret passages went, the one leading into the subbasement of the Irithlium was a masterwork. Concealed beneath the only false column among the thousands of real ones supporting the floor above, the entrance was nearly undetectable, with the door seams concealed by the column's base stone and the hinges hidden in the capital twenty feet overhead. Had Vala not seen the two-foot centipede crawling out from beneath the base as she approached, it was doubtful that she would have noticed anything unusual about the pillar at all. It looked just like every other support column she had passed, complete with mildew and moss-filled cracks. The elf builders had even taken the precaution of concealing the latch in a crack on the opposite side of an adjacent column.

"Scout, why are you stopped?" The demand came from ten paces back, where Parth Gal—Vala refused to call the Shadovar a lord, even in her own mind—stood peering out from behind a column. "Have you found something?"

"A secret door," Vala said, motioning him forward.

Parth raised a hand to halt the rest of the patrol and remained where he was. "Open it."

"This place was built by elves," she said. "It'll be trapped, and I don't have the word of passing."

Parth shrugged and did not come out from behind his column. "That is what scouts are for." He paused, then said, "Unless you would rather contact Prince Escanor and tell him where your friends are?"

Vala glared daggers at him. "One of you must have a spell for disarming traps."

"Of course—we are a reconnaissance patrol," Parth said. "Which means we should be locating phaerimm, not assaulting them. If you will just contact the prince, I am sure we will *all* live longer. Until then, I am afraid I must insist that you perform your duties."

A muffled thump sounded in the darkness somewhere behind Parth, then a strangled voice cried out in alarm. There was the sharp crack of a dark blade slicing through a thick carapace, followed by a sort of buzzing snarl and a wet crunch. Vala glimpsed a handful of Shadovar slipping through the columns toward the struggle, but the sounds died away almost as quickly as they started, and the warriors arrived too late to help their comrade.

"Balpor," someone announced. "Gone, except for his head and one arm."

It was the patrol's fifth casualty, and they had not even seen a phaerimm. Vala felt a sudden chill. Though the sensation seemed likely to be her own reaction to another casualty, she took the precaution of glancing around the immediate area to make certain nothing was creeping up on her. She thought she glimpsed a gray figure slipping behind the pillar where the latch was hidden but found only empty darkness when she stepped around the other side.

"What is it?" Parth called.

"My imagination," Vala answered. "Still want me to open that door?"

"Unless you've changed your mind about telling the prince what he wishes to know," he replied.

"Sorry." Vala dropped to her haunches and slipped the tip of her dagger into the crack where the latch was hidden. "Listen, if this goes bad for me, send word to Sheldon that I died for my word."

"Sheldon?"

"My son," Vala said.

"Ah . . . that would not be necessary, if only you would—"

"Can't do it," Vala interrupted. She had to suppress a shiver. The chill she had experienced earlier just wouldn't go away. "One more thing—if this leads to a treasury instead of a phaerimm lair, don't touch anything. There's nothing elves hate more than artifact thieves."

"Thank you for the warning," Parth replied.

"I wasn't thinking of you," Vala said, "but you know how fond I am of elves."

She took a deep breath, then, stretching her arm as far as she could, crouched down around the side of the pillar and flicked the latch.

Eltargrim.

So softly came the word that Vala was not even sure she had heard it. She spun on her heels and saw nothing behind her, but the chill remained. If anything, the cold felt deeper than before, though perhaps only because of the icy sweat running down her chest and sides.

"Vala?" Parth sounded as frightened as she was.

"Still here," she said. "Watch yourselves."

Vala rose slowly and went to the column. Half-expecting the Shadovar to tell her to wait for him to send someone forward to check for traps, she took a deep breath, then gave it the gentlest of pushes. The entire shaft swung aside, revealing a narrow staircase spiraling down into the darkness beneath its false base. When no clouds of poison gas came billowing out, she waved the tip of her darksword around the entrance to check for motion activated traps, then pushed down on the first stair.

Nothing happened.

"Well?" Parth called.

"No traps so far," she reported, "and no cobwebs. Something comes down here, and it doesn't leave tracks."

The Shadovar stepped out from behind his hiding place and motioned her down the staircase. "We're right behind you."

"Sure you are," Vala muttered.

Deciding Parth and his comrades deserved no warning about the gray figure she might or might not have glimpsed and the whispered word she might or might not have heard, Vala crouched on her heels and dropped to the fifth step down.

The steps continued to spiral downward through another ten feet of solid stone, then opened up into a grand corridor running parallel to the base of the stairs. By crouching on her heels and craning her neck, Vala could look far enough up the passage to see a series of arched doorways opening off to either side at irregular intervals, but the magic of her darksword did not allow her to see all the way to the end of the hallway. When nothing came charging up the stairs to meet her, she descended the first ten feet in two quick bounds, braced her hand on the banister, and leaped into the corridor facing the opposite direction she had been descending.

Vala found herself facing a large round silhouette with a wriggling crown of bulbous-ended tentacles. She had just enough time to recognize the silhouette as that of a large beholder before several eyestalks began to swing in her direction. Leaping into a foot-first slide underneath the thing, she flipped her darksword toward its huge central eye and grabbed for her dagger.

Vala hit the floor at about the same time her darksword found its mark—though, without the weapon in her hand, she could no longer see in the dark and knew that she'd hit the beholder only by the bloodcurdling screech that echoed down the corridor. She was showered in warm gore as she slid under the still-floating eye tyrant. Knowing better than to think even a perfect slash to the central eye could kill a monster this big, she reached up and caught the bottom of the cut with her free hand, then jerked its wounded side to the floor and smashed it into the stone. At the same time, she was bringing her dagger up behind it, driving the steel blade through its thick skull once, twice, half a dozen times, until the trapped beholder finally collapsed in a limp heap atop the arm that had been holding it pinned to the floor.

Vala pushed the thing aside.

"Vala?" Parth called down the stairs, then more loudly, "Vala?"

"No such luck, Parth," she yelled back. "Still here."

A deep rumble reverberated through the ceiling as the secret pillar was pushed back over the stairwell.

"Coward," Vala muttered.

She extended her arm to call the sword back but felt its hilt under her knuckles already. Counting herself lucky she had not found the blade instead, she rolled to her knees and took the weapon in hand—and, once she could see in the darkness again, found herself looking into a huge, toothy mouth surrounded by four arms. Even at this unfortunate angle, she recognized it instantly as a large phaerimm.

"Tempus give me strength!" she gasped.

Why pray to Tempus, my dear? I am your god now. The raspy voice came to Vala inside her head, not like the single whispered *Eltargrim* she had thought she heard earlier but definitely inside her thoughts. *Set aside your sword, and we will talk.*

Vala gathered her legs beneath her and sprang to her feet—then found herself rolling head over heels down the dark corridor.

What don't you understand, human? the voice demanded. *Put down your weapon.*

Showing no fear of the darksword whatsoever, the phaerimm continued to come down the corridor, two of its four arms pointing at the mossy floor. Puzzled by the thing's strange behavior, Vala wavered between doing as it ordered and throwing her sword at it—though she felt sure it was ready with magic to bat the weapon out of the air the instant it left her hand.

She made no move to do either, and the phaerimm stopped just beyond her sword's reach.

Obey!

Parth's muffled voice began to reverberate down the stairwell, demanding explanations and shouting threats about what would happen if she didn't open the door—

and suddenly Vala understood. The phaerimm did not want to kill her. It had trapped her alone, believing that it could turn her into one of its mind-slaves—but Vala's helmet protected her against that.

"Y-yes," she said. Moving very slowly, she dropped to her haunches and set the sword on the floor. "I want to talk."

As soon as her hand left the hilt, she was plunged into blindness again. Unaware of the phaerimm's presence, Parth and the others continued to yell for her to open the door. Silently cursing them for fools as well as cowards, Vala kicked her darksword away and backed down the corridor. She was so terrified that her whole body was shaking. Without the sword, she could no longer see what the phaerimm was doing.

A bony hand clamped her shoulder. *That is far enough, child.*

Vala stopped and prayed it would not remove the helmet Escanor had given her. Without it, she would become the thrall it believed she was. Unless she lulled it into a false sense of security, she had no chance of killing it anyway. The things could cast spells as fast as she could think—maybe faster.

You are not one of the Shadovar.

It was not a question. Did the phaerimm expect an answer?

What are you?

"V-Vaasan," Vala replied. "My people owe them service."

Vala? the phaerimm asked. *The one Escanor favors to carry his egg?*

Vala had to concentrate to keep from gasping and asking how the phaerimm knew such a thing; instead, she merely nodded.

What are you doing here?

"I refused him," Vala said, "and so he sent me to kill phaerimm."

At the top of the stairs, Parth had finally realized something was wrong and stopped pounding on the column.

And could you?

Vala shook her head. "No!" At the moment, it was an honest answer. "Never again."

Again? The phaerimm seemed astonished, then said, *But I forget who you are. How do you feel about him now?*

"I hate him." It was not far from the truth.

Can you betray him?

"Perhaps," Vala said. A low rumble shook the ceiling as the false column began to slide aside. "He is very powerful."

I will help you with that, the phaerimm said. *Hold out your hand.*

Vala extended both arms, palms up. She felt something small and round pressed into her palm.

You will allow him to mount you, then press this to his back, the phaerimm said. *It will rob him of his power. Do you understand?*

"Vala?" Parth called down the stairs. "Are you there?"

Vala did not dare shout a warning. "I understand," she said.

"What?" Parth called.

She ignored him. "Then what, my master?" As she asked this, she called to her darksword in her mind. "Do I kill him?"

No! You sneak him into the woods, the phaerimm said. *This will make it easy.*

"Vala, answer me, or we're coming down!"

The darksword arrived.

"Hurry!"

As Vala yelled this, she was already bringing the darksword across the phaerimm's midsection. Her dark vision returned and she saw a fang-filled mouth the size of a cavern yawning before her. Instead of trying to back away or strike again, she twirled along the phaerimm's thorny body and saw a fiery column scorch the stone where she had been standing. Reversing her grip as she moved, she drove her black blade through the thornback's midsection and rolled back in the opposite direction, using the edge of the wound as a fulcrum to pry the darksword through three feet of tough flesh and scaly thorn.

The corridor exploded into howling winds as the phaerimm bellowed its rage and brought its barbed tail around in a classic distraction maneuver. It was a fatal mistake. Vala was already vaulting onto its thorny back, lopping off first one, then two more flame-shooting hands. She brought the darksword down on the rim of its mouth, and the phaerimm dropped to the floor, its tail lashing ineffectually at the stone where it had expected her to be standing. She spun around and risked another blow from her same location, this time slicing the creature cleanly in two behind her.

The tail struck at the stone twice more, then fell limp and lay motionless. Vala took the precaution of slicing the thing into a few more pieces, then finally heard boots pounding down the stairs and turned to find the first pair of Shadovar legs descending into view.

"Parth, take your time. The hard work—"

A loud thrum sounded from the stairwell, and a chorus of Shadovar voices cried out in astonishment. The first pair of legs buckled, then Parth's limp body tumbled into view. It was followed by Carlig's, Elar's, and four more, all that remained of the reconnaissance patrol.

Vala slipped over to the wall beneath the stairwell and pressed her back to the stone, darksword ready to lop off the next foot that came within reach. When none did, she hazarded a glance at the bodies at the base of the stairs. All seven Shadovar were dead, their faces, necks, and other areas of unarmored flesh flecked with tiny, cone-shaped darts. She waited a moment longer, then peered up into the spiraling stairwell itself. The steps were littered with spent darts, and the walls were flecked with the tiny holes from which they had come.

A voice at the top of the stairs, a voice so wispy that it seemed barely a hiss, called, "Eltargrim."

Vala ducked back out of sight, her heart pounding so hard that she could barely hear the darts clattering down the stairs as the newcomer kicked them out of the way. She wanted nothing more than to flee down the corridor as fast as her legs would carry her, but that would have been the worst thing she could do. The stranger knew she was there—had in fact whispered the password that kept her from meeting the same fate as the Shadovar—and whoever it was, he obviously knew the Irithlium far better than did Vala.

A chill came over Vala again. She raised her sword toward her helmet, wondering if Escanor would arrive quickly enough to save her if she touched the blade to one of the horns. Probably not—but maybe he would avenge her death or die himself at the hands of whatever was coming. Either way was fine, as far as Vala was concerned.

A bare foot appeared on the stair above Vala's head. Small and fine boned, it reminded her of an elf's foot, except that the flesh was so thin and white she could see the bone beneath, as well as the tendons and ligaments that made it move. The foot's mate appeared, also small and pale, with long broken nails hanging off the ends of the toes. Above the ankles hung the ragged cuffs of a pair of long-rotted trousers.

Vala grew so cold her flesh broke into goosebumps. Whatever this was, it could not be good. She took a deep breath and spun away from the wall, then brought her darksword around to strike the feet off at the ankles—and barely stopped her blade in time to keep it from burying itself in the stone steps.

The feet were gone.

But the cold was not.

Vala stepped away from the wall and found a small figure with alabaster skin and a willowy build watching her from the base of the stairs. Clothed in the tattered remains of what had once been a fine cowled robe, the stranger's features were sunken and shriveled, his eyes glowing orbs of pure white.

He pointed at Vala's sword, then wagged a bony finger and said, "You do not seem very fond of elves."

CHAPTER TEN

19 Mirtul, the Year of Wild Magic

The white elf turned his back to Vala and the dead Shadovar and started down the murky corridor.

"Come."

Vala stood where she was and didn't move. She didn't even lower her sword.

"Come?" she gasped. "After you killed Parth and everyone else?"

"I did not kill them, woman. I saved *you*." The elf continued away, but his head turned to face her, his neck giving a mushy crackle as it traveled the last few inches to sit backward on his shoulders. "From what I saw, I will be of more use to you than they were."

"Doing what?" Vala asked, starting after him.

"Surviving."

The elf rotated his head forward again. Deciding there was truth in what he said, Vala lowered her guard and moved to within four paces of him, where his chill aura grew so uncomfortable she began to shiver. She had seen enough undead in the past six months to recognize him as some sort of lich, but his presence did not engender the same sense of fear and corruption she had experienced back in Karsus when she and Galaeron and their companions had fought the lich Wulgreth. What she wouldn't have given to have Galaeron at her side, with his Tomb Guard's knowledge of all things unliving—but the old Galaeron before he fell victim to the corrupting influence of the Shadow Weave. Gods, how she missed that one, the Galaeron who had been so steady and earnest and noble.

The lich-elf turned down a smaller side corridor—still so wide three Vaasans could have stood abreast—and sent a spider the size of a pony skittering along the wall. Hanging in its web overhead were several silk-wrapped packages, some with clawed feet or beastly snouts poking out. From one dangled a halfling-sized boot, the toe still twitching. As she passed beneath this cocoon, Vala slowed and raised her sword to cut the halfling free.

"Leave him."

Vala looked up to find the lich-elf's head turned backward on his shoulders again, watching her.

"He is a relic thief and has met a relic thief's end," the lich-elf said.

Vala lowered her sword. She knew firsthand how elves felt about treasure thieves, and the last thing she needed was an angry lich . . . of any sort. She mouthed a silent apology to the halfling and followed her guide a hundred paces down the corridor to an iron door, which he opened by means of an ancient bronze key and a word of passing. They descended a long iron staircase filled with dog-sized rats and knee-high centipedes, all of which fled before the chill aura of the white elf.

"I'll say this, you make this place a lot safer," Vala observed.

The elf didn't respond.

The staircase descended into a natural cavern filled with limestone formations. The place stank so foully of offal and mold that Vala had to cover her mouth and nose to keep from retching. When they stepped onto the floor of the chamber, she recognized a strange regularity to many of the largest formations, where the stalactites and stalagmites met to form a wall of cagelike columns. Peering out from between many sets of bars were glowing red eyes of various shapes and sizes, some the size of Vala's fist, some no larger than pinheads. One of the nearest cages had no eyes, only a mold-covered skull with six ebony fangs propped against the bars with the tip of one dark horn poking out to touch the ground.

A chorus of low groans and rasps arose from the nearest cages, gradually mounting toward a din of bestial growling and rumblings. Though Vala was holding the hilt of her darksword, she could see nothing beyond the stone bars but red eyes.

"Mind the prisoners," the lich-elf warned. "They'll be hungry."

Vala eased away from the cage she had been peering into, only to hear a wet plop as something struck her armored thigh. The lich-elf cursed in some ancient language she did not understand, then spun toward the source of the saliva and loosed a flight of golden energy darts. When the bolts passed through the bars and exploded into her attacker, Vala glimpsed a bristly muzzle with long curved tusks, a pair of fan-shaped ears, and a set of folded wings rising up behind its shoulders.

The creature roared and tore at the inside of its cage with four huge claws. When the energy bolts faded, it vanished back into the darkness inside its prison.

The lich-elf pointed at a glob of green mucus bubbling on the surface of Vala's armor. "Wipe that off before it takes root," he said. "The last thing I want is you spreading devil spawn through my Irithlium."

"*Your* Irithlium?" Vala tore a strip from the hem of her undertunic and wrapped it over the back of her darksword, then scraped the stuff off and flung the cloth into the creature's cage. "Who were you?"

The lich-elf's eyes brightened. "*Were?*"

"No offense meant," Vala said. "It's just that I'm not friends with many undead."

Nor was she friends with this one, as the lich-elf made clear when he turned and continued through the chamber without speaking. Taking care to avoid the occasional glob of mucus that came flying her way, Vala followed as closely behind as her tolerance for cold allowed. They passed through the strange prison and wandered the dark caverns beneath the Irithlium until her legs grew weary with exhaustion. Periodically, she would try to learn more about her guide by engaging the lich-elf in conversation, but he only spoke to utter a word of passing or warn her about some deadly hazard into which she had nearly stumbled. Twice they were ambushed by spell-flinging dark nagas, one of which actually succeeded in wrapping the lich-elf in a web spell before Vala diced it into six three-yard pieces. Before continuing on, her guide was grateful enough to inform her that his name was Corineus Drannaeken.

Finally, they ascended a vertical shaft into the sub-basement levels, emerging in what had once been the central fountain in an elaborate two-story complex of work chambers. Clambering past a giant constrictor snake that had been immobilized by Corineus's aura of cold, they slipped out of the basin and sneaked down a narrow service corridor. Near the back, the white elf stopped and pulled a loose wall stone out of place. A section of stone wall grated open and rumbled aside. He uttered a word of passing, then motioned Vala through the opening.

Ever the cautious one, she dropped to a knee and peered around the corner—and found herself looking underneath a floating beholder into a large room filled with wands, crowns, bracers, and other items even she recognized as magical. There was also a mind flayer, whirling toward Vala's door, and half a dozen confused bugbears scrambling for their weapons.

Cursing herself for a fool and Corineus for a faithless double crosser, Vala whipped her darksword at the mind flayer. Waiting only long enough to see that the spinning blade was flying toward its target, she launched herself forward and rose beneath the beholder, pinning it against the ceiling of the opening while she drew her dagger.

"Ressamon, you idiot!" the beholder screamed. "Stun it—stun it before—"

Vala drove her dagger into the monster's underside. The resulting shriek was more angry than pained, and the mordant smell of powdered stone filled the air as the beholder began to spray the rock above with its disintegration ray.

"Ressamon!"

But Ressamon, if that had been the mind flayer's name, was already lying on the floor beside its amputated head. Finally gathering their wits, the bugbears sprang over the illithid's body to charge Vala.

Driving her dagger into the beholder's underside again, she extended her free hand to summon her sword. It flashed between two of the charging bugbears, slashing open a furry knee and buckling the leg. The astonished brute collapsed in front of two companions and sent them sprawling, prompting the rest of the band to stop and whirl around to see who was attacking from behind.

The darksword arrived in Vala's hand, and the beholder's disintegration ray finally cut through the keystone of the hidden archway. With a thousand tons of stone settling on her shoulders, she had no choice except to leap into the chamber ahead and let the wounded eye tyrant escape behind her. She tucked into a diving somersault, taking a bugbear's legs off at the knees as she rolled past, then came to her feet and brought her dagger over her head, driving it to the hilt in the nearest furry back.

The roars of the wounded bugbears were lost to the sound of the collapsing doorway. Vala ducked a massive axe as the quickest of the bugbears whirled to attack, then removed the arm holding it and opened its chest on the backstroke. She glimpsed another axe coming and barely managed to pivot away, though not before the blade slashed along her chest, denting steel scales and hurling her into a pair of hairy arms as big around as her waist. With her arms pinned at her sides, Vala brought her feet up over her head and smashed her booted feet into her captor's face.

The blow was not sufficient to drop a bugbear, but it did startle it. The creature's grasp loosened enough for her to bring her sword around beneath her. So weak was the attack that not even the sharpest steel would have penetrated the bugbear's thick hide, much less the apron of leather armor it wore over its loins.

The darksword's glassy blade slashed through the leather like gossamer. The bugbear bellowed in shock and started to squeeze, and Vala cocked her wrist, driving the tip of her weapon deep into its abdomen. The hairy arms went limp and dropped her on her shoulders, her captor's huge body doubling over above her face. Reaching up behind it, she grabbed a handful of fur and pulled herself through its legs and to her feet.

A huge hand axe came tumbling through the air and smashed into her helmet, breaking one of the horns off and knocking it from her head. Sure of only the direction the attack had come from, Vala spun around to the opposite side of the bugbear she'd just wounded and found another big axe swinging toward her throat. Barely flipping her darksword up in time, she caught the weapon near the top, using the attack's own momentum to cleave the shaft and send the head spinning off to lodge itself in one of the attacker's wounded companions.

Faster than the others, this bugbear followed its first attack by slamming a huge fist into Vala's armored ribs, launching her across the room into a shelf full of artifacts. She dropped to the ground in a limp heap, still holding her sword and struggling to get the wind back in her lungs.

Snorting in triumph, the bugbear snatched a weapon from a wounded companion and stomped toward Vala. Behind it, she saw a spherical form float out of the dust cloud rising from the collapsed doorway. Of Corineus, there was no sign.

Vala bounced to her feet and raised her darksword to throw. The bugbear pivoted away and brought its big axe around to block. Vala hurled the blade anyway. As the weapon sailed past the astonished brute to split the beholder down the center, she charged after it. Seeing its mistake too late, the bugbear swung back into the attack, but Vala was inside the arc of its weapon by then, her boot heels driving for its face in a flying side kick.

The bugbear leaned aside in an attempt to slip the blow. Vala kicked her feet apart and caught its head between her ankles. As she swung into its torso, she scissored her legs and swung herself around to the side. Though the bugbear was easily three times her size, the weight of her body acted like a pendulum, pulling it down face first. It slammed to the stone floor with a heavy thump and immediately began to push itself up again.

Vala's sword was already returning to her hand. She brought it down on the back of her attacker's neck, then leaped up and dispatched the wounded bugbears in a series of cautious, darting attacks from the rear. By the time she finished, the dust in the fallen doorway had cleared enough for her to see Corineus standing in the service corridor on the other side of the rubble.

"Well done, woman." he said, pointing past her toward an iron door on the adjacent wall. "Above the door, you will find a holy symbol painted in black blood. Break it."

Vala turned in the direction he pointed. When she'd had a chance to examine the room, she could see that it was divided into two sections. She had entered the front area, which the bugbears, beholder, and illithid all shared with the assortment of magical items she'd noticed earlier. In the back, opposite the door Corineus was pointing at, an assortment of gem-studded scepters, rods, rings, tomes, and other powerful artifacts of magic—even a diamond ball the size of a halfling's head—floated inside a field of green spell light. Vala's throat went dry, for she understood the phaerimm well enough to realize when she was standing in one of their lairs—and to know that had the creature been present, she would have been too busy fighting to take in all that she was seeing.

"What are you waiting for?" Corineus demanded. "Break the seal."

"Not so fast," Vala said, retrieving her helm. She had no idea whether it would still protect her from the phaerimm mind control with only one horn, but it was worth a try. "Not until you answer a few questions."

"The phaerimm who claims this laboratory lair will soon realize it has been broken into and return," Corineus replied. "That is the only question you need answered."

"Afraid not," Vala replied. "You surrendered your right to claim my trust when you sent me through that door without warning."

"You had to be tested."

Vala bit back the rage she felt rising inside and said, "I passed."

She turned toward the nearest shelf and picked up a pair of fabulously decorated silver bracers.

"Put that back!" Corineus started forward, only to encounter a field of flashing blue energy that hurled him back against the wall. "You've no right!"

"No?" Vala raised her brow and considered threatening the lich-elf, then recalled how touchy elves could be about their ancestral treasures and decided to try a different tactic. "Consider these a token of good faith."

She tossed the bracers through the door.

Corineus's eyes went wide, and he nearly let the bracers fall. "The symbol, woman! You've no idea what you just did."

Vala's mouth went dry, but she managed to meet the white elf's gaze without shaking. "Don't be too sure."

Corineus's white eyes glared at Vala for a moment, then drifted to the symbol over the door.

"Have you ever heard of a baelnorn?" the white elf asked.

Vala shook her head. "I take it I'm looking at one."

"Sworn to a duty more sacred than you can know."

A dull clunk sounded from the other side of the door.

"The time has come for you to choose," he said. "Without my help—"

"One moment," Vala interrupted, jerking the iron door open.

A teleport-dazed phaerimm tumbled into the room, its four spindly arms windmilling wildly. Vala brought her darksword down across the thick part of its body and clove it cleanly in two, then stepped back and opened both halves along their length. When she was certain the thing was dead, she cut off the wicked tail barb, then finally reached up with her sword and broke the holy symbol painted above the door.

Corineus rushed into the room, his white eyes shining bright with rage. "How dare you disobey—"

"How dare *I*?" Vala tossed the tail barb into the bael-norn's face, then touched the tip of her darksword to his throat. "Let's get something straight, White Eyes. I need you as much as you need me, but if you *ever* send me into a lair again without warning me, it'll be you I'm carving into little pieces. Clear?"

The baelnorn moved closer, enveloping her in his chill aura. "I do not think you understand who you are talking to."

Vala stepped even closer, so close that her face and hands began to ache with cold. She laid a bloody palm on his flesh-freezing face.

"Oh, I understand," she said, "but what you need to know is I mean to see my son again, and I'll gut anything that makes that less likely."

A low groan rolled from beneath the roots of the smoke tree, where Aris lay hidden in an undercut carved out of the dry riverbank by some long-ago flood. Galaeron, standing watch outside, dropped to his haunches and peered inside, where Ruha kneeled beside the unconscious giant's head, using a wet rag to drip water onto his cracked lips. His broken arm was stretched out beside him, splinted to the straightest pair of branches Galaeron had been able to find in a mile of dry riverbed. A shield-sized circle of charred flesh on his chest marked where the dragon's lightning bolt had entered his body, and a blackened foot marked where it had left. Of the most concern to Galaeron, however, were the giant's black and sunken eyes, which Ruha said were signs of the head injury he had suffered.

Aris groaned again, and a gray tongue appeared between his lips. Ruha squeezed the cloth hard, dribbling water directly onto the tip of the tongue, then tilted her head at the pair of empty waterskins resting on the shadow blanket beside the giant.

"More water," she said.

"More?" Each skin held two gallons, and Galaeron had filled them twice already since the dragon attack. "That's a good sign, isn't it?"

Ruha shrugged. "How much would a healthy giant drink in a day? I don't know." She placed the rag in a small hollow she had lined with dragon skin and filled with water. "It takes water to heal, and I would say the matter remains uncertain."

The witch did not look at Galaeron as she spoke, and her voice remained cold. He reached into the undercut and pulled the waterskins off the shadow blanket, then left the scant shade of the smoke tree to creep along the edge of the dry riverbed. Ruha's manner had been much the same since she'd used her air magic to float Aris into the shelter of the undercut. She clearly held Galaeron responsible for the giant's injuries, and he was not so sure he disagreed.

The shock of seeing Aris pinned beneath the dragon had jolted his conscience into asserting itself again, driving his shadow self back down into the dark realm beneath his conscious mind, and he had instantly realized how his actions must have seemed to someone else. Even given the spell he had cast to confuse the dragon when it wheeled on Aris, preventing the witch from attacking the dragon's belly must have reeked of cowardice. If Galaeron doubted his own motivations in that first instance, he did not in the second, when he had used a shadow snare to drag the dragon back to ground. At that point, his only concern had been for the shadow blanket, and it had not even occurred to him that Aris would be further injured when the wyrm crashed into the ground.

The dragon's corpse still lay out on the Saiyaddar, surrounded by a ring of glutted predators and blanketed beneath a mountain of flicking feathers. Galaeron longed to move beyond sight of it, and not only because looking at it reminded him of his terrible selfishness. If a Shadovar patrol or another of Malygris's dragons happened across the corpse, he and his companions were certain to be found. Ruha lacked the magic to move Aris a long distance, and Galaeron was determined never again to use his own. He could no longer touch the Weave at all, and he recognized he was far past the point where he could wield shadow magic without yielding control of himself to his shadow. The next time he cast a spell, he feared, even causing a friend's injury would not be enough to bring him back.

Galaeron reached a clump of giant featherwoods growing along the outer curve of a bend in the riverbed and kneeled beside a deep hole nestled down among the tree's roots. Though the bottom was concealed in shadow, there should have been enough light for an elf to see whether it contained any water.

Galaeron saw only murk.

He was not even all that surprised. Since touching the Shadow Weave, he had gradually started to become less and less of an elf. He had lost the ability to enter the Reverie and started to sleep just like a human, and even to dream. He was awakened by nightmares almost nightly and occasionally talked in his sleep, and he no longer felt any mystic connection in the presence of other elves. He could no longer see in dim conditions. It was, he had decided, a symptom of his shadow's growing hold over him. Elves were born with a special bond to the Weave and his connection was being weakened by the Shadow Weave's power over him. The only thing that remained was for his senses to grow as dull as those of a human. He thought of himself running around with a three-day sweat, thinking he smelled as fine as a spring rain, and shuddered.

Galaeron dropped a pebble into the hole and heard only a wet thud. The hole had not yet refilled. He gathered himself up and wandered half a mile down the riverbed to the next well—also in the roots of a featherwood—and found water. Ruha had explained that it was only worth digging under a featherwood, and only when they grew on the exterior curve of a river bend.

Though even this short trip in the hot sun was enough to make Galaeron thirsty, he filled both waterskins first, and by then there was barely a handful of muddy liquid left for him. He quaffed it down gratefully, then shouldered the waterskins and climbed out of the well to find a tall, silver-haired woman in elven chain mail, elven boots, and an elven cloak standing before him, her hand resting on the hilt of a fine elven long sword. The woman, however, was definitely human—and one he recognized from an ancient portrait hanging in the halls of Evereska's Academy of Magic.

"Well met, Lady Silverhand," Galaeron said, holding out one of the waterskins. "If you're not my dying hallucination . . ."

"You should be that lucky, elf," Storm said, not taking the waterskin. "After the evil you brought into the Realms, I'll send you to the Nine Hells to look for Elminster before I let you die a peaceful death in Anauroch."

"The Mage Masters at the Academy always said you were the merriest of the Seven Sisters," Galaeron retorted, concealing the hurt the words caused him behind a facade of cynicism. He hefted the waterskins onto his shoulders and started for the undercut. "If you are about to open a hell-mouth beneath my feet, at least wait until I deliver this water. My friend Aris is in danger of dying."

"I didn't come here to punish you, elf," Storm said, ignoring Galaeron's attempt to elicit her concern for the stone giant. "That is not my place—even were you worth the trouble."

Galaeron glanced up at the blazing sun and licked his cracked lips, then asked, "Well then, if you didn't come to help and you didn't come to punish, what are you doing here?"

"Delivering a message on behalf of Khelben Arunsun," she said. "He asks that I inform you that your sister Keya is well."

Galaeron nearly dropped the precious waterskins. "Keya is safe?" he gasped. "The siege has been lifted?"

"Not exactly," Storm replied, "but the shadowshell has weakened the phaerimm deadwall. Khelben is in the city."

Galaeron was so astonished he couldn't quite think of what to say. The Chosen of Mystra seldom took an interest in the affairs of individual people—how could they, when they were so few and those who needed them so many?—yet here was Storm Silverhand, delivering a message from Khelben Arunsun about his younger sister Keya. It was so far beyond likely that Galaeron grew convinced he was suffering heat hallucinations.

Resolving to waste no more of his energy on illusions, he clamped his jaw shut and fixed his attention on the undercut where Aris lay resting.

The hallucination walked along at his side. "That's all?" she asked. "Not even a 'thank you for your trouble'?"

Galaeron ignored her and continued toward the undercut.

"Well, you would at least be wise to thank Khelben," the illusion said. "He's going to a great deal of effort to undo the trouble you and that shadow wizard unleashed."

"That may be true," Galaeron said, speaking aloud in the hope that the sound of his own voice would lend impact to his logic, "but why would Khelben Arunsun trouble himself to deliver a message about my sister?"

The hallucination made a lifting gesture with her hands, and both waterskins rose off Galaeron's shoulders. Thinking he had dropped them and was simply imagining this to conceal the fact, he cried out and dropped to his knees and began to run his fingers through the sand. The *dry* sand.

The hallucination came over to stand in front of Galaeron, holding both waterskins.

"He feels obligated," she said. "Your father saved his life at the Battle of Rocnest."

"My father?" Galaeron asked. "Did he . . ."

The hallucination shook her head. "He died in the battle." For the first time, a soft look came to her eyes. "I'm sorry."

Galaeron let his shoulders slump and was relieved to feel himself crying. At least he was still that much of an elf.

"None of that, elf—from the looks of it, you don't have the water to spare," Storm said, starting down the riverbed with the waterskins in hand. "Why didn't you levitate these? That's what magic is for."

"Not for me, not any longer," Galaeron said, rising. "I've a friend lying in there injured because I couldn't control my shadow magic, and I'll not insult him by using it now."

Storm glanced over. "Really? Even to save his life?"

Galaeron shook his head. "He wouldn't want it."

"You sound awfully sure of that." She studied him for a moment, then added, "Or maybe awfully scared."

Leaving Galaeron to ponder the truth of her words, Storm stepped into the air and flew the rest of the way to the undercut. She poked her head through the smoke tree's root and began to speak with Ruha. By the time Galaeron arrived, Storm was already inside dribbling her third healing potion into Aris's half-open lips. Though the giant's eyes were open, he remained as pale as a pearl and looked too weak to lift his head, even had there been room.

Storm tossed the empty vial aside, opened a fourth, and began to dribble it into the giant's half-open mouth.

"This is the last one for now, my large friend. They said five would be too many, even for a giant."

"Even for a giant?" Galaeron echoed, starting to realize that there was more to Storm's appearance than she had told him. "Milady Silverhand, exactly how did you know where to find us?"

Instead of answering, Storm exchanged glances with Ruha, and Galaeron suddenly knew the answer to his own question.

He looked at the witch and asked, "Was it Malik you were watching, or me?"

"You have a very large opinion of your value, don't you, elf?" Storm asked, her eyes sparkling in amusement. "It was the Shadovar we sent her to watch. You, we know already."

Galaeron found himself smiling, then—to his own surprise—he began to do something he had not done in a very long time.

He began to laugh.

Keya was in Treetop on her Reverie couch, reliving in her mind the last homeagain embrace she had shared with her brother, when a white snow finch appeared outside her room's theurglass window and politely fluttered its wings. Rousing herself from her daze, she uttered the command word to make the theurglass passable, then swung her feet to the floor and extended her finger to form a perch. On the way across the room, however, the bird noticed Dexon slumbering on the floor and circled the Vaasan's hairy mountain of a body, nearly coming to a bad end when his wingtip brushed the sleeping warrior's nose and a massive hand rose up to swat at the disturbance.

The finch dived to safety, then flew up and, chirping in indignation, landed on Keya's finger.

"That is no concern of yours, Manynests," Keya said sternly. "Besides, he has to sleep somewhere."

Manynests warbled a question.

"*That* is none of your business," Keya retorted, "and I

don't want you spreading it about Evereska that we are."

He chirped an assurance.

"I'm serious about this," Keya warned. "I'm sure you wouldn't want your mate to learn the real reason Lord Duirsar calls you Manynests."

The finch ruffled his feathers, then repeated his promise in a lower tone that, from what Keya understood of peeptalk, indicated a solemn vow. Given what a compulsive gossip Manynests was, she suspected her secret had about even odds of remaining secret.

"Are you here just to spy on me, or does Lord Duirsar require something?"

Manynests ruffled his wings and asked about Khelben's whereabouts.

"Did you try the contemplation?" she asked.

The bird chirped his thanks and flew out the door—then circled back into the room and tweeted a suggestion that she fetch the other Vaasans and join them there. His speech was urgent and rapid, as though he had just recalled the importance of his errand.

"Very well," she said. "We'll be there in a minute."

She roused Dexon and told him to fetch the others, then pulled on a robe and went down to her father's old contemplation, which was serving Khelben as a study and magic laboratory. By the time she arrived, the archmage was interrogating Manynests in peeptalk too rapid for Keya to follow. His battle cloak was spread open on the table, and Khelben was furiously stuffing gem powders, balls of brimstone, glass cylinders, and other spell ingredients into its component pockets. The archmage did not even look up as Keya entered the room.

"Lord Duirsar is calling the city to arms," Khelben said. "The phaerimm are massing outside the mythal."

Manynests tipped his head in Keya's direction and chirped something too fast for her to follow.

"Slow down, bird!" she admonished. "Master Colbathin what?"

"Says you are free to fight in my company, if I have a place for you," Khelben translated. "Welcome."

Manynests added another series of peeps, this time slow enough that Keya understood that the Long Watch would be assembling for battle in the meadow outside the Livery Gate.

"So I am free to choose?" Keya asked.

Manynests chirped a confirmation and took wing, circling toward the window and warbling about all the other messages he had to deliver.

Keya uttered the command word to open the theurglass, then said, "I'll fetch my armor and weapons."

"Good," Khelben said. "We'll assemble in the foyer—I want to conserve my teleport magic for battle."

"Battle?" Dexon echoed, leading Kuhl and Burlen into the room. "What battle?"

"The phaerimm are massing—"

That was as much as Keya said before the Vaasans turned and pounded off to armor themselves. She returned and pulled on her own armor—a hauberk of fine Evereskan chain mail and her father's magic helmet—then gathered her weapons and rushed down to the foyer. Khelben and the three humans were already waiting, looking out the door at the great sheets of spelllight already flashing across the surface of the mythal. As they watched, golden meteors began to rain down into the Vine Vale as the mythal activated its most ferocious—and best-known—defense. The phaerimm assault only intensified.

"What're the Hill Elders thinking?" Dexon growled. "I'd wager my shield arm that shower of magic bolts is what the thornbacks *want*."

"The mythal is a living thing," Keya explained. "The

Hill Elders know better than any of us that the phaerimm are trying to drain it, but no one can prevent it from defending itself—or Evereska."

"Which is all the more reason we should hurry." Khelben stepped through the door and continuing to speak over his shoulder, led the way head-first down the exterior of the tower. "Their success is not certain, but it is very possible. The more we kill—and the faster—the better the mythal's chances of holding."

"We're *attacking*?" Dexon gasped from a few feet above and behind Keya.

"That's what I intend to recommend to Lord Duirsar, yes," Khelben said. He reached the bottom of the tower and dropped off the wall into the Starmeadow, then turned to face Dexon. "Unless you know of a better way to kill phaerimm."

Dexon frowned, then swung his feet around and dropped to the ground beside Khelben. Armed and armored elves were rushing past on all sides, descending toward the juncture of trails at Dawnsglory Pond and continuing from there toward their assigned mustering points.

"I was thinking of Keya," Dexon said. He spoke quietly—though not quietly enough for Keya's keen elf ears to miss. "There's no reason she has to go, is there?"

"Only that this is my home we are defending," Keya said, jumping to the ground beside him. "You wouldn't be trying to rid yourself of me, would you Dex?"

The big Vaasan blushed. "No, of course not."

"Then you must think me incapable of carrying my weight in such an elite band of phaerimm killers." She grabbed one of the barbed trophy tails tucked into his belt and gave it a flick. "Perhaps you think I am not brave enough."

"I know you are brave enough," Dexon said, looking

to his fellows for help—and finding nothing but amused grins, "b-but you don't have a darksword."

"Neither does Khelben," Keya pointed out.

Dexon rolled his eyes. "Khelben is one of the Chosen."

"Dexon just couldn't stand to see you hurt." Kuhl grabbed them by the arms and led them after Khelben, who was already halfway down the trail to Dawnsglory Pond. He leaned closer to Keya, then added in a quiet voice, "If you ask me, I think all those moonlight swims have gone and made him sweet on you."

Keya blushed and, unsure whether Kuhl was joking or really had not noticed how close she and Dexon had become, disengaged herself and glanced over at her Vaasan lover. As large and hairy as a bear, his emotions were in many ways just as alien to her. She had no doubts about the depths of his feelings—she would have known that by the way Khelben frowned whenever he saw them together, if nothing else—but it had never occurred to her that his passion would manifest itself in such a protective streak. To an elf, such paternalism implied that he believed her incapable of making her own decisions, and elves were not in the habit of falling in love with those whom they held in such low regard.

But humans were different. She had seen the way Dexon glowered when the other Vaasans looked at her during their swims, and she had noticed how he often tried to keep them away from her when the water games began. His affection for her seemed to manifest itself as though she were a treasure he feared someone might steal—and, with a sudden rush of comprehension, she understood that was almost true.

Their love *was* a treasure—and humans viewed treasure not as beautiful artwork to be shared with others, but as coins and gems to be hidden safely away. They were like dragons that way—and they would fight just as ferociously to protect their hoard. If, on the battlefield, Keya were to be threatened, Dexon would forget all else—his own safety, his duty to help Khelben, even the many thousand Evereskans whose lives were at peril—and rush to defend her.

They reached Dawnsglory Pond, where Khelben turned uphill toward Cloudhome, Lord Duirsar's citadel. Burlen and Kuhl started after him at once, but Keya stopped and turned down the slope toward the Livery Gate.

Dexon caught her arm and motioned up the hill. "Lord Blackstaff went this way."

"I know," Keya said, pointing down the hill, "but I must go that way."

"Then you're not coming with us?" Dexon looked almost as confused as he did relieved.

Keya shook her head. "My place is with the Long Watch."

"The Long Watch?" Dexon gasped. "But they've no training!"

Keya frowned. "More than you know," she said, raising her chin. "Our hearts are brave. We'll give a good accounting of ourselves."

"For as long as it takes the phaerimm to cast one spell!" Dexon objected, trying to pull her up the hill. "The Long Watch is fodder. You're coming with us."

Keya twisted her arm free. "No, Dex, you were right. I don't belong in Khelben's company."

She grabbed his shoulders and pulled herself up to kiss him on the lips, then let go and dropped back to the ground a pace away.

"I'll see you after the battle," she said.

"*If* we win," Dexon said, shaking his head and starting after her. "I can't let you—"

"Yes, Dexon, you can, and you will." Khelben's strong hand caught him by the shoulder and pulled him back. "Say your farewells."

Dexon's eyes grew a little glassy, then he kissed his beefy fingers and turned them toward Keya. "Till swords part."

Keya smiled and returned the gesture. "Back soon for soft songs and bright wine."

Khelben pushed Dexon into the arms of his waiting companions. He made a shooing motion and mumbled something Keya did not quite catch.

"I'm sorry," she said. "What was that?"

"Just the usual," Khelben said, turning away. "Sweet water and light laughter."

To Keya, that didn't sound like what he'd mumbled. Not even close.

CHAPTER ELEVEN

20 Mirtul, the Year of Wild Magic

"Loose!"

Keya released her bowstring on command. Her arrow hissed skyward with a thousand others, passing through the mythal and arcing down toward the thin line of beholders and phaerimm floating out in the Vine Vale. Shimmering rays of disintegration magic swept back and forth across the volley, dissolving hundreds of shafts before they neared the blackened vineyards. One of the mythal's golden meteors came streaking down from the heavens and burned a twenty-foot swath through the sizzling cloud of sticks. Hundreds of missiles missed their targets and planted themselves in the soil like a crop of newly sprouted feather sticks. Of the few dozen arrows that found their marks, most were deflected by powerful shielding magic and clattered harmlessly to ground, but a few enchanted shafts penetrated the phaerimm defenses and lodged themselves deep in enemy bodies.

One phaerimm and two beholders went limp and began to sink toward the ground, then a fierce counterattack blossomed against the mythal and prevented Keya from seeing if they recovered. She nocked another arrow—the last in her quiver—and awaited the next command. Like the rest of the Long Watch, she was standing inside the Meadow Wall with nothing between her and the enemy but the battered mythal and seventy paces of open ground—close enough that when she was not trying to blink the magic-dazzle from her eyes, she could see the big central eyes of the attacking beholders.

What Keya could not see were any bugbears, illithids, captured elves, or any other phaerimm mind-slaves. There were only the thornbacks themselves—less than two hundred in the whole vale, according to rumor—and perhaps a thousand beholders. With a full ten thousand elves ringing the city, it definitely appeared that the odds favored Evereska, but where the phaerimm were concerned, appearances were always deceiving. The mind-slaves could be anywhere, lurking invisibly on the other side of the Meadow Wall or hiding in tunnels under the Vine Vale, ready to burrow under the elven defenses the instant their masters weakened the mythal.

"Loose!" came the command.

Keya set her aim on the eye of the closest beholder and released her bowstring. She lost sight of her arrow as it joined the dark cloud sailing into the Vine Vale, but she chose to believe that hers was the shaft that survived to plant itself between two of her target's writhing eye-stalks. Another phaerimm spell-storm exploded against the mythal.

An arrow runner lifted Keya's empty quiver off her belt and replaced it with a full one. She grabbed the next shaft and was horrified to feel green, moist wood. To save Evereska, even the trees had to sacrifice—not that they would live long if the mythal fell. She slipped the nock onto her bowstring and raised the tip to the air.

The phaerimm began to retreat, fleeing so fast that one flew into a mythal-meteor and vanished in a golden flash. In the next instant, a cone of sparkling gray flame shot out from behind the Meadow Wall, engulfing a pair of phaerimm who had made the mistake of drifting into a single line. They erupted into screeching tornadoes of silver fire.

Khelben Arunsun appeared at the Meadow Wall where the cone had originated, his hand still pointing at the two burning phaerimm. In the next instant, the Vaasans and the rest of the archmage's escort appeared to both sides of him, all grunting with effort as they hurled a flight of golden javelins after the fleeing phaerimm. The beholders caught the first wave of spears in their disintegration rays, which only turned them into pure magic and sent them streaking into their targets with the speed of lightning bolts. The second wave followed a little more slowly, but two dozen weapons found their marks. Three phaerimm dropped to the ground and disintegrated into piles of dust, and two more were injured so badly they teleported away.

The surviving thornbacks came streaking back, driving their beholder slaves ahead of them and hurling such a spell tempest at the mythal that Keya had to turn her face away from the heat of the dissipating magic. Khelben and his escort simply laughed and strolled calmly away from the Meadow Wall, their backs to the enemy. They passed through the Long Watch lines not twenty paces from where Keya stood awaiting the command to loose her next arrow. If Dexon—or any of the Vaasans—noticed her standing in line, they did not betray the fact by looking in her direction.

"Well done, Khelben!" chortled Kiinyon Colbathin. "Five this time!"

"Yes," Khelben answered. "If we had forty hours and a thousand Corellon's Bolts, we could kill them all—but we don't. We're not going to save the mythal by teleporting in to attack once every hour."

"What do you suggest, Lord Blackstaff?" asked a familiar voice.

Keya glanced over her shoulder and found Lord Duirsar standing a dozen yards behind her with Kiinyon Colbathin and what remained of Evereska's Hill Elders. They were surrounded by the Company of the Cold Hand, a hundred hand-picked Spellblades chosen to wield the sixteen darkswords borrowed from the Vaasans who had fallen when the phaerimm escaped their ancient prison. Because the weapons would freeze the hand of any wielder not of the owning family, the idea was that the first warrior would use the weapon until his hand grew too cold to hold it, then pass it to the next, and so forth.

Khelben stepped to Lord Duirsar's side. "We must carry the attack into the Vine Vale, and soon."

"Leave the mythal?" Colbathin gasped. "Do you know how many warriors we'll lose?"

"A fraction of what we'll lose if we let them wear it down and enter Evereska," Khelben countered. "The shadowshell has already weakened it, and this battle is draining it by the minute." He turned to Lord Duirsar. "Milord, even if Evereska had arrows and magic enough to squander in this way, the mythal won't last. We must reduce the enemy."

"You forget that we will be reduced ourselves, tenfold," Kiinyon objected. "Surely, it is better to take what kills we can from the safety of the mythal—"

"Do those pointed ears not hear, elf?" roared Khelben. "The mythal won't last!"

In spite of herself, Keya found her attention wandering from Khelben and the high lords to her cherished Dexon. To her dismay, the Vaasan had noticed her as he passed through the lines of the Long Watch—was, in fact, studying her with the dark look of an angry bear, holding his darksword across his breast and towering over not only the elves, but Khelben and even his fellow Vaasans. Even the night before, when she had spent so many hours climbing over that massive body, she had not realized just how large—how brutish—a man he really was.

When he noticed her watching him, Dexon gave a melancholy smile and extended an index finger in her direction. At first, Keya thought he was trying to use elven fingertalk, but then she sensed someone looking over her shoulder and realized he was pointing. She looked forward again to find Zharilee, the sun elf who commanded her company, standing in front of her impatiently tapping a long finger on her extravagant armor of gold scales.

"Truly, Keya, it is nothing to me if you are attracted to these hairy brutes, but I insist that you leave the flirting until after the battle." Zharilee turned away, then raised her magic command horn to her lips and shouted, "Loose!"

Keya drew her bowstring back and sent an arrow arcing over the Meadow Wall into the blinding storm of flame and lightning that was the Vine Vale. She reached for another of the green shafts in her quiver.

"Hold!"

The command came not from Zharilee, but from Kiinyon Colbathin himself—and he sounded none too happy.

"Split by ranks, swords the first, spears the second, bows the third."

Heart leaping into her throat, Keya slung her bow over her shoulder and pulled her spear out of the ground beside her. Khelben's argument had prevailed, and Lord Duirsar had given the order to leave the mythal to engage the phaerimm. A low, ground-shaking rumble rolled up from the rear as the elite companies trotted up to take attack positions behind the Long Watch.

Even had Keya not learned tactics on her father's knee, she would have known what was happening. As the most inexperienced element of Evereska's military, the Long Watch would lead the charge over the wall and absorb the brunt of the phaerimm attack. With any luck, the elite companies following behind would reach the enemy ranks intact and force the thornbacks to engage in their least favorite kind of combat—close.

Though Keya desperately wanted to steal a last glance over her shoulder at Dexon, she resisted the temptation. Looking at him would only make him worry about her when he should be thinking of killing their enemies. As the rightful wielder of a darksword, he was one of Evereska's most potent weapons against the phaerimm. His shadowy blade could cut through even their mightiest defenses, and he already had three of their tails tucked into his belt to prove he knew how to get close enough to use it.

"Long Watch, charge in three ranks!"

Keya counted a one second delay, then set her spear tip at a slight incline and started forward at a two-step-per-second run—swift enough to cover ground quickly, but not so fast that the charge would disorganize their formation. Instead of starting forward to meet the charge, the phaerimm and beholders hung back, content to hurl spells at the mythal and create a gauntlet of magic for their attackers to struggle through. It was a tactic that would serve them well against the Long Watch—but bring the elite companies behind into the middle of their ranks.

Keya was ten steps from the Meadow Wall when Khelben's voice came to her in her mind. *Nothing to fear, my dear.*

Who's afraid? she retorted. *Just kill the thornbacks—and tell Dex to keep his mind—*

That was as far as she made it before the first rank reached the Meadow Wall. With only their swords in hand and light Evereskan armor on their bodies, they leaped onto the wall in one stride and disappeared over its crest on the second. Keya and the rest of the second rank were slower. They had to brace a hand on top of the wall and swing their legs up beside them—and by then, the first rank was already stopped dead in its tracks, filling the air with eerie wails as their legs crumbled into ash.

Keya kept herself from going over by dropping to her seat and bracing her spear on the other side of the Meadow Wall. In front of her, Zharilee and half a dozen other elves seemed to be melting into the ground as first their legs, then their hips and torsos dissolved into a pile of gray cinders. She nearly fell when the shaft of her spear crumbled as well.

A young Gold elf from the third rank crashed into her from behind, and she grabbed the back of his helmet to prevent herself from going over.

"What's the hold up?" he demanded. "Get a move on!"

"Not wise." Keya pulled his head over the wall and forced him to look at the dissipating ash piles. "Those are our friends."

The young sun elf turned the color of a withered birch leaf, but many in the Long Watch were not so fortunate.

Much of the third rank simply leaped onto the backs of the second rank, forcing them over the wall into the Vine Vale and beyond the protection of the mythal. As soon as their feet touched the blackened ground, their bodies crumbled into cinders and collapsed.

Without the constant rain of arrows from the Long Watch, the phaerimm and beholders finally began to float forward, coming closer to the mythal. Keya glanced back and, over the retching figure of the elf who had nearly pushed her to her death, saw the Company of the Cold Hand charging up to vault the wall behind them.

Still sitting astride the wall, Keya raised both hands. "Khelben, stop them! You made a mistake!"

"*Mistake*?" Khelben's voice boomed across the valley like a clap of thunder. "Impossible!"

"Khelben, it *is* possible—the Vale is a death trap!"

For a long and terrible moment, the Cold Hand continued to rush forward. A golden mythal meteor roared down behind her, cratering the blackened ground and spraying her with so much dirt and stone that she was knocked off the wall back into the meadow. Lord Duirsar's mages launched a volley of lightning bolts and black death rays that streaked overhead and—so far as Keya could tell from where she was cowering down behind the wall—had absolutely no effect on the enemy.

Then, much to her horror, an avalanche of stones shot across the wall above her and found the young Gold who had nearly pushed her into the Vine Vale. The pile took him square in the chest, reducing his torso to a spray of blood and bone, then crashed to the ground behind him and rolled off trailing a spray of crimson.

That was enough to halt the charge of the Cold Hand—and send what remained of the Long Watch scurrying back toward Evereska. The enemy had attacked into the meadow. The mythal was weakening, and fast.

Keya suppressed a gasp and rolled into a crouch, then poked her head up to find a beholder hovering not a spear's length away, its great central eye projecting a powerful antimagic ray into the failing mythal. Behind it, a phaerimm was floating forward to exploit the resulting gap in the LastHaven's magic defenses.

Keya had just time enough to see that the scene was much the same in other places along the wall before the phaerimm pointed in her direction. A stream of stones rose off a vineyard wall and came streaking in her direction. She rolled away. The rocks slammed into the Meadow Wall behind her, smashing through and raining shards of broken granite into the meadow. Finding herself alone next to the breach, she took a deep breath and reached for her sword.

Keya, no! came Dexon's voice.

She started to tell him to mind his own business and let her do her duty, then hesitated when she realized that would be the last thing anyone ever heard from her.

In that moment Dexon added, *Here!*

Keya looked toward the Company of the Cold Hand and saw Dexon's darksword flying toward her hilt-first. Reaching up to catch it, she thought, *Thanks, Dex—love you.*

Deciding those were much better last words than what she had been thinking a moment before, she brought the darksword up before her and spun into the gap in a squat—and came nose-to-mouth with a crawling phaerimm. For an instant, she was almost too stunned to comprehend what she was seeing. Thornbacks did not crawl, they floated . . . and why was she still alive anyway? It had only to think a spell and she would be an elf-shaped cinder.

It opened its toothy mouth and stretched four spindly arms toward her, and suddenly none of that mattered.

She brought Dexon's darksword down, splitting it open for two feet past its mouth, then brought the blade around and slashed it in the opposite direction. The phaerimm whistled and recoiled, grabbing Keya by the shoulders and rearing up on its tail. She kicked at its torso with both feet, hacking herself free of its arms and dropping on her shoulder.

Still using no magic, the thing lunged and snapped at Keya's feet. She kicked free and rolled over her shoulder—then glimpsed one of the beholders shining its antimagic ray over the phaerimm and understood. She drew her dagger with her free hand and flipped it at the eye tyrant in one swift motion.

Keya was no bladesinger. The dagger struck pommel first—hardly fatal, but enough. The beholder blinked, and in that instant, the mythal's magic returned to the gap. The phaerimm screeched and started to retreat back into the Vine Vale, but not quickly enough to avoid the golden meteor that streaked down from the heavens and slammed it to ground—where it quickly dissolved into a pile of ash only a little larger than those left behind by the first wave of the Long Watch.

Before the stunned beholder could recover, Keya leaped onto the Meadow Wall rubble and brought the darksword across the middle of its spherical body. A cascade of dark gore spilled out of the wound, and it dropped to the ground without so much as a curse. Keya brought the darksword around and started down the wall toward the next beholder, then cried out in astonishment when she felt a magic hand pluck her off the crest and carry her back into the Company of the Cold Hand.

"Let's not get carried away, young lady," Kiinyon Colbathin said, stepping to her side. He gestured down the way, to where the survivors of the Long Watch were charging back to the Meadow Wall behind a storm of spears and arrows. "Let someone else have a go at them."

"Yes, you've done your part many times over," Khelben agreed, plucking the darksword from Keya's hand. He hissed at the cold and quickly returned the blade to Dexon, then raised his swarthy brow. "That didn't freeze your hand?"

"As a matter of fact, no." She displayed her hands. Aside from the calluses she had earned in weapons practice, they remained as healthy as her eighty-year-old cheeks. "They didn't even get cold."

Dexon's jaw dropped, and Burlen and Kuhl fell to chuckling.

Khelben frowned. "What are you two laughing about?"

The battle din built to a roar as the Long Watch reached the Meadow Wall and began to assail the enemy at close range. Unable to use their own magic within the antimagic zones created by their beholder slaves, the phaerimm hung back.

Khelben's scowl only deepened. "This is important. If there's a way for the Company of the Cold Hand to wield your comrades' darkswords—"

"The Cold Hand wouldn't care for it much," said Kuhl.

"The Cold Hand will do what it must to defend Evereska," Kiinyon growled. "They are elf warriors."

"It won't work," Kuhl said. "Most of the warriors in the Cold Hand are male—and I doubt even elven magic can get a Vaasan baby on a male warrior."

"B-baby?" Keya stammered. "What are you talking about?"

Burlen grinned and nudged her arm. "Come on, Keya, you know how these things work," he said. "You and Dexon are family now."

From the ruins of the Secret Gate, high in Evereska's Upper Vale, Laeral had watched in horror as the first rank of elves poured over the Meadow Wall and disintegrated into swirling piles of ash. When the phaerimm launched their counterattack, using their magic to hurl half the stones in the Vine Vale through the breaches the beholders had opened in the mythal, she had gasped out loud. As the young warriors of the Long Watch somehow rallied themselves and came charging back to drive off the beholders, she felt tears sliding down her cheeks.

"The stuff of legends, my friend," Laeral said, looking across the window to Lord Imesfor. "If those are raw recruits in Evereska, I shudder to think what will become of the phaerimm when the time comes to unleash your seasoned warriors."

"I just wish I could be there with them," Imesfor said. Though the magic of Waterdeep's clerics had regrown his fingers, they were still too clumsy and stiff to cast spells, or even hold a sword in combat. "It is good to watch, to remind myself that the Tel'Quess never lose hope."

Forcing their mind-slaves to hold at the mythal's edge, the phaerimm continued to hurl whole stretches of vineyard wall into the meadow. The Long Watch fell by the dozens and continued to attack, playing a deadly game of dodge as they tried to avoid breaches in the mythal while continuing to pour arrows into the beholders. One eye tyrant after another sprouted more spines than a hedgehog, then sank to the ground and disintegrated. Some, maddened by pain, finally broke free of their masters' hold and turned to leave, only to be struck down by the phaerimm themselves. Though it would have been a simple matter to send the elite companies forward to support the Long Watch and finish off the beholders, Khelben and the elf commanders wisely resisted the temptation. One way or another, Evereska would need its most experienced fighters later, when victory or death hung in the balance.

Laeral could see just see Khelben in the heart of one of the elite companies, a swarthy figure in black robes, his namesake black staff cradled in the croak of one arm as he discussed strategy with the elf lords clustered around him. How good it was to see her beloved again, even if he was little more than a black speck in a square of gleaming gray mithral.

"Lord Blackstaff seems to have them quite distracted," said Prince Clariburnus, peering out the watchloop adjacent to Laeral and Lord Imesfor. "What say you, Lady Laeral?"

"I would say we dare not wait—the mythal is growing weak," Laeral said, noting that the rain of golden meteors had tapered to a drizzle. "You've seen their trap. We can't dismount."

"That trap we will turn against them," said Lamorak, who was watching opposite Clariburnus, "but let us be alert for more phaerimm trickery. You Chosen are not the only ones who know the value of guile in war."

Laeral met the prince's orange eyes. "Always a good thing to remember," she said, starting downstairs. "I will hold it in mind."

When the phaerimm had made no attempt to stop them from entering the Sharaedim, it had been Laeral who realized the thornbacks would attempt to breach the mythal and take refuge inside Evereska—and who had developed the strategy to take advantage of their plan. After emerging from the shadowshell and using her silver fire to open a gate in the weakened deadwall, she had sent the relief army to attack the enemy rear guard, then summoned Lord Imesfor from Waterdeep to serve as a guide. He had led the Shadovar army through the shadow fringe into the Secret Gate and safely past hundreds of elven traps—a gauntlet so devious and powerful that it had claimed several of the phaerimm before they finally gave up on clearing the passage and simply sealed the entrances—at least those they could find.

Laeral reached the exit vestibule at the bottom of the stairs, where a company of Shadovar cavalry stood beside its mounts in a long line stretching back across a marble bridge into the murky recesses of the Passing. With little more than lances, darkswords, and black helms, the veserab riders were lightly armed and thinly armored. Behind the cavalry, Laeral knew, ran an even longer line of infantry equipped just as sparingly. Against the magic of the phaerimm, massive blades and heavy armor counted for less than the swiftness of the strike and the agility with which one dodged.

Lamorak came and gave his orders, then turned to Laeral and said, "This is your plan. Would you care to launch the attack?"

"By all means—thank you." As Laeral waited for the riders to mount their veserabs, she turned to Lord Imesfor. "I know you'd like nothing better than to see the outcome of the battle, but the Shadovar infantry will need someone to lead them back to the relief army."

Imesfor raised his hand, displaying a set of stubby white digits that did not yet look quite like fingers. "Say no more. It will be my pleasure to guide them through the Passing."

"Once the outcome is apparent, of course," Lamorak clarified.

Imesfor nodded. "Of course."

Since the infantry would not be able to step foot into the valley below without being disintegrated by phaerimm magic, the prince's plan called for them to return to the holding action in the mountains and catch the enemy from behind. Given the tremendous advantages of holding the high terrain, the tactic was certain to save a lot of lives in the relief army.

The cavalry commander reported his readiness, and the two Shadovar princes mounted their own veserabs. Laeral cast a flying spell on herself, then raised her arm and led the way out of the Secret Gate down a hanging gorge that opened into the High Vale itself. The life-draining magic of the phaerimm had reduced the slopes to barren pitches of rock and dirt, lacking even a rotted stump to hint at the forest of old growth spruce that had once covered the valley.

As soon as Laeral cleared the shelter of the hanging vale, she turned and streaked for the Vine Vale as fast as she could fly. The cavalry came behind her, fanning out across the slopes in a great blanket of flapping black wings. Mistaking the Shadovar and their mounts for a legion of some new, hell-spawned horrors come to aid the phaerimm, the elite companies of Evereska raised their voices and weapons and started to press forward.

Khelben raised his arms and staff and called out something in a thunderous voice that brought the Evereskan companies up short, but the damage was done. First one, then a dozen, then half the phaerimm at the Meadow Wall drifted away from the mythal and swung their toothy jaws toward the descending Shadovar. Laeral reached the highest terrace of the Vine Vale.

A scintillating wall of colors rose in front of her. Foolish phaerimm—still didn't know who they were dealing with. Laeral dispelled it with a gesture, then did the same to the curtain of flame that appeared next. By then, the Shadovar were sweeping past to both sides, spraying dark bolts into the enemy. The valley ahead became a storm of shadow magic and black flapping wings. Laeral saw a dozen thornbacks drop out from beneath the tempest and disintegrate into long mounds of ash. An instant later, she was in among them, flashing past scaly, wormlike bodies and deflecting barbed tails with her quarterstaff.

Climb! Lamorak's voice came to Laeral as a bare, faint whisper inside her head. *Cast the shadow zone!*

Laeral and the Shadovar ascended high into the sky. The phaerimm started after them, but their floating magic was no match for the swift-climbing wings of the veserabs. Even Laeral had to extend a hand and allow herself to be drawn along by a passing shadow lord. Blasts of silver lightning and golden magic chased the riders skyward, filling the air with black blossoms of blood, wing, and shadow armor.

Clariburnus, Lamorak, and several powerful Shadovar spread out over the Vine Vale, then released the reins of their mounts and began to drop wads of shadowsilk. They spread their hands palm downward and called out something in ancient Netherese she could not quite catch. The wads flattened into translucent disks of darkness and fell to the valley floor, forcing the phaerimm and beholders down beneath them. As the first creatures touched ground, they wailed in pain and crumbled to ash.

Perhaps two dozen thornbacks and twice that many beholders perished before the disintegration spell was nullified. The survivors writhed about under the disks for a moment, then finally broke the surface of the shadow like fish rising from a pond. The Shadovar were already diving on them, peppering them with shadow bolts as they emerged from the darkness, their mounts spraying them with streams of noxious black mist. Laeral released her escort to join the assault and curved back toward the Meadow Wall, concentrating her own attacks on the beholders. Unlike the Shadow Weave spells of her allies, the phaerimm were less likely to be injured by anything she hurled at them than they were to absorb it and heal themselves. Of course, a blast of her silver fire was sure to slay even the mightiest phaerimm, but she could use that only once an hour, and so it seemed wisest to hold that particular attack in reserve.

A flash of silver light lit the vale behind Laeral. Her entire body erupted into fiery nettling as a bolt of lightning caught her in the flank and sent her tumbling through the air head over heels. She bounced off the mythal and quickly brought herself back under control, then turned to find a pair of cinder clouds settling to ground where the attack had blasted through two Shadovar warriors before exhausting itself on her.

About twenty yards away floated the phaerimm that had hurled the lightning, its toothy mouth turned in her direction and hanging agape. The bolt had been a powerful one. By all rights, it should have torn through her and continued on to another five or six targets, but Laeral was one of the Chosen. She could use the Weave to protect herself from many forms of magical attack, and this was one of the most obvious ones.

Laeral raised her hands and was about to blast her attacker with silver fire when a pair of Shadovar warriors swooped down on it from behind, their veserabs engulfing it in a cloud of noxious black fume that made Laeral's eyes sting even at a distance.

Guiding their mounts with their knees, they poured shadow bolts into it with one hand and raised their black swords with the other, hacking it into three pieces as they flashed past. Laeral waved her thanks and praying that Waterdeep's hippogriff riders never found themselves taking the sky against such a deadly air cavalry, she turned back to the mission she had assigned herself.

Not far ahead, a pair of beholders were using their antimagic beams to cover each other as they retreated from the Meadow Wall and laced the sky above with disintegration rays. Laeral cast a quick invisibility spell on herself and dropped to a few inches above the ground, then came up beneath the creatures, pouring golden streams of magic into them. Both beholders erupted into crimson starbursts, coating her head to toe in foul-smelling gore.

Laeral only hoped that Pluefan Trueshot still allowed humans into the Hall of the High Hunt. She had not seen Khelben in nearly four months, and she could see that she would need a long dip in the Singing Spring before their reunion could be a proper one.

Khelben's first glimpse of Laeral in the battle came when she emerged from the starburst of viscera and entrails that, until a few moments earlier, had been two beholders holding Keya Nihmedu's company of the Long Watch at bay. Even smeared in crimson, she was a sight for weary eyes—and not only because she had broken the siege of Evereska. Never had he spent four months as long as the last four, when he had not known when he would see his beloved Laeral—or even whether he would survive to do so. The Chosen did die, and—as he had so nearly learned at the Rocnest—the job of killing them required far fewer than two hundred phaerimm.

Khelben watched Laeral vanish back into the magic storm, then stood staring into the flashing bolts and scintillating sprays for a few minutes longer. Though the sheets of fire and swirling clouds of veserab breath made it impossible to catch more than glimpses of the action, the battle roar was as ferocious as ever, and the number of Shadovar wheeling up into sight was steadily diminishing. The phaerimm were standing their ground, no doubt because they understood what was at stake in this battle as well as Khelben did.

"Lord Duirsar, the time has come to commit Evereska's army," he said, speaking to the Hill Elders as much as he was to Duirsar. "We must break the siege now, while the phaerimm are still reeling."

"What remains to us is hardly an army," Kiinyon objected, "and even less so, after we followed your advice the last time."

"The attack cost more than I had anticipated, but it was also a crucial diversion." Khelben pointed at the Shadovar swirling above the vale, then started toward the Meadow Wall. "Now, with the Shadovar and the rest of the North's forces operating inside the Sharaedim, this is the phaerimm's last chance to breach the mythal. If we can make them withdraw now, we can break the siege and hunt them down at our will."

Unconvinced, Kiinyon grabbed Khelben's arm and tried to hold him back. "If we fail—"

"If we fail, we lose everything," Lord Duirsar interrupted. "We have been failing for the last four months, it's time to take a chance." He nodded to Khelben. "Call the charge."

Khelben used a spell to carry his voice to every corner of the vale. "Ready the charge! Long Watch, stand down!"

At the Meadow Wall, the young elves of the Long Watch began to disengage and fall back, clustering around trees, granite monoliths, and deep ravines where they would not hinder the charge. The process took several long minutes, for they were as inexperienced as they were exhausted, with casualties that would have reduced even the most stalwart company of veterans to a disorganized horde. At Khelben's side, however, Keya Nihmedu was cinching her chin strap and checking her armor. He turned a disapproving eye on her and was rewarded with a glare that could have cracked stone.

"If you say one word about my condition—"

Khelben raised his hands. "Wouldn't dream of it," he lied.

In contrast to Dexon, who was hanging at her heels with a dazed look in his eyes, she seemed to be taking the news of her condition in stride. Khelben removed the magic bracers on his wrists and tossed them to her.

"I want you to wear these for me—and stay close," Khelben said. "I may need them."

"Of course." Keya's expression changed to dutiful, and she slipped the bracers onto her biceps. "What are they?"

"When the time comes," Khelben said. He raised his staff and waved it toward the Vine Vale. "To battle!"

Unlike every human charge he had ever led, this one started in near silence and seemed to grow quieter. There was no yelling, no banging of arms or clanging of armor, only the soft patter of thousands of graceful feet—and the much louder sound of the Vaasan boots pounding along behind.

They came to the Meadow Wall, and Khelben cast a spell of flying. He sprang into the air on the run, sweeping his black staff across a line of beholders floating out of the haze, their writhing eyestalks spraying all manner of rays and beams at the first rank of charging elves. Khelben held his staff across his body and caught half a dozen rays directed at him, then spread the fingers of his free hand and sent a stream of golden bolts pouring back at his attackers. Three of the eye tyrants sank to the ground with clusters of smoking holes drilled clear through their spherical bodies, but one of the creatures managed to sweep its antimagic beam up in time to block Khelben's counterattack.

A tumbling darksword split this one down the center, then the Company of the Cold Hand was streaming past into the Vine Vale, leaping the bodies of deflated beholders, wounded veserabs, and groaning Shadovar . . . even a few hacked and mutilated phaerimm.

Khelben sensed his bracers drifting off to the left and turned to see Keya Nihmedu leading Dexon and the other two Vaasans through the remains of the vineyard gate. Cursing her impetuousness, he circled around to meet her from the other direction—and found himself somersaulting backward through the air as a flurry of golden magic bolts caught him in the chest.

Sting though they might, the attacks harmed him no more than had the lightning bolt that had sent Laeral tumbling. He righted himself and returned more cautiously, weaving and bobbing, coming in fast and low, staff at the ready and silver fire crackling on his fingertips. He found Keya and the Vaasans battling a pair of phaerimm, the elf dodging and somersaulting as black death rays and tongues of fire erupted all around her. Dexon barely stood on a withered, smoking leg, Burlen had one arm hanging limp at his side, and Kuhl was still attempting to sneak up behind the nearest creature for a killing blow.

Khelben loosed a bolt of silver fire into the nearest phaerimm. That was all it took. As the first crumbled to cinders, the second creature attempted to teleport away—attempted, because Kuhl was already leaping on it from behind, driving his sword down into its mouth. The Vaasan landed face first on the ground, his sword coated in foul-smelling gore.

Khelben circled the vineyard once to make certain there were no more unseen threats, then dropped to the ground beside Keya, who was examining Dexon's mangled leg and assuring him—or perhaps herself—that Pluefan Trueshot and Hanali's priestesses were perfectly capable of restoring the limb. Dexon's face was pained, but he seemed more concerned about the possibility of another attack than his gruesome injury.

"I told you to stay *close*, young lady," Khelben said.

As he spoke, he noted that the battle roar had all but vanished. Shadovar veserab riders were flying toward the edges of the valley, swarming around the tentacled orbs of fleeing beholders—the phaerimm had abandoned their mind-slaves and teleported away.

Looking back to Keya, Khelben gestured at the bracers. "What if I had needed those?"

"If you had *needed* them, you wouldn't have given them to me." Keya pulled the bracers off and thrust them into his hands, then, slipping a supportive arm around Dexon's waist, stretched up to kiss Khelben on the lips. "But thank you."

"Y-you're welcome," Khelben stammered. He felt himself blushing and smiled to cover it. "Very welcome, my dear."

Keya's eyes shifted past his shoulder and suddenly widened in surprise, as did Dexon's, and Khelben heard a familiar "ahem" behind him. He turned to find Laeral standing there, tapping the tip of a smoking wand against her crimson-streaked armor.

She cocked her brow, then shifted her gaze to Keya. "Tell me, young lady—what does a girl need to kill to get a kiss around here?"

CHAPTER TWELVE

21 Mirtul, the Year of Wild Magic

Vala hung motionless in the ceiling spider webs, watching in silence as Corineus spun around the sanctum below, slashing eyestalks from beholder heads and cratering illithid chests with bolts of golden magic, somersaulting under bugbears and diving over kobolds. All the while, he somehow kept himself between his enemies and the four spellbooks resting on a dusty oak table in the corner, amidst a pile of crowns, scepters, rings, bracers, and other magic relics recovered from the lairs of the phaerimm they had slain so far. The monster bodies were beginning to pile up, slowing the baelnorn's bladedance to the point that he began to take hits. It hardly mattered. Steel weapons only bounced off his white flesh, and he absorbed disintegration rays and mind blasts the way leaves drank sunlight. Even antimagic beams had no effect. The beholders casting them never lived long enough for their blade-wielding comrades to take advantage.

Finally, there were just too many bodies for Corineus to continue his bladedance. He stumbled spinning in for a kill, and two kobolds bounced across the carnage into the corner, each grabbing for one of the spellbooks on the desk. Though they were no more than twelve feet below Vala, close enough that she could smell their musky odor even over the charnel stench that filled the room, she continued to hang under the ceiling, her arms and legs aching from the strain of holding herself in such an unaccustomed position. This time, Corineus had told her to be a spider, to let the prey twist itself into their web before striking.

As Corineus struggled to regain his balance, a pair of bugbears leaped onto his back and bowled him over. He started to throw them off, and more started to squeeze through the doors one after the other, adding their weight to the heap. The pile continued to rise, but more slowly, then finally sank back toward the floor. The bael-norn's muffled voice called out an incantation, and a brilliant spark flashed somewhere under the tangle of hairy limbs.

A sheet of silver lightning fanned across the room, momentarily blinding Vala. There was a single communal death-growl, then the room fell silent. The reek of scorched flesh pervaded her nostrils, and her chill-numbed flesh began to prickle as the baelnorn's cold aura suddenly vanished. She blinked the dazzle from her eyes to find the sanctum piled three layers deep in scorched body halves, many pouring smoke into the air and some still twitching.

Corineus was encased in a shimmering sphere of force, his withered face twisted into a mask of agony as he struggled to his feet. He was moving only slowly and with great effort, with his eyes bulging out of their sockets and lines of black blood running from his ears and nostrils. The sphere was contracting visibly, crushing the baelnorn in its inexorable grasp.

Vala remained where she was, all too conscious of the shiny red diamonds starting to peer at her from the corners of the web-strewn ceiling. The giant spiders had vanished through their hidden bolt holes the instant Corineus entered the sanctum, but with his chill aura gone, they were eager to return and reclaim their webs. Her goosebumps rose again, though this time they had nothing to do with being cold.

Finally, the object of her ambush appeared, the largest phaerimm yet, with amber scales and a tail-barb as long as the blade of her darksword. The creature paused a moment in the door, then floated over to the sphere in which Corineus was imprisoned and stopped. The baelnorn turned his head in its direction. His eyes were bulging so badly they were about to pop their sockets, and the black stuff running from his nose and ears had fanned across his entire lower face. The undead elf began to fumble through the gestures of an enchantment.

So clumsy were his efforts that even Vala knew the spell would never go off. The phaerimm simply floated there before him, and eventually Corineus stopped trying. The pair simply stood beside each other and did nothing. Vala was confused for the first several moments, until the baelnorn's gaze shifted to the captured spellbooks, and she recalled that phaerimm communicated with their captives telepathically. The thing was interrogating him, no doubt trying to learn how he had been slipping past the wards designed to keep him at bay.

Vala prayed to Tempus to give Corineus strength—then remembered herself and asked Corellon Larethian, the elf god of war, for the same thing. They had taken care to leave behind no trace of her presence in the lairs they had broken so far. If the baelnorn betrayed the secret, she would not survive long enough to realize their plan had failed.

A tremble in the web drew Vala's gaze to the opposite corner of the ceiling, where a wolf-sized spider was creeping out of its bolt hole. She fixed it in place with a glare but did not dare do more. Corineus had warned her not to move until the instant she attacked. Her only camouflage was spidersilk and darkness; any magic that the baelnorn might have used to hide her would have drawn the phaerimm's attention as surely as a flame.

Emboldened by the first, a second spider crept out onto the web, this one only half a dozen yards from Vala's feet. She glanced toward the phaerimm, trying to gauge her chances of making the leap. Not good. The thornback was over by the main door with the baelnorn; she was in the opposite corner, above the spellbooks. Corineus had said the thing would not be able to resist such a treasure. So far, it seemed to be withstanding the temptation all too well.

A third spider crept onto the web, this one in the corner above Corineus, who was enduring long past the point when a living elf would have been crushed. His eyes were hanging out of their sockets, flattened against his cheeks, while his arms and legs were bent at impossible angles and pressed back against his body. Vala wanted to yell at the baelnorn to give up and let himself be destroyed already, but she didn't even know if that was possible. Besides, he had to make it look real. If he gave up too easily, his tormentor would grow suspicious—and few things were more dangerous than a suspicious phaerimm.

The web began to tremble violently as the first spider darted for Vala, fangs dripping venom and pedipalps reaching out. The second made a dash for her legs but stopped to face the other one when it changed its direction.

Vala started to throw her sword in desperation—then had a better idea and looked back to the spiders. She ran her blade through the spider web, cutting a huge crescent around the bottom of her feet. The web came free with a series of brittle pops, and she swung down from the ceiling, descending toward her target in a swift-moving arc. The phaerimm swung its huge mouth toward her.

Vala leaped straight at it, whipping the darksword around for a vicious, two-handed downstrike. She heard scales cracking and felt the blade splitting flesh. A pair of phaerimm hands caught her by the throat and began to squeeze. She turned the blade and began to drag it through the thing's body. The barbed tail arced up, clanked off her backplate, and drew back to try again.

Vala knocked a phaerimm hand from her throat—only to have it replaced by two more. Her vision began to fade, and her right leg erupted into fiery pain as the tail barb penetrated her armor and began to pump its poison into her body. She pried her darksword free, swinging the blade up through two feet of tendon and flesh. Her vision darkened to something darker than black, and Vala's stomach suddenly rose into her chest. A bitter chill stung her flesh, and there was an endless eternity of falling. She grew queasy and weak and heard nothing but the pounding of her own heart, slowing with each beat, then even that was gone.

Vala's first hint that she was not . . . well, *gone*, was the reek of battle gore. The second was pain. Something was lodged in her leg, holding up her whole body by the big thigh muscle and flicking across the bone. She thought for a moment that she was dead and in the Nine Hells with no memory of how she had come to be there. Then she saw a huge, amber-colored phaerimm lying flayed and motionless on the floor above her—no, *below*—and recalled the fight in the sanctum.

Vala was not in the sanctum. Instead of the four captured spellbooks and great heap of recovered magic she and Corineus had piled in the corner, there was a single open book floating in a green spell field and several shelves of neatly arranged relics. There were the mind-slaves' sleeping palettes lined up along the wall, and the ward symbol above the door that kept her baelnorn ally at bay. Most of all, there was the thornback itself, lying motionless and gutted on the floor beneath her, its long tail preventing her from floating to the ceiling by the painful barb lodged in her thigh.

After Vala's attack, the thing had attempted to teleport to the safety of its lair and arrived dead. At least she thought it was dead. She brought her arm down to cut herself free—or, rather, tried to bring her arm down. It didn't move in response to her will, nor did her legs or neck when she tested them—or even her tongue, when she attempted to curse.

Eventually, Vala knew, the crushing sphere would destroy Corineus's body and free his spirit to seek one of the spare bodies he had hidden in the Irithlium—but that was not going to help her. Until she broke the warding symbol above the door, the baelnorn could not enter the lair. There was nothing to do but hang there in pain until the poison wore off.

❂ ❂ ❂ ❂ ❂

The Shadovar were not conspicuous in Arabel—or rather in what had been Arabel before the ghazneths and their orc hordes reduced it to rubble—but they were there. On the dark side of a broken tower, a pair of swarthy masons were using a shadow saw to size blocks. Through the window of a bakery, a potter with gleaming amethyst eyes was fashioning an oven from darkclay. In an alley, a tall and gaunt carpenter was installing an ebon-wood door.

None of them more than glanced in Galaeron's direction as he passed by with Aris and Ruha, but that meant nothing. With an elf, a Bedine witch, and a stone giant traveling together, the Shadovar had to know who they were looking at.

Aris stooped down to within three feet of Galaeron and Ruha. Though the giant had spent much of the past two days sipping Storm Silverhand's healing potions, he remained unsteady enough that Galaeron would rather he wasn't leaning over them.

"This is going to be harder than we thought," Aris said quietly. "I keep seeing Shadovar."

Galaeron nodded. "Sent to watch for us."

"So many?" Ruha shook her head. "The Shadovar have easier ways of watching than rebuilding a whole city."

"What do you know?" Galaeron snapped. "With the information I have about the phaerimm, the Shadovar would do anything to get me back."

"I am sure they would," Ruha said patiently.

She pointed at the base of a nearly rebuilt tower, where the foundation had been patched with the same dark amalgam that served as mortar in Shade Enclave.

"They have been here for some time," the witch

continued. "Their purpose here is to make an ally of Cormyr, not find us."

Galaeron considered first the foundation, then the rest of the broad street, and had to nod. While the city still looked like a rubble heap at first glance, the outlines of its former shape were beginning to re-emerge. Many of the larger buildings were already rising to the second or third story, and most showed signs of Shadovar work—if not in the mortar then in the precision fit of the stones and the dark wood of the balconies, or even in the depth of the shadowed window alcoves.

"You're right, of course," Galaeron said, transferring his ire from Ruha to Storm Silverhand. "Even the Shadovar couldn't do this overnight—and Storm had to know it when she teleported us here."

"Most likely," Ruha admitted.

"So why send *us*?" Galaeron demanded. "It would have made more sense to teleport us to Waterdeep and come to Cormyr herself."

"Perhaps you have answered your own question," Ruha said. "That is what the Shadovar would expect. Or matters in Waterdeep may be more complicated than we know. I am given to understand that Storm's sister Laeral is friendly with the Shadovar."

"Say no more," Galaeron grumbled.

Storm's reaction to him in Anauroch had convinced him how unlikely he was to persuade any of the Chosen of anything. For loosing the phaerimm on the world, they might have forgiven him eventually, but for bringing the Shadovar into the world after them, and getting Elminster banished to the Nine Hells—never.

"We're better off taking our chances with the Cormyreans," Galaeron admitted.

"Then you accept that Storm did the wisest thing?" Ruha asked.

Galaeron shrugged. "How can I know? But she has to have a better hope in Waterdeep than I do. Lord Piergeiron certainly isn't going to take my word over Laeral's."

An approving twinkle came to Ruha's eyes. "You may survive this yet. I think you are finally learning to control your shadow self." She glanced over at a pair of Shadovar stone cutters who had stopped work to watch them pass, then added, "But perhaps we would draw less attention if we disguised ourselves and found a safe place to leave Aris."

"At this point, speed is better than stealth," Galaeron said. "The sooner we present ourselves at the palace, the more difficult it will be for Telamont Tanthul to have a troop of his lords spirit us back to the enclave."

"Well said," Aris agreed, glancing out over the half-built city. "Besides, there isn't a place to hide a stone giant within twenty miles of here."

It was no exaggeration. Though Storm had teleported them into a field only a quarter mile outside Arabel, the walk to the gates had been plenty long enough to bear witness to the devastation wrought by the dragon Nalavarauthatoryl and her ghazneths and orcs. Even a year after the terrible war, nothing grew in the once-lush fields except a few black thistles and carpets of foul-smelling moss, while the great forest that had once flourished to the south and west of the city was still struggling to put the first spindly leaves in its canopy.

Despite their presence in Arabel, the Shadovar were not helping matters. With the melting of the High Ice carrying so much rain and cool air west toward Waterdeep, a steady wind had been blowing northward through Cormyr, carrying with it the heat of the southlands and the mugginess of the Dragonmere.

Had the zephyr but dropped a fraction of its moisture

on its way over the kingdom, the change of weather might actually have helped matters. Instead, the air remained miserly with its water until it crashed into the northern Stormhorns and abruptly cooled. As a result, the kingdom was enduring its worst, hottest, most miserable drought in a thousand years, while at the same time its two largest rivers, the Starwater and the Wyvernflow, were flooding their banks and washing away whole villages.

Galaeron was far from certain that he would be able to secure an audience with the rulers of the kingdom, much less persuade the Cormyreans that Shade Enclave was causing their problems. But, as Storm had said, they would be eager for an explanation and inclined to listen. All he had to do was get the shadow blanket into Vangerdahast's hands. After that, the royal wizard would convince himself.

They reached the city palace, which—to Galaeron's great disappointment—had been rebuilt from the second story in the same pearly stone as Villa Dusari. Atop the highest spires, dozens of Shadovar polishers were crawling over the turrets like spiders, putting the final touches on the magnificent building. Fortunately, the guards at the door still wore Cormyr's purple dragon, or Galaeron would have concluded that the Shadovar had claimed Arabel for their own and left immediately.

As the trio ascended the steps, two of the guards crossed their halberds in front of the entrance. The sergeant—no older than his comrades, but with a badly scarred face and an eye patch—stepped forward to address them.

"You have business with Lord Myrmeen?" he demanded.

Galaeron shook his head. "Our business is with Princess Alusair and her wizard," he said. "It concerns the abnormal weather Cormyr has been suffering of late."

The sergeant seemed not to hear the last part of his explanation. "This is the palace of Myrmeen Lhal," he said. "The Steel Regent keeps her home—and her wizard—in Suzail."

Alarm bells started clanging inside Galaeron's mind. "You are saying Arabel is no longer part of Cormyr?"

The sergeant's one eye narrowed. "What I'm saying is that unless you have business with Myrmeen Lhal—"

"We have it on good authority that Princess Alusair and Vangerdahast are inside," Ruha interrupted. She removed the Harper's pin from inside her robe and pressed it into his hand. "Please deliver that to her with the message that our lives may depend on a swift audience—and perhaps the fate of Cormyr's growing season, as well."

"Harpers?" The sergeant barely glanced at the pin. "Why didn't you say so?"

He turned and vanished into the palace, then returned a moment later with a gangly, horse-faced man in a scarlet cape and purple sash of office. The newcomer returned Ruha's pin and waved them into the palace's grandiose reception hall—so large that, after crawling through the entrance, even Aris could stand upright.

"Welcome. I am Dauneth Marliir, Her Majesty's High Warden," the man said. "I'm sorry for the delay, but we have learned to be cautious with information about Her Majesty."

"We understand," Ruha said, returning the pin to its place. "I am Ruha—"

"Yes, I know." Dauneth flashed a big smile.

Galaeron ignored him and looked down the long arcade of pillars, where he was disappointed to see more Shadovar than humans polishing and buffing.

Dauneth continued to speak with Ruha. "There are not many Bedine witches in the Harpers."

"Only one, I am certain," Ruha laughed. She waved a hand at Galaeron. "This is Galaeron Nihmedu."

Dauneth's brow rose in shock, but he managed to recover himself. "Well met, Galaeron. I have heard of your bravery." He extended a hand and clasped Galaeron's wrist in the human fashion. "Prince Rivalen tells me that his father has been most concerned since your disappearance."

"Yes, I'm sure he has," Galaeron replied, surprised by the coldness in his own voice. "He has good reason to be."

Dauneth's brow rose, prompting Ruha to say, "It is related to our visit." She half turned to wave at Aris. "And this is—"

"Aris of a Thousand Faces," Dauneth finished. He paused and bowed deeply. "When the palace is finished, Myrmeen intends to display one of your pieces, 'The Descent of the Shadow Army,' here in the lobby."

"She does?" The giant's jaw dropped. "How did she come by it?"

Dauneth smiled enthusiastically. "A gift from Prince Rivalen, of course."

The High Warden led the way down a stately side corridor toward a pair of well-guarded double doors, and Galaeron's heart fell. He could see already that Rivalen and his gifts had won the hearts of the Cormyreans, that he had no chance whatsoever of winning Alusair's confidence. Soon, he would either be dead or on his way back to the enclave, and after seeing how close his shadow self had come to getting Aris killed, he knew which he was going to choose. He wanted nothing more than to use his shadow magic to do a sending to Vala and apologize for how he had parted, to let her know that, in the end at least, he had come to his senses and died thinking of her.

And he would have liked to apologize to Takari Moonsnow, as well, for refusing what she had offered. He had always known on some deep level that they were spirit mates and, because of that, assumed she would always be with him, but when he had chosen to help Vala instead of her in the final battle against Wulgreth, he had wounded her more deeply than any lich could have. He knew there could be nothing between them but pain. For the rest of her life, whenever she thought of him, it would fill her with feelings of betrayal and loss.

How could he have been such a coward? Perhaps there had always been a shadow on his heart because of his fear of following it—because in trying to avoid his own pain, he had inflicted it on others. Certainly his father had never turned his back on his feelings. He had loved Morgwais completely from the moment he had met her, all the years they had lived together in Evereska and all the years she had lived apart in the High Forest, and if her absence had caused him anguish, their love had given him the strength to endure it without bitterness or regret.

They reached the double doors and were admitted at once. Aris had to hunch his shoulders to squeeze through this entrance, but inside lay the palace's formal audience hall, with an arched ceiling high enough that the giant could still stand upright by walking down the center of the aisle.

In a raised throne at the far end sat a striking woman with oak-brown eyes and amber hair, one arm resting on her knee as she conversed with a huge Shadovar beside her. Even had Galaeron not glimpsed the man's golden eyes and ceremonial fangs, he would have recognized Prince Rivalen by his immense shoulders and narrow waist. Next to the throne and a little behind it stood an elderly, tired-looking man in a voluminous robe and long white beard who could only be Cormyr's royal wizard, Vangerdahast. Adjacent to him stood the final member of the little group, a statuesque woman with dark hair and eyes as blue as a mountain lake.

Dauneth stopped opposite the throne and presented

Galaeron and his companions, introducing the woman on the throne as the Steel Regent of Cormyr, Princess Alusair Obarskyr, and the one on the floor as Myrmeen Lhal, the King's Lord of Arabel.

When she was introduced to Aris, Myrmeen's eyes sparkled, showing flecks of gold almost like an elf's.

"I'm a great enthusiast of your work, Master Aris." She gestured to Rivalen, who was studying the group with a forced smile and said, "The prince has gifted me with 'The Descent of the Shadow Army'. I intend to display it prominently in the lobby."

"It will be an honor," Aris said with a certain practiced ease. "I only hope it will do your palace justice."

"It will *make* my palace," she said. "The way you impart a sense of the army's whirling descent while using the veserab wings to support the enclave is pure magic. But I find a hint of menace in how the riders fan out at the bottom, as though you found the coming of the Shadovar just a little frightening."

"You are very perceptive, Milady." Aris glanced in Rivalen's direction, then added, "Were I to do the same sculpture today, there would be more than a hint of menace."

"Really?" Myrmeen furrowed her brow. "I was under the impression you were quite content in the city of Shade."

"So were we," Rivalen said smoothly, "but we understand how temperamental artists can be. If Aris was unhappy, we would have been glad to transport him to any place he wished. There was no need for him to brave the desert with these thieves."

"We are not the thieves in this room," Galaeron began. "The Shadovar—"

"Myrmeen did not ask you to speak," Princess Alusair said, raising a hand to cut him off. She moved to the edge of her seat and addressed Rivalen. "So what'd they steal?"

Vangerdahast laid a restraining hand on her shoulder. "Princess, this matter really has nothing to do with Cormyr."

Alusair scowled. "They're in Cormyr now, Vangey." Her glance strayed in Myrmeen Lhal's direction ever so briefly, then looked back to Prince Rivalen. "At least I think it's still Cormyr."

"Shade would not recognize any other claims to Arabel," Rivalen said, not rising to the bait, "and we would certainly be very grateful if you would return these thieves to Shade Enclave for judgment by the Most High."

Alusair continued to watch the prince, and Galaeron began to see that there was more going on in Arabel than the rebuilding of the city—or at least the Steel Regent feared there was.

"Must I ask again, Prince?" Alusair said. "What did they steal?"

Rivalen hesitated just a moment, then gestured at the shadow blanket draped over Aris's shoulder. "The umbral mantle, to begin with. Also a flying disk and a veserab . . . that I know of."

Alusair looked to Ruha. "Is that true?"

"In its essence," she said. "I was not—"

"In its fact," Rivalen insisted. "You were all part of the plan from the start. Malik confessed all."

"Malik?" Alusair asked. "Would this be Malik el Sami yn Nasser, the Seraph of Lies?"

Rivalen nodded. "A despicable little man, but it is well known that Mystra's curse prevents him from lying." He looked in Galaeron's direction and sneered. "He was with Galaeron when we rescued his party from the Dire Wood. We should have taken that as a suggestion of what to expect when we realized who he was."

"Indeed," Vangerdahast said. "I am surprised you didn't. Malik was captured in the escape?"

"It was not an escape," Rivalen clarified. "Until they began stealing, they were free to leave at any time."

"Princess Alusair," Ruha said, "if you will permit me—"

"I will not," Alusair said, raising a hand to silence the witch. "The prince is speaking."

Ruha's face fell, and Galaeron could tell that she was feeling as hopeless as he had earlier. He caught her eye and smiled in encouragement. It was impossible to see how she responded beneath her veil.

When Rivalen did not continue, Alusair asked, "Do you have anything to add, Prince? Perhaps they murdered someone in the escape?"

Rivalen considered this a moment, then shook his head, "There were some injuries—but only to Malik, and he survived. Their only crime in Shade Enclave was theft. The Most High will be grateful when they are returned to answer for it."

"Of course," Alusair said. She turned to Ruha. "Have you anything to say before I return you to the prince?"

"Only that it is a mistake to do so in such haste." Ruha looked to Myrmeen Lhal for support—then let her shoulders slump as the lady lord looked away. Turning her gaze back to Alusair, she began, "On my word as a Harper—"

"If I may," Galaeron interrupted. Even in Evereska, he had seen enough of politics to realize that truth was seldom the most valued currency in such discussions. Addressing himself directly to Alusair, he said, "The gifts of the Shadovar come with a price—"

"Every gift comes with a price," Alusair shot back. "If you mean to waste the crown's time on such tripe, I'll have your tongue before I return you to Rivalen."

Galaeron's confidence of a moment earlier vanished. He had read the situation correctly—he was more sure of that than ever—but he had failed to anticipate just how astute the Steel Regent really was and how quick to anger when she thought she was being manipulated. He swallowed and tried again.

"The price of this gift is higher than you think." Galaeron sneaked a glance at Rivalen, who caught him looking and made a derisive motion for him to continue. He did. "The droughts and floods Cormyr has been suffering, they are the Shadovar's doing."

Myrmeen and Dauneth sighed audibly, and Vangerdahast looked as though he were struggling not to laugh.

Alusair turned her gaze to Prince Rivalen. "Well, Prince, what say you to that?"

Rivalen rolled his golden eyes. "I wouldn't think it necessary to say anything."

"It is true," Galaeron insisted. "Surely, you've heard about the troubles on the Sword Coast? The Shadovar are melting the High Ice. It's affecting the weather all across Faerûn."

"Melting the High Ice?" Vangerdahast scoffed. "The fire spell that powerful hasn't been written, even in Azuth's spellbook."

"They're not using a spell—they're using that." Galaeron pointed to the shadow blanket hanging over Aris's shoulder. "They're spreading them over—"

"Princess Alusair," Rivalen interrupted. "It pains me to see this thief wasting the crown's time with this nonsense. If you will allow me to summon a few of my lords—"

"Only a minute longer," Alusair said, raising her brow at the note of concern that had crept into the prince's voice. "Cormyr's law requires that the accused be allowed to speak before I can turn them over to you."

The princess nodded Vangerdahast toward the blanket, and Galaeron breathed a quiet sigh of relief as the old man shuffled out from behind her. Aris spread the blanket obligingly and draped it down where Vangerdahast could reach it, turning the darkest side toward the window so that it would absorb the sun's heat. The wizard rubbed his hand first over one side of the surface, then the other, and the way his eyes widened made clear that he had noted how efficiently it trapped heat.

Galaeron glanced over at Rivalen and found the prince's golden eyes locked on his face. In that moment, he knew that he had succeeded—and the prince knew it, too. Were it not for the knowledge Melegaunt had secreted inside his head, Galaeron had no doubt that Rivalen would have killed him on the spot and fled into the shadows. As it was, however, the prince had no choice but to play the game a little longer.

After a time, Vangerdahast removed a wand from inside his robe and waved it over the shadow blanket, then put it back and repeated the process three more times. Finally, he stepped away, folded his hands behind his back, and said nothing.

A full minute passed before Alusair growled, "Well?"

Vangerdahast jumped as though she had startled him out of a dream, looking around with an alarming expression of confusion on his face.

"Well, what?" the royal magician asked.

Alusair nodded at the shadow blanket. "The umbral mantle," she prompted. "Can it do what the elf claims?"

Vangerdahast turned and studied the blanket as though seeing it for the first time, then shrugged and turned away. "How should I know? I don't understand shadow magic."

The only thing that fell farther than Alusair's expression was Galaeron's heart.

"What's there to understand?" Galaeron cried, stepping toward the throne. "Just put your hand—"

"That's far enough, elf," Dauneth Marliir said, catching Galaeron by the arm and pressing a dagger tip to his ribs. "You've had your say."

Rivalen flashed his fangs in Galaeron's direction, then turned to Alusair. "If they have had their say, Princess, I will summon my lords."

Alusair lifted her hand in consent—until Vangerdahast gave a short, "Ahem."

Finally unable to contain himself, Rivalen spun toward the wizard. "What now?"

Vangerdahast gave him a synthetic smile. "Nothing to upset yourself over—a mere formality, really," he said, turning to Alusair, "but the law requires due regard for anyone seeking judgment before the crown."

Alusair frowned in confusion. "And?"

"This is not due regard," the wizard explained. "For that, you must consider the matter overnight."

"She must?" Myrmeen asked, puzzled. "Where does it say that?"

"In the *Rule of Law*, of course," Alusair said, somehow at once smiling at Vangerdahast and frowning at Myrmeen. "Do you mean to tell me one of the King's Lords doesn't know her Iltharl?"

Myrmeen's face fell. "No, er, of course not," she stammered, frowning. "I, uh, just hadn't considered that the, uh, passage applied to this situation."

"Well, it does," Alusair said. She turned to Rivalen. "I'm sorry, Prince Rivalen, but you'll have to wait until morning. You understand—laws can be such pesky things."

"Yes, can't they?" Rivalen smiled thinly and inclined his head. "I trust you have secure facilities."

"Oh, *very* secure." Alusair looked to her High Warden and said, "Dauneth, see to it that these prisoners are lodged in the citadel—and put them in the deep dungeon. When Prince Rivalen comes for them in the morning, I want them to be there."

CHAPTER THIRTEEN

21 Mirtul, the Year of Wild Magic

Slapping the warding symbol off the wall as she left, Vala ducked out of the tiny lair and scuttled down the ancient sewer in a low crouch. A knot the size of a fist was throbbing atop her thigh, and the wound itself oozed a steady stream of hot fluid. Fortunately, the cause of Vala's injuries had died without depositing its egg. She found the thing in the phaerimm's tail when she cut off the barb to add to her collection. After the levitation magic had finally lapsed, she'd fallen onto the dead creature and had to wait for the paralyzation poison to wear off. If the egg had been implanted, she would still have been lying atop the dead phaerimm with her face buried in its entrails.

As it was, Vala was so feverish that catching up to her quarry was out of the question. It required all of her strength just to limp down the tunnel in such an awkward stoop and avoid splashing her bandage with the cloudy fluid standing stagnant in the bottom. Though the sewer had not been used for its intended purpose in six centuries, the filth that filled it had been spawned of constant death and decay and reeked even more horribly than the offal it had been intended to carry. She came to a **T** in the passage and, ten paces up the right branch, glimpsed a short length of thorny tail disappearing around another corner.

Vala stepped into the mouth of the opposite fork and brushed her shoulder and arm against the filthy wall, leaving a broad drag mark in the mildew, then retreated back to the intersection and pressed her back to the wall. Having predicted the little phaerimm would flee to the right, Corineus was waiting a hundred paces up the tunnel, ready to drive the thing back toward its lair. Vala would have preferred to force the thornback into the baelnorn's ambush, but his aura of cold made it impossible for him to surprise anything in the dungeon.

The crack and rumble of an approaching spell battle heralded the return of the phaerimm. Vala kissed the blade of her darksword and said a prayer for her son in case Tempus should decide to take her in this rank place, then held her weapon ready next to the intersection. A few moments later, a brilliant orange light erupted from the tunnel mouth, blinding Vala and scalding her skin. She turned away, raising her free hand to shield her face as a crackling ball of flame hissed past and vanished down the opposite passage.

Vala opened her eyes and saw only circles of popping orange. The phaerimm could have been three inches from her face preparing to sink its tail barb into her throat, or it could have been lurking ten feet up the passage, waiting to see what its spell flushed out. Guessing the phaerimm would be a little behind its spell, she counted three seconds, brought her sword down, and hit something solid.

A fierce wind gusted through the sewer and died almost instantly. When Vala's sword fell free and touched the floor and she found herself still alive she deduced that she had at least hit the thing and began to slash about the intersection at random, weaving her blade through a blind figure-eight defense and trying to blink the orange spots from her eyes.

"You killed the phaerimm," Corineus said from up the passage. "Are you trying to kill its ghost as well, or do you have no further use for me now that we have destroyed the last phaerimm?"

"It's dead?" Vala stopped weaving but did not return her sword to its scabbard. Phaerimm were tricky creatures, and even if the Shadovar helmet protected her from its mind control, it would be an easy matter for it to use its magic to impersonate the baelnorn. "You're sure?"

"I am sure." An icy hand grabbed hers and guided the darksword back toward its scabbard. "Put that away. I have something I want to give you."

Vala sheathed the weapon, certain of the baelnorn's identity. She had grown so accustomed to his chill aura that she'd scarcely noticed it until he'd taken her hand.

"You'll have to tell me what it is," she said. "I'm afraid my eyes are still a bit dazzled from that fireball."

"It is a treasure from Myth Drannor."

Corineus slipped a ring onto her finger, and she could see him—not the withered baelnorn she had come to know during her trials in the Irithlium, but a tall sun elf with gold-flecked eyes and a long mane of silky red hair.

"When you wear it this way," the elf said, "you will see things as they truly are."

He turned the ring a quarter turn, and Vala's vision returned to normal—which was to say that she couldn't see a thing, since her hand was not on her darksword.

"When you wear it this way, no one will know you are wearing it." He turned it another quarter turn. "And when you wear it this way, no one will see you."

Corineus started to remove his icy hand, but Vala caught it between hers.

"You know I killed the phaerimm for my own reasons," she said. "It's not necessary to gift me."

"I think it is, Vala Thorsdotter." Corineus freed his hands from hers and stepped away. "I have seen a little of the future while we were together."

The chill aura began to fade rapidly. Vala turned the ring and saw the dead phaerimm floating in the water in two pieces, neither as long as her arm. She nudged them aside and peered down the tunnel from which it had come, where Corineus's noble figure was wading into the darkness.

"Thank you, Corineus," she called after him, "and not only for the ring."

Corineus turned his head around on his shoulders and gave her a broad grin that reminded her of Galaeron's joyful smile—back when he had one.

"Thank you, Vala Thorsdotter," he said, "and not only for killing the phaerimm."

☉ ☉ ☉ ☉ ☉

As dungeons went, the one beneath the Citadel at Arabel was kinder than most—certainly kinder than the cramped cells of the Evereskan Tomb Guard, where crypt breakers were forced to kneel with their arms locked in stocks and gags in their mouths. Here, Galaeron and Ruha sat in side by side cages, with Aris chained to a wall in the interrogation chamber outside. There were no rats and only the typical human infestations of fleas and lice. Save for the acrid stench of the impure oil used in the wall lamps, the place didn't even smell that bad.

But it was secure. Aris had been scratching at the mortar around his chain mountings for half the night and done nothing more than bloody his fingertips. Ruha had tried half a dozen spells, only to have the magic sputter away as soon as it left her hands. Galaeron had kicked at the latch of his door until an ominous rumble sounded from above and he looked up to realize that the cell ceiling was a set of interlocked drop-blocks, with the keystone supported by the same jamb he was kicking. Fearful that ill-considered attempts might cost his life, he had given up trying to escape the cell at all.

Galaeron pressed his face to the bars and strained to see if there was anyone in the guard station, which was positioned at the end of the row of cages where it was almost impossible to see from inside a cell. He could see flamelight dancing on the walls, but no shadows that suggested someone upright and moving.

"No one there," Aris hissed, his whisper as loud as wind in trees. "The last check was about an hour ago."

"Confident in their dungeoncraft, aren't these Cormyreans?" Galaeron said.

"They have every reason to be," Ruha said, speaking from the corner of her cell. "I don't hear you kicking any more, and the spell-guard has defeated everything I've tried."

"Then we really don't have any choice, do we?" Galaeron stepped back from the door and, hoping the guards had missed a few strands of shadowsilk when they searched him, began to fish through his cloak pockets. "I can get us out of here."

Aris's eyes grew round and alarmed. "How?"

"Their spell-guard won't stop shadow magic," he said, "and since it didn't occur to Rivalen to erect his own—"

"Galaeron, no," Ruha said. "It is too risky for you to cast another shadow spell."

"What's too risky is waiting here for Rivalen." He found a strand of shadowsilk and began to tie it into a closed loop. "I'll have us out of here with one spell."

"And then what?" Aris demanded. "Wait until we are counting on you again, then let your shadow get us all killed?"

Galaeron stopped tying and looked across the chamber. "I'm sorry about the Saiyaddar, Aris, I truly am. Had I let you drop the shadow blanket, you wouldn't have been so eager to reach water—"

"And you would have had nothing to show Storm," Aris interrupted. "It is not what you did, my friend, but *why*. When your shadow self takes control, you lose sight of what is right and think only of vengeance."

"I'm entitled," Galaeron said, growing irritated with the giant's lecturing. "Telamont was trying to bring out my shadow, and Escanor . . . well, never mind Escanor."

"You were going to say that Escanor stole Vala," Aris said, "but you know that isn't so. You know you drove her away."

"You're right," Galaeron replied, "but I can see that now. I'm in control."

Despite the admission, Galaeron began to knot the shadowsilk again. Aris exchanged concerned gazes with Ruha, and the witch pushed a hand through the bars to grab Galaeron's arm.

"You're not in control now, Galaeron," Ruha said. "Your shadow is trying to tempt you into another mistake."

She slipped her hand down to his and tried, gently, to pluck the shadowsilk from his fingers. He held tight.

"Storm will send help," Ruha said. "I have told her of our troubles."

Galaeron started to demand how she could get a message past the spell-guard but answered his own question when he recalled that the guard was fashioned of Weave magic. Because Storm was one of the Chosen, Ruha merely had to speak her name, and the Weave would carry the next few words directly to her ear—no spells required. What it would *not* do, however, was carry a reply.

"You know she is coming?" Galaeron asked. "You know that for certain?"

Ruha's eyes remained locked with his. "No, but it is wiser to trust in her than to believe you can control your shadow when it is so plainly controlling you. At the moment, I would rather place my life in Malik's hands."

The witch's frank words were enough to remind Galaeron of his remorse after Aris was wounded and to make him see that he was only using their situation as an excuse to cast a spell and feel cool shadow magic rushing through his body. It was an almost physical sensation, like being thirsty and longing for water or being exhausted and yearning for sleep, and it was just as hard to deny. The Shadow Weave was always there, within easy reach, inviting him to reach out and touch it.

Galaeron released the strand of shadowsilk, then watched as Ruha rolled it into a tiny ball and flicked it toward a lamp flame. She missed, but the wad bounced off the wall, then landed in the murk and was lost.

"You know what will happen if Rivalen takes me back to Shade?" Galaeron asked, talking to both Ruha and Aris. "I won't be able to stop Telamont from bringing out my shadow. It would be better to get us out of here and let it happen now, where you two can still do something about it."

"Only a fool would think us capable," Aris said. "Your shadow is still tempting you, Galaeron. If you yield to it— even for a minute—we are lost."

"Trust in Storm," Ruha urged. "I do, and I will die first if we are returned to the enclave."

That much was true, Galaeron knew. Aris's talent would probably buy his life, at least if he could find it in himself to continue sculpting. Galaeron himself would be kept alive and corrupted and might eventually find a way to overcome his shadow, but Ruha had nothing to offer the Shadovar except trouble. The interrogation that followed the trio's return would reveal that she was an agent of the Chosen—if Telamont didn't know it already—and Galaeron didn't even want to contemplate the fate that awaited spies in Shade Enclave.

Galaeron nodded and said, "Very well." He stepped away from the bars, and sat on the stone bench that served as his cot. "If you are willing to trust in Storm to save us, then I ought to be, too."

"But are you?" demanded Aris. "You must promise not to use shadow magic again, even if it means our deaths."

Galaeron shook his head. "I can only promise to try."

"That is no promise at all," Ruha retorted. "Trying is easy. Doing is hard."

Galaeron looked away. He had already broken that promise once, so he knew how difficult it would be to keep—even harder than the last time, perhaps impossible— but Ruha was right. Trying was easy, and doing the easy thing had been leading him deeper into disaster from the beginning. He had breached the Sharn Wall and released the phaerimm when he ordered his patrol to attack with magic bolts instead of swords. He had allowed his shadow to sneak inside him when he ignored

Melegaunt's warning and used more shadow magic than he had the strength to control. He had loosed the Shadovar on Faerûn when he brought their flying city into the world to save Evereska from the phaerimm. He had lost Vala when he had been foolish enough to believe that Telamont Tanthul would teach him to control his shadow self. And he had nearly lost his closest friend in pursuit of an easy vengeance. The time had come to start doing the hard thing.

Galaeron looked across the interrogation chamber and said, "You're right. On my word as a Tomb Guard, I promise never to use shadow magic again."

Aris gave a curt nod. "Good, then you have already defeated the Shadovar."

"The defeat is in the keeping," Ruha said, "but it is a start."

She returned to her own bench, and they fell into silence again. Aris went back to tugging at his chains and scratching at the mortar around the mountings. Ruha and Galaeron tried to think of some way to escape that didn't involve using shadow magic. A little later, two night sentries came in and sat down at the table at the guard station. Constant companions through this night and no doubt many others, they exchanged a few stale words in a half-hearted attempt to stay awake, then fell to snoring within a few moments of each other. Galaeron was not surprised. Boredom was ever the watchman's curse and one that would be especially potent in a dungeon where escape seemed such a remote possibility.

A quarter hour later, the snoring came to a gurgled end. A pair of armored bodies clanged to the floor, and Aris's eyes grew wide. Galaeron pressed himself to the bars and looked toward the guard station. The sentries lay with their feet in view, surrounded by a circle of murk that might have been blood or shadow—without darksight, it was impossible to tell which. Rivalen and half a dozen Shadovar lords were stepping out of the shadows behind them.

Galaeron's throat went dry. The moment had come sooner than expected, but he knew that his temptation would have been the same in the morning—or anytime. His body was fairly aching for him to cast a spell. He felt feverish and hollow and thirsty for the cool sensation of the Shadow Weave, but even aside from his promise, it was too late for that. He could never hope to best Rivalen in a duel of magic. Still, when their eyes met, Galaeron maintained a calm composure and gave a nonchalant tip of his head.

"Rather early, aren't we?" the elf said.

"I grew tired of waiting for you."

Rivalen motioned a trio of warriors toward Aris and two more toward Ruha, then had the last one accompany him to Galaeron's cell.

"As a matter of fact," the prince said, "I was beginning to fear you had found some way other than shadow magic to leave the dungeon."

Galaeron shook his head. "No, just stopped using shadow magic."

Rivalen gave him a disbelieving smirk. "Of course you have." He came to Galaeron's door and studied his cell for a moment, then motioned him toward the back. "If you don't mind kneeling."

Galaeron did as the prince requested, though he took care to tuck his toes under him so he could spring to his feet quickly. To avoid letting his gaze stray toward the keystone in the ceiling and give away his plan, he kept his eyes locked on Rivalen.

"Why the hurry?" he asked. "A few more hours, and you wouldn't have to kidnap us."

The prince drew a set of lockpicks from his cloak pocket and kneeled in front of the door. "In a few more hours, you would have escaped and been in another realm betraying the Most High to someone else."

"Not actually," Galaeron said, "but I see your point."

He fell silent and allowed the prince to work. On the other side of the interrogation chamber, Aris's escorts finished binding his wrists and ankles with shadow line and set to work on the chains binding him to the wall. The giant kept jerking his arms and legs away, complicating their task to the point that one of them was drawing his sword.

"Aris, don't get yourself hurt," Galaeron ordered. He was beginning to see how he might help Aris and Ruha escape, but he needed the giant free of the chains. "It isn't worth it."

"Yes, you must be careful with those hands," Rivalen called, still working on Galaeron's lock. "The Most High values them nearly as highly as he does the secrets Galaeron carries from Melegaunt."

Ruha's escorts succeeded in opening her cell and motioned the witch out. As she approached the door, she glanced over her shoulder and raised her brow.

"At least you'll be in the same city as Malik," Galaeron said, nodding her out into the interrogation chamber. "Assuming he's still alive."

"He is, indeed," Rivalen said. "After betraying your plan, he is a favorite of the Most High."

The tumblers in Galaeron's lock clicked open. The prince smiled and withdrew the picks.

Galaeron leaped to his feet and launched himself at the doorjamb with as much force as he could gather in two steps.

"Run!" he yelled. "Save your—"

The prince waved a dark hand at him, and Galaeron

slammed into the back of the cell so hard his breath left him. He slid halfway down the wall, then found himself floating out the door still gasping for breath.

"Did you think I would fail to see the trap?" Rivalen asked. He held Galaeron suspended in front of him. "You are foolish as well as ungrateful. If you try something foolish again, Weluk will cut the witch's throat."

One of Ruha's escorts pressed a glassy dagger blade to her throat, and Rivalen's assistant began to bind Galaeron's wrists.

"You Shadovar have a strange sense of gratitude," Galaeron said. "If you think I'll help you destroy Faerûn to save Evereska, you are wrong."

"Your thinking will change," Rivalen assured him. "And we have no wish to destroy Faerûn."

"Then your wishes are different from your actions," Ruha said, ignoring the knife at her throat. "You have seen for yourself what the melting of the High Ice is doing to the Sword Coast and the Heartlands. You are starving whole nations out of existence."

"The Shadovar have spent seventeen centuries starving, and we endure," Rivalen shot back. "If the Faerûnian kingdoms are too weak to survive a few decades of hunger so the Netherese lands can grow fertile again, then they were not meant to last."

"I would take issue with that," said a familiar—and very angry—female voice. "As would Waterdeep, Silverymoon, the Dalelands, and even Thay, I'm sure."

A tremendous clanking filled the dungeon as an entire company of Purple Dragons literally stepped out of the opposite wall of the interrogation chamber, followed closely by Alusair Obarskyr, Vangerdahast, and Dauneth Marliir. Galaeron was almost embarrassed to realize that he had been staring at an illusion the entire night without realizing it.

Galaeron looked over to Ruha, and she shook her head. The issue remained in doubt. Her confidence in Storm had not been because she knew they were being watched.

Alusair turned to a wiry priest who followed her out of the wall and gestured toward the two sentries lying on the floor over at the guard station.

"Owden," she said, "would you mind. . . ."

"Of course, Princess."

The priest scurried away. Alusair, attired in a full suit of battered plate armor, clanked across the interrogation chamber to where Rivalen stood.

"You will be kind enough to return the prisoners to their cells, Prince," she said, pointing to Galaeron and Ruha. "It is not yet morning."

Rivalen looked around the room and, finding several dozen crossbows not quite trained in his direction, seemed confused. He bowed but did not give the order—apparently deciding that since he was not yet under attack, Alusair had either not heard everything he had said or did not find it indefensible.

"I beg your forgiveness, Majesty," he said. "I did not mean to be presumptuous, but fearing the elf would use his shadow magic to escape, I assigned certain of my lords to keep a watch on their prison."

Alusair said nothing and looked to the guard station, where the one she had addressed as Owden was kneeling over the fallen sentries. He looked up and shook his head.

Rivalen was quick to cover. "As it happened, my caution was well-warranted. We spied a shadow whorl outside and followed it down to this dungeon." He waved a hand at the fallen guards. "Alas, we were too late to save your men, but we did capture the elf and his accomplices as they were attempting to leave."

"That's a lie!" boomed Aris. "We were—"

Vangerdahast made a motion, and the giant's lips continued to move without sound. Aris scowled and shook his head in angry denial. If Alusair noticed, she paid him no attention and kept her attention focused on Rivalen.

"Cormyr is grateful for your vigilance," said the princess, "but the prisoners have not yet been returned to their cells."

Ruha's escorts started to return her to her cell. Rivalen snapped something at them in ancient Netherese that prompted them to stop in their tracks, then he turned to Alusair with a smile.

"It is nearing dawn, Princess. Given how close the prisoners have come to escaping already, surely we can steal a few hours from the night."

Vangerdahast scowled and tottered forward. "That is not how the law works in Cormyr, Prince Rivalen." He pointed an ancient and crooked finger through the bars behind Galaeron's back. "Remove your bindings and return the prisoners to their cells—or take their place."

Rivalen's golden eyes glowed almost white at the threat. He sneered at the old wizard a moment, then turned to Alusair. "If that is the crown's wish, then, of course, we will obey."

Vangerdahast pointed a serpentine finger at Ruha's guards and spoke a word of magic, and the two lords were hurled into the cell's back wall with enough force to shatter their black armor and leave them slumped on the floor.

"The crown has already stated its wish," Alusair said, motioning a squad of Purple Dragons forward to surround Rivalen and the others. "Will you unbind the prisoners, Prince?"

Rivalen hesitated, and Galaeron felt the cold magic of the Shadow Weave welling up as the prince prepared to carry him to the enclave.

"Go ahead, Rivalen," he said. "Abduct me now, and all Faerûn will know I am telling the truth."

The swell of cold magic faded, and Galaeron instantly regretted his words. Another second, and he would have been back in Shade Enclave, with no choice except to immerse himself in shadow. The restraints came free of Galaeron's hands of their own accord, and Rivalen shoved him through the door of the cell with enough force to bounce him off the far wall and drop him to the floor.

"You will give the prisoners to us at dawn." Though Rivalen attempted to phrase it as a command instead of a request, the mere fact that he said it made the question implicit. "The Most High would find it difficult to understand why a friend would harbor fugitives from his justice."

"Would he?"

Alusair nodded, and Vangerdahast made a motion with his crooked finger. The doors slammed shut, locking Galaeron in his cell and the two Shadovar in the one adjacent. The Purple Dragons escorted Ruha away and placed themselves between Aris and the Shadovar who had been holding him prisoner.

Alusair watched Rivalen watch this, then said, "But he would understand allowing his friends to starve." She gave him a cold grin, then echoed his earlier words. "After all, if the Faerûnian kingdoms are too weak to survive a few decades of hunger, they are not meant to last."

Rivalen's face turned so dark it almost vanished. "Majesty, to understand any comment, you must know the context."

"I suppose that is true." Alusair stepped toward the prince, her attitude more that of a warrior challenging another than a potentate delivering a message. "So the Shadovar are not melting the High Ice?"

Rivalen cast a disparaging look in Galaeron's direction, then said, "The princess surely knows that every kingdom has its disaffected. A discontented elf saying a thing does not make it true."

"That is not an answer," Alusair pressed. "Are the Shadovar responsible for changing the weather of Faerûn or not?"

"Us, Majesty?" Rivalen gasped. "We are only one city."

"A Netherese city—and Netherese cities have done worse," Alusair said, no doubt referring to the hubris that had caused the fall of the goddess Mystryl and altered the Weave itself forever. She turned her head over her shoulder and called, "Myrmeen, have you seen enough?"

"I have, Majesty."

Myrmeen Lhal stepped through the illusionary wall, bringing with her half a dozen Arabellan nobles bearing the shadow blanket confiscated from Galaeron and his companions. She directed the nobles to drop the blanket at the prince's feet.

"There is Shade Enclave's stolen property," she said. "You and the rest of the Shadovar in Arabel may return it to your father with my compliments."

"I don't understand," Rivalen said, stalling for time to think. "You are ordering us out of the city?"

"I am ordering you out of Arabel—and the entirety of Cormyr, you and all Shadovar," Alusair clarified. "You won't be welcome here until you stop the melting of the High Ice."

"You would begrudge us our birthright?" Rivalen gasped, changing tactics the instant it grew apparent his lies had been discovered. "By what right do you dare?"

It was the wrong thing to say to Alusair Obarskyr. She stepped forward until she was standing nose to breastplate with the huge Shadovar.

"By the right of law—and of arms." She shoved him back into Galaeron's cage, then turned to Dauneth Marliir and waved at the two Shadovar locked in the cell that had been Ruha's. "Are those the ones who killed our guards?"

Dauneth shrugged. "Perhaps, Majesty. These Shadovar are difficult to tell apart."

"Well, it matters not," she said. "They were at least party to the deaths of two of our guards. Execute them."

"Of course, Majesty."

Rivalen opened his mouth to object, but Dauneth was already dropping his arm. Two dozen crossbows clacked, peppering the two Shadovar inside with iron bolts. Both warriors fell without a scream, their faces and throats studded with expertly placed quarrels.

Alusair turned to Rivalen. "I believe that makes our position clear, does it not?"

❧ ❧ ❧ ❧ ❧

Vala limped out of the Irithlium's shadowed entranceway to find Prince Escanor standing with a full company of Shadovar in the tree-choked courtyard. Their armor was fastened and their glassy swords held at battle ready. They were divided into squads of a dozen, each commanded by a fang-mouthed shadow lord. As Vala approached, an astonished—or perhaps relieved—murmur ran through their ranks, and the tips of their swords began to drift toward the ground. Raising her brow at the unexpected reception, she checked the ring Corineus had given her to make certain it was in the undetectable position, then removed the phaerimm tails from her belt and presented herself to Escanor.

"Come to keep your promise, Escanor?" she asked.

Escanor closed his gaping mouth. "My promise?"

"For killing the phaerimm beneath the Irithlium." Vala slapped the tails into his hand. "There are six tails there. Count them."

The prince glanced down at the tails and gave a wry smile. "Most impressive, but no. When I made that promise, I actually didn't think you would be returning."

"What you thought matters less than what you do about it," Vala said. "Are the Princes of Shade men who honor their words?"

"Unfortunately, that won't be possible," Escanor said, smile vanishing. He returned the phaerimm tails, then caught Vala by the wrist. "I was just on my way to fetch you for the Most High. It seems he has finally located Galaeron."

The prince turned away and dragging her after him, started to walk. Within two steps, his body had grown diaphanous and ghostly. Another two steps, and they were completely immersed in shadow, the ground beneath their feet as soft as water. Vala tried to pull away but stopped struggling when she experienced a strange sensation of falling and her captor's arm stretched into a writhing rope of darkness. She turned her magic ring so that it would show affairs as they truly were.

The swirling darkness around her became a pearly, motionless void, more colorless than it was gray. Escanor was a black heart beating inside a cage of black ribs, with no limbs or skull, but two coppery flames where there would have been eyes and a sheaf of finger wisps wrapped around Vala's arm.

The prince's fiery eyes swung in her direction. She quickly thumbed her ring back to its concealed position, and he became the shadowy figure of a moment before.

"Walk," he said.

The prince took a step and became solid again. Vala followed. The ground grew hard beneath her feet, and wisps of shadow started to coalesce in smoky ribbons. The voices of unseen whisperers rose and fell in the surrounding darkness. Gradually, a set of murmurs hardened into the fuller tones of normal speech, and Vala recognized the sibilant voice of Telamont Tanthul Most High. He was speaking harshly to someone—shouting, in fact—and there was an angry murmur in the air around him.

The figures of several shadow lords appeared in the murk surrounding Telamont's throne. Standing closest to the dais were the princes Rivalen and Lamorak, with Hadrhune a quarter of the way up the stairs. To Vala's astonishment, Malik was on a step between the seneschal and the princes, his cuckold's horns no longer hidden by his customary turban. Galaeron was nowhere in sight. Escanor brushed past the lords and stopped at the base of the dais.

". . . allow her to dictate terms to me?" the Most High was raging. "After all I have done to rebuild that wreck of a kingdom?"

"Most High, had the harlot dared utter a word against you, I would have stricken her down myself," Rivalen said, cringing visibly in the heat of his father's anger. "As her outrages were merely directed at me, I thought it best to endure them and return to consult."

"Return without the elf?"

"It was impossible to bring him," Rivalen said.

The Most High waited in expectant silence.

"When it remained possible, I still had hopes of salvaging our relationship with Arabel," the prince continued. "I know the value you place on controlling the border cities."

The Most High remained quiet, though the sense of expectation that had hung in the air was gone. Vala folded her hands in front of her, covering the gift from

Corineus, and thumbed her ring around. The murk paled to the color of fog, thin enough for her to see that the throne room was really a vast courtyard surrounded in the distance by dark bands she took to be walls. Beyond the dais in front of her rose the shapes of many other platforms, their silhouettes growing progressively more indistinct with distance, but each surrounded by a crowd of shadow lords similar to those ringing Vala and the princes.

The shadow lords themselves were wrinkled, ghoul-like figures with sunken, red-rimmed eyes and leathery black skin often pocked by white sores. Rivalen and Lamorak appeared much the same as had Escanor when Vala looked at him during the journey from Myth Drannor, varying only in how much of their skeleton remained attached to the black ribs that enclosed their black hearts. Surprisingly, Hadrhune appeared the same as before Vala had turned the ring—as did Malik, save that he held himself more erectly and seemed far more wiry than Vala had grown accustomed to thinking of him.

Finally, Telamont sent Vala's heart jumping into her throat by crying, "Betrayer!"

It was at first impossible to tell whom the Most High was addressing, for he was only two platinum eyes floating in a vaguely man-shaped pillar of darkness. The gray fog that filled the throne room seemed to be flowing through him, entering his "body" in the general area of the feet and leaving at the hands. In the area behind one of the eyes, in what should have been the temple area, there was something black and wrinkled, about half the size of Vala's fist, pulsing in beat to the Most High's words.

"This is your doing, ungrateful Vaasan!"

Vala spun the ring to its concealed position and found the Most High's murk-filled cowl turned in her direction, his empty sleeve raised and pointing down the stairs at her.

Praying that Telamont had not sensed her magic ring, Vala raised her chin and forced herself to meet his angry glare. "Mine, Most High? I have not been anywhere near Cormyr."

"You knew of his plans before he left, did you not?"

The last thing Vala wanted to do was admit her complicity in Galaeron's escape, but Malik had almost certainly revealed her role already, and she knew better than to think the Most High would be swayed by any lie she could tell.

"I did," she said.

The Most High remained silent, and she felt the weight of his next question as tangibly as that of a fallen comrade's body.

"I wanted him to leave," she said. "You were giving him over to his shadow, not teaching him to control it."

"Yet you went to Myth Drannor with Escanor."

"So you wouldn't grow suspicious and stop him from leaving," Vala said.

Again, the silence, heavy and demanding.

"He didn't want to leave without me," Vala admitted. "I had to convince him that he had vexed me and that I was enamored of Escanor. He left swearing vengeance on you, Escanor, and Shade in general."

Telamont finally looked away and, shaking his head in disbelief, descended the dais to stand in front of Escanor.

"The blame in this lies in part with me," the Most High said. "I had not thought his shadow so much in control, but you were blinded by a woman's cajolery and allowed her to use you against the enclave—and for that, you should be executed as well."

Vala's knees grew instantly weak at the pronouncement, but Escanor only inclined his head. "If that—"

"Execute?" Malik interrupted, stepping to the Most High's side. "You cannot execute Vala!"

Telamont's platinum eyes grew as cold as winter hail. "You object, cuckold?"

"Of course not . . . only Vala is my friend, and it would break my wretched heart—whatever the One may still let me have of it—to see her killed." Malik frowned at the curse that compelled him to keep speaking when it would have been so much wiser to let the matter drop after the first few words, then apparently saw that he had nothing to lose and plunged ahead. "And even more importantly, it would break Galaeron's heart."

"Why should the One care about that, little man?" asked Hadrhune, descending the dais to stare down over Telamont's shoulder. "The elf is an ingrate and a traitor to all the enclave has given."

"True," Malik said, "but he is an ingrate and a traitor that Shade Enclave needs. If you slay Vala, you will make him an implacable enemy who will no doubt die in some foolish manner seeking vengeance against you."

Telamont rolled an empty sleeve, gesturing for Malik to continue.

"On the other hand," the little man said. "If you keep Vala here, holding her in some terrible manner certain to cause her great pain, letting it be known that she truly does love Galaeron and only went to Myth Drannor so he would leave and save himself, Galaeron is certainly the type of noble fool to return and try to rescue her."

"The fault in your thinking is that his shadow has almost certainly taken him already," Hadrhune pointed out. "If that is so, he will see through your plan and avoid us all the more."

"He seemed well in control of himself in Arabel," Rivalen said. "In point of fact, he seemed to be avoiding shadow magic altogether, even when he might have used it to free himself and escape us."

"If that is so, then perhaps our plan will work," Hadrhune said, as much the idea thief as ever. He stepped around to bring himself in line with Telamont's gaze. "May I suggest the drop pits? Surely, no torture can be worse than keeping those clean and clear—at least no survivable torture."

Vala had an unpleasant feeling that she knew what the drop pits were, but it hardly mattered. Any torture that kept her alive to return to her son was one she could endure.

Telamont considered Hadrhune's proposal for a moment, then gave a thoughtful half-nod. "It would certainly give the elf cause to come for her quickly." He turned his platinum eyes upon Malik and added, "What do you think, my short friend?"

Malik's brow rose. "Me?"

"The plan is yours," Telamont said. "Do you think the drop pits the worst we can do?"

"Milord, I really do not know Shade Enclave well enough to name the worst torture it has to offer."

Malik fell silent for a moment, then his face twisted itself into a familiar expression of distress, and Vala had a sinking feeling.

"Only, it occurs to me that the torture most likely to draw Galaeron back in a rush is to make Vala a scullery maid in Escanor's palace and to let it be known that he is using her horribly at night."

Vala swallowed. As terrible as was Malik's suggestion, it was still something she could survive. To return to Sheldon, she could endure anything.

"And, of course, you must put her darksword away someplace where she cannot call it," Malik added. "For Vala, the worst torture of all will be not looking in on her son at night."

Until then, Vala had felt a debt of gratitude to the little man for saving her life. For telling them to take her visits, she could have killed him—in fact, she might have, had Escanor's powerful hand not closed around her wrist and prevented her from drawing her sword.

"If you please," Escanor said, "leave it in the scabbard when you pass it over."

Telamont's eyes sparkled with delight. "I think Malik is correct." He turned his gaze on the little man. "You are proving yourself a surprisingly capable advisor."

Malik beamed. "I am glad you are pleased with my humble services."

"Yes, I would never have thought one of Mystra's curses would be of such benefit to Shade Enclave." Telamont left the dais and started across the throne room. "Come to the world-window with me, my friend. We must make an example of Cormyr and show Faerûn what it is to betray the generosity of Shade Enclave—and you will tell me how we are going to do it."

CHAPTER FOURTEEN

25 Mirtul, the Year of Wild Magic

Through the magic of the scrying ball, Galaeron felt as though he were an eagle on high, circling the walled city of Tilverton in search of some garbage-loving raccoon to feed the nestlings in its aerie. He had a view of the entire town and the four roads leading into it, yet he could still make out details as fine as shield insignia carried by the growing number of warriors encamped among the mansions and temples of the Knoll District. There were plenty of Cormyr's Purple Dragons, of course, but also the Twisted Tower of Shadowdale, the White Horse of Mistledale, even the Raven and Silver of Sembia and dozens of other symbols Galaeron did not recognize.

According to Vangerdahast, Cormyr's neighbors had sent more than a hundred companies to help persuade Shade Enclave to rethink its melting of the High Ice, some as small as twenty well-mounted riders, but several numbering in the thousands—and with a generous mix of clerics and battle mages. To Alusair's dismay, the most enthusiastic response had come from the merchant princes of Sembia, some of whom stood to lose their entire fortunes if the weather disturbances continued. Always suspicious of Sembian designs on Cormyrean lands, the Steel Regent had not even informed the merchant princes of the alliance she was forming. They had sent large forces anyway, threatening to form their own alliance if she failed to accept their troops.

What Galaeron did not see were any companies on the roads outside the city. Though warriors were pouring into the Knoll District by the hundreds, trampling the grounds of the great estates in search of bivouacs, they were not entering through Tilverton's gates. The companies seemed to be sprouting from the city itself, marching out of shadowy cul-de-sacs or emerging from some ancient tower or keep to form up in the street.

Galaeron raised his gaze and looked over the scrying ball to Vangerdahast's bushy-browed eyes.

"It won't work," the elf said. "If you can scry this, so can the Shadovar."

"Not so." Vangerdahast raised his head, revealing a confident smirk not quite hidden beneath his beard. "This is what they will see."

He waved his hand over the scrying ball. When Galaeron looked back, the soldiers were gone, and the residents seemed to be having some sort of festival in the Knoll District.

"You can annul shadow magic?" Galaeron gasped. The

implications for Evereska were distressing. If Vangerdahast could find a way to negate the Shadovar's spells, so could the phaerimm. "How?"

"I *am* a wizard of some power, elf."

"It's not a question of power." Galaeron gestured at the ball. "May I?"

"If you don't think it will draw out your shadow." Vangerdahast's voice was mocking. He had been trying to persuade Galaeron to demonstrate his shadow spells since Rivalen's departure and could not seem to understand why Galaeron refused. "I wouldn't want to be responsible for unleashing such a demon."

"I'll be fine."

Galaeron envisioned the world-window in the Palace Most High and waved his hand over the scrying ball. The crystal filled with dark clouds, then a circle of light opened in the center and several murky Shadovar figures grew visible along the edges. The image in the middle was that of a great lake ringed by desert mountains.

"This is Telamont Tanthul's scrying window," Galaeron said, disappointed that he had not caught the Shadovar looking in on Tilverton. "If shadow magic and regular magic were capable of annulling each other, don't you think this room would be warded?"

Vangerdahast studied the image for a moment, then said, "Of course the room can't be warded. The Weave is mightier than the Shadow Weave."

"Mightier, perhaps," Galaeron said, "but also different. They can spy on you as easily as you spy on them."

Vangerdahast's face appeared inside the crystal ball. "I am experienced in such matters, you know."

Realizing he would never win this argument, Galaeron decided to try another approach. "Even if you're right, the

Shadovar do use spies—thousands of them, I am sure."

"Not in Tilverton—or any other Cormyrean city." Vangerdahast displayed a tile with a magic ward etched onto the surface. "My war wizards have been busy."

Galaeron took the tile and ran his fingers over the symbol. It was a variation on an ancient Cormanthorian sigil he had studied in Evereska's academy of magic, used to keep spirits of darkness and cold at bay. The workmanship was exquisite and the magic so powerful that the presence of his shadow self caused it to burn his hand. When he returned the tile to Vangerdahast, he was surprised to discover the symbol burned into his palm. Finding that even this copy of the ward made his eyes burn, Galaeron closed his hand.

"Impressive, but useless," he said. "All a Shadovar need do is enter the fringe, and your ward will have almost no power over him."

Vangerdahast's eyes flickered with alarm. "Really?" He turned the ward toward Galaeron. "Show me."

Galaeron had to look away. "I can't. You know that."

"I certainly do," Vangerdahast snorted.

"I've explained how it can be defeated," Galaeron said, raising a hand to block his sight of the symbol. "There is no need for me to prove it. The cost of satisfying your curiosity is too dear."

"Very well." Vangerdahast lowered the tile and set it aside—facedown, thankfully. "By the way, the last time I spoke to Storm Silverhand, she asked me to pass along a message from Khelben."

"From Khelben?" Galaeron's heart was immediately beating faster. "About Keya?"

"I believe that was the name mentioned, yes."

Galaeron waited for the wizard to continue—then, when he did not, asked, "What is it?"

Vangerdahast's eyes slid toward the ward.

Galaeron rose in disgust. "You're no different than the Shadovar!"

"There you are mistaken, elf," Vangerdahast said, peering at Galaeron over the shadow ball. "I am very different. What I do, I do for the good of Cormyr."

"Then you would do well to stay clear of the Shadow Weave." Galaeron started for the door. "You are already half shade yourself."

"Probably." Vangerdahast's tone was thoughtful. He remained silent until Galaeron reached for the latch, then said, "You're going to be an uncle."

Galaeron stopped, then turned. "What?"

"According to Khelben." Vangerdahast shrugged. "Your sister is getting married."

"Married?" Galaeron gasped. "She's only eighty!"

"And fighting the phaerimm on the front lines of the siege, from what I hear." Vangerdahast steepled his gnarled fingers. "People mature quickly in the face of death."

Galaeron studied the old wizard, trying to figure out what the human hoped to gain by making up such an outrageous story.

Finally, he gave up and said simply, "It won't work, old man. It takes years for elves to fall in love. An engagement can last a decade."

"I have found that war tends to speed matters of the heart," Vangerdahast said, eyes twinkling. "And humans are not so reticent. Especially Vaasans."

"Vaasans?" Galaeron released the door latch and stumbled into a nearby chair. "One of the Vaasans did this?"

"Someone named Dexon, as I understand it."

"The ice-hatched bastard!" Galaeron hissed. "I'll slit him from groin to gullet!"

"Really?" Vangerdahast chuckled. "I thought you were trying to control your 'shadow self.' "

A deep barbarian bellow, muffled by distance and the thick walls of the tent, sounded down in the camps. Always concerned about friction between the disparate companies of her motley army, Laeral cocked an ear toward the sound. The voice was angry and a little bit puzzled, as though demanding an explanation. Probably just one of Chief Claw's warriors still trying to figure out the magic latrines the clerics insisted on whenever the army was encamped.

Khelben, lying on the camp rug beside Laeral, took her chin in hand and gently turned her face back toward his so he could resume kissing her. Though it had been several days since they had trapped the phaerimm in the Vine Vale, they had been so busy securing Evereska's defenses and hunting down survivors that this was the first night they'd found for each other. Khelben, who had after all nearly died at the Rocnest and been the one trapped by the thornbacks for all those months, seemed to feel the need to shut out the war even more keenly than did Laeral. With the dexterous fingers of a magician, he used one hand to undo the knot holding her jerkin closed and began to unlace her.

A tremendous fluttering sound pulsed somewhere high above the tent. Laeral rose to her elbows and looked up through the smoke hole and saw nothing but the starless mantle of the shadowshell.

"Do you hear that, Khelben?" she asked.

Khelben pushed her back down and rolled astride her body. "I hear nothing but the fervid drumming of my heart, beating its joy in anticipation of our first night together—our first *undisturbed* night together—since all this began."

Laeral smiled. To everyone else, Khelben might be the stern and dour Blackstaff, Lord Mage of Waterdeep and founder of the Moonstars. To her, he was a hopeless romantic, given to outrageous professions of love and a touch so gentle it wouldn't break soap bubbles.

She whispered, "Come here, you."

Deciding the fluttering sound had probably just been a hippogriff patrol trying to duck a flight of veserabs—Aelburn's scouts had learned the hard way that the things had a taste for anything with feathers—Laeral pulled Khelben down on top of her.

"I want to feel that heart drumming," she said.

Khelben kissed her again, then slipped off to the side and set to work on her laces with his dexterous fingers. By the time the next sound came—this time the distinctive crackle-boom of a lightning bolt—he had Laeral out of her doublet and her trouser laces untied.

"*That*, I heard," he growled, rising.

Laeral jumped to her feet and, throwing her cloak around her shoulders, followed him out the door of the tent. Scattered across the plain at the foot of their rise were hundreds of campfires, by the light of which it was possible to see thousands of silhouettes milling about in confusion, pulling on armor and buckling sword belts. Though no one seemed to have any more idea what was happening than Laeral and Khelben, an increasing number of figures appeared to be looking toward the area of inky darkness that marked the Shadovar camp.

Laeral turned to call for a messenger and found two of Khelben's Vaasan escorts, Kuhl and Burlen, rushing up fully armored—as always. Vaasans, as far as Laeral could tell, slept in armor. The third of their number, Dexon, was back in Evereska with Keya Nihmedu, recovering from his wounds.

"They're gone!" Burlen exclaimed.

"Gone as in 'departed'?" Khelben asked, not even bothering to clarify that the Vaasan was talking about the Shadovar. "Or gone as in 'dead?' "

"Gone is in 'not there,' " Kuhl growled. "What's the difference? An Uthgardt lookout noticed that the Shadovar tents were empty, and when he went to check on the veserabs, they took a fright and flew off."

"Weren't they hobbled?" Laeral asked.

"Not even a piece of twine," Burlen confirmed. "At least not on the one Yoraedia's sentry bolted down."

Laeral exchanged a worried glance with Khelben. The sound of arguing voices drifted up from the middle of the dark camp, and dancing lines of torches began to stream in from all sides. Khelben extended a hand and summoned his staff, and Laeral did the same for her broadbelt. Then, while Khelben sent the Vaasans to check on the night pickets and call the companies to alert, she tied her trouser laces and belted her cloak closed.

Once she had her clothes tied, she extended a hand to Khelben and said, "Shall we, my dear?"

Khelben sighed and took her hand. "If we must."

Laeral eyed a spot near the center of the converging torch streams and used a spell to open a small translocational door. She and Khelben stepped through into a tumult of shouting voices and bobbing torches. So belligerent was the argument that, during the moment it took the afterdaze to clear, she grew convinced she had emerged into the middle of a tavern brawl. She drew a fighting wand from her belt.

Khelben was even more alarmed. He began to whirl his staff around them in a practiced defensive pattern that sent a pair of elves and a Waterdhavian sergeant tumbling to the ground.

A pair of the sergeant's subordinates came rushing up, "You there, wizard!" Instead of stopping to help their superior, they stepped over his groaning figure and split up to come at Khelben and Laeral from opposite sides. "Who do you think you're batting around with that thing?"

Laeral's assessment of the situation took a decided turn for the worse. She leveled her wand at the nearest figure and said, "Hare."

The man took one more step, then curled to the ground and began to sprout fur. She pointed the wand at the second fellow, who was still trying to dance past Khelben's whirling staff, and said, "Ass."

He dropped to all fours, his nose and ears already beginning to lengthen.

Laeral waved the wand past the others in the growing knot of warriors. "Has our arrival offended anyone else?"

When no one else stepped forward, Khelben said, "Good."

He lowered his staff and led the way past half a dozen empty Shadovar tents to the assembly square in front of the command pavilion, where Lord Yoraedia was standing nose to belly with Chief Claw, his face twisted into a very unelflike scowl.

"Will someone tell us what's going on here?" Khelben asked.

Both leaders turned their gazes on Khelben and Laeral and began to speak at once, gesturing wildly and pointing at the other.

"One at a time," Laeral ordered. "You first, Lord Yoraedia."

The elf cast a superior smirk at Claw, then said, "This oaf's sentries fell asleep and allowed the Shadovar to slip past them unseen."

"Liar!" Claw deliberately stepped into Yoraedia, bumping the elf with his stomach and sending him stumbling half a dozen steps back. "My lookouts only *found* that the camp was empty. Your watchers are the ones who fell asleep."

"Elves," Yoraedia sneered, "do not sleep."

"Then they are blind!" Claw bumped the elf with his belly again. "The Shadovar did not leave by our side."

Yoraedia caught himself after three paces and stepped back toward the barbarian, his hand dropping toward his dagger. "One more time, walrus, and I'll slit that gu—"

"That's quite enough, Lord Yoraedia." Laeral stepped between the two. "The Shadovar were not prisoners. No one is to blame for their departure."

"You will both be to blame if this continues," Khelben said, stepping to Laeral's side and using the butt of his staff to push Yoraedia back. "What madness has taken hold of you two?"

The solemn glance he cast in Laeral's direction was hardly necessary. She had already guessed the reason behind the group's anger and was searching her cloak pockets for a spell component.

Khelben continued, "No one could have stopped the Shadovar from sneaking away. As soon as it was dark, the cowards probably melted into the shadows and walked off."

Skarn Brassaxe and his dwarves marched into the assembly square, shouldering past elves and barbarians alike.

"It's bright enough to blind Lathander!" Skarn complained. "Are you all this stupid, or are you fools trying to light yourselves up for enemy long-casters?"

"Be careful who you call stupid, Beltwatcher," said Aelburn, stepping into the light from the opposite side of the gathering. "Some of us need the light. Not everyone has goblin blood running in their veins."

"Goblin blood!" Skarn stormed, reaching for his axe. "I'll show you gob—"

Khelben's staff crashed down, knocking the dwarf to his seat and causing his arm to go limp. Claw and Yoraedia continued to trade insults, with most of their followers adding their own voices to the tumult, and the dwarves and hippogriff scouts were starting in as well. It would have been a simple matter for Laeral and Khelben to start dispelling whatever magic was causing this madness, but until she knew whether the casters were Shadovar or phaerimm, it was better to let them believe their tactic was working.

Laeral found what she was looking for and unobtrusively began to sprinkle diamond dust in each direction, at the same time mouthing an incantation and running her fingers through the gestures of her most powerful spell. As the magic took effect, she had to bite her tongue to keep from gasping.

On the western side of the square, Skarn's dwarves were stomping in from their own camp flanked by the silvery blurs of well over a dozen invisible phaerimm. The scene was much the same on the north side, save that it was Waterdhavian volunteers and Aelburn's scouts who were being marched in. The situation to the east and south was even worse. With most of the barbarians and elves already in the square, the thornbacks had already formed themselves into battle ranks.

"Uh, Khelben?"

"Yes?"

With more leaders marching their companies into the dusty square every minute, Khelben had given up on ending the argument between Yoraedia and Claw and was using his magic to intervene in actual outbreaks of violence.

Khelben pointed at a scowling dwarf in the gleaming armor of the Knights in Silver who was charging toward the center of the quarrel with a drawn hand axe and asked, "Would you mind?"

"Not at all."

Laeral pulled two beads of tar from her cloak pocket. Voicing a short spell, she flicked first one, then the other bead at the scowling dwarf, whose progress immediately slowed to a sluggish crawl.

"As I was saying," Laeral said, "do you remember those detection amulets we passed out so the sentries would be able to see invisible infiltrators?"

Khelben frowned and used his black staff to sweep the feet from beneath one of Claw's barbarians who was reaching for one of Yoraedia's elves.

"I remember," he said. "You brought twenty of them—"

"Twenty-five," Laeral corrected. "They don't seem to be working."

Khelben grimaced, then asked, "How badly?"

"Fifteen," Laeral said. "On each side."

Khelben considered this for a moment, then growled, "The bastards! The slippery, shadowy, betraying bastards!"

"I wouldn't go so easy on them."

Laeral had already done the math. After the battle in the Vine Vale, they had estimated that there could only be a hundred phaerimm left inside the shadowshell. Over the past few days, they had hunted down and killed another twenty, which meant there were only about eighty thornbacks left in the entire Sharaedim.

Somehow, most had converged on the relief army's camp within a few hours of the departure of the Shadovar. Clariburnus and Lamorak had not only abandoned their allies, they had invited the enemy to destroy them.

"What now, Khelben?" Laeral asked. She saw an elf reaching for his sword and waved her wand, turning him into a sleek hart. "Start dispelling and hope for the best?"

Khelben shook his head. "This requires something more . . . wondrous. Can you distract the phaerimm while I raise a sphere?"

"Of course," Laeral said, pulling a second wand from her belt. One of Khelben's favorite spells, the sphere of wonder created an area in which only one type of magic—chosen by the caster—would function. "But that won't hold forever."

"I'll open a teleport circle from inside," Khelben said.

"Good," Laeral said. "We'll meet at the Halfway Inn."

"Meet?"

"Somebody has to bring the rest of the army."

Laeral started across the assembly square, using one wand to paralyze anyone shouting and the other to turn those holding weapons into rabbits and raccoons.

"Quiet!" she called. "I have heard quite enough of this bickering!"

No one obeyed, of course, and several people were actually foolish enough to guarantee a shake of a wand in their direction by turning to argue. The distraction seemed to work, holding the phaerimm's attention so Khelben could raise his arms in the necessary circles and voice what was really rather a long and drawn-out incantation—an incantation that most of the Chosen except him agreed could use some editing.

Laeral paralyzed and polymorphed so many warriors that they were actually beginning to take notice of her commands and fall into a grudging silence, which all but guaranteed that the thornbacks would have to attack openly instead of using mind-slaves to goad the others into doing it for them—and that Laeral would be their first target.

Finally, a dome of faintly shimmering golden light rose up in the middle of the assembly square, prompting the phaerimm to reveal themselves by vainly hurling magic bolts and flame strikes against its wall. The dazed warriors stopped arguing and looked around with stunned expressions and arched brows. Leaving it to Khelben to help them recover, Laeral turned toward her tent and opened another translocational gate.

There was the familiar instant of falling before she emerged adjacent to the worst battle din she had ever heard. Blades were clanging off armor in mad cacophony and anguished voices were shrieking their pain. The air reeked of blood and opened guts, and warriors were streaming past in a torrent of dark silhouettes. A few were doubled over and some were missing limbs or pieces of limbs, but none had weapons in their scabbards or hands.

Still struggling with afterdaze and unable to make sense of what she was seeing, Laeral nevertheless responded instantly. She pulled a vial of granite dust from her cloak pocket and sprinkled it over her head, speaking the words of an armoring spell. Her skin grew cold and numb and as hard as rock. She turned toward the furor and found herself looking across the body-strewn cloth of a collapsed camp tent and finally recalled where she was and what she had come to do.

She was too late.

A whirling tornado of blades was coming across the tent toward her, plucking the swords and daggers from the hands and scabbards of the soldiers fleeing before it. A handful of brave warriors stopped to fire crossbow bolts or hurl spears into the heart of the vortex, but these were plucked up with the rest of the weapons and came flying back around to slash the brave souls into a spray of blood and shredded armor. There had to be a thousand weapons in the storm already, with a dozen more flying into it every second, and the whirling cloud of steel was so thick that Laeral could not see to its heart.

The edge of the blade-storm reached her side of the tent. Swords and daggers began to shatter against her spell-hardened skin. The shards were sucked back into the tornado, more deadly than before. Laeral waded into the tempest, staggering under the constant hail of weapons slamming into her from the side. The tent cloth was slick with blood and strewn with bodies and pieces of bodies, some still animated enough to reach out and clutch her ankles. Several times, she stumbled and nearly fell, and once she had to kick herself free of a blood-soaked half-elf who managed to wrap both arms around her legs begging for her to save him.

Finally, Laeral began to glimpse the heart of the storm, where the cone-shaped silhouette of a phaerimm was floating toward her at an oblique angle. She raised her hand and loosed her silver fire. In the same instant, the terrain opened beneath her feet as the thornback tried to suck her into the ground. Quick as the counter-attack came, the tactic was a tired one against which Laeral had long ago developed a magic immunity. The Weave simply kept her suspended over the hole until it closed.

In all likelihood, the phaerimm never knew its attack had failed. It was engulfed in silver fire and spent the next few seconds whirling around madly as it disintegrated into ashes. The blade-storm came to a sudden halt, covering Laeral's collapsed tent in a steel carpet as a thousand swords clanged to the ground.

By the light of the fires raging in every camp, Laeral could make out the broad swath of motionless silhouettes and writhing forms the phaerimm had cut through her army. It was a broad belt beginning over by Silverymoon's Knights of Silver and curving steadily inward, razing the entire camp of the Bloodaxe mercenaries sent on behalf of Sundabar and tearing a broad tract through the tents of the Slugsmashers representing Citadel Adbar before spiraling through the Waterdhavian encampment and coming up the hill to Laeral and Khelben's tent.

Nor was this phaerimm the only one to attack the outlying camps while its companions prepared the main ambush. There were firestorms and lightning squalls everywhere, another blade-storm, and more mind-enslaved warriors fighting each other than the phaerimm. Heart sinking with sorrow and despair—and more than a little guilt at having failed to foresee the Shadovar betrayal—Laeral removed a silver thimble from her pocket, then uttered a spell and held it to her lips like a miniature horn.

"The Shadovar have betrayed us. Take who you can save and flee." Though she spoke softly, Laeral's voice would be heard by every commander and wizard in her army, save those who had fallen under the mental sway of the enemy—she had designed the spell with the phaerimm in mind. "We'll form again at the Halfway Inn. May the gods speed you."

From behind her came the sound of chiming steel as someone approached across the carpet of fallen blades. She turned and glimpsed the hulking form of a Vaasan running in her direction—then cried out in confusion as his sword came tumbling at her. She twisted away and instinctively raised her arm, but trying to block a dark-sword was a bad idea even for one of the Chosen.

A wave of searing cold shot up her arm, and the limb went numb below the elbow. She cried out more in shock than pain and dropped to her knees and nearly fainted when she saw her hand and forearm lying on the carpet of swords in front of her. The black blade that had severed her arm lay a pace or so away, wet with her blood. The darksword rose into the air and started to float back in the direction from which it had come.

Laeral turned her head and saw Burlen's hulking form striding toward her, his hand stretched toward the floating sword. Too dazed to understand why he had attacked her, she nevertheless knew that she had to stop him before he did it again. She reached into her cloak for a spell component—then experienced a wave of excruciating pain and recalled she was reaching with a stump. She reached with her other hand, but the angle was awkward and the movement unfamiliar. Burlen was almost on her by the time she found what she was searching for.

The Vaasan raised his darksword and said, "Your fault."

Laeral pulled the iron bar from her pocket and pointed it in his direction. The steel carpet chimed again as another hulking form came rushing up behind the Vaasan. Burlen dropped to a crouch and started to spin, only to have his guard kicked aside by a big Vaasan boot.

"Kuhl?" Burlen gasped. "What are you—?"

The pommel of Kuhl's sword caught Burlen at the base of the jaw, lifting him off his feet and dropping him flat on his back in the carpet of swords. Kuhl took a moment to make sure his comrade was out cold, then turned to Laeral—who, still in shock and uncertain of what was happening—was pointing the iron bar at him.

"My apologies, Lady Arunsun. There are infiltrators everywhere." He tucked a pair of phaerimm tails into his belt, then picked up Burlen's sword and sheathed it in his own scabbard. "Can you stand?"

Laeral tried and nearly passed out. "No." She pocketed the iron bar, then extended her hand. "Set me over there with Burlen and hold us tight."

"Hold you, Milady?"

Laeral nodded. "For your life." She pointed at her amputated arm. "It could be a rough ride to the Halfway Inn."

❀ ❀ ❀ ❀ ❀

A raw potato in one hand and a drawn throwing dagger in the other, Galaeron stepped off Aris's upraised palm directly onto the sill of the third-story lodging chamber Vangerdahast was using as a council room. The half-dozen war wizards gathered around the table cried out in surprise and reached for spell components, and one actually stood, pointing at the window and opening his mouth to loose a spray of magic bolts. Galaeron bounced the potato off the fellow's head, shocking more than knocking the wizard back into his seat, then turned his attention toward a large blonde woman holding a finger-length cylinder of glass.

"You don't want to point that in my direction," he said, raising his throwing dagger. "This is my good hand."

Vangerdahast, sitting with his back to the window, sighed heavily. He motioned his war wizards to their seats, then braced his elbow on the armrest and turned to look at Galaeron.

"Surely, you can see we're in a conclave?"

Galaeron lowered the dagger. "So the door guards informed me, but the interruption will be a short one. I have only one question: is it true?"

A murmur of alarm rustled around the table, and Vangerdahast closed his eyes and nodded. "I fear so."

Galaeron's heart sank. He could not bear to think of Vala in that place, being abused in that manner. He stepped to Vangerdahast's side.

"Why wasn't I told?" he demanded. "Why did I have to find out through palace gossip? If this is another of your bids to inveigle me into using shadow magic . . ."

"That would be your fourth question, if a question it is," Vangerdahast interrupted. He pointed at the wall, and a chair walked over to place itself behind Galaeron. "Have a seat and explain what you mean by palace gossip. Surely, the whole palace can't know so soon?"

"The whole city knows, as far as I can tell. I heard it from a gate guard." Galaeron ignored the chair. "What I want to know is why wasn't I told? Were you afraid I'd go back to the enclave?"

Vangerdahast cocked his bushy brow. "Actually, that's the last thing I would have expected from you," he said, "but the fact of the matter is that we only found out ourselves a few minutes ago. I was about to send for you to see if you might have any thoughts on their departure."

"Departure?" Galaeron asked. "Whose departure?"

A twinkle of comprehension came to Vangerdahast's eyes. "Then you didn't know," he said. Several of the wizards sighed in relief. "The Shadovar have left the Sharaedim—sneaked out in the middle of the night. Laeral's relief army was decimated, and she was horribly wounded."

Galaeron sat—fell, actually—into the chair. "What?" he gasped. "Is Keya—?"

"The mythal wasn't breached," offered the woman Galaeron had threatened with the throwing dagger. "Your sister and everyone inside Evereska are no worse off than before—better, in fact, since they've been reinforced and resupplied—but with the relief army decimated and Laeral wounded, the phaerimm will be free to focus their attention on the city again."

Vangerdahast laid a wrinkled hand on Galaeron's arm. "I'm sure I don't have to tell you what the shadowshell is doing to the mythal. If you know of anything Storm and the other Chosen can do to breach it. . . ."

"The magic must be renewed," Galaeron said. "All they need do is keep the Shadovar away from the Splicing.

The bonds will weaken over time, and Weave magic will start to flow into the Sharaedim again."

Vangerdahast sighed in relief. "Good. Then our only problem is the additional magic the extra troops will require when the Heartland Alliance attacks the flying city." He looked around the table. "I think we can take this redeployment as Telamont Tanthul's answer to our demand that he stop the melting of the High Ice."

"Actually, no," Galaeron said. "This is about me."

The looks that came to the faces of the war wizards made clear what they thought of the theory.

"It is," Galaeron insisted. "I came here because there are rumors about that Vala has been made Escanor's bed slave. They abandoned Evereska to punish me for leaving Shade."

"You have an awfully high opinion of your worth," said the wizard Galaeron had hit with the potato. "I don't suppose they could be consolidating their forces to defend against an attack from the Heartland Alliance?"

Vangerdahast cleared his throat and said, "The elf may have a point. There are certain, um, secrets in his possession that they may desire to recover."

Vangerdahast and Alusair had elected to hold close the fact that Melegaunt had imbued Galaeron with a vast knowledge of the phaerimm, lest the thornbacks have spies in the Arabel palace.

"The damage he caused them by revealing the shadow blankets was immeasurable," the royal magician continued. "They may very well be doing this to punish him—and to force him to return to Shade."

"Or to force you to turn me over," he said, "and to punish you for harboring me—and daring to threaten them."

Vangerdahast scowled. "Punish *us*? They couldn't possibly—"

"They *could*," Galaeron insisted. "When was the last time you checked on matters in Tilverton?"

CHAPTER FIFTEEN

26 Mirtul, the Year of Wild Magic

Ruha had crossed the Shoal of Thirst once before. It had been a long, thirsty journey over a salt-pan as flat as a mirror, rife with tragedy and hardship, and she had considered herself lucky to reach the other side. Such a journey would have been impossible, save by ship or wing. Where once she had feared death because a camel collapsed and burst a waterskin, there lay an entire lake, vast beyond the belief of most Bedine and blanketed beneath the shadows of an evening rain.

"It is a different desert than when you left, Ruha. Better," said Sheikh Sa'ar.

A powerfully-built man of fifty who wore a gray *keffiyeh* over his graying hair, the sheikh was lying on a ridge crest, looking out over the lake along with Ruha and a Cormyrean war wizard named Caladnei.

"The lake has already brought us good hunting," he added.

The sheikh pointed down the shore, to a broad sweep of desert blossoms with a few young date palms already pushing their crowns above the foliage. Ruha did not see what he was indicating until a herd of gazelle emerged from an expanse of tall grass and began to drink. Apparently, whatever magic had made a lake of the Shoal of Thirst had also removed its salinity, for gazelle did not drink brackish water.

"Easier, perhaps, but not better," Ruha said.

Though it had been many years since Ruha lived in Anauroch—much less crossed the Shoal of Thirst—she felt violated. Undeniable as was the lake's beauty, it was already changing the surrounding desert, bringing with it an abundance and leisure that would destroy the Bedine's nomadic way of life.

"Those waters," she said, "are poison to the Bedine."

The sheikh furrowed his brow. "How can that be? I have drank from its waters many times myself, and you see for yourself that I am stronger than ever."

"So you are," Ruha said, "but how long has it been since your *khowwan* left the lake?"

Sa'ar's face grew stormy. "We are leaving soon." He looked in the direction opposite the gazelles, to where a flight of veserabs were frolicking in a small bay. "Upon the heels of our raid, in truth."

"Stealing mounts from the Shadovar is not very safe, Sheikh," said Caladnei. "Their magic is strong."

An unveiled woman with striking amber eyes and a tall willowy build, she insisted on dressing in a deliberately male fashion, with long tresses of red hair spilling out from beneath her *keffiyeh* and a slender sword hanging from her belt.

"Then it is good I have you." Sa'ar looked away from the lake and locked gazes with the war wizard. "Your magic must be very strong as well, for you to dress as you dare."

Caladnei's eyes flared. "We did not come to Anauroch to help nomads steal—"

"Take only the young veserabs, Sheikh—those still too small to ride." As Ruha spoke, she looked past Sa'ar to scowl at Caladnei. "The others will only spit in your face, and their breath is worse than that of ten camels."

"That awful?" The sheikh's bushy brow rose. "Then they must be fine mounts, indeed."

"So it seems to me," Ruha said, "but Shadovar magic is different from that of the Zhentarim. You must not blame us if the raid goes awry."

Before the sheikh could answer, Caladnei said, "Ruha, did you not tell me that the Bedine don't use magic? If we help, the Shadovar may realize we're here."

"Anauroch is a large desert, wizardess," Sa'ar said, "and the city of Shade well-hidden. By the time you find it on your own, the Shadovar will certainly know you are looking for them."

"Are you threatening to reveal us?" Caladnei demanded.

"Sheikh Sa'ar would never betray his guests," Ruha said.

She glanced down the hill, where the rest of the Cormyrean scouting party stood in dusty *abas*, holding the reins of their recently purchased camels stiffly at arm's length. The handful of women in the company followed Caladnei's example and refused to wear veils, and there was a marked lack of children and saluki dogs.

"But he is right," the witch continued. "We do not

make a very convincing tribe. The sooner we find the Shadovar city, the better our chances of surprising them."

In truth, Ruha thought it likely they had been discovered already. When Vangerdahast had asked her to lead a scouting party into Anauroch to locate the flying city so Cormyr could launch a surprise attack, Ruha had asked for a company of swarthy, brown-eyed volunteers whom she could disguise as Bedine. Instead, the wizard had provided her with Caladnei and her equally stubborn superior, Hhormun, two fools who seemed to believe that riding camels and wearing *abas* was all that was required to disguise a company of fair-skinned Cormyreans as a Bedine *khowwan*. Had she not known that Alusair was preparing to launch a surprise teleport-attack from a secret base in Tilverton, she would have sworn the wizards wanted the Shadovar to notice them.

After a few moments, Caladnei said, "Very well, Sheikh, but you will take us to Shade, no matter how the raid comes out."

She started to back down the dusty slope.

"If you keep your promise, I will keep mine." Sa'ar crawled down beside her, then spit in his palm and offered it to her. "It is a bargain."

Caladnei spit in her own hand.

"You are sure Hhormun will agree?" Ruha asked, sliding down to join the pair before they clasped hands. "The bargain is yours if you make it."

Caladnei clasped the sheikh's hand. "Hhormun will follow me in this."

Ruha was not so sure. Old and portly though he was, Hhormun had proven surprisingly energetic in directing the activities of the company, from picking campsites to dictating the pace of the daily marches. When they reached the bottom of the ridge, however, he surprised her by not protesting at all and even allowing Sa'ar to plan the raid.

A few minutes later, Ruha, Caladnei, the sheikh and a dozen of his men were rubbing themselves and the Mahwa tribe's strongest camels in veserab dung, collected by the warriors a few days earlier for just that purpose.

"You're sure this is necessary?" Caladnei asked, wrinkling her nose at the awful stench of the stuff. "I'm sure someone in the company has a spell that could eliminate our smell."

"It is not enough to eliminate our own odor," Sa'ar said. "We must smell like what we want. It pleases the little gods."

"And puts our camels at ease," Ruha added, explaining in terms Caladnei would understand more readily. "If they think the smell is ours instead of the veserabs, they will cause less trouble as we approach."

"*Less* trouble?" Caladnei grumbled. "I suppose none would be too much to ask for."

They waited until a lookout signaled that the veserabs had come out of the water to rest for the evening, then Hhormun used his magic to render the entire raiding party invisible, while Ruha and Caladnei used their own magic to cast a pall of silence over the group. Though the Mahwa had been part of the coalition that relied on Ruha's magic to destroy the Zhentarim army at Orofin, that had been many years earlier, and even the sheikh's stern glower could not keep the men from grumbling and cringing as the spells were cast over them.

Finally, the raiding party circled around to the downwind side of the ridge and—with the aid of yet more magic—crept out onto the lakeshore. The nearest veserabs were only a few hundred paces away, mostly solitary bulls so cranky and strong that the Shadovar herders left them to stand guard at the edges of the flight, trusting that the creatures' instincts would make them follow when the rest were moved. Ruha, who was leading the raid by virtue of being the only person present with any experience at all handling veserabs, picked a serpentine course around the beasts, giving them as wide a berth as possible.

Once, when they entered an area of tall marsh grass, a nearby bull flared its wings and started over to investigate. Sa'ar released a sand grouse he had brought along as a diversion, and the bird burst skyward with such a riot of flapping wings and terrified screeching that it drew three veserabs into the air after it. Ruha made good use of the distraction, leading the party to within twenty paces of the three Shadovar herders camped on that side of the flight.

A tug on a guideline attached to her waist brought her to a stop. Several moments later, ten fist-sized sling stones appeared in the darkening sky and rained down on the sentries. Two fell unconscious. By the time the third made enough sense of the assault to turn and see the raiding party—rendered visible when they attacked—galloping toward him on their camels, two warriors were already clubbing him senseless. Bruised as the young herder might be when he awoke, Ruha took the fact that the warriors used the butts of their lances instead of the tips as a sign of Sa'ar's concern about angering the Shadovar. Bedine raiders usually killed the sentries, so there would be that many fewer warriors available for the counter raid.

The sheikh and his other warriors were already charging into the flight of resting veserabs, hurling loops of braided rope around the necks of the smallest beasts and securing the other ends to their saddles. Most of them were coughing and reeling, struggling to stay on their mounts as the veserabs filled the air with their nox-ious fumes. Ruha cleared the air with a powerful wind spell, then saw an angry veserab cow leap onto a camel's neck and rip the thing's head off with four sharp-taloned feet.

More veserabs began to rise all around, filling the dusk air with fluttering clouds of dark wings. Most were simply trying to escape, but a few, especially those with calves whistling for help, were beginning to wheel toward the Bedine warriors. A veserab dived low in front of Sa'ar, pulling a grizzled warrior off the camel ahead, then dropping him back to the ground in pieces. Ruha dismissed the silence spell and pointed toward the wadi they had chosen as their escape route.

"Enough, Sa'ar!" she yelled. "Flee!"

The sheikh did not need to be told twice. He sounded three notes on his *amarat*. His warriors—those who were not fleeing already—turned as one, each pulling two or three panicked veserab calves through the air behind them. Ruha hurled a flurry of magic bolts into the air and dusted half a dozen adults off the raiders' tails, then Caladnei raised a force barrier behind them. A dozen veserabs slammed into the invisible wall and dropped to the ground with broken necks and wings. The confused survivors circled away, whistling in frus-tration and sorrow.

Ruha and Caladnei followed. By the time they reached the mouth of the wadi, the veserabs were beginning to find their way over the force barrier. Ruha leaped off her camel and scraped up a handful of sand, then voiced an incantation and blew it toward the growing number of creatures streaming after them. A howling wind rose at her back and, scraping the canyon mouth clean of sand and dust, roared out toward the lake. The veserabs van-ished into a cloud of swirling dust and did not emerge.

"Your magic has grown stronger, witch," Sa'ar observed behind her. "Remind me to be patient with you."

Ruha turned to find him holding the reins of her camel. The rest of his warriors were emerging from their hiding places in the mouth of the wadi, half of them covering the raiders' back trail with bows and arrows, the other half pulling the captured veserabs down out of the air and binding them with leather hoods and wing jackets. Though most Bedine were adept at handling falcons and other birds of prey, veserab calves were both larger and more ferocious. The battle was not all that one-sided, and the warriors were paying in blood for every lace they threaded.

Ruha commanded her camel to kneel, then, as she mounted, heard one roar a little way up the wadi. She pivoted toward the sound and saw a line of tethered mounts collapsing, their throats and bellies being opened by glassy black blades as a Shadovar patrol peeled itself out of the shadows along the gulch. She loosed a lightning bolt at a figure rising up behind Sa'ar's camel and saw the fellow's head come apart before he sank back into the murk. Caladnei cried out in shock behind her, and Ruha turned to find the Cormyrean on the ground, pinned beneath her wounded camel with a ruby-eyed Shadovar warrior leaping over the top. She flung a ball of spider silk at the figure and uttered a spell, and he hit the ground encased in a sticky cocoon.

Finally, there was time to scream, "Shadovar! Defend yourselves!"

Even Ruha could barely hear her voice over the battle din that had already risen in the wadi. Bedine were shouting to each other about demons and djinn and, finding attackers at their backs no matter which way they turned, falling fast. The Shadovar were rising from the shadows to hack off an arm or leg, then vanishing back into the murk before they could be counterattacked.

Ruha grabbed Caladnei under the arms and pulled her from under her camel.

"Are you hurt?"

"Stunned," the wizard replied, mouth gaping at the carnage. She lowered her hand and sent a golden bolt streaking through a Shadovar rising behind Ruha, then shook her head in astonishment. "Where did they come from?"

"Out of the shadows," Ruha said.

She slipped around to Caladnei's back and shot a long stream of fire at a Shadovar rising behind a Bedine camel boy, no doubt holding reins on his first raid. The fireball exploded without harming the shadow warrior, as Weave magic sometimes did, and the dark figure ran his sword through the young warrior, then melted back into the shadows.

"This is how it often is with them," Ruha said.

"Really?" Caladnei gasped. She was silent for an instant, and Ruha glanced over her shoulder to see the wizard rubbing the purple dragon on her signet ring. "Hhormun, come quick. You need to see this!"

"Come?" Ruha cried.

She glimpsed a Shadovar rising up from behind a boulder with a blowpipe in his hands and flung a pebble in his direction, then spoke a single word. The pebble became a bead of magma. When it hit the boulder, the boulder erupted into a thousand drops of molten stone as well, and the warrior vanished in a searing orange spray.

"We should be fleeing!" said Ruha.

"Flee?" Caladnei shook her head. "There can't be more than two dozen left."

"And more where they came from," warned Ruha.

She had no idea how close they were to the city, but she knew the Shadovar well enough to feel certain this was just the first wave of the attack. Even if they didn't realize there were Cormyreans involved in the raid, they would send a company of veserab riders to make an example of any tribe that dared steal from them.

"They're just trying to delay us," Ruha said.

"Yes, so I guessed when they attacked our camels first."

The Cormyrean loosed a silver ray at a pair of Shadovar charging Sa'ar, who was still struggling to slip a hood and wing jacket over the last veserab tied to his dead camel. When the attack succeeded only in stunning the shadow warriors back into the murk, Ruha left Caladnei's side and dodging one black sword and reducing the owner of the second to a cinder even darker than his normally swarthy complexion, stopped at the sheikh's side.

"Are you mad, Sa'ar?" She swatted the creature's head aside as it swung around to bite at her knee, then continued, "Let it go! A few veserabs cannot be worth so many Mahwa lives."

The sheikh did not even look up from his work. "Mounts that can fly across the sky? The Mahwa will be the masters of the desert!"

He finally managed to pull the hood over the creature's faceless head, then was struck from behind by a bolt of shadow magic that pitched him face first over the waist-high calf. His arm went limp and Ruha saw ground through a jagged hole in it. Before she could sweep a pebble off the ground to counterattack, the sheikh had pulled a throwing dagger with his good hand and pivoted around to whip it at his charging attacker.

The throw missed, of course, but it distracted the Shadovar long enough for Ruha to pull her own *jambiya*. She grabbed the laces of the calf's hood and held it beside her for the half second it took the shadow warrior to close. Ruha came up beneath his guard and opened him from groin to ribs. She was mildly surprised to see that the stuff spilling out of him looked much the same as that coming out of the Bedine.

"May Elah smile on you," Sa'ar gasped, his good arm thrown over the veserab's back, supporting him. "How many times have you saved my life, now?"

"Too many times for one sheikh," Ruha said, pulling him to his feet. She took his curved amarat horn and pressed it into his good hand. "Now blow your horn and scatter your warriors. Veserabs are no good to dead men."

Sa'ar thrust the horn away. "They are *my* veserabs now," he said, "and no man steals from Sa'ar, Sheikh of the Mahwa."

Ruha let her chin sink. "You are a fool, Sheikh."

"Almost certainly," Sa'ar said, pushing the calf's head toward her. "Now help me lace this up, before the battle turns against us again."

"Again?"

Ruha looked around and saw that while the battle was continuing to rage, the Shadovar were now being assailed by magic and iron whenever they drew near a Bedine. She glanced up the slopes of the wadi and saw Hhormun standing atop a boulder, his *aba* tossed aside somewhere to reveal the black battle cloak of a Cormyrean War Wizard. He was wielding two wands at once, hurling blazing nuggets of fire or crackling forks of lightning whenever a Shadovar dared emerge from the murk to attack. Flanking him were two full ranks of Purple Dragons, loading and firing their iron crossbows by turn, while a smaller ring of three wizards and two dozen dragoneers stood by staring into the murk, attacking any shadow that so much as flickered.

"The fool!" Ruha hissed. "Does he think no one will see him? Or that the Most High will think the iron bolts came from Bedine crossbows?"

"I do not know what he thinks," Sa'ar said, "only that he is a man of his word. Now, will you help me or not, witch?"

After a quick glance around to ensure they were under no imminent threat of attack, Ruha helped him lace the hood. By the time she finished, Caladnei was standing at the upper end of the battlefield, waving the Bedine survivors up the wadi.

"Come along, and quickly!" The Cormyrean's gaze was fixed on the sky above the lake, where Ruha's sandstorm was still raging. "Be quick about it."

Ruha pushed Sa'ar and the reins of his three veserab calves into the arms of a group of stunned-looking warriors, then turned in the direction Caladnei was facing and saw a large company of veserab riders approaching from the north, flying high above her sandstorm. They were still too distant for her to tell much more than that there were several hundred of them, but she would have bet her veil that a force of that size was being led by a Prince of Shade.

Hhormun and his dragoneers began an orderly withdrawal toward Caladnei—and Ruha was not at all sorry to see the Shadovar survivors concentrating their efforts on the Cormyreans instead of Sa'ar and his Mahwa. The shadow lords were being more careful now, emerging from the murk just long enough to fling a shadow bolt through a warrior's knee or hamstring a wizard, clearly attempting to delay their retreat until the veserab company arrived.

Ruha ran up the wadi and joined Caladnei, who was busily spraying magic into the hillside shadows in an attempt to help her struggling companions. With her attack magic all but exhausted, Ruha prepared a sand dragon spell, but held it in reserve in case Caladnei irritated the Shadovar enough to draw an attack.

Between the wizardess's attacks, Ruha said, "Had Hhormun been waiting here with the rest of Sa'ar's warriors, the Mahwa might have lost fewer lives."

"Or we all might have lost more," Caladnei said. "This way, it was the Shadovar who were surprised, not us."

"And you had a chance to watch them fight." Ruha did not bother to keep the bitterness out of her voice.

Caladnei sprayed a pair of Shadovar with some sort of green ray Ruha was not familiar with, reducing both warriors to smoky wisps and opening the way for Hhormun's battered company to join them in the bottom of the wadi.

She cocked her brow and glanced at Ruha. "We had a chance to watch them fight, but it was their idea to steal the veserabs."

"True—and you took advantage." Ruha was fighting to keep from yelling. The story was an old one, the *berrani* from outside Anauroch entering the desert and using the nomads for their own purposes. "Sa'ar would never have attempted such a thing without Cormyrean magic."

"It sounds to me like we took advantage of each other." Caladnei shrugged and pointed up the wadi, where Sa'ar and his warriors were leading their new veserabs into the teleport circle that would carry them to safety—at least temporarily. "I don't see the sheikh complaining."

Hhormun and the rest of the Cormyrean scouts arrived, with half a dozen Shadovar close on their heels. Caladnei took out two with one of her green rays, then Hhormun and another wizard killed three more. The last warrior glanced over his shoulder and, finding the veserab company still too distant to aid him, began to run for the nearest shadow. When no one else started a spell, Ruha scraped a handful of sand off the ground and started hers—only to be interrupted when Hhormun brought his arm down across her wrists.

"Let him go," he said. "He's not hurting anybody now."

"Hurting anybody?" Ruha gasped. "He's seen your wizard's cloak. He'll run straight to the Most High and confirm that we're a scouting party from Cormyr."

"Will he?" A faint smile came to Hhormun's bearded lips, and he turned up the wadi. "Then we had better hurry to our next campsite, hadn't we?"

Ruha's jaw fell behind her veil. She stood there staring after the old wizard until Caladnei took her arm.

"Come along," the Cormyrean woman said. "The point has been made. Vangerdahast wouldn't be happy if you stayed behind to confirm it . . . not happy at all."

❧ ❧ ❧ ❧ ❧

Rivalen had battled three phaerimm at once, toe to thorn and with no chance to call for help. He had dallied with twin succubae and awakened to find them—well, he didn't want to relive that again. He had fought demons—bare-handed, by Shadow—and been the one who flew away. And never, not in eight-hundred years—not even when he gave his spirit over to the shadowstuff—not once had he been frightened. Not like this.

"How?" the Most High asked. His voice was calm, gentle—even reasonable—in that terrible tone it assumed just before he condemned someone to an eternity of wandering the Barrens of Doom and Despair. "Can someone please explain this?"

They were looking down at the camp of the Harper witch and her Cormyrean scouts. Not scrying it through the world-window, mind you, but looking straight down on it from the Most High's personal observation balcony in the Palace Most High. Staring down through the shadow mists at an imminently defensible camp, located in a maze of canyons so narrow a veserab's wings would touch both sides. A maze of canyons flooded by magic light with no particular source, where the few shadows that did exist were guarded by a squad of sentries armed with both magic and steel. A maze of canyons where the Shadovar would have to fight their way in like common orc footsoldiers, and a maze of canyons with plenty of room for more Cormyreans . . . and Sembians . . . and Dalesmen . . . and the Hidden One only knew who else, all determined to deny the lands of lost Netheril to the Shadovar.

The witch could not see them, of course. Certainly, her Bedine vassals had reported to her the stream of veserabs that constantly dropped into the lake there, and no doubt remarked on the dark storm cloud that never seemed to leave the area, but she could not *see* Shade Enclave. There were still the shadow mists and the thousands of feet above ground and, not least of all, the Most High's magic, but Rivalen was not so sure.

"Rivalen?"

Rivalen felt the weight of the Most High's gaze upon him. He did not bother to look up. There was nothing there to see anyway. He simply swallowed his fear, then addressed his father.

"There is a reason Ruha hides her face behind a veil, Most High," he said. "Of all the races on Toril, the Shadovar have more reason than any to know the power of the hidden."

"True, but that explains nothing."

Rivalen swallowed—hard. "Most High, who can explain the will of the Hidden One? The witch is down there; that is all that matters—save my own failure in stopping her in Cormyr."

It was this last that saved him. The weight of the Most High's scrutiny vanished at once, and the air grew still and cold as he came to Rivalen's side.

"You did as you thought best, my son," Telamont said, and Rivalen's shoulder grew numb with cold. "I am sure you will make it up to us."

"As am I," Rivalen said.

"Good." The Most High squeezed his shoulder until Rivalen thought it would break. "Now, we must concern ourselves with what to do next."

"The answer is clear, Most High," said Clariburnus. "We must kill the witch."

The Most High was silent.

Clariburnus continued, the words spilling out of him like breath. "The magic of the Weave is impure and weak, no match for the Shadow Weave. All we need do is drop a shadow blanket—"

"And that will help us how?" the Most High asked, his voice alarmingly reasonable and calm. "By disposing of your mistake?"

"*My* mistake, Most High?"

"Was she not your guide, brother?" Rivalen asked. "Yours and Brennus's?"

"She was," Brennus answered, "and *we* controlled her."

"Enough!" the Most High spat. "There is no use in blaming each other. I am disappointed in all of you."

The Most High remained silent.

Escanor was the first who dared to speak. "What does the witch matter? If she cannot enter the city, what does it matter if she camps below us for a century?"

"It only matters if you are wrong," the Most High responded.

The question hung in the air as heavy as lead. None of the brothers dared answer.

Finally, the Most High said, "You have all failed me. All of you princes." The shadow mists briefly obscured the tents of the Cormyrean camp, and when they cleared again, the princes were looking at a circle of white rocks. "Do you see that circle?"

"A teleportation circle," Rivalen said.

His knees nearly buckled under the weight of the Most High's question.

"For retreat, I believe," Rivalen said.

More silence.

"But I could be wrong," Rivalen admitted.

"If he is, there will be an army below us in hours," Clariburnus said. "Laeral required less than three hours to transport her entire relief army to the Sharaedim."

Rivalen glowered into Clariburnus's lead-colored eyes. As the Eleventh Prince—and the youngest still surviving—he was an ambitious one, always eager to raise himself at his brothers' expense.

"Do not blame your brother for your failures, Rivalen," Clariburnus said. "In Cormyr, the Steel Regent bested you handily."

Escanor, always Rivalen's favorite brother, said, "We have all underestimated the enemy."

"You certainly have," Clariburnus said.

Escanor took a step toward the junior prince—only to find Hadrhune blocking his way.

"Dear princes, if we allow the enemy to divide us like this, we have lost already." The seneschal—more ambitious than any of the princes and, in his own way, more dangerous—turned toward the Most High. "Mighty Telamont, if I may—"

"If you must."

Hadrhune continued, nonplussed, "If I may suggest a

more conservative strategy, perhaps we should call our armies home and defend the enclave."

Telamont remained silent.

"Yes, Most High, I *do* believe the witch might know a way into the enclave," the seneschal added, glancing in the direction of Clariburnus and Brennus. "We do not know what she learned when she was brought here. You are aware of where I found her."

The Most High whirled away from the rail and stabbed an empty sleeve at Hadrhune's face. "The Faerû-nians are not being reasonable!" he stormed. "What do we want, but what was Netheril's to begin with? By what right do they deny us?"

Rivalen breathed easier and settled in for the rant. Having not been born for seven hundred years after Shade left Faerûn, he did not feel the same sense of entitlement as the Most High, but he recognized the power it held over his father. The dream of reclaiming Anauroch and driving out the phaerimm was really all there was of Telamont Tanthul. At times, it made Rivalen wish he had been alive to see the glory that was Netheril, if only so he could understand his own phantom nature.

"Netheril was the most beautiful, the highest and mightiest, the worthiest civilization that Faerûn ever spawned!" Telamont complained. "And the Heartlands balk at a few decades of starvation! I would not hesi-tate—not hesitate at all, I tell you—to wipe them all from the face of the world if it meant the return of the floating cities. And the elves—I would *give* Evereska and Ever-meet both to the phaerimm, for just the century of peace we need to restore Anauroch to its glory."

Brennus stepped forward, head bowed and ceremo-nial fangs displayed. "If it pleases the Most High, I would be happy to go to the Sharaedim to open—"

"Negotiations?" The Most High cuffed him—actually

struck him—and sent the prince sprawling. "*That* I ought to allow."

The Most High turned to Rivalen, platinum eyes burning with a question.

"The alliance could have their army here all too soon," Rivalen reported. "Our agents in Tilverton report that it is already many thousands strong, and growing by the hour."

The Most High turned to Clariburnus.

"Our army from the Sharaedim is passing south of the Shadow Sea as we speak," Clariburnus said. "It will reach Tilverton by tomorrow evening."

"How soon could it be here?" asked Hadrhune. As usual, the seneschal's impudence was beyond belief. It was as though he believed that because he was not plane-spawned he had nothing to fear from the Most High's wrath. "In time to stop the Cormyreans?"

Clariburnus inclined his head. "It is but an hour away."

Hadrhune turned to the Most High. "Perhaps we could split the army. Recall enough to ensure against an assault."

"That way lies defeat in both battles," Rivalen said. "There are more than ten thousand enemy soldiers in Tilverton, many of them war wizards and clerics. If I am to defeat them, I will need our entire army."

"Even the army in Myth Drannor?" Escanor asked.

In truth, Rivalen thought it would take that army as well, but he did not dare alienate his closest ally among the princes—and his only older brother.

He inclined his head to Escanor and said, "Any troops you were able to spare would certainly add to the victory."

"Unfortunately, I fear it will be impossible to spare any," Escanor said. "The Myth Drannor phaerimm are proving as obstinate—"

"I am sure you can spare half your troops," the Most High said. "Our victory in Tilverton must be quick. We must return our largest army to the Sharaedim within the month, before the shadowshell fails. The phaerimm are our greatest threat."

Escanor glanced at Rivalen, his coppery eyes burning with anger. "But if our losses are heavy—"

"We will be surrounded on all sides," Hadrhune confirmed. "Surely, a conservative approach is wiser."

The Most High considered this for a moment, then said, "You are half right. I will send princes to treat with polities more sympathetic to our cause. Lamorak, you will go to see the Red Wizards of Thay. Yder, you will seek out the true leaders of the Cult of the Dragon . . ."

The Most High continued on, outlining a strategy that would envelop the forces currently surrounding the Shadovar.

When he finally finished, Hadrhune tried again to assert his influence. "You have taken every wise precaution that can be taken, Most High . . . but what of my suggestion? Certainly, it is wisest to defend Shade Enclave first."

"Wait." The Most High turned to the Seraph of Lies, Malik. To the great credit of the little man's willpower, he did not seem to feel the weight of any unspoken questions, and Telamont was forced to ask, "You know Ruha better than any of us. Do you think she knows a way into the city?"

Malik's eyes grew as round as coins, and Rivalen thought he would have thrown himself over the balcony rail, had the prospect of a painful landing not been so great.

"In my experience, that witch can get into anywhere," Malik said. "She has intruded upon me many times in many delicate moments—and sometimes when

I could have sworn she was a thousand miles away."

The Most High considered this, then nodded. "I suppose it would be safer to assume that she knows a way into the enclave." His platinum eyes flared in Clariburnus's direction, then he looked back to Malik and asked, "So you would advise me to call Shade's armies home?"

"Indeed."

For a moment, Rivalen thought Malik would leave the matter at that, then the little man's face contorted into a mask of displeasure, and he said, "Only, I think it would be wiser to advise you to give all your troops to Rivalen and order him to attack."

The Most High's hood turned in the little man's direction.

"Because that is what you truly want to do, Most High," Malik blurted, "and a wise advisor always tells his master what his master is eager to hear."

"Is that so?"

Telamont's empty hood swung in Rivalen's direction, and Rivalen felt the weight of his father's question pressing down on his shoulders.

He inclined his head. "I will capture Tilverton and destroy the Alliance army," Rivalen said, "or I will die trying."

"Die if you must, but death does not excuse failure," the Most High said. He turned to Malik, and Rivalen could have sworn he saw a smile beneath the Most High's hood. "Thank you, little man. Not only are you my wisest advisor, you are the most honest."

CHAPTER SIXTEEN

27 Mirtul, the Year of Wild Magic

To the west lay the setting sun, its orange fury igniting a rusty blaze across the darkening sky and painting the jagged Stonelands in a fiery copper glow. Behind the lonely trees and distant monoliths, the shadows were lengthening, stretching their pointed tips across the parched pasturelands toward the city of Tilverton. To the north, purple darkness already cloaked the Desertsmouth Mountains. To the south, a lake of umbral murk was spreading outward from the foot of the Stormhorns. The attack could come from any direction or from all three, and with no more warning than the time a shadow needed to sweep across the plain. Or it might not come at all, though Galaeron knew better than to count on that.

Along with Vangerdahast, Alusair, Lady Regent Alasalynn Rowanmantle, and more aides than was safe, Galaeron was atop an unfinished wall tower in the Knoll District of Old Town, standing on a makeshift scaffolding that creaked every time someone shifted his weight, watching the darkness for the first hint of the enemy. Vangerdahast's attention was fixed on the south, as that was the only side of the city without a gate and he was convinced the Shadovar would want time to form ranks before the battle began. Most of the aides were convinced they would come out of the Desertmouth foothills, since that was both the shortest route to Anauroch and one of the most sheltered. Alusair was keeping her eye—and her archers' arrows— trained on the sky, for she was troubled by the descriptions of veserab riders and the fact of the Shadovar's alliance with Malygris and his blue dragons. Galaeron didn't know what to expect, but he felt sure that whatever the Shadovar did, it would be as unexpected as it was devastating.

A soft clatter sounded below as the bodyguard companies at the base of the tower ran through the procedure of admitting a runner. Finally, a herald called for permission to send up one of Vangerdahast's wizards, and a surprised murmur rose atop the keep as the aides nearest the ladder saw who it was. Galaeron looked down to see a willowy woman in a red cape ascending the long ladder. With red hair and golden eyes, even he recognized her as Vangerdahast's favorite aide—and, some said, lover—Caladnei.

The old wizard stepped over to the ladder and, as she neared the top, extended a hand. "About time, my dear," he said, pulling her onto the scaffolding. "What news?"

"Good news." She turned away and bowed to Alusair, then made her report directly to the regent. "Ruha has found the flying city, and it appears but lightly defended."

"Where is it?" Vangerdahast asked. "On the new lake?"

Caladnei nodded. "Floating above the north end. There is fresh water, and a defensible camp. Hhormun is preparing a translocational circle now."

Alusair considered the report for a moment, then said, "There's a reason the city is only lightly defended."

Vangerdahast nodded. "Either Galaeron is right and they're readying an attack . . ."

"Or they're hoping to lure us into a trap," Alusair finished. She turned to Galaeron. "What do you think?"

"The Shadovar are cunning warmakers," he said, "but the phaerimm are their most ancient enemies. Telamont Tanthul would risk freeing them only if he's allowing his anger to guide him."

"And angry men don't lie in wait," Alusair agreed. "They attack."

"Unless that's what he wants us to think," Caladnei pointed out. "Perhaps Telamont is confident he can defeat us quickly and return his army to the Sharaedim in time to keep the phaerimm in check."

"In which case, he can't let us set the pace," Vangerdahast said. "Either way, he's attacking *us*. Everything points to it."

Caladnei inclined her head to the old wizard. "I'll send word to Hhormun to save his spell."

Alusair raised a restraining hand. "Hold a moment." She bit her lip in thought, then turned to Vangerdahast with a half smile. "What if we could beat them to the strike?"

Galaeron's brow rose. "Beat them? If you timed matters wrong, Tilverton would be lost."

"True," Alusair said without losing enthusiasm, "but Cormyr has many cities. The Shadovar have only one."

Alasalynn Rowanmantle gasped aloud. "You would sacrifice Tilverton?"

"No, but I'd surely wager it," Alusair said, not grinning. "You do have an evacuation plan?"

Alasalynn's already pale face grew even paler. "I'll activate it."

She thumbed a ring on her middle finger and vanished in a crackle of magic.

Vangerdahast cocked his bushy brow and started to say something, then caught Alusair's warning glance and cleared his throat instead.

Alusair smiled. "Vangey, can you. . . ."

"Of course, Princess." Too plump and rickety for the ladder, Vangerdahast simply stepped to the edge of the scaffolding and looked for a clear place to land. "I'll prepare the device for transport at once."

Galaeron frowned but bit his tongue and managed to avoid asking about the "device." Their departure from Arabel had been delayed nearly a day and a half to give Vangerdahast and the war wizards time to "prepare." Galaeron had assumed that they were gathering magic items and memorizing spells, but he had realized this was not the case when the wizards emerged from their armory pulling a huge wagon covered with a tent of black canvas. The wizard had ignored Galaeron's repeated inquiries about the thing, saying only that it would prove once and for all that the Weave was mightier than the Shadow Weave.

When Galaeron made no move toward the ladder or Vangerdahast, the wizard grabbed him by the arm.

"Come along, young fellow." Vangerdahast pulled him off the scaffolding, and they floated down the hollow interior of the unfinished tower. "You'll want to see this."

At the bottom, they gathered Aris and Vangerdahast's troop of bodyguards and threaded their way down the knoll past company after company forming up for the short march to the translocational circle. The officers were engaging in no bluster or bravado and offered relatively few words of encouragement. Everyone knew the Shadovar were a strange and powerful enemy, and most wise commanders had prayed that the mere fact of the Heartlands Alliance would force the princes to reconsider the melting of the High Ice. That the Alliance was being marshaled for a night march put to rest any hope of ending the matter without a fight.

At the base of the hill, where the mansions of the Knoll District gave way to the exorbitant shops and inns that populated the rest of Old Town, Vangerdahast turned through the gate of the Windlord's Rest, which he had appropriated to serve as the headquarters of the war wizards. Instead of entering the cozy inn itself, he led the way past a mixed troop of war wizards and Purple Dragons into the livery.

Inside, the "device" sat covered in its wagon, fans of golden light spilling through the slats of the cargo bed to illuminate the stable floor. The light was incredibly bright, though it did not seem to burn the eyes of either Vangerdahast or the guards the way it did Galaeron's. He had to shield his face, and his palm began to nettle.

Vangerdahast smirked at Galaeron's reaction, then removed from his pocket a ring bearing a crude copy of the Purple Dragon of Cormyr.

"Sorry for the workmanship," the royal magician said, "there wasn't much time." He passed it over. "Put it on."

Galaeron slipped the ring onto his finger and immediately felt better. He also saw that the light was not nearly as bright as he had thought, barely showing through the slats at all.

"Interesting," he said. "How does it work?"

"I'll explain at the circle," Vangerdahast said. He turned toward the main doors, where Aris was crouched on hands and knees peering into the stable. "I would be indebted if you would draw the wagon for us. Translocational magic tends to make draught horses panic."

"My pleasure."

The giant stretched an arm through the doorway to grab the hitch—then a cry of alarm sounded from the courtyard behind him, and he stopped to look over his shoulder.

"Stonebones shield us!" Aris cried.

Galaeron stepped to the door and saw a company of dark forms peeling themselves out of the shadows, spraying the astonished guard companies outside with darts of black glass and bolts of shadow magic.

Aris cried out as a dark ray lanced out to pierce his forearm, then lashed out at his attacker with the same hand. Before the giant could close his fingers, the Shadovar changed back to shadow and drained away, then emerged behind him and pierced his thigh with another beam.

Aris screamed and whirled around. Galaeron saw a trio of Shadovar emerging adjacent to the door and could pay no more attention to the giant. He drew his sword and, waiting until the warriors began to assume a semblance of solidity, beheaded the nearest one. The body simply drained back into the shadow, but the dead man's companions whirled on Galaeron, their hands rising to unleash shadow spells.

Galaeron ducked back into the stable. "Warn the princess!" he yelled. "They've found me!"

"They've found my device," Vangerdahast corrected, peering past Aris's dancing legs into the courtyard. "But how? This city is warded!"

His bodyguards were beginning to counterattack with lightning bolts, crossbow quarrels, and—Galaeron was disappointed to see—bolts of raw magic. Even after hearing how the Sharn Wall had been breached, Vangerdahast had ignored Galaeron's suggestion that the War Wizards strike all spells of raw magic from their battle lists.

"I told you those wards were useless," Galaeron said, "as the Shadovar are about to prove."

The shadows inside the building began to undulate as more shadow warriors arrived. Galaeron tapped Vangerdahast on the shoulder, and the wizard glanced over his shoulder into the thicket of silhouettes rising behind them.

"Vexatious beings, aren't they?" the royal magician said.

Vangerdahast pointed at his device and made a lifting motion. The canvas cover rose to reveal a globe of living light, its exterior etched with hundreds of black glyphs similar to the warding tile Galaeron had seen two days before. The glyphs were swimming over the surface like water striders on a pond and casting dark shadows of themselves across the interior of the stable. As the silhouettes fell on the Shadovar warriors, the corresponding glyph stopped moving and affixed its shadow firmly in the center of the target's chest.

The Shadovar wailed in agony and tried to dodge aside or drop back into the shadows. It was difficult to say what happened to those who retreated into the fringe, but the others screamed in agony as their glyphs moved across the orb to keep the dark emblem painted on their torso. A second later, the symbol burst into golden flames, and they dissolved into sooty black smoke.

Galaeron noticed that, despite the ring Vangerdahast had given him, he was growing uncomfortably warm himself. He took shelter behind the wizard's ample form.

"Impressive." He glanced around behind them, expecting the ones who had retreated into the Shadow Fringe to reemerge at their backs. When the shadows remained as still as shadows should, he said, "Using a shadow to project the symbol prevents them from escaping into the fringe."

Vangerdahast beamed. "Imagine what I could have learned, had you actually demonstrated shadow magic." The wizard went to the front of the wagon and picked up the hitch. "Help me get this out where it will do some good."

Galaeron went to the other side and began to push against the crossbar. The wagon was incredibly heavy, as if the orb it carried were made of gold metal instead of gold light.

"Corellon's bolts!" he gasped. "Wouldn't it be faster to use magic?"

"It is folly to rely on magic for things your own strong back can do better," Vangerdahast said, frowning across the bar at him. "A wise woman taught me that."

"So you're saying you'll need your telekinesis spells later," Galaeron surmised.

"Exactly." Vangerdahast leaned into the hitch. "Now put your back into it."

Galaeron braced his feet and did as the wizard commanded. The effort was almost enough to make him break his promise not to use shadow magic. The floor was slick with dust and there was a slight incline at the threshold, and the battle raging in the courtyard had already become a desperate one. Purple Dragons lay two and three bodies deep, and Vangerdahast's war wizards were having to stand back to back to keep their Shadovar attackers from slipping through the shadows to attack from behind. Even then, the Shadovar were far more adept at using their defenses to stop Weave spells than the Cormyreans were at using their magic to stop shadow spells, and more than a dozen of the kingdom's battle mages already lay among the fallen dragoneers.

Aris was staggering around like a drunken fire dancer, bleeding from a dozen wounds, alternately trying to stomp enemy warriors flat or kick them out over the inn's roof.

"Aris!" Galaeron yelled. "Help us!"

The giant crossed the battle in a stride, scattering a trio of shadow warriors with a sweep of his large foot. He dropped to a knee and pulled the wagon across the threshold so quickly that Galaeron and Vangerdahast had to leap aside to keep from being crushed under the wheels. The silhouettes of the old wizard's glyphs danced over the surrounding walls for less than a second, then began to settle on their targets. The wispy screams of anguished Shadovar filled the air, then a thicket of golden flames flared to life across the courtyard, and their attackers vanished as quickly as they had appeared.

Galaeron rolled to his knees and found Vangerdahast lying against the opposite doorjamb, his chest heaving and his face contorted with pain. Galaeron's mind leaped immediately to the worst possible conclusion.

"Vangerdahast?" He scrambled across the doorway and pulled the portly wizard into his lap. It wasn't easy. "Are you hit?"

"No . . . just getting . . . old," the old wizard groaned. He rubbed a shoulder, then looked from Galaeron to one of his assistants who had come running and extended a hand. "How bad?"

"We lost thirteen war wizards and most of your dragoneers." The fellow used both hands to pull Vangerdahast to his feet—then grinned broadly. "But you were right about those ward tiles, milord. They lured the Shadovar in through the fringe just like you—"

"Yes, well, we've no time to waste congratulating ourselves," Vangerdahast growled, casting a sidelong glance in Galaeron's direction. "Let's finish this."

He rubbed his signet ring, then looked into the sky and said, "Alusair, the time has come. Are you in position?"

The wizard was silent for a moment, then nodded and looked back to his assistant. "The attack is citywide. Leave them no place to hide. Demolish any building they enter, if you must."

"I'll pass the word." The assistant acknowledged the order with a bow, then turned to cast a spell.

A weary look came to Vangerdahast's eyes. He motioned Galaeron to follow and shuffled toward Aris and the orb of light. Seeing that the battle had already taken more out of the wizard than the old fellow cared to admit, Galaeron offered a hand in support . . . and was not rebuffed.

"You planned this?" he asked. "You picked one of your own cities as the battlefield?"

"We certainly didn't let them take us by surprise, if that's what you were thinking," Vangerdahast snapped. "Cormyr *has* fought a few wars . . . and won them all."

"If I underestimated you, I apologize," Galaeron said, "but all that talk on the wall tower—"

"For the spies," Vangerdahast said. "The Shadovar do use spies, you know."

"I know," Galaeron said. "I thought you weren't listening to me."

Vangerdahast fixed Galaeron with a rheumy eye.

"Who says I was?"

Galaeron was too stunned to laugh. Though Tilverton's evacuation was under way, he had seen for himself that there had still been hundreds of women and children in the city earlier that evening—and the Cormyrean plan risked them all. How hard, he wondered, had been the lessons they learned in their last war against the dragon Nalavarauthatoryl? Had they truly grown so cold that they would knowingly sacrifice so many to win a quick victory—and save how many more? Perhaps that was what it required to defeat the Shadovar, and, more importantly, the phaerimm.

They reached the wagon, and the wizard stopped beside Aris's knee. "Stay close," Vangerdahast said. "I may have need of your talents."

Without waiting for a response, Vangerdahast cast a quick spell and lifted his hand heavenward. The golden orb shot high into the air, its glyphs growing motionless as they found their first targets. The battle din beyond the courtyard continued unabated for a moment, then slowly changed pitch as the symbol silhouettes began to take their toll. The wizard cocked his head as if listening to a distant voice, then moved his hand a few inches. The golden sphere floated a hundred yards across the sky.

"Come along. We need a better vantage point."

Vangerdahast laid a hand on each of them, spoke a magic word, and pulled them through the dark square of a magic door. There was a timeless instant of falling, then Galaeron found himself standing in bright golden light, feeling very hot and dizzy, listening to the sounds of a battle far below.

"Don't worry about being seen," said a familiar voice. "I've cast a couple of spells that will keep us hidden."

Galaeron recovered from his afterdaze enough to

recall that he was somewhere in the middle of the battle for Tilverton.

Vangerdahast was shaking him by the arm and pointing down at the ground. "What's that he's doing?"

Galaeron looked down—a *long* way down—and grew so dizzy that it took him a moment to find what the wizard was pointing at. It was a dark figure more than a hundred paces from the tower where they stood looking out over the raging battle. Barely visible beneath the canvas awning of a patio tavern, the figure was waving his outstretched arms in small circles, apparently summoning the black fog that was rising out of the cracks of the flagstones at his feet and spilling out into Old Town—much to the confusion and distress of the companies of Alliance warriors rushing about the streets flushing Shadovar from their hiding places.

"It's hard to tell without seeing how he cast the spell," Galaeron said, "but he seems to be summoning shadow-stuff."

Vangerdahast raised his brow. "Shadowstuff? Would that be raw—"

"Don't tell me!" Galaeron had a sinking feeling. "The glyphs—"

"Not the glyphs, or their silhouettes," Vangerdahast said, "but the sphere itself is raw magic."

"And the light?" Galaeron asked.

Vangerdahast shrugged. "Not in itself, but born of raw magic."

"Close enough," Aris said. He was kneeling on the other side of Vangerdahast, his elbows resting on the tower's stone crenellations to take some of his weight off the roof. "There is a disruption already."

He pointed into a street around the corner from the Shadovar, where the black fog was rolling out of the shadow of the building into the orb-lit street—and swirling about the shins of a company of Sembian mercenaries who had been attempting to sneak up on the object of their attention. Though the general battle din was too loud to hear their screams, their writhing arms and contorted postures left no doubt about their pain.

As Galaeron and the others watched, the warriors plunged to mid-thigh in the fog, then fell prone and vanished entirely. A moment later, the light of Vangerdahast's orb turned the shadowstuff itself to ash. It sank to the ground, covering the street in an inky stain of darkness devoid of shape or texture—or even any apparent substance.

Vangerdahast pointed at the fog and cast what Galaeron recognized as a spell of magic dismissal. The shadowstuff continued to roll out of the Shadovar's hiding place, floating across the dark stain to brush against the orb-lit foundation of the mansion across the street. The stone disintegrated as had the legs of the Sembian mercenaries, and the building itself collapsed into the inky murk that had been, until a few moments earlier, a cobblestone street.

It vanished without raising so much as a dust plume.

Another building on the other side of the Shadovar spellcaster collapsed, then a company of Purple Dragons came charging into view with a tide of the shadowstuff rolling down the street behind them. It appeared they would be fast enough to reach safety—until the rear rank threw up their arms and fell, bringing down those in front of them, and so on until the entire company was gone.

Trees and buildings began to vanish in a widening circle as the shadowstuff spread, first creating lacy paths of nothingness where the black fog worked its way into orb-lit areas, then gradually developing into a solid disk of murk as adjacent areas were exposed to the golden light. The battle at the edge of the circle grew wildly intense as Shadovar and Alliance warriors fought for control of the escape lanes, filling the dusk sky with flashing lightning bolts and hissing rays of darkness. Only the patio where the fog-summoner himself stood remained untouched, revealing a huge figure in a horned helm still waving his outstretched arms, calling more shadowstuff up into the streets.

Galaeron clasped Vangerdahast's arm. "You're destroying the city!" he said. "Annul your spell, or at least move it out over the plain."

"And let the Shadovar destroy our armies?" Vangerdahast scoffed. "Better to lose a city than a kingdom."

Galaeron stared out over the collapsing city and thought of all the dying warriors, of all the innocents who would perish if the shadow fog continued to spread. Vangerdahast had tried to dispel it and failed.

But Vangerdahast could not use the Shadow Weave, and Galaeron could. What kind of person would turn his back on the deaths of so many—even if it meant the return of his shadow self? Galaeron had recovered from it once, and with Aris and Vangerdahast, and the entire kingdom of Cormyr to stand with him this time, he could certainly do so again. Even if he could not, what was he sacrificing, really? Only his life, and hundreds had done that already.

Galaeron took a deep breath, then raised his hands and started to open himself to the Shadow Weave—and found Aris's big hand reaching over Vangerdahast to pluck him off the rooftop.

"Galaeron, you are forgetting your promise."

"Not forgetting," Galaeron said, "but I can't let thousands die while I do nothing."

"So your shadow would have you believe," the giant replied, "but you know better than to think you can dispel the magic of someone like Prince Rivalen."

"That's Rivalen?" Vangerdahast gasped.

Aris nodded. "I would recognize that face anywhere. Can you not see his golden eyes?"

Galaeron was undeterred. "I have to try," he said. "If there's any chance I can save Tilverton—"

"There is not, and you know it," Aris said, "but the choice must be yours, or your shadow has already won."

He placed Galaeron on the roof beside Vangerdahast. Galaeron watched another mansion tumble into nothingness, then the golden blaze of a dozen Shadovar warriors burning into ash beneath the light of the war wizards' artificial sun.

Vangerdahast glanced into the street below. "Fog's coming this way," he observed. "Our tower will go soon."

Galaeron started to lower his arms, then felt such a pang of guilt that he realized he would not be able to live with himself if he just let all those innocent people die.

"I have to try—"

"No you don't." It was Vangerdahast who knocked Galaeron's arms down this time. "You're no match for Rivalen, and we both know it."

"But—"

"There are other ways," Vangerdahast said. There was an emotion unaccustomed to the wizard's face in his expression, something sad and contrite, almost kind. "If you're going to throw your life away, at least do it wisely."

He placed Galaeron's hand on his sword, then motioned him to wait and looked into the sky. "Caladnei, I need you. We're on the Tower of Wond—"

Vangerdahast had barely finished before the air hissed with her arrival.

"My dear, what took you so long?" Vangerdahast mocked. As the wizardess struggled to recover from her afterdaze, he guided her hand to Aris's knee. "Take the giant and go to Alusair. If that shadow fog does not stop expanding in the next few minutes, you are to sound the retreat, then teleport to safety with the princess and as many others as you can take."

Caladnei's eyes remained vacant. "Fog? Retreat—?"

"I understand," Aris said. He clapped a big hand over Galaeron's shoulder. "Till swords part, my friend. Good luck."

"Good luck?" Galaeron asked. "What am I doing?"

"We'll decide that later," Vangerdahast said, taking his arm. "Just have your sword ready and start cutting when we get there."

The wizard spoke a mystic word, and Galaeron felt again the timeless falling of translocational magic. He was growing almost accustomed to the feeling, but that did not make the afterdaze any less disorienting when his stomach finally settled back into its proper place. The ground beneath his feet felt unsteady and yielding, almost as though he were standing on a soft human bed instead of anything like a street or floor.

Cut!

Vangerdahast's voice came to Galaeron inside his head. He felt the ground bouncing under him as the old wizard hobbled away. He recalled, dimly, that they were in some sort of battle and that his last instruction before the teleport had been to start cutting, so he jammed his sword into the softness beneath his boots and began to—

A loud ripping noise sounded between his feet and he found his stomach turning somersaults again, this time more normally as he plunged through a canvas awning. Something sharp punctured the chain mail on his leg and sank deep into his thigh, sending a bolt of fiery agony shooting up through his body. He hung for a moment high up beneath the awning, until whatever he had landed on toppled over and dropped, crashing, onto a wooden table.

A raspy voice screamed in agony. The sharp point pulled free of Galaeron's thigh. He fell off the table onto a hard stone floor, then rolled to his knees and found himself peering over the table at the figure of a hulking Shadovar holding a horned helm in his hands.

"Elf!" Rivalen said, tossing the helm aside. "I thought we would need to look for you in Suzail by now."

"Here I am." Galaeron rose from behind the table and, glancing at the broad swath of orb-light that separated them, tried to appear confident. "All you need do is come get me."

Rivalen peered up at the rip in the canopy. "Yes, I'm certain you would like that." He smiled, then glanced over Galaeron's shoulders. "I think I will have my guards do it. Seize him!"

Heart sinking at the sudden clamor that erupted from the patio edge behind him, Galaeron vaulted the table into the swath of orb light, landing so that he had the prince on one flank and the approaching bodyguards on the other. Of course there were guards.

There were always guards.

Wondering what was taking Vangerdahast so long, Galaeron glanced up at the ripped awning. He had a chance of leaping high enough to grab hold and climb to safety—but, with one wounded leg, not much of one.

"Don't let him get away!" Rivalen ordered, starting forward from his side—apparently unaware that Galaeron had come with company. At least that much of Vangerdahast's plan was working. "Take him now!"

The guards, already rushing across the patio, began to vault tables and kick chairs aside. Galaeron leaped as high as he could and slashed at the torn edge of the awning.

The canvas, already weakened by his first cut, split down its length. More Shadovar than Galaeron could count in a glance howled in anguish as the orb light poured through and fixed them with the silhouette of a death glyph. Those closest to the tavern walls turned and dived for shade, their bodies bursting into sprays of golden flame as they tumbled through the windows. The rest perished where they stood, setting the wooden chairs and wooden tables alight as they died.

Galaeron pivoted into the sunlight and brought his sword around into a guarding position. Where the devil was Vangerdahast? Rivalen stopped a safe distance back beneath the remaining half of the awning, his golden eyes burning almost white with rage.

"Enough, traitor. You will drop your sword and come to me." He pointed his finger at the far edge of the patio behind Galaeron and spoke a word of command, then continued, "Or you will perish with your friends."

Galaeron glanced over his shoulder and saw a plume of shadowstuff rising from a corner of the patio still shaded by a dangling flap of torn awning. It was slowly spreading across the flagstones toward him, bringing its tide of oblivion steadily closer. He looked back to the prince.

"You wouldn't dare," Galaeron said, trying to sound confident. "The Most High—"

He was interrupted by the sudden eruption of Rivalen's chest. Galaeron danced quickly aside as the dregs of the purple death ray shot past, then looked back to see the prince's body crashing to the floor and Vangerdahast standing behind him with ten smoking fingertips. Galaeron stepped into the safety of the awning shadows.

"Took you long enough," he said.

"I'm old," Vangerdahast replied, and he sounded it. His gaze remained fixed on the far corner of the patio, where wisps of shadowstuff continued to pour from whatever fissure Rivalen had opened into the shadow plane. "I thought that would stop when he died."

Galaeron frowned, then looked down to discover that all that remained of Rivalen was a long black spine and an ebony heart beating in a broken cage of black ribs. To his horror, it was rolling onto its back and rising in Vangerdahast's direction.

"Vangerdahast, watch your—"

The prince's remains—if that was what they were—hurled themselves at the wizard. A deep gash appeared across Vangerdahast's collarbone, and blood began to spurt from the wound in great red arcs. Vangerdahast cried out in pain and stumbled back, one hand crackling with fire and the other with lightning. Galaeron leaped to the attack, slamming his sword into the ebony spine with enough force to fell a fair-sized sapling.

The bone did not even chip, though the ribs did pivot slightly as an unseen heel slammed into his stomach. He doubled over and flew backward, his sword flying away as the air left his lungs. He crashed down just beyond the awning's shadow, less than an arm's length from oblivion's advancing edge. Behind him, the far wall of the patio crashed down and vanished into darkness.

Vangerdahast thrust one hand forward and poured lightning into the dark heart. It stopped beating—but only for as long as the lightning continued. A red gash opened in the wizard's cloak, and a sword-shaped spray of blood came out the back.

Vangerdahast bellowed—more in rage than pain—and filled the cage of black ribs with magic fire.

The wizard's head snapped sideways. Vangerdahast's arms dropped to his side, and Galaeron, already leaping back into the fray with a drawn dagger, screamed. The ribs half turned toward him, and for a moment Rivalen's golden eyes appeared in the air above the writhing vertebrae of the neck.

Vangerdahast's weary arms came up, wrapping themselves around the skeletal body, and he uttered a familiar command word. They vanished in a sizzle of teleport magic—

—and Rivalen's raspy voice erupted in anguish on the orb-lit patio. Galaeron spun around to find the prince—or, rather, the prince's ribs and heart—erupting into golden flame as Vangerdahast tried to push the black thing into the inky darkness creeping toward them both.

Galaeron was there in a leap, arriving heels first to kick Rivalen over the edge. The ribs and heart vanished, burning, into black nothingness—and Vangerdahast started after them, suddenly spinning around on his back, sleeve stretching over his head into darkness. Galaeron landed alongside him facing the wrong direction, but grabbed the wizard's belt and pulled himself around, then hacked the cuff free.

Vangerdahast let out a pained gasp and jerked his hand back. All that remained of it were the fingers, thumb, and a small piece of flesh connecting it to the wrist. The rest was simply not there, as though it had been rendered invisible or lost to the bite of some very strange creature.

The adjacent wall of the tavern crumbled into oblivion,

leaving only the corner with the shadowstuff fountain standing upright. Galaeron pulled Vangerdahast back under the awning and began to go through the pockets of the wizard's cloak.

"Do you have any healing potions?" Galaeron asked, tossing aside feathers and satchels full of iron filings.

With sunken eyes and skin as gray as a snow cloud, the wizard looked like he had died already. Galaeron could see at least two life-threatening wounds, and suspected there were other injuries he could not even guess at.

"Any way to get us to help?" asked Galaeron.

Vangerdahast's gaze grew vacant and slid away.

"Vangerdahast?" Galaeron placed his ear close to the wizard's mouth and was relieved to hear a soft, steady wheezing. "Vangerdahast?"

When the wizard still made no reply, Galaeron stanched the bleeding as best he could, then stood on a table to search for help. He was not surprised to discover that the fighting was already over—cataclysmic magic had a way of ending battles swiftly—but he was astonished at the extent of the destruction. Much of Tilverton—all of Old Town below him and the rest of the city out past the Moonsea Ride—already lay beneath a sea of shadowstuff, and the stain was continuing to spread. The great Council Tower in the center of town was sinking into oblivion even as he watched, and he could hear warriors from both sides calling to each other in the dark streets beyond, all more concerned with saving their own lives than taking anyone else's. Whether Lady Regent Rowanmantle had succeeded in evacuating the rest of her citizens, Galaeron could not say, but he took the lack of matronly voices and sobbing children to be a good sign—one of the few of the day.

Finding no possibility of help there, Galaeron hopped down and went to the uphill side of the patio. The scene there was much the same as below, save that most of the shadowstuff had rolled downhill into the lower city, sparing much of the Knoll District, the jagged ruins of Tilver's Palace, and a lengthy section of wall.

It was there, atop one of the as yet unfinished wall towers, that he found their salvation. Atop one of the spires, no more than two hundred paces distant, stood Aris's looming figure, illuminated in the yellow light of Vangerdahast's orb, one hand raised to his brow as he searched the city. Galaeron stepped as near the edge of the awning as he dared and waved. For a moment, there was no response, and he began to fear that even the stone giant's keen sight would not be able to see him beneath the canopy.

When Aris pointed in his direction, Galaeron knew they were saved. He waited a couple of moments for the giant to return his wave, then dropped off the table to return to Vangerdahast's side—and found Caladnei already kneeling there, pouring a healing potion down the wizard's throat one drop at a time.

As Galaeron limped over, she looked up with an angry scowl on her face. "When you need help, call for it." She pointed her chin at the ring Vangerdahast had given him. "That's what the purple dragon is for."

❧ ❧ ❧ ❧ ❧

"What in the name of all the drow gods," the Steel Regent demanded, pacing back and forth in front of Galaeron, "did you do to my Royal Magician?"

It was almost dawn, and they were encamped—hiding, really—with what remained of the armies of the Heartlands Alliance, a mile outside of what had once been

Tilverton. The shadowstuff had consumed the city almost completely, spreading well beyond the walls to engulf even the outlying stock pens and caravan campsites. All that remained of the city was the wall atop the Knoll District and the jagged ruins of Tilver's Palace, now back lit by the sinking sphere of Vangerdahast's magic orb.

Alusair waved a hand at the golden ball. "He won't look at anything but that damnable globe, and he keeps asking if we won. What do I tell him? That we won because we had more survivors than the Shadovar? Or that we lost because we lost our entire army? How do I snap him out of this?"

"Tell him the truth," Galaeron suggested. "Tell him that no one won."

"That would not be the truth," Aris said.

Alusair whirled on the seated giant and, despite the fact that she had to crane her neck to see his face, somehow still seemed to be looking him straight in the eye.

"Are you saying Shade won?" she demanded. "Because I know *we* didn't. Not if we've lost Vangerdahast."

"I am saying that the phaerimm won," the giant answered. "They still control Evereska, and now they will soon be free."

Alusair's already stormy face turned absolutely tempestuous. "Thank you for making an insufferable loss seem even worse." She whirled on Galaeron. "This is your doing, elf. Had Vangerdahast had a better understanding of shadow magic—"

"He would have done exactly as he did, Majesty," said Caladnei, stepping to Galaeron's defense. "You can ask a warrior to lay down his life for you but not his soul."

"Elves don't have souls," Alusair shot back, "but I see what you mean." She cast a sidelong glance in Galaeron's direction. "That's as much of an apology as you're going to get, elf."

"And more than is required," Galaeron replied. "All I ask is that you let me assist when you do attack."

"Still thinking of Vala, are we?" Alusair asked.

Galaeron nodded. "Always."

The truth was that since escaping Tilverton, he had been able to think of nothing but the thing Vangerdahast had killed, wondering if Escanor was something similar, and of what Vala must be suffering in service to such a thing. However great her pain, whatever her humiliation, he was to blame. He had allowed his shadow self to drive her away, and it was because of his weakness—*that* weakness—that she was imprisoned in Escanor's palace.

"I have much to answer for," Galaeron added.

Alusair's expression grew almost sisterly. "We all do, Galaeron." She reached out and squeezed his arm, then turned to face Tilverton, where Vangerdahast's orb was just sinking behind the Knoll District wall. "We all do."

As the globe vanished from sight, a terrible rumbling rolled across the plain, shaking the ground so hard that the wounded—what few they had been able to evacuate—began to groan. The glow over Tilverton darkened for a moment, then returned in an exploding fan of golden light.

With that Vangerdahast was up and standing tall, looking as regal and powerful and truly frightening as the mighty wizard Galaeron had come to know—and perhaps even love—in his short time in Cormyr.

"To arms!" Vangerdahast's voice boomed across the plain. "Summon my War Wizards! Call out the Purple Dragons! Azoun calls, and we ride—for king and Cormyr!"

Alusair and Caladnei were at the wizard's side almost instantly, taking him by the arms and soothing him with gentle words. Galaeron did not hear exactly what they said, for his attention was fixed on Tilverton, where the entire Knoll District was rapidly sinking into the dark plain, taking with it the last bitter reminders of the Heartlands Alliance—and all of Faerûn's hopes for a season without starvation. Soon, all that remained of the city were the back lit ruins of Tilver's Palace, surrounded by smaller piles of dark rubble. The last rays of Vangerdahast's light paled to darkness, and eventually even they were lost.

Shandril's Saga

Ed Greenwood's legendary tales of Shandril of Highmoon are brought together in this trilogy that features an all-new finale!

SPELLFIRE
Book I

"Director's cut" version in an all-new trade paperback edition!

The secret of Spellfire has fallen into the hands of Shandril of Highmoon. Now the forces of the evil Zhentarim are after her.

April 2002

CROWN OF FIRE
Book II

All-new trade paperback edition!

Shandril and Narm are on the run from the Zhentarim. As they make their way toward Waterdeep, aided by a motley band of fighters and mages, the danger grows.

June 2002

New!
HAND OF FIRE
Book III

*Ed Greenwood's latest novel brings
Shandril's Saga to its thrilling conclusion!*

The forces of the Zhentarim and the terrifying Cult of the Dragon converge on Shandril, but there may be a worse fate in store for her.

September 2002

R.A. Salvatore's
War of the Spider Queen

New York Times best-selling author R.A.
Salvatore, creator of the legendary dark elf
Drizzt Do'Urden, lends his creative genius to
a new FORGOTTEN REALMS® series that delves
deep into the mythic Underdark and even
deeper into the black hearts of the drow.

DISSOLUTION
Book I
Richard Lee Byers sets the stage as the delicate power structure
of Menzoberranzan tilts and threatens to smash apart. When
drow faces drow, only the strongest and most evil can survive.

July 2002

INSURRECTION
Book II
Thomas M. Reid turns up the heat on the drow civil war and
sends the Underdark reeling into chaos. When a god goes silent,
what could possibly set things right?

December 2002

THE DRY ROT PROBLEM

THE RENTOKIL LIBRARY

Sporophores often give the first indication of the presence of the Dry Rot Fungus *(Merulius lacrymans)*. The timber in the photograph looks sound, but when removed, it was so badly damaged that it fell to pieces.

THE
DRY ROT
PROBLEM

NORMAN E. HICKIN

Scientific Director
Rentokil Limited

HUTCHINSON OF LONDON

HUTCHINSON & CO (*Publishers*) LTD
3 Fitzroy Square, London W1

London Melbourne Sydney Auckland
Wellington Johannesburg Cape Town
and agencies throughout the world

First published 1963
Reprinted 1965
Second edition 1972

Produced by Hutchinson Benham Ltd

This book has been set in Times type, printed in Great Britain
on coated paper by Anchor Press, Tiptree, Essex and
bound by Robert Hartnoll Ltd, Bodmin
ISBN 0 09 113850 7

CONTENTS

PREFACE

This is an account of the problem of fungal decay of wood in buildings in the United Kingdom. Dry Rot and Wet Rot affect a large number of buildings in these islands as the result of one or a combination of many reasons which are stated and discussed in this book. This is all the more remarkable in view of the fact that, unlike woodworm attack, the onset of both forms of fungal decay may be prevented by good design and satisfactory maintenance. But in the United Kingdom we have about eight million buildings which were built before the First World War and a high proportion of these are without damp-proof courses; thus the hazards of wood decay are constantly with us in these buildings. Happily this particular design consideration has become a legal requirement in building by-laws, but exigencies due to the acute shortage of timber during, and for a period after, the Second World War caused timber to be used in constructions again of unsatisfactory design. An example of this was the laying of wooden floors in bitumen and even in cement, which either allowed excess water to be absorbed by the wood or did not allow the over-moist wood to give up its excess water with sufficient rapidity, and thus conditions for fungal spore germination and the subsequent thriving of a fungal infection were present.

For centuries fungal decay has been accepted almost as a natural consequence of the use of wood in a number of circumstances. But the age of the village carpenter and building repairer spending a high proportion of their time in continually replacing such timber in buildings is coming to an end.

We now not only know very much more about the environmental conditions required by wood-rotting fungi, but much work is now largely undertaken by specialist servicing companies employing trained technologists who correct the unsatisfactory environmental conditions and destroy the fungal growth so that a 'once and for all treatment' is accomplished.

Fungal decay of wood is a biological phenomenon, but this little book is for the non-biologists, so that the necessary explanations are made as simply as possible.

Finally, the author hopes he has made a contribution to the conservation of timber in buildings.

7

PREFACE TO SECOND EDITION

This second edition includes some corrections and amendments to the text and some new photographs to bring it more into line with current practices. I wish to thank my colleague Dr. David Dickinson for the comments and suggestions he has made, and Mr. Robin Edwards for the new colour plate and jacket, and the black and white photographs.

N.E.H.

ACKNOWLEDGEMENTS

A number of acknowledgements must be made: Mr. E. M. Buchan and Mr. W. H. Westphal, Managing Directors of Rentokil Limited, have encouraged me to write this account and have kindly given me permission to publish statistics concerning the occurrence of Dry Rot and Wet Rot from commercial sources.

Miss Daphne Linscott of the Rentokil Research Laboratory has read through the typescript and proofs and made a number of valuable suggestions.

Mr. W. J. Holmes, the Technical Controller of the Woodworm and Dry Rot Division of Rentokil Limited, has given me much help, especially concerning the electro-osmotic system of preventing rising damp, and I have drawn widely on his experience of building practice.

Pieces of decayed wood are notoriously difficult subjects for photography, but Mrs. E. R. Winslow has placed her skill and experience at my disposal and I am very grateful to her for this.

Some of the material in this book, particularly in Chapters 4, 5 and 6, has already appeared in *Wood, International Pest Control* and *The British Wood Preserving Association Newsletter*, and I am grateful to the Editors of the two former journals, Mr. J. Richardson and Mr. Philip Burton, and to the President of the British Wood Preserving Association, for permission to publish this material in its present form.

I wish to thank my friend and colleague, Mr. E. H. Brooke Boulton, who has given me permission to use some photographs from his extensive collection (Figures 11, 12, 65, 66 and 69) and has encouraged me in other ways in writing this account. Mr. K. J. Course provided me with photographs for Figures 5, 10 and 43. Mr. R. A. Woods of J. W. Faulkner & Sons Ltd. gave me permission to use Figures 59 and 60. Mr. John Woodhouse of Rentokil East Africa Ltd. sent me the photograph which is the subject of Figure 21.

I am indebted to all these gentlemen for their help so freely given.

1

THE IMPORTANCE OF WOOD IN BUILDINGS

A brief summary of the nature of wood—The moisture relations of wood—What causes
wood to decay

Wood is one of the most important materials used in buildings. A very high proportion of the sixteen million houses in the United Kingdom are of partly timber-framed construction. The very great majority of our homes have the roof-construction in wood. The floors, both at ground level and above, are constructed of wood, together with doors, window frames and skirting boards. The annual outlay for timber, which is paid mainly in currencies other than sterling, has averaged about £180 million each year over the past five years. In addition to this, a small proportion of home-grown wood is used, a proportion which will increase in the coming years as plantations come to maturity. What may be called the national investment in wood in buildings is therefore of colossal proportions and every new house that is built adds something in excess of one standard of timber to this investment (a standard of timber equals 165 cubic feet).

Wood has many virtues as a building material: it can be cut and fashioned easily and rapidly to predetermined sizes and individual wooden sections can be fastened together with the greatest of ease, and if the timber is adequately preserved from the depredations of wood-destroying organisms, then the timber in a building will last for the useful life of the building. Indeed, the more durable hardwood timbers have even outlasted the buildings for which they were hewn.

As time goes by, wood becomes more costly; the higher standard of living demanded by people throughout the world means that the cost of extracting the logs from the forest, their transport, conversion to timber and fabrication into the desired shapes and distribution to the customer is progressively more costly. In addition to this, the more accessible forests have long since been cut, so that sizeable timber must be sought for in inaccessible situations, and not always has there been replanting of timber trees when the forests have been cut. This makes conservation of existing timber in our buildings of prime importance.

Wood and Trees

There are some 44,000 species of trees which produce wood. Trees are plants which have adopted a form of growth by producing 'woody' tissues

11

by means of which the plant or tree may reach a much greater height towards the light than plants that are non-woody; these latter are known as herbs. The woody tissues carry out vital functions for the tree in transporting sap and storing food reserves. As the wood tissue becomes older it loses the ability to convey the sap but forms a core of high mechanical strength.

Hardwood and Softwood

The timbers of the world are divided into two groups known as hardwoods and softwoods. Hardwoods are the timbers converted from the Dicotyledon group of the flowering plants (Angiosperms), whereas, the softwoods are the timbers converted from the naked-seeded plants (Gymnosperms), and almost all of which belong to the CONIFERAE. Most of the species in this group bear cones and needle-shaped leaves. It will be seen, therefore, that the terms hardwood and softwood are technical terms having an exact meaning, and although historically the hardwoods were usually hard and the softwoods soft this is now not invariably the case, as some species of hardwood are relatively soft and some softwoods are quite hard. In our buildings softwood is by far the most important type of timber used for constructional and carcassing purposes on a gross tonnage basis. Hardwood is used for joinery and floors which are to undergo heavy wear, whilst furniture is almost invariably of hardwood.

Wood production by the tree

The actively growing layer of the tree is known as the 'cambium'. In the trunk of the tree it consists of a cylindrical sheath of extreme thinness, only a few cells wide, lying beneath the bark and phloem. The dividing cells are passed either inwards, where they become modified into various wood elements, or to the outside to form the phloem. This growth continues year after year, and seasonal differences in the sizes and distribution of some of the wood elements give rise to the phenomenon of growth rings, which are usually annual, at least in those temperate forests, where there is one fast-growing season each year.

Fig. 1 (*opposite*). Moisture in wood. The oak square illustrated is 3 ft. 6 in. in length and $2\frac{3}{4}$ in. $\times 2\frac{1}{2}$ in. in section. When freshly felled the moisture content was about 90% (calculated on the dried weight) equal to 5.17 pints. When dried to a moisture content of 12% for furniture manufacture it would contain 0.69 of a pint. If the moisture content rose to 20% when fungal attack might commence, this would be equal to 1.15 pints of water.

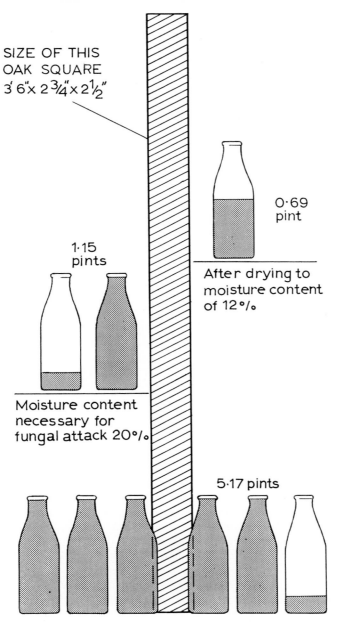

SIZE OF THIS
OAK SQUARE
3´6˝ x 2¾˝ x 2½˝

1·15
pints

0·69
pint

After drying to
moisture content
of 12%

Moisture content
necessary for
fungal attack 20%

5·17 pints

When freshly sawn, moisture content in Oak
about 90%

The microstructure of wood

All plants are composed of a number of minute box-like elements which are known as cells. The simplest form of construction of the cell is found in the cambium when it has been freshly split off from the actively dividing tissue. The cell in its young stage consists of a thin cell wall composed entirely of cellulose and containing the vital living material; the latter is known as cytoplasm, and a much more concentrated body, usually near the centre of the cell, is known as the nucleus.

Softwoods

In softwoods, the cells which develop into conducting tissue also have considerable mechanical strength. They become needle-like and are known as tracheids. They are usually about one-tenth of an inch in length, but may be a little longer. During modification of the cell, the cell wall becomes thickened, not only by the deposition of more cellulose but because other substances are secreted in addition. This thickening is not uniform, as a number of circular-shaped areas are left in the original condition. These are known as pits, and it is through the pits that conduction of the nutrient materials and other substances takes place from cell to cell and thus from one part of the tree to another.

The tracheids are packed so tightly together that in the transverse sections the appearance is that of honeycomb, but zones of smaller, thicker-walled tracheids (more concerned with the mechanical rigidity) alternate with longer thinner-walled tracheids (more concerned with sap conduction). In addition to tracheids certain cells, much less modified than the tracheids, which are concerned with the storage of food reserves, are present. Resin is a gummy aromatic secretion characteristic of many softwoods.

Hardwoods

The conducting tissue in hardwoods consists of 'vessels' or 'pores'. These consist of rows of highly elaborate cells running the length of the trunk or branch. They lose their connecting walls and thus form long tubes, although in some species the connecting walls remain but are perforated. There are many different cell-forms found in hardwoods and it is not proposed to make a detailed study of them here. For our purpose it is sufficient to add that the strengthening tissues consist of pointed cells or fibres which are usually furnished with a few pits, and the cells concerned with food storage are often quite simple, although numerous, and their distribution in the wood gives characteristic patterns.

Wood is a chemical substance and it will have been realized that wood consists of a mass of hollow tube-like structures cemented together. The chemical composition of the cell walls varies greatly amongst the different tree species, but in general cellulose is the main substance present, and although the cellulose molecule is highly elaborate it is based on the rather simple substance glucose. Lignin is the next most important substance present. This is rather less stable than cellulose and it can be removed from wood pulp by the use of steam or warm weak acids, which are the processes used in paper manufacture. Wood also contains a number of other substances in varying quantities, but they need not be referred to here.

Fig. 2. Chemical decay. In general, wood is durable with regard to chemical decay but prolonged contact with a weak alkali (washing soda) has caused this 'dolly stick', used on washing day for fifty years, to have a woolly appearance due to defibration.

The moisture relations of wood

Wood always contains a certain quantity of water. This water is always present in the cell walls as thin films in between the cellulose layers. There is a maximum amount of water which the cell walls can contain, and this varies according to the species of timber, usually between 25 and 30%. This maximum is known as the fibre saturation point.

In addition to this the cavities of the cells and fibres contain moisture, but whereas the amount of water in the cell wall has a bearing on the physical properties of the timber, the water content in the cell cavities has no bearing on the physical properties, except, of course, that of weight. When a tree is felled and sawn into planks the moisture content is very high. In oak this is about 90% when reckoned on the dry weight of the wood. (Moisture content of wood is always calculated on the dry weight of wood.) The wood, when freshly felled and converted, immediately starts to lose moisture, and indeed this process continues, gradually slowing down in rate of loss until the equilibrium moisture content is reached with respect to the relative humidity of the atmosphere. If, subsequently, the wood is placed in a damper atmosphere, it will commence to absorb water until again the equilibrium is reached. In practice, wood is continually losing or gaining water according to the relative humidity and temperature. A piece of oak furniture in a centrally-heated room still contains about 8% of water.

Fig. 3. Fungal Decay. The floor of this building has been completely rotted by the fungus *Merulius lacrymans*.

The moisture content of wood may be estimated in two ways:

1. *In a constant-temperature oven*. The piece of wood is weighed and then placed in the oven at 60°C for a few hours and then raised to 102°C. After staying at this temperature overnight, it is re-weighed and re-heated until a constant weight is obtained. Actually, between 1–2% of the moisture present is not expelled by this method, but this is not considered to be important.

2. *By moisture meters*. Two main types of moisture meters are in use: both rely on the measurement of some other property of the wood which varies in proportion with change of moisture content. The first relies on the electrical resistance of the wood sample as an index of its moisture content. In this type of instrument spikes are forced into the wood and the conductivity in terms of moisture content is read on a scale. In the second type plates are clamped on opposite sides of the piece of timber and the capacitance is balanced against a variable condenser. There are limitations in the use of each type of meter and they require delicate handling.

What causes wood to decay

Wood is a natural substance which has been produced by plants for some hundreds of millions of years. The cellulose in wood, its major constituent, has been produced by the process known as 'photosynthesis'. Carbon dioxide from the atmosphere and water, with the aid of energy from sunlight, and in the presence of the green pigment, chlorophyll (why plants are green), have built up this vast storehouse of wood. But during the evolutionary history of living organisms, both plants and animals have been evolved which bore into or destroy wood by one means or another, either consuming it for food or using the inside of a gallery in a tree trunk as a safe harbourage. If these organisms had not been produced the world would have a very different appearance. But the organisms mentioned above have brought about an equilibrium between the decay of wood and the production of new wood, and unfortunately many of these wood-destroying organisms occurring naturally out of doors often find suitable conditions for flourishing indoors.

The living organisms which cause wood to decay are classified into two main groups:

1. *Wood-rotting fungi.* If all the timber in the world is envisaged then wood-rotting fungi are the most important organisms causing it to decay.

2. *Wood-boring animals.* Many different groups of animals contain species which are able to utilize wood as a foodstuff, either directly or indirectly. In fact, very few animals appear to be able to digest cellulose except in the presence of wood-destroying fungi or other primitive plant forms. The important destroyer of wood floating or submerged in the seas, the Shipworm or *Teredo*, is a bivalve mollusc, in the same group as the oyster and the mussel. The Gribble, another important destroyer of timber in the sea, is a Crustacean, in the same class of animals as the crab and shrimp. On land, the most important class of animals destroying wood is the **Insecta**. Wood-boring species are found in the LEPIDOPTERA (Butterflies and Moths), COLEOPTERA (Beetles), HYMENOPTERA (Ants, Bees and Wasps) and ISOPTERA (Termites). In the United Kingdom the most important wood-boring insects are beetles, but in many countries in tropical and sub-tropical areas a group of rather primitive insects, the Termites, is of paramount importance.

In addition to the two factors involving wood-destroying organisms a number of physical factors cause the breakdown of wood. These are heat, chemical degradation and mechanical wear. However, it is not proposed to discuss in detail these latter forms of wood decay; mechanical wear is easily identified by changed shape and smaller volume, usually without loss of any other physical property in the remainder. Where wood is decomposed by certain chemical reagents, the wood becomes 'woolly' in

B

appearance owing to the individual wood fibres becoming loosened from each other. This type of wood decay is sometimes of importance in buildings where sulphur-dioxide gas has caused the chemical breakdown of the wood owing to escaping flue gases in broken or faulty chimney systems.

THE SPECIAL FEATURES OF FUNGI

Their evolution, biology, and physiology, with special reference to the Dry Rot Fungus

---

Fungi are plants, members of the vegetable kingdom, and this is the group to which the organisms responsible for the particular decay of wood called Dry Rot belongs. The fungi are, however, primitive in their development and they must have evolved very early on from the most primitive of the green plants, the algae, and this very early in the history of living matter on the earth. The fungi have developed to form a group of organisms of the greatest importance, and something like 90,000 different species are known, although only 5000 species of green algae have so far been identified.

Green plants and photosynthesis

Green plants contain a complex substance called chlorophyll. This is contained in small ovoid bodies called chloroplasts which move about in the cell sap. Carbon dioxide, which is a colourless gas occurring to the extent of 0.03% by volume in the atmosphere, is absorbed by the plant, and with water absorbed by the roots and the aid of the chlorophyll and energy derived from sun-light, simple carbohydrate substances (that is substances containing carbon, hydrogen and oxygen) are built up by synthesis. More complex organic substances are built up by the plant from these simple carbohydrates. One of the more complex carbohydrates is cellulose, which goes to form the walls of the box-like 'cells' of which plants are composed. Cellulose consists of relatively large molecules but nevertheless is built up from relatively simple units of glucose. This is by far the most important process which takes place on earth, as all animals are directly or indirectly dependent upon green plants. With the possible exception of Man the fungi are surely the next most important group because they bring about the destruction of green plants and bring other nutrient materials composing them back into the earth. Besides the chemical elements already mentioned which are present in the tissue of plants, a number of mineral substances are also present, although in much smaller quantities. These mineral salts are soluble in water and are absorbed by the plants through the root system. These salts are present only in small quantities in the soil and therefore, unless plants died and the nutrients dispersed in the soil through the action of the decaying or scavenging fungi, life would inevitably come to an end.

19

The fungi are plants without chlorophyll and therefore must obtain their nourishment from other organic matter. If they obtain their nourishment from living organisms they are known as parasites. A large number of

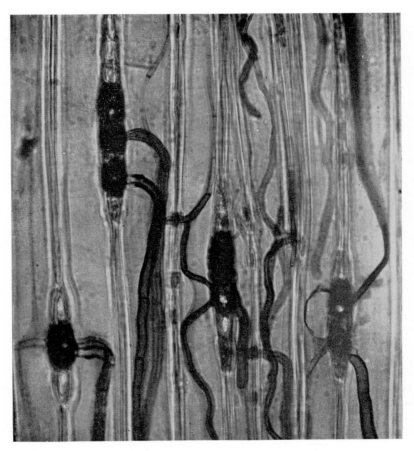

Fig. 4. Photomicrograph of section of softwood showing hyphae of a wood-rotting fungus. The hyphae have been stained. Very much enlarged. (Crown copyright reserved).

species of fungi are known to be living in a special relationship with living animals or plants in which they are mutually beneficial. This special relationship is known as symbiosis; the individual partners are known as the symbionts. An example are the yeast-like fungi habitating the gut of the larva of the wood-boring beetle *Anobium punctatum*. The yeast-like cells

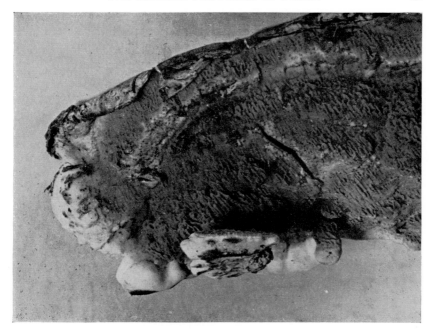

Fig. 5. Sporophore of Dry Rot Fungus, *Merulius lacrymans*, showing the corrugated spore-bearing area in the centre.

play a part in the nutrition of the larva. On the other hand, the yeast-like fungal cells are maintained in an environment in the gut of the larva which is beneficial to them. The other group of fungi, those which obtain their nourishment from dead organic matter, are known as saprophytes, and it is to this group that the wood-rotting fungi with which we are concerned, the Dry Rot fungus, the Cellar Fungus, and others belong. These types of fungi obtain their nourishment from the dead woody tissues of plants; in fact, the timber in our buildings.

The fungal plant body

The plant body of a fungus or 'thallus' has no resemblance to the shape of a higher plant form. Stem, root and leaves are absent, but the fungus consists of a number, sometimes a very large number, of very slender branched thread-like cells. Each of these thread-like cells is known as a hypha, the plural being hyphae. The mass of interlacing hyphae is known as a mycelium, and this is the vegetative part of the body which carries out all the necessary functions of the fungus except, in general, reproduction. The mycelium is often not visible because the individual hyphae are growing within the substance which it is decaying, and this is true of the wood-rotting fungi, except that in conditions of high humidity and often in darkness the mycelium may grow on the surface of the material. This is also true of the Dry Rot fungus.

The fungus-plant organization

There are several points of interest in the organization of the fungus thallus. In the first place, the cell walls, unlike those in the green plants, are not usually composed of cellulose. Several substances are present, one of the important ones being chitin. This is the substance of which the exo-skeleton of insects is composed.

Fig. 6. Mycelium of Dry Rot Fungus, *Merulius lacrymans*, growing over wood from a packing case in a damp cellar. (Crown copyright reserved).

The wood-rotting fungi produce an enzyme cellulase which breaks up the cellulose into simpler substances, with the liberation of vital energy for the plant. It is easy to realize that cells which secrete cellulase cannot very well be composed of cellulose. Another point of interest in fungi is that the hyphae are sometimes in a multinucleate condition, that is, the separating cell walls break down and a number of nuclei appear to be present in each cell. Another feature of many of the higher fungi is that small connecting tubes are present, connecting adjacent cells, and nuclear substances are passed from one cell to another. These are known as clamp connections. Another characteristic obvious in many fungi is that the mycelia are of different sexes. They are then said to be *heterothallic*, and before spores can be produced from a fruiting body a fusion of the hyphae from two distinct sexual strains must take place.

Fig. 7. Basidia arising from the hymenial layer of the sporophore of *Merulius lacrymans*. Side view. Each basidium bears four stalks (Sterigmata) on each of which a spore develops. Much enlarged and diagrammatic.

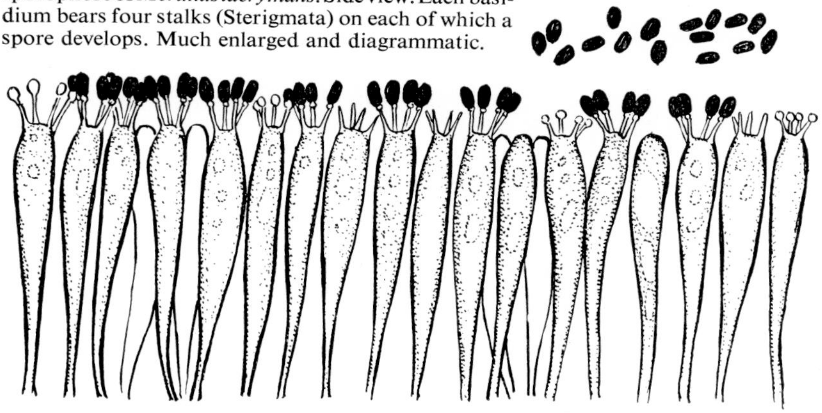

The fruiting body

When the fungal mycelium has accumulated sufficient food reserves, a special organ is produced consisting of hyphae packed very tightly together and in a characteristic shape and colour, according to species. This is the fruiting body or sporophore from which the spores are produced.

Fungi are normally only recognized by their sporophores. The mushroom, toadstool, puffball and bracket fungus are examples of these.

The delicate interlacing hyphae forming the vegetative part of the fungus plant are usually not visible and have already been described. In the Dry Rot fungus, *Merulius lacrymans*, the sporophore is usually flat and pancake-like, the whole area normally being adherent to a surface. The surface on which it is formed determines, to a large extent, the shape of the sporophore. For example, if a sporophore forms in a corner of a room it may grow in three planes at right angles to each other. On the other hand, if it grows on a vertical wall it often forms bracket-like thickenings. The sporophore is white in colour round the edges, sometimes with a little canary-yellow staining. The centre is corrugated and mustard yellow in colour or rusty-red, and it is from this central area that the spores are produced. The size of the sporophore also varies greatly. It may be only a couple of inches in diameter, but on the other hand sporophores have been observed up to 6 feet in diameter. It has been mentioned that sporophore production only takes place when sufficient food reserves have been stored, but although little is known about the precise mechanism of the sporophore production it often takes place under 'stress' conditions. The hyphae may have been penetrating long distances away from the original wood

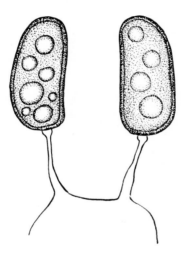

Fig. 8. Two spores of *Merulius lacrymans* still attached to their stalks (Sterigmata). Very much enlarged and diagrammatic.

decay until a situation in the light is encountered when sporophore formation occurs. Very occasionally this may be on the exterior wall of a building, although the fungus *Merulius lacrymans* is never found decaying wood in such a situation.

The spore

Undoubtedly one of the principal factors causing fungi to be so successful in decaying organic matter throughout the world concerns the nature of the spore and the numbers of these which are produced. Spores are minute structures invisible to the naked eye, although when present in large numbers are seen as a fine dust. This happens in the case of the spores of the Dry Rot fungus, where the rusty-red dust is a common characteristic of wood decay by this species. A single spore of the Dry Rot fungus seen under a microscope is grain-shaped and very light yellow in colour. The size of the spore is about 0·01 mm. and its weight is in the order of 1×10^{-11}g. Unlike the seed, the spore does not contain an embryo of the young plant. The extremely small weight of the spore enables it to be suspended in an air current for a very long time and thus it can be distributed with great ease. Another remarkable feature of the fungal spores is the very great quantity which is produced. It has been estimated that a sporophore of the Dry Rot fungus one yard square will produce fifty million spores per minute over a period of many days. Other fungi decaying wood have been estimated to be even more fruitful and to produce between eight hundred and nine hundred million spores per hour. This fact, together with their extreme lightness, means that any moist wood will be infected by one or more species of wood-rotting fungi.

3

HOW TO IDENTIFY DECAY

Decay due to wood-rotting fungi—Decay due to wood-boring insects—Dry Rot and
Wet Rot—The Dry Rot Fungus in buildings

In examining timber in buildings for evidence of deterioration it is essential
to be able to distinguish between decay due to wood-rotting fungi and that
due to wood-boring insects. In the following table the main differences in
decayed timber due to these two factors are given. In each case the wood
is considered quite apart from the decaying organisms present; i.e. mycelium or the larvae of wood-boring beetles. The association, however, between certain species of wood-boring beetles and fungal decayed wood must
be kept in mind. The Furniture Beetle, *Anobium punctatum*, attacks only
sound wood, although in the laboratory it has been demonstrated that
superficial fungal attacks initiated by soft rots help the young larvae to
gain admittance into the wood and flourish afterwards. The House Long
horn Beetle, *Hylotrupes bajulus*, develops only when fungal decay is absent,
and the Powder Post Beetle, *Lyctus*, likewise. In the case of the Death

Decay caused by fungi	*Decay caused by larvae of beetles*
Well-defined tunnels absent	Well-defined tunnels often of constant shape in transverse section
No comminuted wood particles present	Tunnels partly or entirely filled with frass—comminuted wood particles
Change of colour of wood, usually darker	Colour of wood unchanged
Loss of strength throughout whole mass of wood and friable	Strength of wood not affected except for tunnels, not friable
Circular or oval flight holes on external surfaces absent	Circular or oval flight holes on external surface on completion of one life-cycle
Considerable loss in weight of whole wood mass	Considerable loss in weight of wood not tunnelled, not usual
Transverse and longitudinal fissures present—often breaking into cubes	Transverse and longitudinal fissures absent. Not breaking into cubes

Fig. 9. Rhizomorph of the true Dry Rot fungus *Merulius lacrymans* travelling over the surface of well-decayed wood. Note cuboidal cracking of the decayed wood.

Fig. 10. A large sporophore of the Dry Rot fungus *Merulius lacrymans*. Note the white edge. It is five feet in length.

Fig. 11. Dry Rot in a London club caused by war damage.

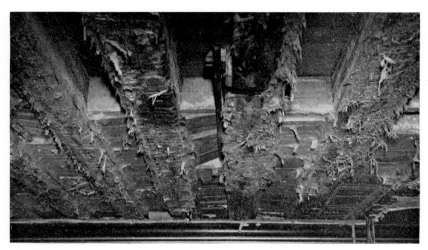

Fig. 12. Dry Rot in a ceiling caused by a burst water-tank.

Watch Beetle, *Xestobium rufovillosum*, and the two wood-boring weevils, *Euophryum confine* and *Pentarthrum huttoni*, these insects can develop only in wood that is supporting an active fungal attack or in wood which shows evidence of being attacked at sometime in the past. There is also another feature which must be kept in mind; that is, wood decayed by the wood-boring beetle *Anobium punctatum* and then exposed to damp conditions when the fungal attack occurs. This usually kills off the insect infestations, but the tunnels and flight-holes remain in the fungal decayed wood.

Dry Rot and Wet Rot

Dry Rot is the name given to a particular decay of timber brought about by the activity of one particular species of fungus, *Merulius lacrymans*. The term Dry Rot is descriptive of the dry and friable condition of the rotted wood. The characters by which the decay caused by the Dry Rot fungus can be identified are summarized below.

1. The spores, when in very large quantities in the vicinity of the sporophore, are rusty-red or mustard yellow in colour. The spores only accumulate in still, unventilated conditions, as otherwise they are blown about on account of their great lightness. They may, however, sometimes be seen caught in a spider's web.

2. The mycelium external to the timber occurs as thin sheets of silvery grey or mouse-grey appearance, tinged here and there with lilac patches; bright yellow patches may also occur. This type of sheet mycelium is mostly found where conditions are drier.

Fig. 13. Mycelium of Dry Rot fungus *Merulius lacrymans* with floor cut away to show extremity of attack.

3. In damp humid conditions the mycelium grows rapidly and is snowy white, rather like cotton wool, but where the edge of such mycelium comes into contact with rather drier air or exposure to light, the bright yellow occurs.

4. The specific name, *lacrymans*, refers to the characteristic which it shows in damp conditions when in active growth. Innumerable globules of water are seen which sparkle in the light of a torch like a large number of tear drops—*lacrymans* means 'weeping'. The generic name, *Merulius*, refers to the bright yellow coloration which occurs on the mycelium, being similar in colour to the beak of a male blackbird (*Merula*).

5. Wood decayed by the mycelium shows deep transverse and longitudina' fissures and the wood breaks up into cubes, sometimes of large dimensions, several inches in length. Such cracking is seen on the surface of the wood.

6. The wood becomes very light in weight owing to the extraction of the cellulose by the fungal hyphae.

7. The wood becomes darker in colour, usually brown; it is friable when rubbed between the fingers and the wood loses its characteristic fresh resinous smell.

8. The appearance of the sporophore has already been described. It is thin and pancake-like, white round the edges, with the centre thrown into corrugation; the colour of the spores is rusty-red; and when in active growth the sporophore and the mycelium have a strong mushroomy smell.

9. A very important characteristic of *Merulius lacrymans* is the ability of the fungus to produce water carrying strands or 'rhizomorphs'. These strands are formed from hyphae and modified to form vein-like structures. They may be as large in diameter as a lead pencil. The importance of the rhizomorph is that it conveys the water from damper wood which has been decayed to drier wood elsewhere, the strands passing over brickwork, stone or metal. It is in the hyphae constituting the rhizomorphs that food reserves are stored, so that even if the affected wood is taken away the rhizomorph is still capable of further growth and infecting new wood. The rhizomorphs are also able to penetrate soft brickwork and mortar.

The Cellar Fungus *Coniophora cerebella*

The next important wood-decaying fungus in buildings is the Cellar Fungus, *Coniophora cerebella*. The particular decay it causes is known as Wet Rot. This is due to the fact that wood must be considerably wetter

Fig. 14. Mycelium of the Wet Rot Fungus, *Coniophora cerebella.*

for an attack of *Coniophora cerebella* to take place than for an attack of *Merulius lacrymans*. It has been stated that 95% of all wood decay caused by wood-rotting fungi in the United Kingdom is brought about by *Merulius lacrymans* and *Coniophora cerebella*, and although decay caused by the Cellar Fungus is far more common than in the case of that brought about by the Dry Rot Fungus (see Chapter 4), attacks by the Cellar Fungus are almost always but not invariably much less severe. The special characteristics by means of which *Coniophora cerebella* and the decay caused by it can be identified as follows:

1. The fungal strands are never as thick as those of *Merulius lacrymans*, being usually less in diameter than is twine. These strands are brownish or black, but when freshly produced are yellowish brown. The fungal strands when growing on the surface of the wood, or sometimes plaster, are vein-like in appearance and said to be similar to the blood-vessels of the cerebellum, hence its specific name.

2. Mycelium is rarely produced, but in some locations (e.g. under linoleum and behind skirting boards), a thin sheet may be present. The sporophore is rarely found in buildings, although it may be common out of doors. It consists of a thin plate, olive-brown in colour, of indeterminate shape covered with small tubercles.

3. The spores, because of the comparative absence of sporophore indoors, are rarely found but they are nevertheless ubiquitous, so that wood of the required moisture content is almost certain to be rotted by this species in buildings.

RECORDS OF THE OCCURRENCE OF DRY ROT AND WET ROT ATTACKS IN THE UNITED KINGDOM

The comparative incidence of Dry Rot and Wet Rot

Although there have been estimates from time to time of the annual cost of Dry Rot eradication, there have so far been no attempts to estimate the frequency with which Dry Rot and Wet Rot attacks are found in buildings.

The incidence of the two types of decay is an important fact which should be known. From it can be deduced the amount by which the total national investment in wood must be reduced and the desirability of pre-treatment of timber for new buildings assessed.

The meaning of 'incidence'

The incidence of Dry Rot and Wet Rot can be expressed as the total number of occurrences of these two forms of wood decay compared with the total number of buildings. Obviously the figure for the total number of fungal decay occurrences is impossible to obtain. A 'random' or truly representative sample of buildings, therefore, should be examined and the proportion of such buildings containing Dry Rot and Wet Rot attack would be deemed to be the same in the total number of buildings as was present in the sample.

The size of the sample is of importance; it must be large enough to have ironed out many of the unusual figures given by probability and chance, which could be the case if the size of the sample was unduly small. This would give, in the language of statistics, a *significant* result.

Difficulties of choosing a random sample

In choosing the random sample of buildings we must keep in mind the object which it is serving. Complexities are very soon apparent. Buildings are of all ages, of many types of construction and materials, and are sited in every type of topographical situation. The nature of the sub-soil and the underlying geological strata are clearly of importance as influencing drainage. The concentration of the buildings can be seen also to influence the results we might expect to obtain from any particular case. If an attack of Dry Rot occurs in a building in a heavily built-up area we might expect the spores to be distributed and be blown or otherwise carried on to

C

33

Fig. 15. Symmetrical fruiting body of *Merulius lacrymans*, the true Dry Rot fungus.

Fig. 16. Bracket-type fruiting body of *Merulius lacrymans*.

Fig. 17. Hand circular-saw for cutting inspection board for underfloor inspection.

susceptible wood in adjacent property more rapidly than if the attack occurred in a sparsely populated neighbourhood.

The social factors

There are also what may be called the social factors. To some extent these are influenced by the density of population, but we see that at both ends of the social scale something like the same result ensues. In some of the larger cities, where the population is crowded together in large buildings, maintenance is virtually either non-existent or exists at the level required by the local Public Health Authority.

On the other hand, extensive Dry Rot and Wet Rot are the common fate of many of our large mansions which have been in the possession, even if not in the occupation, of our landed families. The owner-occupied house, by virtue of several extraneous factors, is probably the best maintained of all dwellings.

The Timber Decay surveyor

One of the difficulties in the way of obtaining accurate counts of the number of occurrences of fungal decay is the great scarcity of trained timber decay surveyors outside the staffs of the major commercial servicing organizations. Indeed, no statistical survey of the problem in the United Kingdom is possible without their help. The examination of all the timber in a building involves timber in situations where it is difficult of access; indeed, this is the timber most likely to be affected by fungal decay. Thus it is essential for the timber decay surveyor to have had considerable building experience so that he is familiar with the siting of all timber in all types of buildings in his particular territory.

Of equal importance is, of course, the ability to identify the more important wood-rotting fungi and wood-boring insects with accuracy, coupled with facilities to discuss those wood-rotting organisms which show unfamiliar characteristics, with scientifically qualified and experienced colleagues.

Any survey of the timber in a building which is to show any useful results must be a painstakingly thorough one. But this is a time-consuming operation, and whereas in buildings of rather similar type of construction, such as Local Authority-owned housing estates, several units may be inspected and reported on in the course of a day, not more than two or

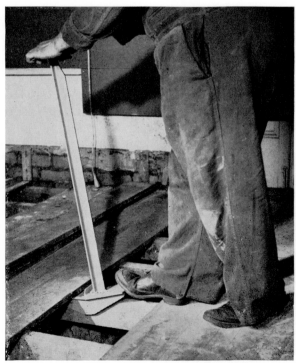

Fig. 18. Floor-lifting device for rapid floorboard removal without damage.

three four-bedroomed detached owner-occupied houses are possible in a day's work, if adequate timber examination and report is undertaken.

Although the true incidence of Dry Rot and Wet Rot attack has so far not been estimated owing to the difficult and complex nature of the surveying problems as mentioned previously, during the last few years accurate accounts of many types of timber decay in various regions of the United Kingdom have been made by a large servicing organization, the Woodworm and Dry Rot Division of Rentokil Limited. The numbers of occurrences and the *comparative* incidence and variation in distribution of

Fig. 19. Typical 'pancake' fruiting body of *Merulius lacrymans*.

the various wood-boring beetles have already been published from this source, but given below are the details concerning Dry Rot and Wet Rot attacks which were found in the period January to June 1962. However, before giving this actual number of occurrences, some notes of explanation are thought to be necessary.

In the first place, the term Dry Rot was used in the surveys exclusively for decays caused by the fungus *Merulius lacrymans*. The identification of this fungus is a relatively simple task for the trained Timber Infestation Surveyor. All other rots were deemed to be Wet Rot, no matter what species of fungus was involved. In some official leaflets issued a few years ago as many as four fungus species are listed as causing Dry Rot, but this practice has, during the last few years, largely dropped out of use.

THE AGE OF BUILDINGS IN THE SURVEY

Obtaining the exact age of a building is a difficult task, often considerable questioning being required even to obtain an approximation. Often house-owners do not know the date of erection of their own homes even if built since the Second World War if the building has changed hands since it was erected.

It was decided, therefore, for the timber surveys which were to be conducted that buildings would be placed in three age categories only.

1. Built pre-1919—in effect this means built before the First World War.
2. Built 1920–39, i.e. between the wars.
3. Built 1940 to the present.

It is a relatively easy task for a trained surveyor to place every building in his territory into one or another of these groups with the minimum of questioning and yet it gives the information with as much precision as is required.

The age classes of the buildings which were surveyed during the period January to June 1962 were as follows:

TABLE 1

		Approximate total of buildings (in millions) in these age groups in Britain
1. Pre-1919	52·2%	8
2. 1920–1939	41·5%	4
3. 1940–present	5·4%	4

TABLE 2

The Types of Buildings Surveyed	
Private dwelling-houses	84·8%
Commercial buildings, factories, shops, etc.	6·4%
Churches, historic buildings	4·6%
Licensed premises	1·0%
Farms, country estates	3·2%

Apparent discrepancies in percentage totals are due to a small element of indecision, parts of buildings having been erected at different times, etc.

The total number of timber surveys in buildings during the six-month period was 9810, distributed throughout England, Scotland, Wales and Northern Ireland, and for this purpose these countries were divided into eleven regions as follows:

TABLE 3

The United Kingdom divided into 11 districts: the total number of dwellings in each district and the proportion of timber surveys to dwellings

District No.	Region	Total Number of Dwellings	1 Survey in Every
1	London, Middx.	2,784,273	1478
2	Surrey, Hants., I.O.W.	806,632	672
3	Kent, Sussex	745,609	855
4	Glos., Bristol, Wilts., Dorset, Somerset, Devon, Corn., Channel Islands	932,526	1430
5	Berks., Oxon., Bucks., Northants., Hunts., Beds., Herts.	692,975	771
6	Cambs., Isle of Ely, Norfolk, Suffolk, Essex	950,867	2270
7	Salop, Staffs., War., Worcs., Hereford, Radnor, Cardigan, Pemb., Carmarthen, Brecon, Glam., Mon.	1,759,274	2900
8	Lancs., Ches., Flintshire, Denbigh, Anglesey, Caernarvon, Merioneth, Montgomery, Isle of Man	2,041,008	3325
9	Northumb., Cumb., Westd., Durham, Yorks., Derby, Notts, Lincs., Leics., Rutland	3,016,998	3017
10	Scotland (excluding Zetland)	1,369,701	2760
11	Northern Ireland	408,000	5440
	Total	16,250,000	Av.: 1900

TABLE 4

The number of timber surveys in each district and the number of records of Dry Rot and Wet Rot in each district, and their percentage of the total number of timber surveys

District	No. of Surveys	Dry Rot	%	Wet Rot	%
1	2055	304	14·8	700	34·1
2	1300	90	6·9	340	26·1
3	926	55	5·9	191	20·6
4	757	81	10·7	129	17·0
5	964	52	5·4	207	21·5
6	463	51	11·0	165	35·7
7	728	94	12·9	191	26·2
8	753	143	19·0	198	26·3
9	1183	234	19·8	286	24·2
10	583	142	24·4	118	20·2
11	98	28	28·6	22	22·4
Total	9810	1274	13·0	2547	26·0

CONCLUSIONS

1. In these figures of the recorded occurrences of Dry Rot and Wet Rot, no claim is made that this represents the true incidence of these forms of decay throughout all buildings in the United Kingdom. The figures are only true of the sample, the nature of which has been described.

2. A total of 1274 records of Dry Rot and 2547 records of Wet Rot during a six-months examination of buildings leads to the conclusion that fungal decay of wood in buildings in the United Kingdom is widespread and on such a scale that it must inevitably result in heavy economic losses.

3. Taking the United Kingdom as a whole, Wet Rot occurs almost exactly twice as commonly as Dry Rot.

4. Dry Rot occurs most commonly in the larger cities in the North (Glasgow, Edinburgh, Manchester, Liverpool, Bradford, etc.). It is least common in Surrey, Kent, Sussex and the South Midlands.

5. Wet Rot is most common in London, Essex, Suffolk, Norfolk and Cambridgeshire and is least common in the Southern counties of England and also Scotland.

THE LESS IMPORTANT SPECIES OF WOOD-ROTTING FUNGI FOUND IN BUILDINGS

Poria, Phellinus, Lenzites, Daedalia, etc.

By far the most common wood-destroying fungus found indoors in Britain is *Coniophora cerebella*, the Cellar Fungus. This is the fungus which brings about decay usually called Wet Rot. Next in order of importance in number of occurrences is *Merulius lacrymans*, which causes the wood decay called Dry Rot. The economic importance of Dry Rot, however, is much greater than that of Wet Rot, although statistics obtained from a commercial undertaking controlling Woodworm and Dry Rot show that Wet Rot occurs almost twice as frequently as Dry Rot, as described in the previous chapter. The same figures confirm the statement of Findlay that these two fungi together are responsible for something like 95% of all fungal decay in buildings in Britain. It should be mentioned that whereas the decay termed Dry Rot is caused by the fungus *Merulius lacrymans* alone, Wet Rot is the name given to the decay caused by all other fungal species indoors. The less common species of wood-rotting fungi found indoors— those other than the two species already mentioned—show many interesting features although collectively they only amount to about 5%.

These fungi are able to live and develop only because excess moisture is present in the wood, that is, there is more moisture present than is normally the case for wood indoors. There are a number of causes of such excess moisture such as leaking pipes, defective plumbing, water coming through walls from outside owing to stopped-up gutters and hopperheads, broken downpipes, covered ventilation bricks preventing ground floor joists, wallplates and flooring from giving up moisture, and rising damp where damp-proof courses are absent or defective.

The fungi which develop under these conditions can be divided into two groups: firstly those fungi already present in the timber when it was converted, but where on drying the fungal mycelium assumes a moribund condition. When the timber becomes wetted again owing to one or more reasons as given above, then the fungus springs into life again, often producing a sporophore. The second group consists of fungi which were not present in the timber, but spores, usually produced in great quantity are blown about and reach the surface of the damp wood, germinate and produce new fungal mycelia.

Next in importance to the two species of wood-rotting fungi already mentioned is the White Pore Fungus, *Poria vaillantii*. Eighteen occurrences in North London, eleven in Scotland and a rather scattered distribution in buildings in the remainder of the British Isles became known to the writer during 1962.

Brief biological details of sixteen species which all belong to the BASIDIOMYCETES group of the fungi are given below.

Fig. 20. Rhizomorph of the White Pore Fungus, *Poria vaillantii*. It is white and curling, and only half the diameter of that of *Merulius lacrymans*.

Poria vaillantii (D.C.) Fr. The White Pore Fungus

Reference to this species in the literature has sometimes been given under the name *Poria vaporaria* and hitherto there has been a certain amount of confusion in identification nomenclature. It is a common species in wet mines but sometimes occurs also in buildings in situations where the timber has been exposed to very damp conditions. The moisture content of the timber required by this fungus species to flourish is higher than that required by *Merulius lacrymans*. In addition it continues to flourish up to a temperature of 36°C, conditions which would bring the growth of *Merulius lacrymans* to a halt, and this explains its general occurrence in many mines both in the United Kingdom and in Continental Europe, and indeed in many other parts of the world.

Fig. 21. Mycelium and abnormal fruiting bodies of *Poria vaillantii* under a ground floor of a building in Nairobi.

Fruit Body. The production of a fruit body is a rare occurrence in buildings. It is white and consists of an irregularly-shaped plate adhering to the timber. On close examination it is seen that it is covered with pores, the tubes of which vary in depth from one-sixteenth to half an inch. The individual pores are angled to a greater or lesser degree, sometimes resembling honeycomb. It is usual for a number of strands to run off from the fruiting body.

Mycelium. This is always white or cream in colour and never shows the patches of lilac and canary-yellow coloration which are present on the mycelium of *Merulius lacrymans*. When freshly growing over a wooden surface the mycelium is fern-like, and this is an important character for identification. Rhizomorphs or water-carrying strands are much smaller than those of *Merulius lacrymans* and remain flexible when dry. They are also less successful in penetrating loose brickwork and lime mortar than those of *Merulius lacrymans*.

Wood Decay. Only softwoods are affected and the rot produced is very similar to the Dry Rot caused by the true Dry Rot Fungus. The cuboidal cracking, however, is not quite so pronounced as that caused by *Merulius lacrymans*. The decayed wood is generally darker in colour than when undecayed. Although in mines where conditions are ideal for mycelium production the mycelium spreads over the rock and coal-face, in buildings it never seems to have quite the same ability of spreading to drier parts which *Merulius lacrymans* possesses.

Paxillus panuoides Fr.

This species occurs from time to time in buildings where softwood timber has been allowed to remain in very damp conditions, although like *Poria vaillantii* it is of common occurrence in damp warm mines. It also occurs out of doors on old heaps of sawdust and on coniferous stumps.

Fruit Body. This is brownish or dingy yellow and is fan-, funnel- or ear-shaped, measuring from one to three inches in diameter. The pileus is soft and fleshy and the pronounced gills are dichotomously branched. The fruit body is at first concave but later becomes lobed and undulating.

Mycelium. The mycelium which occurs on the timber surface has been variously described as hairy or woolly, and fine branched strands are present. It is yellow in colour with occasional violet patches, a character it shares with *Merulius lacrymans*, but the mycelium never darkens with age

Fig. 22. An abnormal form of the fruiting body of *Lentinus lepideus*. Such sterile and antler-shaped sporophores are usually found under floors in complete darkness.

as does that of *Coniophora cerebella*. Maximum temperature for growth is 29°C, which is a little below that for *Poria vaillantii*. The required moisture content of the wood and the optimum are said to lie between 50% and 70% of the dry weight of the wood, and in addition it requires ample aeration, so that in very wet wood the decay is confined to the surface layer.

Fig. 23. A collection of abnormal fruiting bodies of *Lenzites sepiaria* (some doubt is attached to the specific determination). The normal form is bracket shaped.

Wood Decay. This is characterized by the wood first becoming stained a vivid yellow where the mycelium is in contact with it. The outer layer of wood then assumes a cheese-like consistency, and when this commences to dry longitudinal cracks, which are deep and broad, appear, but the transverse cracks are very fine. The deep transverse cracks which are characteristic of Dry Rot are absent.

Control. Two points on control of this species of wood-rotting fungus are worthy of mention. In the first place, drying of the timber rapidly kills the fungus, as it can only exist in very wet wood. Secondly, it is very easy to kill with fungicidal fluids.

Phellinus megaloporus (Pers.) Heim

This species has, until relatively recently, been known as *Phellinus cryptarum* in the United Kingdom. It can cause a serious rot in oak and first achieved some importance when serious damage to the Palace of Versailles was reported as caused by this species. In the United Kingdom it is known as attacking only oak and chestnut indoors, although in Continental Europe it occurs in mines and on bridges. It has however been found occasionally on softwood timbers. It is fairly common in large-section oak timbers in old mansions and other large buildings where leakage of water has taken place over a long period and where conditions generally are rather warm, and it is said that the decay always takes place in darkness.

Fruit Body. This is variable in shape but is usually plate-like up to about ten inches in length and about an inch thick. It often consists of several layers of pores, which give it a stratified appearance in section. The pores are usually only 0·25 mm. in diameter. The whole fruit body is hard and woody and is rather variable in colour from buff to rich dark brown.

Mycelium. A surface growth of mycelium of usual form is absent but when the fungus is growing actively it forms what has been described as a thick matted crust, yellow to red-brown in colour. It exudes a yellowish brown liquid.

Wood Decay. The decay caused by this fungus causes the wood to be reduced to a loose white fibrous mass which does not powder when pressed between finger and thumb. This type of decay is known as a white stringy rot. Another character of the decayed wood is its extreme lightness. The decay is often hidden within a large beam or the fungus may attack a beam where the end is embedded in masonry or plaster, so that attack by this species sometimes proceeds undetected until the fruiting body is produced. The optimum temperature for growth of *Phellinus megaloporus* has been found to be about 27°C, the maximum temperature is about 35°C, whilst at 10°C the growth is very slow. It has been said that this

Fig. 24. Top surface of a normal fruiting body of *Ganoderma lucidum*. This fungus attacks oak and the fruiting body sometimes possesses a stalk.

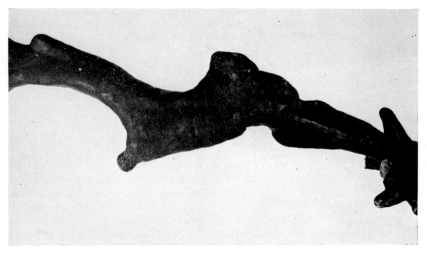

Fig. 25. An abnormal fruiting body of *Ganoderma lucidum*. The surface has a varnished appearance.

fungus causes a more rapid decay of oak in buildings than any other species, but the absence of strands prevents the fungus from travelling over inert materials such as brickwork and masonry, so that the attack is more or less confined to the damp area.

Lentinus lepideus Fr.

This species is not commonly found under natural conditions in Britain although it is of widespread occurrence both in Europe and North America. In this country it is found rather infrequently on coniferous stumps. It is, however, commonly found in softwood timber which has not received sufficient creosote during pressure impregnation. Telegraph poles, railway sleepers and paving blocks are attacked quite frequently by this species on account of its tolerence of comparatively high concentrations of creosote. Although most frequently found in the situations detailed above, and also in mines, it is sometimes found in very damp conditions in buildings.

Fruit Body. Two forms of the fruit body occur, and indeed may occur within a few inches of each other, together with intermediate forms. In the typical form the pileus, or cap, is well developed, circular, up to about four inches in diameter, and the stem is mostly bent. When fresh, although it is tough, it is somewhat elastic. In colour it is pale brown, with the base of the stem, and sometimes elsewhere, purplish. The spores are colourless. The abnormal form occurs in dark damp situations, usually under floors. The stem becomes elongated and twisted; sometimes the pileus becomes much reduced and contorted. At other times the pileus is completely absent and the stem branches, each branch ending in a sterile point, the general effect being antler-like.

Mycelium. White mycelium is first seen in the cracks of the decayed wood, but later, when the wood is at an advanced stage of decay, a sheet of soft whitish mycelium may be present, sometimes tinged with brownish or purplish brown. A feature of the mycelium is the frequent occurrence of long needle-shaped crystals on the surface.

Wood Decay. At first there is little alteration in appearance but later the wood darkens in colour and cuboidal cracking occurs. The decayed wood becomes sticky and when freshly decayed there is a strong characteristic balsam-like smell.

Other species of wood-rotting fungi which have been more rarely found indoors in Britain are described below. These species are all most likely to be present in the timber either in the standing tree or when the log was on the ground before collection and conversion. In these cases the fungal mycelium becomes moribund when the moisture content of the timber drops on seasoning, but when the moisture content rises again owing to damp conditions brought about by the faulty design, faulty maintenance or accident, the mycelium commences to grow again and brings about the decay of the wood.

Fig. 26. The dried fruiting bodies of *Peniophora gigantea* are sometimes found indoors on oists and rafters. When fresh they resemble spilt candle-grease.

Fig. 27. An abnormal fruiting body probably of a species of *Stereum*. The cap is completely aborted, only the hymenial layer being visible.

Lenzites sepiaria (Wulf.) Fr.

This species is very common in Continental Europe, attacking converted softwood out of doors. It is uncommon for it to occur naturally in Britain, but it is often imported. From each imported timber occasional outbreaks of decay take place if the timber is used in an exposed situation where periods of wet and dry alternate rapidly. The typical fruiting body is a corky bracket, but in dark, damp situations in buildings abnormal forms in a wide range of shape occur. *Lenzites trabea* (Pers.) Fr. is also a common wood-rotting fungus on the Continent, occasionally imported into Britain.

Peniophora gigantea (Fr.) Massee

This is a very common species attacking coniferous logs, but, when the converted timber is dried, the decay is arrested and killed. Nevertheless, a fruiting body is sometimes produced in the dying stages of the fungus. It has been described as an irregular waxy crust which, when wet, appears like spilt candle-grease. It is creamy white in colour when fresh but brownish or tinged with lilac when older.

Trametes serialis Fr.

This is a common cause of decay in coniferous logs and is also identified as causing a heart rot in standing trees. The fruit body is tough, corky and

D

usually elongated. The pore surface, which is usually irregular when found in a building, is cream or buff in colour and if any part corresponding to the pileus is present, then it is brown. The individual pores measure 1–8 mm. in length.

The rot caused by this species is brown and cubical and crumbles at the touch. There are marked similarities between this species and the rot which it produces and *Poria monticola.*

Poria monticola Murr.

Poria monticola has had a rather chequered history in its naming and much confusion still arises in its identification. Although this species does not occur under natural conditions, it is imported from North America in Douglas Fir and Sitka Spruce. If the timber is used in a dry and well-ventilated situation the fungus soon dries out, but if the situation is damp and ill-ventilated then the fungus can cause an extensive brown crumbling rot.

Poria medulla-panis Pers.

The rot caused by this fungus is indistinguishable from that caused by *Phellinus megaloporus* and occurs in rather similar situations on oak in buildings. The tough fruit body is whitish or light buff in colour. The small pores measure about 4 or 5 to the millimetre.

Merulius tignicola Harmsen

This species is rare in buildings. The fruit body is thinner and the colour paler than *Merulius lacrymans*. It is much more concentrated in its attack than is usual in the latter species.

Merulius pinastri (Fr.) Burt.

This species is found only in wet situations. The fruit body is thin and fragile and an important character shown is the tooth-like projection on the pore edge. It also is unusual on account of being able to form sclerotia (round bodies about 1–2 mm. in diameter), on the strands. It produces a brown cubical rot which is confined to the area of moist wood.

Phellinus contiguus (Pers.) B. and G.

This species, which is one of the most common fungi decaying timber in buildings in New Zealand, is sometimes reported in buildings in Britain, where it is usually found attacking window sills and frames. It causes a stringy white rot, usually in oak but sometimes in softwood.

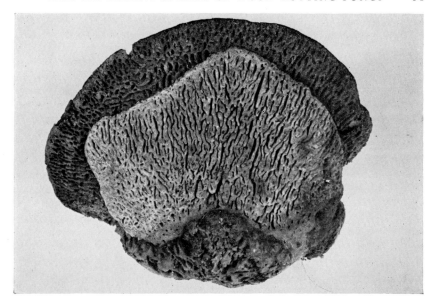

Fig. 28. The hymenial layer (spore-bearing surface) of the fruiting body of *Daedalia quercina*. It is sometimes perennial in character, a fresh hymenium being developed in succeeding seasons. This is clearly shown in the illustration.

Ganoderma applanatum (Pers.) Pat.

This species is most usually found on living beech trees but in addition it attacks a large number of different hardwood species, where it produces a heart rot. The fruiting body is a typical broad flattened bracket, sometimes growing to a large size, eighteen inches across being not uncommon.

Ganoderma lucidum (Leyss.) Karst.

This species is fairly common, causing a white rot of oak. The fruit body is red in colour, the cap is polished and a long stalk is often present. Occasionally an abnormal fruit body of this species is found indoors which is warped, twisted and stick-like.

Polyporus sulphureus (Bull.) Fr.

The importance of this widely distributed species lies in the fact that although normally it is commonly found causing decay of old living oaks (and many other timber species) it can live for a considerable period deep in the woody tissues of large oak members. The moisture content of such timber only very gradually falls, and the moisture gradient is such that even when dry on the outside large-dimensioned timber still retains considerable moisture inside. Again, in such large-section timber considerable fissures open up on drying, and if water accidentally gets into such situations, this species of fungus can again flourish.

The normal fruiting body as it occurs out of doors is large, yellow and orange, consisting of whorls of finger-like structures, but when it occurs indoors in darkness it assumes antler-like shapes. When decayed the wood cracks into cubes and skin-like mycelium is often present, filling the cracks.

Daedalia quercina (Linn.) Fr.

Daedalia quercina is a common wood-rotting fungus found attacking felled hardwoods throughout the world. In the United Kingdom it is found on oak, but chestnut, beech and other species are sometimes attacked. In buildings the timber infestation surveyor is more likely to find this species decaying window sills in damp situations where rain is not drained away quickly. The writer has found it to be not uncommon on oak window sills of houses with a south-west aspect on the south coast.

Fruit Body. This takes the form of a thick bracket which may be simple and regular or irregular and lumpy. In special circumstances it can attain rather bizarre forms, even twisting spirally. In colour it is greyish-buff, often remarkably similar to the colour of the wood it is decaying. The pores are elongated, sometimes pale in colour, and have rounded edges. The pore-bearing surface is tough and cork-like. In a number of cases the fruit body is perennial, zones of growth being clearly observed. The spores are colourless.

Mycelium. Mycelium is visible only in the splits and fissures in the decaying wood. It is present in thin sheets. In culture it is white at first but later turns 'maize yellow'.

Wood Decay. A reddish-brown cubical rot is produced by this fungus not unlike that produced by *Merulius lacrymans*, the individual cubes being sometimes quite large. It is friable and crumbling to the touch. The optimum temperature for growth is about 23°C, and the maximum temperature at which growth occurs is somewhat below 30°C. The optimum moisture content for its growth in wood has been found to be about 40%. The sapwood is relatively quickly decayed by *Daedalia quercina*, but whilst the heartwood is more resistant it nevertheless decays in time if the conditions required by the fungus are favourable.

6

SPECIFICATIONS FOR DRY ROT AND WET ROT ERADICATION

Fungicides—Notes on special cases

Dry Rot is a particular decay of timber, most often softwood, caused by the fungus *Merulius lacrymans*. It is now usual in the United Kingdom to refer to Wet Rot as the decay of timber caused by all other species of woodrotting fungi, to the exclusion of *Merulius lacrymans*, even though some species of fungi concerned produce wood decays not unlike, in some characteristics, the decay caused by *Merulius lacrymans*. The most common wood-destroying fungus is *Coniophora cerebella*, the 'cellar' fungus. It is just about twice as common as the first-named species, and the two species together are responsible for something in excess of 95% of all fungal decay in buildings in the United Kingdom. Of the remaining species *Poria* is the most usually encountered.

Dry Rot and Wet Rot are today widespread and generally distributed, being especially important in London, Glasgow, Edinburgh and other large cities. In the immediate post-war years, during acute timber shortage, there were numerous cases of timber being used in inappropriate circumstances, such as flooring battens embedded in cement or bitumen which caused Dry Rot to occur. In general, however, Dry Rot is uncommon in buildings erected since the end of the Second World War. This is due to the high standards of building design, many of such standards being incorporated in building by-laws, such as the insistence on the provision of damp-proof courses. In addition, supervision during building works is of a much higher order than existed hitherto.

One of the most heartening features, however, of recent years has been the success of the specialist Dry Rot control companies in eradicating this fungal pest. In some situations timber has been replaced time and time again by local building firms without any real check on the growth of the fungus. When, however, the environmental conditions required for the establishment and growth of *Merulius lacrymans* came to be studied in detail, convenient and efficient fungicidal materials such as pentachlorophenol and sodium pentachlorophenate were made available at roughly the same time, and these two factors made possible a great stride forward in timber conservation in buildings.

It is in connection with the environmental conditions necessary for the establishment of wood-rotting fungi in buildings that the important duties

Fig. 29. No difficulty is experienced in identifying this as an attack of Dry Rot but there is considerable difficulty in defining the exact limit of the peripheral growth of the fungus without considerable exposure work.

Fig. 30. Sheet mycelium of the Dry Rot fungus *Merulius lacrymans* overlying a concrete bedding in which fixing fillets of flooring have been almost covered.

Fig. 31. In damp, still conditions, the mycelium of *Merulius lacrymans* assumes a heavy cotton-wool appearance, here seen over a stone floor, brick wall and pieces of steel conduit pipe.

of the Timber Infestation Surveyor should be considered. This is because it is virtually impossible to write a specification for the control of Dry Rot and Wet Rot without including the survey of the property concerned by a trained Timber Infestation Surveyor.

THE TIMBER SURVEY AND THE SURVEYOR

The purpose of the survey is to discover and identify all attacks of wood-rotting fungi so that a report may be submitted on the identity, situation and degree of attack, and the methods to be used for their eradication. The surveyor must inspect all reasonably accessible timber surfaces within the building to an extent sufficient to achieve the object of the survey.

This will include the lifting of convenient traps for inspecting the under-floor. Where traps are not present and the floorboards are square-edged, one or two will be lifted for this purpose. In the circumstances of a Dry Rot attack it may often occur that the cause, the point of origin and peripheral extent of the attack cannot be determined during an initial survey. In such cases the surveyor will recommend that the subsequent work be carried out in stages and he will submit an estimate only for Stage I.

Stage I. This includes only the exposure of the full extent of growth of the fungus so that it can be mapped and reported on. In order to do this, however, considerable areas of plaster may have to be removed and con-

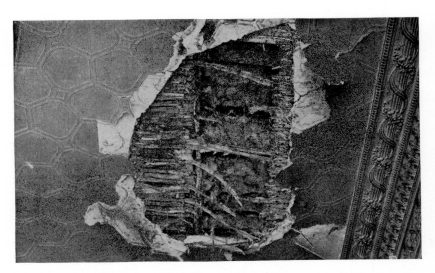

Fig. 32. The Timber Infestation Surveyor must trace the growth of the Dry Rot mycelium both vertically and horizontally. In some circumstances this is not without some danger. The ceiling illustrated supported a heavy fire-hearth which caused the collapse of the ceiling soon after this photograph was taken.

Fig. 33. In older property heavy plaster mouldings are often only held in position by a few wooden battens. This is quite satisfactory until a Dry Rot attack occurs. The moulding illustrated fell in a room when a Timber Infestation Survey was in progress.

siderable superficial damage may take place. But until this is done it is impossible to give a full report on the extent of the damage or to give an estimate for its eradication.

Stage II. When the peripheral extent of the mycelial growth of the Dry Rot fungus has been traced, it is possible to give an estimate for its eradication, the renewal and sterilization and any reinstatement required.

Fig. 34. Portion of the plaster moulding shown in Fig. 33. Fragments of the Dry Rot fungus mycelium can be seen adhering to the plaster.

General Notes

Unless a client makes a specific request, neither outbuildings, gates nor fences outside the buildings, nor furniture inside the buildings, will be inspected by the Timber Infestation Surveyor. The identity and distribution of wood-boring beetles found in the building will, however, be reported on in detail and a control specification with an estimate for carrying out the work will be included.

It is in a client's general interest to co-operate with the Timber Infestation Surveyor so that the survey is conducted not only with the minimum of inconvenience to both parties, but so that a high standard of accuracy is attained. Attention to the following items by the client will materially assist the surveyor.

1. Fitted carpets, stair carpets, lino or other fixed floor coverings should be loosened and lifted where possible.

2. Cases or bulky stored articles in roof spaces should be moved sufficiently to allow access for inspection of roof timbers.

3. Accumulation of stored articles should be removed from cupboards under stairways, as these cupboards are particularly susceptible to attack.

Fig. 35. The mycelium of *Coniophora cerebella* is easily identified from that of *Merulius lacrymans* by its darkening to a vein-like appearance.

Fig. 36. Extensive sporophores of *Merulius lacrymans* shown in this illustration were caused by non-attention to burst water-pipes.

4. Adequate long ladders should be available where large buildings are concerned.

THE SPECIFICATION AND THE SERVICING COMPANY

Below are given model specifications for the control of Dry Rot and Wet Rot for the purpose of enabling the owner of a building who faces the necessity of employing a specialist servicing company to make a comparison between one company and another. There are two important reasons for doing this. In the first place companies vary in the amount and extent of the necessary carpentry, joinery and building work which they are equipped or prepared to carry out, and often this is not made clear in reports and estimates. Thus it sometimes happens that, in comparing estimates, like is not compared with like. Whilst the building owner may select one estimate on the basis of lowest price, he may find himself in the position of having to pay substantial sums to his builder for opening up and replacement of flooring, replastering, etc., which, together with the servicing company's cost, would exceed by a substantial amount the estimate submitted by the second firm which covered *all* the necessary work required for the elimination of the Dry Rot or Wet Rot outbreak.

The second reason, which is related to the first given above, concerns the ultimate reponsibility for eradicating the fungal attack. In the writer's opinion this quite clearly belongs to the specialist servicing company who carry out and report on the findings of their original survey, and, indeed, submit an estimate for all necessary work even though they specifically exclude the joinery, carpentry and building work.

A most important and indeed essential section of the Full Dry Rot Treatment specification is Section IX. It provides for the correction of two interdependent environmental factors necessary for the fungal attack: the improvement of the ventilation and the elimination of the cause or causes of chronic excess moisture; for example, absence of damp-proof courses. These are essentially within the province of the conventional building trades, but even though this work is sub-contracted to a building company, the responsibility must lie on the shoulders of the servicing company.

The scope of the specification

The specification given in this chapter is a general one. The fungi responsible for Dry Rot and Wet Rot are biological phenomena which, although existing under a narrow range of environmental conditions, are found in a very wide range of circumstances in buildings. The specification cannot, therefore, take the place of the trained Timber Infestation Surveyor, but it

Fig. 37. The rotten floor-joists covered with the mycelium of *Merulius lacrymans* are being removed prior to burning.

Fig. 38. When all infected wood has been removed, the walls are brushed and treated with a fungicidal fluid.

will be adapted by him to fit the requirements of the particular case. The use of special paints and plasters which inhibit fungal growth, as given in Sections VII and VIII, may be necessary if large-dimension replacement timbers are to lie adjacent to a thick wall of brick or masonry in which it can be conjectured that inaccessible timber is buried. Apart from this hazard, the large-dimension timbers referred to above may not have been dried down to the equilibrium moisture content appertaining to conditions in the situation in the building in which they are to be employed. Only the Timber Infestation Surveyor, knowing all the conditions of the fungal attack, is in the position to emphasize or elaborate one or more sections in the specification, or indeed to minimize or eliminate others. He will do this in the knowledge that the work carried out to the detail of his report and specification must stand the test of time.

A specification for control of Dry Rot

I. Cut out all timbers showing transverse or cuboidal cracking, brown coloration, presence of white mycelium, etc., and all apparently sound timber within a radius of three feet of the nearest visibly decayed timber.

Carefully remove all such decayed timber from the premises by the shortest practicable route and burn.

II. Hack away all plaster and rendering coats and remove any skirtings, linings, studdings, panelling and ceilings necessary to trace the fullest extent of mycelium, etc., over or through adjacent brick, block, concrete or timber surfaces.

III. Thoroughly clean with a wire brush all such surfaces as walling, partitions, sleeper walls, surface concrete, and also all adjoining timber, and any steel and pipe work within the area up to a radius of five feet from the furthest extent of suspected infection. Carefully remove from the premises by the shortest practical route all dust and débris existing and ensuing from the operation and burn.

IV. Apply fungicidal fluid to all such brick, block, concrete and earth surfaces at the specified rate.

V. Apply two liberal coats of fungicidal fluid to all timber surfaces adjacent to cutting away, to a distance of five feet from cutting away, allowing first coat to be absorbed before applying second coat.

VI. Select thoroughly dry, well-seasoned timber for replacement; cut to size, give two liberal brush coats of fungicidal fluid to all surfaces. Stand ends of timber in a pail of the fluid for a few minutes before placing and fixing.

VII. Re-render in cement, lime and sand (1:1:6) all previously rendered surfaces, including any necessary dubbing out. Then apply quarter-inch floating coat of Zinc Oxychloride Plaster over the rendering coat (where a setting coat of wall plaster is subsequently to be applied) to an area extending twelve inches beyond any previously attacked timber (or up to two feet maximum in extremely severe cases). Render all adjacent surfaces around Z.O.C. with a second coat of cement, lime and sand to receive setting coat of retarded hemi-hydrate plaster (board finish) and leave set ready for client's decorator.

VIII. Alternatively, for areas not to be replastered, apply two coats of Z.O.C. paint in lieu of Z.O.C. plaster. Renew any ceilings or soffits taken down in the course of eradication works in plaster board and scrim and set in retarded hemi-hydrate plaster (board finish) and leave ready for client's decorator.

IX. Cut away for, provide and fix and make good to air bricks or make alternative arrangements necessary to provide adequately increased ventilation. Remove any defective damp courses from sleeper walls and provide and lay new lead-lined bitumen D.P.C. or carry out alternative arrangements to prevent rising damp before fixing any pre-treated replacement joists.

This treatment is referred to as **Full Dry Rot Treatment.**

A Specification for Control of Wet Rot

Provided that the cause of damp can be removed and the timber allowed to dry out, no further attack will develop in timbers not already attacked. The following treatment deals with:

1. the renewal of timber which has already suffered breakdown.

2. the protection of timbers already attacked but still retaining adequate structural strength.

3. the protection of adjacent timbers in which attack may be latent.

I. Timbers in the area of fungal attack are to be tested with a strong-pointed instrument to determine the extent of sub-surface breakdown, and all timber which has suffered surface or sub-surface breakdown due to fungal attack is to be cut out and removed from premises and burnt, together with all dust, dirt and débris existing in the area of attack, or ensuing from cutting-away operations.

II. Select thoroughly dry well-seasoned timber for replacement, cut to size, and give two liberal brush coats of fungicidal fluid over all surfaces of those replacement timbers and of adjacent surfaces of existing timbers and brick, block and concrete areas before placing the replacement timbers in position and fixing.

III. Remove any defective damp courses from sleeper walls and provide and lay new lead-lined bitumen D.P.C. before fixing pre-treated replacement timbers.

IV. Re-render in cement, lime and sand (1:1:6) and float and set in anhydrous (wall finish) plaster any wall surfaces in the area of attack. Renew in gypsum plasterboard, and scrim and set in retarded hemi-hydrate plaster (board finish) any ceiling surfaces removed in the course of the timber treatment and leave ready for client's decorator.

This treatment is referred to as **Full Wet Rot Treatment.**

7

THE CORRECT ENVIRONMENT FOR WOOD IN BUILDINGS

Reasons for excess moisture in buildings—Accident, poor maintenance and poor building design

---

The special relationship of wood to water has already been explained in Chapter 1. Water, either from a humid atmosphere where the amount of moisture is above that normally experienced in buildings, or from excess free water introduced into the building from accidental causes or bad design, will be absorbed by wood until equilibrium has been reached. In such circumstances the moisture content of the wood may reach that required for the germination of spores of one of the wood-rotting fungi and their subsequent development. If, however, the condition of high humidity or the available free water is temporary only, i.e. if the humidity changes rapidly back to normality or the excess water drains away rapidly and the wood loses the water which it has absorbed, the equilibrium moisture content again becomes normal and the fungus will die. A sudden fluctuation of moisture content in wood is normally not a hazard with regard to fungal decay, although it may cause physical difficulties, such as buckling or the lifting of strip flooring owing to the expansion of wood with increase in moisture content.

On the other hand it has often been the practice in the past to use, or perhaps more correctly abuse, wood in buildings by fixing it in such situations that when excess water has been absorbed owing to some reason given above, it cannot readily be lost when conditions are drier. There could be a variety of reasons for this, an important one being the placing or even embedding of the timber in such materials as masonry, brickwork or concrete. In such materials, which may themselves be water-absorbent, the timber has no chance of losing its absorbed water quickly and thus conditions are right for fungal attack of timber.

In buildings, therefore, wood must be used only where these conditions do not prevail. Where wood comes into contact with building materials such as masonry, brickwork and concrete it must be insulated from them by impermeable membranes, such as slate, bitumen or plastic sheeting. In addition the timber must be ventilated by currents of air.

It is significant that in all-timber buildings, Dry Rot and Wet Rot are seldom a hazard. This is because of the absence of building materials which are capable of absorbing and holding water for prolonged periods, so that if the wood in an all-timber house gets wet it dries off relatively rapidly.

Fig. 39. This wall was completely covered with dense creeper, the fallen leaves of which, over several years, had filled and clogged the hopper heads and drains. In addition the creeper has caused the rendering to fail. The Dry Rot Fungus flourished in the woodwork inside. (Crown copyright reserved.)

We shall now discuss the reasons for the presence of excess moisture in buildings.

Damp-proof courses

The presence or absence of horizontal damp-proof courses in the walls of buildings is an important factor influencing the incidence of fungal attack. A damp-proof course consists of a waterproof layer of a material inserted in to or on to a wall of a building in order to prevent water from passing that particular point. Damp-proof courses (often called D.P.C.s) may be horizontal or vertical. In the former case they are designed to prevent

E

vertical movement of water either upwards from ground level or downwards after penetration through parapets, chimney stacks or window
openings. Vertical damp-proof courses, on the other hand, are designed
to prevent lateral movement of water. Damp-proof courses are usually
referred to as such when they are inserted into walls or are of relatively
narrow width. Where a floor, a flat roof or other large area is made
impervious to the passage of water by the insertion of an impermeable
membrane, it is referred to as a damp-proof layer or damp-proof membrane.

Perhaps numerically the most important type of damp-proof course, as
influencing the onset of fungal decay, is the horizontal one at ground
floor level for prevention of upward movement of moisture in walls. The
prevention of *downward* movement of moisture in walls at many other
levels, however, must not be lost sight of.

Nature of damp-proof courses

Horizontal damp-proof courses can be placed in two categories, rigid or
flexible. The various forms of these two types accompanied by notes are
given below:

Rigid

Slate. Two overlapping courses of good quality slate (laid breaking joint)
in cement mortar are effective in preventing *upward* capillary movement

Fig. 40. An example of poorly maintained guttering. (Crown copyright reserved.)

Fig. 41. The cuboidal cracking and buckling of this window-frame is very evident of an attack of Dry Rot. (Crown copyright reserved.)

and also, as a vertical damp-proof course, lateral water movement where no undue pressure is exerted. No reliance, however, can be placed on a slate damp-proof course preventing water moving downwards.

Vitrified Stoneware. One course, normally perforated and laid in cement mortar with open vertical joints, is sometimes found combining the functions of a damp-proof course with ventilation of the sub-floor cavity.

Impervious bricks. Two or more courses of very dense bricks, e.g. Staffordshire Blue and Southwater Engineering, laid in cement mortar and often with open joints, are commonly found at ground-floor level functioning as a damp-proof course. This type is, of course, not reliable in preventing downward movement of water.

Cement. Neat cement or cement containing a waterproofing additive as a continuous bed joint varying in thickness from 1–2 inches is commonly found in older buildings. It is sometimes difficult to be certain whether slates have been incorporated in this type of damp-proof course.

Flexible

Sheet metal. Lead and copper are commonly used, both being flexible enough to accommodate slight structural movements. Lead, however, is subject to chemical corrosion when in contact with fresh lime or Portland cement and should, therefore, be protected by bitumen or bitumen paint. Copper does not require such protection. Neither are likely to squeeze out under normal wall loadings. They can be identified by scraping their edge, and in addition, copper is easily identified by the green staining.

Fig. 42. If the decayed wood is removed from the window-frame shown above the copious skin-like mycelium of *Merulius lacrymans* is revealed. (Crown copyright reserved.)

Sheet metal is suitable as a damp-proof course against upward movement when the joints are lapped, and, with welted joints, against downward movement.

Asphalt Mastic. When laid by experienced specialists this material is a durable, completely impervious damp-proof course without jointing problems. It has, however, only a limited resistance to distortion and is liable to squeeze out under heavy pressure, especially during hot weather.

Bitumen Felt. The current British Standard for bitumen felts for damp-proof courses (B.S. 743) includes six types, based on hessian, fibre felt or asbestos, each of which may be with or without a core of sheet lead. All are flexible enough to accommodate slight movement but are liable to squeeze out under heavy pressure. The hessian and fibre felt bases are liable to decay, but provided the bitumen remains undisturbed the efficiency of the damp-proof course is unimpaired. It is important to note, however, that very large numbers of dwelling houses constructed during the 1920's and 1930's will be found to have horizontal damp-proof courses of this type of material but of a quality very much below current B.S. requirements, and with a life expectation of only about 30–40 years.

Absence of damp-proof course

In the absence of a damp-proof course the hazard of fungal decay is present to a very much greater extent and during the life of such a building there is grave risk of woodwork having to be renewed from time to time owing to the onset of fungal decay. Today all local building by-laws require efficient damp-proof courses to be incorporated into all new buildings. However, something like eight million buildings in the United Kingdom were built before the First World War and are devoid of such means of preventing rising damp from reaching ground floor and other woodwork. Even so it must not be imagined that 'rising damp' is inevitable in such circumstances. A building erected on naturally well-drained soil has little need of further protection. Cases are known, however, of Local Authorities condemning houses as 'unfit for human habitation' on the grounds that they had no damp-proof courses, despite the fact that, standing on exceptionally well-drained soil, they were not damp and had suffered no ill effects from the omission.

Many older buildings lacking damp-proof courses are free from rising damp by virtue of the nature and slope of the soil and by the existence of properly constructed and well maintained systems of rain water and surface water drainage. In properties such as these, damp conditions often develop simply from some recent damage or obstruction to the drainage arrangements. The repair or removal of this is all that is necessary to correct the trouble.

The excavation of a trench around the footings of a house will sometimes reveal the presence of a silted-up ballast drain or some obstruction to its discharge. When these conditions are found it is only necessary to remove the obstruction and restore a free flow or, where silting-up has occurred, to remove the silted ballast and replace it with clean new material. In the latter circumstances, earthenware land drain pipes could be incorporated with advantage. Open trenches or ditches have often, in the past, sufficed to protect walls against damp for centuries.

The presence of damp in an old building may frequently be dealt with successfully by the repair, or possibly the complete removal, of old and now defective rainwater disposal systems.

Vertical slate damp-proof course

In a building without a damp-proof course it is advisable, where finance permits, to construct a vertical slate damp-proof course extending from the foundations up to about six inches above soil level. It should consist of two overlapping courses of slate laid with the grain of the slate vertical.

Fig. 43. Above: This pine panel shows no evidence of decay from the exterior.
Below: But if it is pulled away from the damp wall the cuboidal cracking is very evident.
The position occupied by the skin-like mycelium can be observed on the left of the panel.

Defective damp-proof courses

Failure of a damp-proof course can take place through a variety of causes, the more important of which are listed below, with notes where appropriate:

Soil Shrinkage. This is very evident in heavy clay soils. A long hot and dry summer often causes severe breakage in damp-proof courses in districts

Fig. 44. The oak panelling shown here was covered with Dry Rot mycelium although the oak did not appear to have been decayed. It was carefully cleaned and soaked in a solution of pentachlorophenol before being reinstated. Aston Hall. (City of Birmingham copyright.)

with this type of sub-soil. The condition is sometimes worsened where large trees of various species stand close to buildings and the efficient way in which the moisture is absorbed by these trees from the clay causes shrinkage and subsequent settlement of foundations.

Differential settlement. This can come about by made-up ground settling to differing extents according to the nature of the in-fill material. Mining subsidence and flooding can also cause this defect.

Vibration or Earth Shock Waves. Heavy traffic, civil engineering and building activities such as pile-driving and deep excavations can cause vibrations sufficient to damage damp-proof courses in the vicinity. War-time bombing and gunfire caused a considerable number of damp-proof courses to be inefficient.

Geological phenomena. Underground streams or drainage and variations of the natural water table can cause 'washouts' and can cause considerable soil movement. Natural earth tremors, if sufficiently severe, are also responsible for some shifting and settlement of foundations with the consequent disruption of damp-proof courses.

The above causes of damp-proof course failure refers not only to the rigid type but also to the flexible type, if acting beyond their capacity to accommodate wall movement.

Corrosion. This can cause failure of a lead damp-proof course if it is unprotected, as already mentioned.

Puncture, Splitting, Tearing and Cracking. All these faults can occur in the careless laying of flexible type material. When being laid bituminous felts are particularly susceptible to cracking in cold weather unless very carefully unrolled.

Squeeze-out. Some flexible damp-proof courses can fail owing to disruption caused by pressure and thermal expansion and contraction unless adequate reserves of thickness are present.

Bridging

By far the most common bridging defect in a damp-proof course is caused by the level of the external soil or paving being raised sufficiently to cover it over. Bridging may also be caused by other means, such as (a) rendering over or pointing the damp-proof course, (b) allowing mortar droppings or brick rubble to fall into the cavity of a cavity wall or (c) substitution for a solid floor laid to a higher level than that of the wall damp-proof course by a suspended timber floor without taking adequate steps to provide the required vertical damp-proof course.

Reasons for excess moisture in buildings

An important reason why timber in buildings sometimes has a moisture content higher than normal is because of accidental damage to either the actual fabric of the building or to the water drainage system. Damage to the damp-proof course is dealt with above.

Tiles and slates are sometimes broken or missing and the flashing which normally protects the junction of vertical brick or stonework with roofing is on occasion found to be damaged. In either of these eventualities water can gain admittance to the building. Perhaps the most frequent cause, however, of damp wood in a building, at least above ground floor level, is due to the faulty functioning of drainage hardware (or drainage goods as they are usually referred to in the Building Industry). Guttering, downpipes and hopper heads can corrode or fracture. It is quite common to find iron guttering completely useless, due to rusting through, which in turn has been caused by faulty fixing, whereby insufficient fall was allowed for, and water, instead of draining rapidly away, remained lying in the gutter. Fracturing of downpipes is often observed, and this is usually caused by freezing when water has not been allowed to drain rapidly away due to an obstruction or stoppage. Hopper heads are also likely to fracture for the same reason. Vertical stains arising from the fracture often show the position of the latter, sometimes accentuated by the washing-out of mortar or even by the presence of green algae.

When a Timber Infestation Surveyor visits a building in order to give a report on the presence and extent of fungal decay, it is always a good plan for him initially to make an unhurried general examination of the outside of the buildings and see how it fits into the landscape. Even if all the drainage hardware appears to be present and functional many important faults may be observed only by the surveyor turning up in a rainstorm! After all, that is the test of the drainage system. Here again the lie of the land may well be quite revealing to the surveyor who has a 'feeling' for buildings.

RISING DAMP AND ITS CURE

New damp-proof courses—Improved ventilation

Broadly speaking, if a damp-proof course is not present in a building, and it becomes desirable to insert one, there are two methods by which it can be accomplished. In the first place a mechanical barrier to the movement of water can be introduced, the material of the impermeable layer being conventional or unconventional.

Insertion of conventional damp-proof course
This consists of the traditional methods of undercutting and insertion of slate, lead, copper or bituminous felt. Even when modern power tools are employed, the method is usually slow, difficult, inconvenient and often extremely expensive, and at present limited to wall thicknesses in the region of 21 inches.

Chemical injection methods
Claims are made in favour of damp-proof courses formed by injecting into the damp walls, through holes made for the purpose, substances such as aqueous siliconate/rubber latex and similar materials which when acidified form an impermeable layer in the wall. Such methods, however, rely on the complete distribution of the chemical throughout the wall's thickness at the level being treated for any degree of success; a situation which is indeed suspect for walls over nine inches thick. The writer has had no opportunity of testing these methods under practical conditions.

Insertion of electro-osmotic damp-proof course
The principle of electro-osmosis, by which name is known the movement of water through a porous medium under the influence of an electrical potential, has been known for about 150 years. Today, a number of indus-trial processes and manufacturing developments employ this principle. From time to time electro-osmotic methods have been put forward in an effort to resolve the problem of preventing rising damp in the walls of old buildings, and at the time of writing considerable interest is being taken in the Rentokil method of electro-osmotic damp-proofing of buildings. This account is illustrated by a series of diagrams which will render the basic

Fig. 45. The new drain has bridged the damp-proof course and almost covered the ventilator. Ideal conditions are thus created for Dry Rot.

principles of the method self-explanatory to those readers who have some knowledge of elementary physics.

The following brief explanation, however, will suffice for the purpose of this book.

It was first observed as long ago as 1807 that the passage of water through clay soils produced electrical phenomena. Since that time it has been established that a linear relationship exists between the speed at which a liquid moves through a capillary system and the resulting electro-osmotic potential. In addition, the size of the resulting electro-osmotic potential is influenced both by the cross-sectional area and length of the capillary system and the electrical properties of the moving liquid. These latter are (a) its dielectric constant; that is, its specific inductive capacity, and (b) its specific resistance and, therefore, its conductivity (which can be expressed as the reciprocal of its specific resistance).

The speed of liquid movement is influenced by the following factors:

(a) The co-efficient of viscosity of the liquid.

(b) The potential gradient per unit length of the given capillary system.

A potential gradient, it should be noted, arises in any capillary system in consequence of current flow. The latter will result from the application of an external electromotive force to the capillary system or the discharge

Fig. 46. The roots of this Lombardy Poplar (*Populus serotina*) have caused breakage of the damp-proof course and severe movement of the structure.

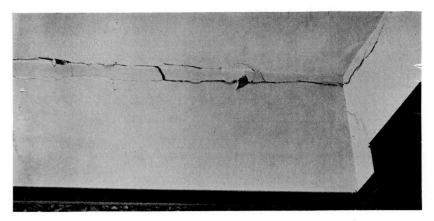

Fig. 47. The structural damage to this house caused by the roots of a Lombardy Poplar tree (see previous illustration) can be gauged by the severe fracturing of the walls.

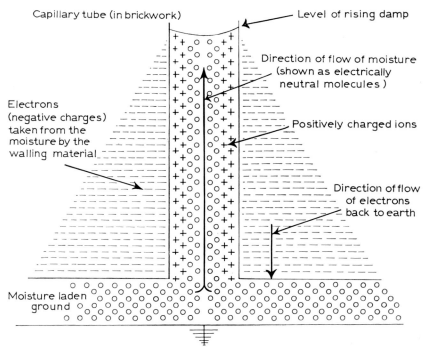

Fig. 48. Why a damp wall is electrically charged.

of the electro-osmotic potential. This discharge is *internal* in every case, though *external* where there is a short-circuiting conductor, the resistance of which is less than the internal resistance of the capillary system. The size both of the current flow and potential gradient depends upon whether the applied potential and the electro-osmotic potential are of similar or opposite polarity.

A capillary or capillary tube literally means a tube with a very fine bore, indeed only a hair's breadth in thickness. A capillary in the context of a blood-vessel has the same meaning. In the context of the soil or a porous building material such as brickwork or masonry, however, the meaning is extended to cover an intricate network of fine interlacing hair-like tubes.

The practical task is then to reduce the electro-osmotic potential to a negligibly small proportion of its original value and to secure the corresponding and consequent reduction in the speed and, therefore, the quantity, of liquid moving in the porous substance. It is now widely held that this can be accomplished successfully by the method given in British Patent 892,906 if the capillary system producing the electro-osmotic potential (that is, in consequence of a capillary *movement* of liquid through the porous medium), has applied to it a conductor system which short-circuits

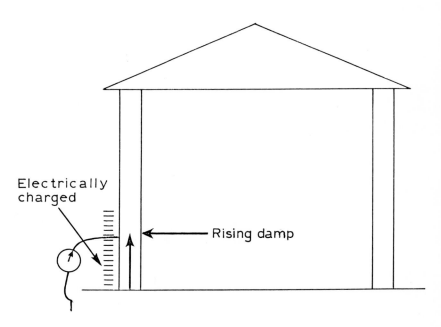

Electrically
charged

Rising damp

Fig. 49. Damp walls are electrically charged with respect to their underlying sub-soil.

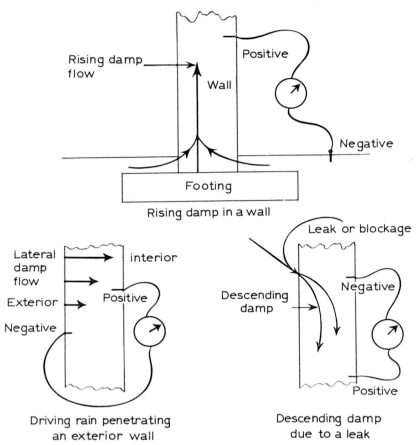

Rising damp flow

Positive

Wall

Negative

Footing

Rising damp in a wall

Lateral damp flow

interior

Exterior

Positive

Negative

Driving rain penetrating
an exterior wall

Leak or blockage

Negative

Descending damp

Positive

Descending damp
due to a leak

Fig. 50. Milli-volt readings reveal the direction of flow of the capillary moisture.

this potential. The applied conductor must have a resistance value which is lower than, or at maximum not more than equal to, the internal resistance of the porous medium which is generating the electro-osmotic potential.

These then are the principles on which the electro-osmotic system of damp-proofing is based. How then is it carried out in practice?

Is rising damp caused by capillarity?

The first task is to decide whether in fact the dampness in the wall is definitely rising damp and whether the water is rising in the porous building medium solely owing to capillarity. If the rise of water in the wall is due to causes such as hydrostatic pressure, a head or weight of water forcing the

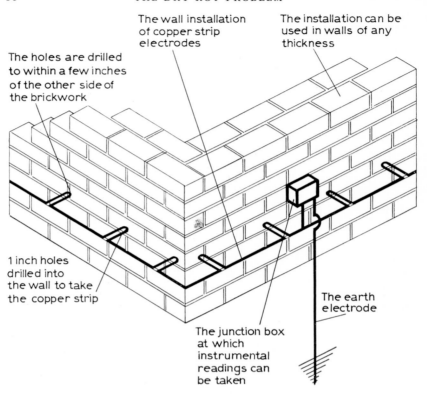

The wall installation
of copper strip
electrodes

The installation can be
used in walls of any
thickness

The holes are drilled
to within a few inches
of the other side of
the brickwork

1 inch holes
drilled into
the wall to take
the copper strip

The earth
electrode

The junction box
at which
instrumental
readings can
be taken

Fig. 51. An electro-osmotic installation.

water through or up the porous medium, or perhaps to still other causes, the electro-osmotic system in its simplest form is not applicable. Hydraulic pressure, that is pressure of water in motion, can produce 'rising damp' in unprotected porous walls also. An example would be when an underground water course has been diverted, perhaps by a blocked or silted-up drainage system, and now flows past the foundation walls of the building.

Efflorescent or deliquescent mineral salts are often present in damp walls, and it must be decided by the surveyor whether these hygroscopic salts have been carried into the wall by 'true' rising damp from the underlying soil or whether they were present in the original wall material and have *not* had their origin in the soil. Unwashed sea sand used for mortar and, more commonly, salty brick earths from which the bricks have been manufactured, are among the sources of efflorescent salts in walls.

The installation

The most common type of electro-osmotic damp-proofing installation will be to provide a horizontal damp-proof course just above soil level but below the level of internal floor framing and wall plates, in the same sort of situation as a damp-proof course of conventional design. A number of holes are drilled at predetermined calculated spacings in the external wall at the horizontal level required. The angle at which the installation is inserted into the wall may be as is most convenient. Unlike the conventional form of damp-proof course, it can, if need be, slope steeply downwards or upwards. Due regard, however, must be paid to the exact position of the internal timber to make sure that it is all protected.

The depth of penetration of the drillings is a factor to be calculated in respect of the number of drillings required and will vary with the wall thickness, but in no case will they extend to the inner face, so that no internal damage or disturbance is caused by the work.

Fig. 52. Fungal decay has always been present in skirtings against this wall due to rising damp. There was no damp-proof course. Earlier attempts at repair are also visible.

F

Fig. 53. Measurement of electrical potentials between wall and soil under the conditions of capillary movement in the porous wall.

A continuous length of copper strip is looped and mortared into holes drilled in the wall and along its length. This forms a bank of transverse and longitudinal wall electrodes which is then connected to copper-covered steel rod earth electrodes driven into the sub-soil to designed depth and location requirements.

The design of the installation is based upon scientifically planned methods for determining the nature of the damp conditions in the wall and on measurements of the electric properties of the sub-soil. The data obtained from these observations is then referred to other pre-calculated design data and read off in terms which enable the surveyor to specify the numbers, sizes and location of the precise details of the installation.

The effect of the installation

The immediate effect of the electro-osmotic damp-proof course is to prevent any further quantity of water from travelling into the porous building material from below or horizontally from the surrounding sub-soil. Water already in the wall must in these, as in any other types of installation, dry out by evaporation, and this may take from a few weeks to several months, depending upon the wall thickness, the degree of dampness, the quantity of soluble salts present, and of course the rate of evaporation. In the case of new buildings, for example, it is a general rule that it takes one month for every inch of thickness, i.e. a 9-inch wall will take 9 months to dry. However, for older buildings where the wall may contain an appreciable quantity of soluble salts, the drying period may be considerably increased; in fact where hygroscopic salts are present the wall may never dry completely, although the level achieved is usually satisfactory for redecoration.

Fig. 54. One of the several stages of measuring the electrical specific resistance, i.e. the resistivity, of the soil, to a depth of many feet, using the internationally known 4-electrode Wenner method.

F*

Advantages of electro-osmotic damp-proofing

One of the most important advantages of this system is its practical use in walls of a greater thickness than is possible by conventional methods. It is an economic process when compared with the laborious conventional method. It is rapidly and conveniently executed and, in external walls, involves no disturbance to occupants or to the internal decorations. Of corrosion-resistant high conductivity copper throughout, the installations are designed to last the life of the building and are, in fact, guaranteed for twenty years.

Provision of improved ventilation

The exact part which ventilation (by ventilation we mean rate of change of air) plays in the growth of a fungal attack is not known, but there is no doubt that a relationship exists. Of course, ventilation could produce a more rapid change in moisture content of wood and well-ventilated wood could be expected to have a lower moisture content (and therefore to be less prone to fungal attack) than if it were not ventilated. In other words, ventilation could exercise a purely moisture-decreasing function.

On the other hand a rapid rate of air change could cause a more direct

Fig. 55. Drilling one-inch diameter holes at calculated intervals through the major part (but not right through) of the wall thickness to receive the transverse loops of the continuous copper wall electrode.

Fig. 56. The earth electrode is connected to the longitudinal wall electrode through a junction box.

biological effect detrimental to the growth of the young hyphae. The correct environment for wood, therefore, requires a degree of ventilation, or a number of changes of air per hour, such as will accelerate the rate of loss of water from damp timber to such an extent that fungal decay does not occur.

The sum total of this adds up to the fact that in any Dry Rot and Wet Rot attack an important part of the eradication and future protection must involve the provision of a higher degree of ventilation. In such outbreaks of fungal decay increased ventilation must always be provided.

There cannot be too much ventilation for the protection of timber against fungal decay, but draughts and freezing cold may impose some reasonable limits on the amount of underfloor ventilation!

British Standard 483 for cast-iron airbricks and gratings requires that their total unobstructed area shall not be less than one-fifth of the total area calculated from the overall dimensions. As a general scale the minimum provision of one square inch of unobstructed open area per foot run of external wall would be reasonable. This amounts approximately to a 9 in. × 3 in. air-brick per 4-foot run or a 9 in. × 6 in. air-brick per 7-foot run (for air-bricks giving only the minimum of one-fifth unobstructed area). This minimum provision is nevertheless honoured, perhaps, as much in the breach as in the observance. But where thought advisable in the individual circumstances of eradicating fungal decay, that minimum at least should normally be observed and in very damp conditions rather more bricks should be provided in order to afford an adequate flow of ventilation currents throughout the underfloor void. The air vents should be placed as high as possible above ground level in relation to the internal floor levels.

It is important to make sure that sleeper walls do not obstruct the free flow of air, and honeycombing is the usual effective way of carrying this out. Ducts should be provided where necessary to avoid blind spots created by areas of solid floors.

TIMBER PRESERVATION

Natural durability—Properties of a wood preservative—Methods of wood preservation
—Pre-treatment—Fungicides

It is not proposed to give here any historical review of wood preservation but only to give information concerning the types of preservatives and methods of preservation in use at the present time in connection with Dry Rot and Wet Rot in buildings. To give a comprehensive account of the preservation of railway sleepers and telegraph poles would only confuse the reader. This aspect of wood preservation is dealt with in several recent works which are referred to in the list of references.

Natural durability

The different species of wood show great variation in their resistance to fungal decay. Ash and beech are rapidly decayed by several species of wood-rotting fungi if conditions are suitable. On the other hand, some timbers are resistant to fungal decay even when conditions are otherwise suitable. Examples of such timbers are oak, teak and greenheart and these are said to be durable. In all timber species the sapwood is much less resistant to fungal decay than is the heartwood, but the former is relatively easy to treat with wood preservatives, as absorption normally takes place readily. It often occurs that preserved sapwood of a non-durable timber species is made much more durable than the untreated sapwood of a 'durable' species.

Wood preservatives

In our desire to preserve woodwork in buildings, we can examine the problem in two ways. First, we should ensure that all timber is situated in its correct environment. This we have already explained in Chapter 7. This environment, however, will be its normal environment, which may not alter significantly for a number of years. Temporary increases in moisture content, due, for example, to high atmospheric humidity, can be taken care of by moderately rapid evaporation when the humidity drops again.

If, however, a building has to endure a period of poor maintenance when drains are clogged, metal downpipes fractured, or perhaps when there are constant plumbing leaks, then woodwork in the vicinity retains the absorbed water and the moisture content rises to a point when fungal decay can occur. The same circumstances can arise with flooding, and even from fire when a large volume of water has been used to extinguish it, so that chemical protection of the timber is a logical conclusion. Such a chemical material, affording protection to wood in that it allows the wood to last longer or be preserved, is known as a wood preservative. There are two modes of action of wood preservatives in the wide sense. Any material applied to wood which will afford a physical barrier to the absorption of water will preserve the timber, at least against the onset of fungal decay. Paint and water-repellents carry out this function, and can also serve for decoration.

Properties required by a wood preservative to be used in buildings

Before dealing further with the protection of wood we ought to define the properties of a wood preservative.

I. *Fungicidal activity.* The wood preservative must possess pronounced fungus-killing properties or so affect the properties of the wood that fungal hyphae are unable to feed on it and thus the wood is protected. The latter property could be called 'fungistatic' or 'fungal inhibiting'. It is of interest

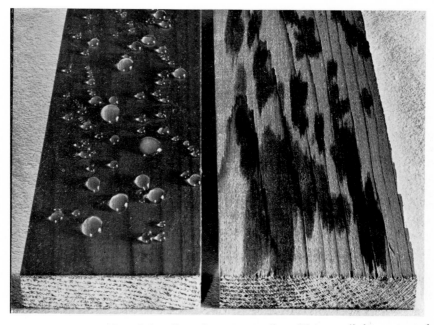

Fig. 57. Demonstration of the effect of a water repellent. Water applied to untreated wood on right has been absorbed, that on the treated timber (left) has formed into droplets and remains on the surface.

to note that a certain amount of confusion exists in the wood preservation industry concerning this. The British Standard Laboratory method for assessment of wood preservatives in respect of the fungal decay hazard refers to *toxicity*, whereas no measurement of the ability to kill the fungus is made, only the ability of the treated wood to remain undigested by the fungus.

II. *Insecticidal activity*. The wood preservative, if it is to be used for application to wood already suspected of harbouring wood-boring insects, must possess pronounced insecticidal properties with regard to these insects. If the wood preservative is to be used against a particular species of wood-boring insect, then the wood preservative must be known to have pronounced insecticidal properties against this particular species. This is because it is known that the various wood-boring insects have different susceptibilities to the different chemicals used as insecticides. Again, a distinction exists between the desirable properties of a wood preservative that is to be used against wood already infested with an insect and a wood preservative that is to give future protection. In the former case the insecticidal activity must be pronounced in respect of all life stages—eggs, larvae, pupae and adults. The latter stage is included because the preservative fluid might be applied at the time when the ecloded adults are within the wood and just about to bore their way out.

III. *Permanence*. The wood preservative must convey its properties to the wood in a permanent or at least semi-permanent form. Timber must remain protected from the hazards of wood-rotting fungi and wood-boring insects for upwards of twenty years or so. This is a property which the public expect, although such a requirement is quite exceptional if the use of fungicides and insecticides in agriculture and public health is considered. Wood preservation, compared with other insect and fungus-killing activities, has several great advantages. The chemicals used are absorbed by the wood, often to a considerable depth, and are thus outside the effect of sunlight, which would decompose them. Volatilization certainly takes place, but at a much slower rate, so that insecticidal chemicals which, as the superficial film, might retain their properties for a few months, are known to retain them for upwards of ten years or considerably longer when absorbed into wood. *Chemicals so absorbed are also placed out of human contact and domestic animals cannot come to harm.* In addition, wood preservatives used in buildings are not subject to leaching by rain or very humid conditions, so that there are never any residues to be washed away or to get into the soil with undesirable effects as have been described in the case of agricultural insect pest control. A wood preservative used in the first place for eradication of a fungal or insect attack must afterwards give prolonged protection. Fumigation and heat-treatment are lacking in this regard, so that such treatments must always be used in conjunction with the longer-lasting chemical wood preservatives.

Fig. 58. Automatic pressure impregnation plant for the pre-treatment of timber by the Celcure process. The entrance and open door of the pressure cylinder can be seen behind the control panel. Timber is wheeled into the cylinder along rails which enter shed through a hole at right.

IV. *Penetration.* It is conventional to emphasize the property of deep penetration of wood preservatives into wood. This is a property, however, more concerned with out-door conditions. Deep penetration of the wood preservative is to guard against fungal infection of wood originating in cracks in the wood; cracks occurring *after* the application of the wood preservative and deep enough to reveal wood into which the preservative has not permeated. Such cracking of wood indoors, at least in timber of the usual dimensions, is probably of uncommon occurrence. Even so, such cracks would be only a potential hazard in respect of fungal attack. In the case of the very much greater hazard of Common Furniture Beetle, *Anobium punctatum*, even if eggs were laid in such a crack or fissure, which would be most unlikely, as this beetle does not select this sort of crack as an egg-laying site, the resulting beetles would have to bore their way out of the peripherally treated layer and would succumb. Their statistical chance of finding the original unpermeated crack for emergence would be negligible.

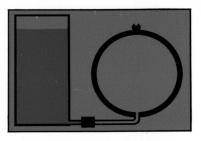

SCHEMATIC DIAGRAM OF THE FULL-CELL
VACUUM-PRESSURE IMPREGNATION
PROCESS

1. Treatment plant before use, with
storage tank filled with preservative.
Pressure chamber empty.

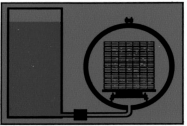

2. A charge of wood has now been
moved into the pressure chamber; the
chamber is then sealed.

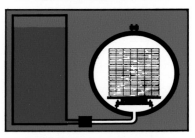

3. The pressure chamber and wood is
evacuated by means of the vacuum
pump.

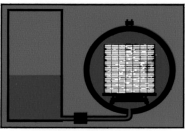

4. Preservative is drawn into the
pressure chamber by the vacuum.

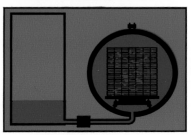

5. Pressure is applied to the preservative
in the chamber; preservative is forced
deep into the wood.

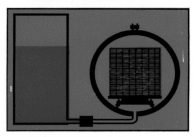

6. Surplus preservative is pumped back
to the storage tank, leaving preserved
wood ready for removal from the
pressure chamber.

There is a more general aspect to penetration which is perhaps best set down here. When a chemical material like a wood preservative is absorbed by wood, and we find out where the chemical is at any given time afterwards, we find that it is more highly concentrated at the surface of application.

Hereafter, as we take slices deeper and deeper into the wood, the chemical becomes less and less concentrated. If we think of the individual molecules we can conceive an intricate reticulation with the molecules further and further apart as we get deeper into the wood. If we consider the larva of a wood-boring insect coming into contact with wood with only the slightest trace of wood preservative in it, it may bore for some distance before it has taken up a lethal dose. It would appear that the most efficient way to present a wood preservative is in a relatively narrow band within the wood, but in as concentrated a form as possible. This is, in fact an argument against *deep penetration* when the wood preservative is to be applied indoors.

V. *Freedom from harmful effects on wood.* The wood preservative must have no harmful effects on the wood itself. Although wood, in general, is a non-reactive substance, certain acids and alkalis cause the individual wood fibres to dissociate, and the wood is given a woolly appearance. In addition there must be no harmful effects on associated metal fittings—nails, screws and hinges, etc.

Paint as a wood protector

Paint is well known as giving a protective coat to timber, especially those based on white lead. With such a paint film, water cannot be absorbed by the wood nor are fungal spores capable of germinating and penetrating the paint film. The paint film, to remain effective, must be renewed at regular intervals because when it cracks, or the blisters rupture, water and fungal spores can rapidly initiate an infection. In the main, the foregoing explains outdoor conditions because indoor paint is used for decoration only and seldom to protect wood. For example, skirting boards are painted on their outer face only, whereas on the inner face, against the wall, the most likely situation to get damp, the wood is left in its original condition. The paint film on the outer side prevents moisture which has been absorbed by the inner face from being evaporated from the outer one. Patches of Wet Rot are of common occurrence in such situations. It would, therefore, with fungal decay in mind, be very much better to paint the inner (wall) face of the skirting to prevent water absorption and leave the outer face unpainted.

Methods of Wood Preservation

Timber in buildings, or desired for use in buildings, may be treated by one of the following methods:

Pressure Impregnation. In this method the wood preservative is forced into the timber under pressure and deep penetration is obtained. Most timbers may be treated by this method, notable exceptions being Douglas Fir and Spruce. The amount of wood preservative taken up by the charge of timber in the specialized heavy chambers which are required can be controlled. (See Fig. 58.)

Fig. 59. This old wall has been treated (right) with two full coats by brush of Zinc Oxychloride paint to inhibit the growth of the mycelium of Dry Rot fungus present in the wall.

Dipping. This method consists of immersing timber in a tank of the wood preservative for relatively short periods. This latter period varies from ten seconds to about ten minutes. The timber is then allowed to lie on a ramp for a short period to allow excess preservative to drain back into the tank.

Steeping, on the other hand, is defined (in British Standard 1282 : 1959) as submerging timber in cold preservative for a period varying from a few hours to days or weeks, depending on the species and the size of the timber. It is not usual to use steeped timber in buildings, as the process is inconvenient and slow.

Steeped or dipped timber, however, shows a deeper penetration of preservative than is shown by sprayed timber and in addition dipping is almost independent of errors of omission which could be made by a spraying gang.

Spraying and Brushing. These methods are those usually employed in buildings on *in situ* timber. In general, spraying is to be preferred to brushing because timber that would otherwise be inaccessible by brush can be so treated. When spraying, a coarse nozzle should be used so that the droplet size is large and the fluid settles swiftly on the timber, saturating the surface without producing a fine mist which would cause difficulty to operators.

Fungicides

As will be seen from the section dealing with the desirable (and undesirable) properties of wood preservatives, a fungicide is a special type of wood preservative, specifically formulated to possess toxic properties in relation to wood-destroying fungi; that is, in the context of wood. In addition, however, the word 'fungicides' in a wider sense, of course, means a material which is toxic to any sort of fungus, and indeed the word is much more often used in its agricultural or horticultural sense than in the field of wood preservation.

This book describes the problem of the wood-rotting fungi present in buildings (and what is done about their eradication) and only deals with those wood-boring insects associated with fungally-decayed wood. It has already been mentioned, however, that the wood-boring insect, Common Furniture Beetle (*Anobium punctatum*), is very widely distributed in the United Kingdom. So wide is its distribution that it is believed to occur in at least half the buildings in the United Kingdom. It would seem, therefore, that when using a fungicide in wood preservation it would be prudent to ensure that the fungicide is also insecticidal, with Common Furniture Beetle in mind.

Type of wood preservatives used in buildings

Wood preservatives are best classified according to the British Standard 1282 : 1959 (Classification of Wood Preservatives and their Methods of Application). They are first divided into three main groups; tar-oil types, organic solvent types and water-borne types. These are again sub-divided, the basis of the classification being the main chemical base of the preservative. This serves as a good guide, as most of the preservatives used in buildings, either as proprietary products or materials used by specialist serving companies, can be allocated to one or other of the groups, although there is an increasing tendency for many products to include such substances as water-repellents (whose use has already been mentioned), special insecticides, anti-bloom agents, surface-active ingredients, etc. Water-repellent substances, it should be added, although limiting or controlling water absorption and therefore decreasing the risks of fungal infection, are usually added to a wood preservative formulation in order to confer dimension stabilization properties on the wood.

The Classification

This is as follows:

Type TO—Tar-oil types
TO1   Coal tar creosote to British Standard 144
TO2   Coal tar-oil types to British Standard 3051

Type OS—Organic solvent types
OS1   Chlorinated naphthalenes and other chlorinated hydrocarbons
OS2   (a) Copper naphthenate
        (b) Zinc naphthenate
OS3   Pentachlorophenol and its derivatives

Mixtures of OS types are also used.

Type WB—Water-borne types
WB1   Copper/chrome
WB2   Copper/chrome/arsenic
WB3   Fluor/chrome/arsenate/dinitrophenol
WB4   Others, e.g. copper sulphate, mercuric chloride, sodium
        fluoride, sodium pentachlorophenate, zinc chloride and
        organic mercurial derivatives

Tar-oil types (TO)

The tar-oil wood preservatives consist essentially of coal-tar distillates. These materials are not now generally used in buildings. This is because of the difficulties in connection with paint-staining, objectionable odour and tainting of food. This type of wood preservative, however, is generally suitable for exterior woodwork, although if the latter is in contact with the ground, special methods must be employed in order to obtain deep penetration, such as pressure impregnation, or hot and cold open tank treatment.

Organic solvent types (OS)

These wood preservatives consist of substances, usually organic (in this context meaning containing carbon) and often in relatively low concentration, dissolved in an organic solvent. The solvent is volatile as a general rule, but there are important exceptions to this, as some more deeply penetrating preservatives employ high-boiling solvents which volatilize very slowly. Most modern OS type wood preservatives are formulated from more than one chemical substance. As an example, pentachlorophenol, which has very good fungicidal properties and is widely used against the fungi *Merulius lacrymans* and *Coniophora cerebella*, nevertheless has relatively poor insecticidal properties when used against *Lyctus* beetle infestations. It is usual, therefore, to incorporate an insecticide such as lindane into the pentachlorophenol solution.

There is an important exception to the point made earlier that OS type wood preservatives often consist of low concentrations of the fungicidal and insecticidal chemicals in the solvent. Certain wood-boring insects, notably the House Longhorn, *Hylotrupes bajulus*, appear to be more readily exterminated by substances with high 'fumigant effect', so certain OS type wood preservatives contain relatively high proportions of fumigant chemical substances. This point primarily concerns wood-boring insects and not wood-rotting fungi, but the reader may want to know the reason for this.

Most OS wood preservatives are not corrosive to metals but some have a characteristic odour when first applied. Tainting of foodstuffs may occur with certain types. Those products utilizing solvents in the higher boiling point range are not readily inflammable, in fact one case is known of a church where a fire occurred in the roof of a few weeks after treatment with such a material. Only those timbers not treated with the fluid were burnt. Problems of staining or 'creeping' occasionally arise. This is due to the desirable property of penetration becoming undesirable, when the preservative penetrates too far! Painting woodwork treated with some preservatives may occasionally give difficulty.

These points may appear confusing to the layman and are strong arguments in favour of Dry Rot control being carried out by specialist servicing organizations who can make the necessary decisions as to which fungicidal fluids to use in the individual circumstances.

Water-borne types (WB)

Wood preservatives in this category consist of all those soluble in water. The chemical substances are either inorganic, such as the WB2 types (based on copper/chrome/arsenic), organic (sodium pentachlorophenate, for example) or mixtures of inorganic with organic (e.g. the WB3 types based on fluor/chrome/arsenate/dinitrophenol). In general it can be said that they have certain advantages, such as cleanliness of the treated timber and ease of painting after treatment. They do not creep or stain when dry and they are mostly odourless. They are non-inflammable, but a few in group WB4 corrode metal. Some are easily leached, such as those based on a sodium fluoride, but others resist leaching, for example those containing chromate. The fixation of the wood preservative chemical to the cellulose of the wood by means of chromate is not fully understood, but an important group of water-borne preservatives rely on this mechanism for prevention of leaching.

Fig. 60. Application of Zinc Oxychloride plaster to cement rendering to inhibit the growth of the mycelium of Dry Rot fungus present in the wall.

HOW FUNGICIDES ARE TESTED FOR EFFICIENCY

A well-established test has been employed in the United Kingdom for evaluating the fungicidal efficacy of wood preservatives since 1939 when British Standard 838 was first published. This is titled 'Methods of Test for Toxicity of Wood Preservatives to Fungi'. As previously mentioned, however, this is, in reality, a test assessing the degree of inhibition of fungal attack produced by the wood preservative; it does not assess its fungal killing power. In 1961 the Standard was revised to include both the initial 'toxicity' and residual 'toxicity' after leaching and evaporation, and included a test embracing the soft rot microfungi. The following description of the test, which is given so that all those who have to deal with the use of preservatives in buildings can understand the general picture, is not of course the official Standard, which would have to be consulted if tests were to be carried out.

The principle of the test

Test pieces of wood susceptible to fungal decay are treated with the fungicide and exposed to pure cultures of several species of wood-rotting fungi under controlled conditions. In addition, some of the wood pieces are tested, but are untreated, and act as controls. Yet a further group is treated, where appropriate, with the solvent of the fungicidal material used in the test.

The two methods of wood preservative application—impregnation under pressure and brushing or steeping—are catered for in the test by slightly different comparisons. In the case of preservatives which are to be applied by impregnation under pressure, the minimum quantity of preservative which inhibits attack by the species of wood-rotting fungi used in the test is determined. This is expressed as kilogrammes per cubic metre of wood, or pounds per cubic foot. In the case of preservatives which are to be applied by brushing and steeping, the basis of comparison is whether or not the test pieces are attacked by the species of wood-rotting fungi when they have been treated by surface application. The extent to which fungicidal efficiency of the wood preservative is lost by leaching, and also evaporation, is estimated by comparing the residual toxicity to the wood-rotting species after subjection of leaching (as determined later) with the initial fungicidal properties.

Preparation of the wood block test pieces

The test pieces are made of two timber species. For a softwood, the sapwood of Scots pine, *Pinus sylvestris*, is used and for a hardwood the outerwood (that is the wood taken from the outer three inches) of beech, *Fagus sylvatica*, is employed. Both these timbers are non-durable in respect of the wood-rotting fungi used in the test. They are also both easily impregnated with wood preservative. The test wood blocks are finished to a size of $5 \times 2 \cdot 5 \times 1 \cdot 5$ cm. and the cutting is so arranged that the grain of the wood follows the long axis. The blocks are prepared for test by drying and sterilizing them in an oven for about eighteen hours at 100–105°C. Their weight immediately after this is known as the 'initial dry weight'. Beech is so easily attacked by certain fungi that in order to ensure sterility it is necessary to subject the test pieces to 15 lb./in.² (1·1 kg/cm²) steam pressure for twenty minutes before the oven-drying treatment.

Fig. 61. Kolle flasks containing standard wood blocks and cultures of a wood-rotting fungus (*Coniophora cerebella* in this case). Some of the blocks are treated with preservatives, others are untreated (controls). The amount of decay caused to the blocks is evaluated by loss in weight and gives a fair indication of the fungicidal activity of the preservative used.

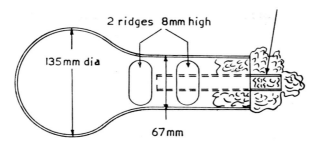

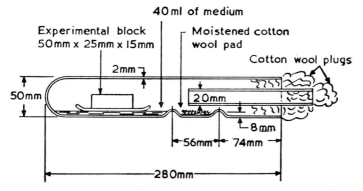

Fig. 62. Kolle flask for wood block test of toxicity of wood preservative.
Above: In plan.
Below: Diagrammatic section showing wood block in position.

Species of wood-rotting fungi employed in the test

When pine sapwood is used as test blocks the following fungi are employed:

I. *Coniophora cerebella* (Pers.). This species is not only very widespread in buildings in the United Kingdom, but it is moderately resistant to many wood preservatives. In the culture flask it forms a soft mat which tends to form fine branching strands. Pale yellow at first, it later produces dark brown patches.

II. *Poria monticola* Murr. In the 1939 edition of B.S. 838 this species was referred to as *Poria vaporaria*. It is resistant to copper compounds. In culture it forms an even, soft, white, cotton-woolly mat.

III. *Lentinus lepideus* Fr. This species is particularly resistant to tar oils. It is slow to get going in culture. It forms a thin colourless mat which later becomes tufted and woolly, showing pale or purplish brown tints. In older cultures cylindrical outgrowths often develop at the upper end of the slope. It always has an aromatic odour.

IV. *Lenzites trabea* (Pers.) Fr. This is an arsenic-resistant species. It forms a soft whitish fluffy cushion at first but quickly assumes a buffish colour.

When beech outerwood is used the following fungus is employed:
V. *Polystictus versicolor* (Linn.) Fr. In culture it forms a thin mat of colourless mycelium and later forms a thin white skin.

All the above species of fungi are of economic importance, although in buildings the species *Coniophora cerebella* is of extreme importance, whilst *Polystictus versicolor* is only found out of doors. They all grow fairly quickly and vigorously under culture conditions and cause a rapid loss of weight of the unpreserved wood.

The culture flasks

Two types of culture vessels may be used in the test. The flat culture flask or Kolle flask is the conventional vessel used, but screw-top square bottles with wide mouths are also permissible in the British Standard method. The illustrations give the dimensions of the Kolle flask, which is seen to be flattened, nearly twelve inches long and two inches deep, with a bulbous body and an elongated neck. At one side of the neck, at the inner end, there are two ridges, formed in such a way that a small reservoir of water may be maintained by a pad of cotton wool soaked in water. The neck of the flask is plugged with cotton wool but a glass tube of 20 mm. external diameter is inserted through the plug through which the inoculum is introduced. This is then plugged separately.

If bottles are used instead of Kolle flasks they are of square cross-section, each side being about 70 mm. wide externally. The bottle is about 170 mm in length and the neck must have an internal diameter of at least 45 mm The aluminium screw-cap engages with an external thread on the neck of the bottle. A hole about 15 mm. in diameter is cut in the screw-cap and when in use is plugged with cotton wool.

The culture medium

The nutrient on which the wood-rotting fungus is to grow before it has access to the test block is made up of malt extract (or dry powdered malt), powdered agar and distilled water. A measured quantity of the made-up medium is introduced into each flask, sterilized and inoculated with the test fungus.

Treatment of wood blocks with preservatives

The treatment of the wooden test blocks varies according to the method of application of the wood preservative in practice, whether by pressure impregnation or surface application. In the former case a series of about six dilutions of the preservative are made so that half the dilutions will fall above and half below the expected toxic limit. Some idea of the toxic limit, therefore, requires to be known, so a preliminary test must be carried out. If the preservative is water-soluble, then the dilutions are made up with water, but if it is not soluble in water, then a solvent must be chosen for dilution that does not, of course, leave a fungicidal residue on the wood block. Light petroleum, acetone, benzene and ethanol have been found to be suitable solvents.

Impregnation of wood blocks

The blocks are weighted down in beakers and then exposed to reduced pressure in a vacuum desiccator for ten minutes. The aperture leading to the pump is then closed and the treating solution is then admitted. The illustration shows a suitable arrangement for the apparatus. When the blocks are completely covered, the vacuum is released and the test pieces

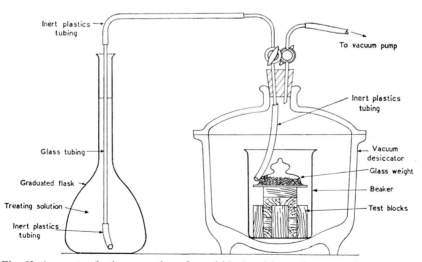

Fig. 63. Apparatus for impregnation of wood blocks with wood preservative.

G

in the beaker are removed from the desiccator. The blocks are fully saturated after the lapse of two hours. Weighing gives the amount of preservative taken up which is expressed as kilogrammes per cubic metre or as
pounds per cubic foot. The control blocks are treated similarly but using
only the solvent employed for dilution. The vigour of the test fungi should
also be tested in untreated test blocks from time to time.

Surface application treatment of blocks

Wood preservatives that are intended for use by surface application, such
as use on woodwork in buildings where a Dry Rot outbreak has taken
place, can, of course, be applied to the test blocks by pressure impregnation. In this way a toxic limit can be assessed but British Standard 838
considers this unrealistic if, in practice, the preservative is not to be applied
in this way.

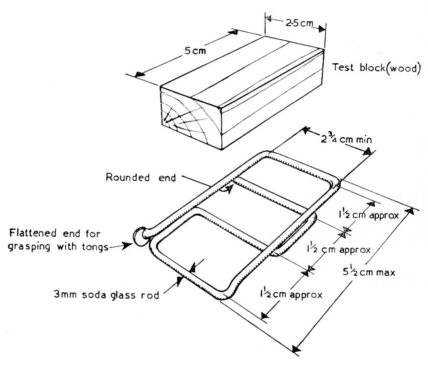

Fig. 64. Above: Wood test block.
Below: Glass frame for supporting test block.

Figs. 62, 63 and 64. From B.S. 838:1961, *Methods of Test for Toxicity of Wood Preservatives to Fungi*, are reproduced by permission of the British Standards Institution,
2 Park Street, London, W.1. from whom copies of the complete standard may be
purchased.

The wood blocks, which have been oven-dried and weighed, are immersed in the wood preservative for 10 seconds (believed to give a retention approximating to that achieved by one application by brush) and another set of blocks is immersed for ten minutes (believed to give a retention approximately equivalent to that achieved by three applications by brush). After draining, the blocks are re-weighed and the uptake of fluid calculated, but the absorption is not in this case expressed as kilogrammes per cubic metre.

Conditioning of blocks after treatment

It is very important that the test blocks are 'conditioned' after treatment. In the case of water-soluble preservatives there is no problem, but there is difficulty with the oil-soluble preservatives in order to remove the oil solvent, and a ventilated oven operating at $50 \pm 1°C$ is employed. After conditioning, the blocks are sterilized by subjecting them to the vapour of propylene oxide. They are then ventilated in sterile conditions and transferred to the culture vessels. Each block stands on a glass frame so that the fungal mycelium can envelop it without the wood coming into contact with the nutrient medium.

The necessity for some types of water-soluble wood preservatives to stand for at least three weeks after the dipping treatment, whilst the fixing of the salts to the cell walls of the wood takes place, is important.

Test blocks infection

Two test blocks of identical treatment are placed in each culture vessel in which there is an actively growing fungus. Four blocks treated at each dilution of wood preservative are used, and all the test blocks remain exposed to the fungus in the culture vessels at $22 \pm 0.5°C$ for three months, the incubator being maintained at 65% relative humidity.

Examination of blocks after test

The blocks are taken from the culture flasks and adhering fungal mycelium is carefully removed. Any visible signs of fungal decay are carefully noted after testing with a knife. The blocks are then weighed, then dried at 100–105°C for eighteen hours and then weighed again. The latter weight is known as the 'final dry weight', and the moisture content is again estimated. The moisture content should not be less than the fibre-saturation value, which is about 27%, otherwise the fungus has not been exposed to the optimum environmental conditions for fungal decay.

The true loss in weight, due to the loss of wood substance brought about by decay, is obtained by subtracting the final dry weight from the initial dry weight. Allowance is made for the dry weight of wood preservative retained by the blocks and for any part of the wood preservative which is volatile at 100°C. This loss in weight due to decay is expressed as a percentage of the initial dry weight of the wood.

How results are evaluated

In the case of those wood preservatives to be applied by pressure impregnation, the minimum quantity in the wood which inhibits decay by the test fungi is the expression of fungicidal efficiency and it is expressed as kilogrammes per cubic foot of wood. It is necessary to state also the 'dilution', (in British Standard 838 this is given as the 'concentration') of the treating solution necessary to give this figure, as well as the species of wood tested. The *toxic limit* is expressed as the interval between that dilution which just permits decay and the dilution next highest in the series which inhibits all decay.

With regard to those wood preservatives applied by non-pressure methods, the results are reported only as the number of blocks that have resisted decay out of the total number exposed to each of the test fungi.

It should be specially noted that British Standard 838 describes a method of testing fungicides in order that their efficiency in inhibiting fungal attack may be assessed. No standards of effectiveness are given nor can they be inferred or implied.

The leaching test

In this test the capacity of the wood preservative to resist being washed out by water is assessed. In buildings this could only take place during the course of erection, either when the timber is stacked outside or when in position, but before the roof has been covered. Heavy or prolonged rainfall at this time could wash out water-soluble wood preservatives and seriously impair their action unless fixation had taken place or sufficient preservative had been applied to allow for a reasonable safety factor for leaching.

Two methods of carrying out the actual leaching are given in the Standard. In the 'beaker' method a set of treated test blocks is subjected to sixteen days' washing and twelve days' drying. The water is changed three times daily during the washing. In the 'Soxhlet' method, which is much more severe, the leaching cycle is 60 minutes and it is arranged that the condensed water has a temperature of $40 \pm 5°C$. For blocks 1·5 cm. thick the total leaching time is 300 hours, but for blocks 0·5 cm. thick it is 100 hours.

Blocks that have been leached are tested against fungal attack in culture vessels and the results compared with the unleached test results.

The wind tunnel test

A very important test, which it is necessary to employ in the United Kingdom, is a test to assess the ageing of wood preservatives. We ought to know how efficient wood preservatives are likely to be in, say, ten, twenty or thirty years' time. Several test set-ups operate in Germany, and the name 'wind tunnel' is taken as a literal translation of the German apparatus. The treated blocks are subjected to alternating temperatures and numerous wind changes.

There is obviously a great need, in the United Kingdom, for research into a suitable test to assess the degree of permanence in wood preservatives.

WOOD-BORING INSECTS ASSOCIATED WITH FUNGAL DECAY

The Death-Watch Beetle—Wood-boring Weevils—The Wharf-Borer

Fungal decay of wood and insect attack

Several wood-boring insects attack wood only when a fungal attack has already taken place. The exact rôle of fungal attack in the biology of certain well-known species is not known, although there is experimental evidence to show that in the case of the most important wood-boring insect in the United Kingdom, the Common Furniture Beetle, *Anobium punctatum*, it has some beneficial effect.

The Death-Watch Beetle

In the case of the Death-Watch Beetle (*Xestobium rufovillosum*), however, fungal attack is a necessary pre-requisite to attack. It is practically certain that attacks by this insect have, or rather had, their origin in standing oak and chestnut trees, while the infested wood was utilized in buildings requiring large-dimensioned timber. The fungi causing the original infestation out of doors have been identified as *Polyporus sulphureus*, *Fistulina hepatica*, *Polyporus fumosus*, *Polystictus versicolor*, *Trametes suaveolens*, *Xylaria hypoxylon*, *Phellinus cryptarum* and *Coniophora cerebella*. Large timbers infested with one or more of these fungi were often sited in situations where dampness was prevalent and ventilation was poor or nonexistent. In many such cases the fungal attack was kept alive and indeed often increased its area of attack, especially in the case of the fungus *Coniophora cerebella*. Again, in such damp and ill-ventilated places the Dry Rot fungus could initiate an attack, although this species normally only attacks softwoods, and it is not uncommon for Death-Watch infestations to be associated with softwood rotted by *Merulius lacrymans*. In the latter case the Death-Watch-infested softwood is invariably adjacent to or very close to the hardwood infestation. An important point, however, is that oak timber attacked by Death-Watch does not necessarily mean that the timber is decayed to the point of substantial loss of strength. Indeed, all who have tried to saw through Death-Watch attacked oak where the fungal decay was caused by the fungus *Fistulina hepatica*, giving the so-called 'Brown Oak', will testify as to its toughness.

Fig. 65. Attack of Common Furniture Beetle, *Anobium punctatum*, in oak. The flight holes are about one-sixteenth of an inch in diameter. Note the small faecal pellets which give the 'frass' a gritty feel. The old sixpence gives the scale of the photograph.

The Wood-boring Weevils

Two common beetles classified in the weevil family, the CURCULIONIDAE, are causing some concern to property owners in London and the Home Counties. These are *Pentarthrum huttoni* and *Euophryum confine*, and they are so similar in appearance that Timber Infestation Surveyors working 'in the field' do not distinguish between them. Indeed, their biologies are thought also to be very similar. The species *Euophryum confine* is native to New Zealand, where it is not found indoors, being confined to rotting tree stumps. It was found in Britain for the first time in 1937, and thereafter it quickly established itself in London and the surrounding counties, but principally in the south-east and east. It has now spread throughout the United Kingdom, although it is still most common in London. It is found infesting badly ventilated and damp wood where a Wet Rot fungus is present. Hardwoods and softwoods are attacked by this weevil, common situations being block flooring laid without an adequate impermeable membrane, wall panelling fitted to a wall without a damp-proof course, and the end of joists and wall plates similarly lying on walls not adequately protected from damp.

Pentarthrum huttoni has been known for a much longer period but it is found in much the same situations as the previous species. The adult beetles of both species are typical weevils in appearance. They are cylindrical, the prothorax is pear-shaped, and the front of the head is prolonged into a long snout or 'rostrum'. The antennae, which arise about half-way along the snout, are elbowed and terminate in small clubs. *Pentarthrum huttoni* measures 2·4–4·0 mm. whilst *Euophryum confine* measures 2·4–4·8 mm. In colour both species vary from reddish-brown to pitchy-brown. The larvae are white, curved and legless. The flight holes which the adult beetles make when biting their way out of the wood are roughly circular, with ragged or indistinct margins. The bore dust made by the larva is finer and the individual faecal pellets are rounder than those of the Common Furniture Beetles, *Anobium punctatum*.

Fig. 66. Attack of Death Watch Beetle, *Xestobium rufovillosum*, in oak. The flight holes are about one-eighth of an inch in diameter. Note the bun-shaped pellets in the 'frass' and the dark coloration of the oak. The old sixpence gives the scale of the photograph.

Fig. 67. Fruiting body (Sporophore) of the fungus *Polyporus sulphureus* out of doors. This fungus causes a rot of oak and other hardwood trees which enables an attack of Death Watch Beetle to take place.

Fig. 68. The ragged, roughly oval flight holes of the Wharf borer *Nacerdes melanura*, in a piece of timber inside a building rotted by the Wet Rot fungus *Coniophora cerebella*.

Fig. 69. A fixing block which has been attached to a damp wall. It is almost completely hollowed out by a wood-boring weevil attack. The old sixpence gives the scale of the photograph.

The present-day importance of wood-boring weevils can be gauged from the fact that in a commercial timber-infestation survey of buildings during 1961, when 18,015 premises were inspected throughout the United Kingdom, 4·1% were found to support an infestation of one or other of the two weevil species. In London the percentage of weevil infestations in buildings was 13·2%, and it is significant that in the same survey it was in London and the south-eastern counties that Wet Rot was found most frequently.

The Wharf-borer

The Wharf-borer, *Nacerdes melanura* (the genus is sometimes given as *Nacerda* and it has sometimes been placed in the genus *Anoncodes*), is a fairly large insect, being from 7 to 12 mm. in length. The adult is yellowish-brown with the tips of the wing-covers black. The underparts of the insect are also black. It is frequently confused with a very common insect of the countryside, the Soldier Beetle *Rhagonycha fulva*, but the presence of three longitudinal raised 'lines' on each wing-cover of the Wharf-Borer, which are absent from the wing covers of the Soldier Beetle, is sufficient to separate these two species. The larva of the Wharf-Borer is very characteristic. It is slender, and may be up to 30 mm. in length and is greyish-white in colour. The deep inter-segmental grooves are said to give a superficial resemblance to a string of beads! The head is large and yellow in colour, whilst the mandibles are black. In addition to the six moderately well-developed true legs there are two pairs of false legs on the third and fourth abdominal segments. On the first five segments of the body are patches of spinules.

The Wharf-Borer, as its name implies, is well known to infest wharf timbers, but in addition it is common in timber which becomes saturated from time to time and in which a fungal attack is taking place. In spite of this the larvae are easily drowned, so that the water-content of infested wood cannot be much above the fibre-saturation point.

The Wharf-Borer has been distributed to many countries in various parts of the world, this obviously being due to infestations in wooden-hulled ships. In the United Kingdom it is mostly found on river and estuarine banks, and although it has been widely recorded, it is most common along the rivers and canals of the south and midlands. It is in London, however, that it is best known as a pest in buildings, and this is probably because of the large amount of partly buried wood on bomb sites present at the end of the last war. Although not nearly so common as it was a few years ago, it still occurs in fungal decayed wood in buildings.

The Wood-Boring Beetles which attack wood partially decayed by fungi accelerate the destruction of timber to the point where it can no longer support the strains for which it was designed, so that the importance of these insects should not be minimized.

REFERENCES

Moisture Content of Timber in Use. (F.P.R.L. Leaflet 9, D.S.I.R., London: 1956.)

Timber Decay and its Control. (F.P.R.L. Leaflet 39, D.S.I.R., London: 1957.)

Dry Rot in Buildings: Recognition, Prevention and Cure. (F.P.R.L. Leaflet 6, D.S.I.R. London: 1960.)

British Standard 838: 1961.

British Standard 1282: 1959.

CARTWRIGHT, K. ST. G. and FINDLAY, W. P. K. *Decay of timber and its Prevention*, 2nd Edition. H.M.S.O. (1958).

FARMER, R. K. *Recalled to Life*. 16 mm colour/sound film. Rentokil Film Unit, East Grinstead (1961).

FINDLAY, W. P. K. *The preservation of Timber*. Black, London (1962).

FINDLAY, W. P. K. *Dry Rot and other Timber Troubles*. Hutchinson, London (1953).

FINDLAY, W. P. K. and SAVORY, J. G. Dry Rot in Wood. *For. Prod. Res. Bull.* 6th Edition. H.M.S.O. (1960).

HICKIN, N. E. *The Insect Factor in Wood Decay*. Hutchinson, London (2nd Ed. 1968).

HICKIN, N. E. *The Woodworm Problem*. Hutchinson, London (2nd Ed. 1972).

HICKIN, N. E. *The Conservation of Building Timbers*. Hutchinson, London (1967).

INDEX

Airbricks, British Standard for, 85
Anobium punctatum, 26, 29, 90, 93, 106, 107, 108
Aston Hall, Birmingham, 71

Bridging of damp-proof courses, 72, 75
Brushing of timber, 93
Buildings,
  correct environment for wood in, 64–73
  excess moisture in, 65, 73
  importance of wood in, 11–18
  records of fungal attack in the United Kingdom, 33–40
  statistical survey of, 33–40

Capillary movement of water, 75–80, 82
Celcure process, 90, 92
Cellar Fungus, see *Coniophora cerebella*
Chemical decay of wood, 15, 17, 18
Common Furniture Beetle, see *Anobium punctatum*
Coniophora cerebella,
  characteristics of decay produced by, 31, 32, 58
  distribution of, 53
  economic importance of, 32, 41, 100
  environmental conditions for, 53
  insect attack associated with, 107, 110
  mycelium of, 31, 58
  records of attack by, 33–40
  specifications for eradication of, 63
  spores of, 32
  used in fungicide tests, 99
Corrosion of damp-proof courses, 72
Cracking of damp-proof courses, 72

Daedalia quercina, 52
  fruit body of, 51, 52
  mycelium of, 52
  wood decay caused by, 52
Damp-proof courses,
  absence of, 41, 69, 70
  defective, 41, 71–2
  electro-osmotic, 74–84
  horizontal, 65–9
    flexible, 68, 69
    rigid, 67, 68
  vertical, 66, 70
Death Watch Beetle, see *Xestobium rufovillosum*

Decay in wood,
  causes of, 17, 18
  identification of, 26–32
Differential settlement of soil, effect on damp proof course of, 72
Dipping of timber, 92
Drainage systems, importance of, 59, 65, 66, 69, 70, 73
Dry Rot Fungus, see *Merulius lacrymans*

Earth shock waves, effect on damp-proof course of, 72
Electro-osmotic damp-proofing, 74–84
  advantages of, 83–6
  installation of, 81–5
  principles of, 74–9
Euophryum confine, 107, 108

Fistulina hepatica, 106
Full Dry Rot treatment, 60, 61, 62
Full Wet Rot treatment, 63
Fungi, special features of, 19–25
Fungicidal properties of wood preservatives, 88, 93
  tests for efficiency of, 97–105

Ganoderma applanatum, 51
Ganoderma lucidum, 51
  fruit body of, 46, 47, 51
Geological phenomena, effect on damp-proof course of, 72
Gribble, the, 17

Hardwood, nature of, 12, 14, 15
House Longhorn Beetle, see *Hylotrupes bajulus*
Hylotrupes bajulus, 26, 95

Insecticidal properties of wood preservatives, 89, 93

Leaching test for fungicides, 104
Lentinus lepideus, 47, 48, 100
  fruit body of, 44, 47, 48
  mycelium of, 48
  wood decay by, 48
Lenzites sepiaria, 45, 49
Lenzites trabea, 49, 100
Lombardy Poplar, damage caused by 76, 77

113